Connecting

Connecting

Adrienne Bellamy

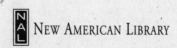

NEW AMERICAN LIBRARY

New American Library
Published by New American Library, a division of
Penguin Group (USA) Inc., 375 Hudson Street,
New York, New York 10014, USA
Penguin Group (Canada), 10 Alcorn Avenue, Toronto,
Ontario M4V 3B2, Canada (a division of Pearson Penguin Canada Inc.)
Penguin Books Ltd., 80 Strand, London WC2R 0RL, England
Penguin Ireland, 25 St. Stephen's Green, Dublin 2,
Ireland (a division of Penguin Books Ltd.)
Penguin Group (Australia), 250 Camberwell Road, Camberwell, Victoria 3124,
Australia (a division of Pearson Australia Group Pty. Ltd.)
Penguin Books India Pvt. Ltd., 11 Community Centre, Panchsheel Park,
New Delhi - 110 017, India
Penguin Group (NZ), cnr Airborne and Rosedale Roads, Albany,
Auckland 1310, New Zealand (a division of Pearson New Zealand Ltd.)
Penguin Books (South Africa) (Pty.) Ltd., 24 Sturdee Avenue,
Rosebank, Johannesburg 2196, South Africa

Penguin Books Ltd., Registered Offices:
80 Strand, London WC2R 0RL, England

First published by New American Library,
a division of Penguin Group (USA) Inc.

First Printing, March 2005
10 9 8 7 6 5 4 3 2 1

NEW AMERICAN LIBRARY and logo are trademarks of Penguin Group (USA) Inc.

LIBRARY OF CONGRESS CATALOGING-IN-PUBLICATION DATA:

Bellamy, Adrienne.
Connecting / Adrienne Bellamy.
p. cm.
ISBN 0-451-21412-9 (trade pbk.)
1. Women—Pennsylvania—Fiction. 2. Philadelphia (Pa.)—Fiction. 3. Female friendship—Fiction.
4. Neighborhood—Fiction. I. Title.
PS3602.E6457C665 2005
813'.6—dc22   2004023292

Set in Adobe Garamond
Designed by Ginger Legato

Printed in the United States of America

PUBLISHER'S NOTE
This is a work of fiction. Names, characters, places, and incidents either are the product of the author's imagination or are used fictitiously, and any resemblance to actual persons, living or dead, business establishments, events, or locales is entirely coincidental.

Thank You

Well, here we are again. *Connecting,* the sequel to my first novel, *Departures,* has been completed and is in your hands. You know I had a bit of trouble placing it there and required the assistance of many. It's Thank You time again—my loves.

Let's start exactly where we are supposed to, thanking God the Almighty for again blessing me with all it took to prepare this novel and for each and every person that he placed in my path to insure another hit and page-turner for us all.

Thank you my Lord for always taking time from your incredibly busy schedule to assist me. I am soo fortunate to have such a great relationship with you and possess the faith to rely on your getting me through. As Luther says "You're So Amazing." Life certainly is a cinch—when I'm working with a partner such as Yourself.

Before I get started on the personals, I'd like to thank Frank Hudak and Four Seasons Publishers for welcoming me and *Departures* in 2002. Without Frank, a struggling first-time author, namely Adrienne Bellamy, who was stressed out with the coldness of the publishing world would not have made it and *Connecting* would not have come to us. Thank you, Frank, for accepting *Departures* and me just on my word that it would be a hit. Thanks for allowing me the freedom to let my characters be real and for putting up with me when I was neurotic, premenstrual, anxious and often just plain crazy. Even though I have moved on and away from Four Seasons, I'd like every budding author to know that when doors are closed in their faces, Four Seasons has the power to make their dream come true. You and I have had a lot of fights—but you know I love you.

Of course, I haven't forgotten my manners and at this time, I'd like to distribute props, recognition, appreciation to all God's little angels who helped us out, bore with me at all hours of the night in consultation, cursed me out when they had to, worried about me and *Connecting,* analyzed the characters to be sure their personalities stayed in line, read their butts off, and, shared their thoughts. These people sacrificed their time to get this novel on the shelves. And, some of these people even grew to love me—and that's a gigantic blessing. We can never have too much of that.

Here, my readers and fans, are the people who worked behind the scenes to keep you riveted, laughing out loud, ready to fight and, loving *Connecting:* The

Thank You list had to be shortened in this book, however the full list of Thank Yous is available on my Web site, www.bellamyadrienne.com.

To thank some of my test readers, whom I love dearly, I have dedicated chapters to them. A much fuller Thank You and more information on the following people is available on my Web site. Thanks to: Alia Bellamy, Regina Bellamy, Ralph Travick, Arlene Sacks, Amy Myers, Shadiyah Hilliard, and Frank Altomare.

ANTHONY MARTHELL HUBBARD: *Aquarius.* Well, people-we've got to do what we've got to do. Many nights, in the middle of the night, specifically between 1:00 a.m. and 7:00 a.m. your author had to go to Kinko's and demand all sorts of things. She would appear in her pajamas and in giant floppy bedroom slippers and her hair would be all over her head. She was in a rush—always. Not an iota of patience. Your author is an expert at being a royal pain in the ass—but can sometimes be charming, too. She now says "Thank You" to Anthony for his patience, understanding and hard work. Chapter 13 is all yours, baby. Thank you so much my love, for inspiring me to write my characters Joel and Angie. Welcome to my life.

ARLENE SACKS: *Libra.* This one just worries about every freaking thing—including the author being the characters. Stop worrying, my sweet—it's fiction. Thank you Arlene for wearing so many different hats for me. You know I have to dedicate Chapter 8 to you. I'll meet you at therapy. Do you think that shrink can really help us?

ROSEMARY REED: *Pisces.* Lord have mercy—please. This one is a piece of work for real. Listen People: I found this one on the Tom Joyner Fantastic Voyage in 2002 while promoting *Departures.* She is as crazy as can be. She is both brilliant and baffling. She is honest and generous and we embraced each other from the very beginning. Hey—you slick little fish—I thank you for your wisdom—and for never backing down just to please me. Thank God you are such a great character analyst as well as a marvelous editor. I appreciate your encouragement, open ears, for hanging tough with *Connecting* and coming through at crunch time to get it to my agents. You are my baby! I have dedicated Chapter 15 to you—and you know why. Luv ya!

LISA NOEL: *Aquarius.* The first time Lisa and I laid eyes on each other was in a parking lot in 2002 shortly before *Departures* was published. She and her family and me and mine were hunting down hard shell crabs in Philly and parked side by side in the restaurant parking lot. You know I started talking. You know that friendly Aquarian jumped right in for conversation. After having a great dinner together, we became not only the best of friends—but Lisa has been instrumental in my books making it to her neck of the woods (upstate New Jersey). I also capitalized on her being an avid reader and one of the smartest people in the zodiac— so I trusted her to test read and edit *Connecting* for me. Hey Lisa: Take Chapter 18 with all my love and thank you for such a warm friendship.

WALTER DIXON: *Libra.* This one came from Children's Hospital of Philadelphia—a dynamic asset to their security force. One night he looked a little bored on the job and we struck up a conversation and I introduced him to *Departures.* Walt later told me that he'd "hit the jackpot" with that novel and was begging for more. Since then, he's become a staunch supporter of my work, read *Connecting* and loved it too. He also contributed and edited my third novel, Arrivals. He's turned out to be a great friend. His favorite character is Emily and believe me he keeps real tabs on her. Thank you, Walt for everything and please accept Chapter 3 as my gift to you. Thanks also for always letting me know how very proud you are of me and for your encouragement. I guess you know now that I can't write without you and how much I depend on your feelings about all of our characters.

JERRY MURPHY, M.D.: *Aquarius.* It really is a shame I became ill so many times, however, a blessing I ended up in your office for treatment. It was there that I learned so many things from you and was inspired to write the character Dr. Pierce (Purdy) Remington. Hands down, everyone has fallen in love with you and you have stolen *Connecting.* Thanks for teaching my daughter Alia and I all about flowers, wine and chocolate from Paris. Thanks for making us listen to opera during our consultations. You are such a loving snob. Since you're born under the smartest sign in the zodiac and know every damn thing, answer this question: What would I do without you? Chapter 2 is all yours. Enjoy.

MONICA JOHNSON: *Gemini.* Well, here's another cousin-in-law that I'm a pain in the butt to. I MADE her read. She tried not to read a thing— she wanted the whole book once it was published. She wanted to be surprised. I couldn't allow that. She was too smart and an avid reader. She had too much of the stuff I needed so I railroaded her into a few chapters for help and feedback. Monica, you have to share chapter 16 with my brother Ralph because you were so "in" on it and I couldn't have gotten through it without your expertise. Thanks for everything and for putting up with me so many weekends. Enjoy the entire book now, baby, and you'll find a lot of new material and many surprises.

SHAUNA RIGSBEE: *Virgo.* Shauna and I met a nailery in Willow Grove, Pennsylvania. We had a lot of fun discussing *Departures,* which she immediately purchased. She got back to me loving it—yep—she read it in all of twelve hours. Shauna and I eventually became friends and she was dying for the sequel, *Connecting.* Since she's a Virgo and literally snuffs out mistakes, you know I snatched this perfectionist up. She is truly phenomenal at test reading my novels. Shauna has worked feverishly on *Connecting* and the soon to be released Arrivals. Thank you, Shauna, for always being your meticulous self and for all your efforts at perfecting my work. You are such a pain in the butt and have made me unable to produce this good stuff without your assistance. With so much gratitude I offer Chapter 25 to you—your very favorite which you must share with Regina Bellamy Johnson. Love ya, baby, you're one smart cookie. And, speaking of cookies—since you so loved it—Chapter 21 is also dedicated to you.

THELMA LEWIS: *Virgo.* Here's another forever friend whom I met on Tom Joyner's cruise in 2002. Thelma purchased *Departures* and laughed her way throughout the cruise and by train from Miami to South Carolina. When she finally arrived back in Philly a few weeks later I received a call to congratulate me on a great novel. Since then we've become best buddies and this Virgo perfectionist has given me great feedback on *Connecting.* Her undying hatred for Paula and her determination to" do her in" kept me searching for things to upset Paula's world. I have gained a great support system in Thelma as well as a wonderful friend. With much appreciation you have earned my gift of Chapter 6. It's yours, baby. I love you.

JONITA MITCHELL MCCREE: *Cancer.* This is the "Cancer with the attitude." Jonita and I met at the George Fraser Power Networking Conference on June of 2002 when she purchased *Departures.* I got not only a fan, I received a sister and a best friend. It is wonderful knowing how proud you are of me and how you love my work. Thank you for reading for me and for loving *Connecting.* Chapter 21 comes to you from me with much love.

SHELLEY SZAJNER: *Pisces.* Shelley is an expert psychic and tarot card reader. As you read through *Connecting,* please know that the tarot card chapters were completed and so carefully done under her watchful eye. I could never have written those chapters without her. Because we both so love astrology, I have dedicated Chapter 25 to you.

TRACY SHERROD: *Cancer.* She makes me laugh. She loves my work. She was my agent and she believed in me. She's cute and sweet and she got the job done. Thank you Tracy for making my deals, trusting me and for teaching me to have a little patience. Thanks for shutting me up and out when you have to. Thanks also for answering your phone at 7:30 p.m. that evening when I took a chance and called to say "I've read up on twenty-two agents tonight and you're the only one I want. Can you take me?" I love you because you had a full load and didn't even need Departures, Connecting or me—and you gave us a shot anyway. Chapter 27 is for you, baby. See ya at the beach house in Boca Raton.

TONY CLARK: *Libra.* Well folks, here's my other former agent. He's the second half of the Tracy Sherrod Literary Agency so he's stuck with me, too. Thank you, Tony, for loving Departures, for your encouragement and feedback and for agreeing to take me on. I've dedicated Chapter 4 to you.

WENDELL BELLAMY: *Leo.* At last—we are friends. Feels real good to me—like a warm pair of socks. Thank you for coming to my rescue, for reading the Big Bird Chapter and for being so very proud of me. And, thank you for saying you are proud. You don't need a chapter, baby—you've got them all after having such a large part of my life. Thank you for that brat of ours—Alia. Thanks for teaching me how to fish and how to properly take care of a cold. Thank you also for June of 2001 when you REFUSED to let me die. I'm going to shut up now—before we both start crying.

KARA CESARE: *Sagittarius.* Thanks for working the crap out of me. Want me to take the trash out, too? I know many days you actually hid from me because you knew I was going crazy and you just didn't want to hear it. Please know I really appreciate your thoughtfulness on so many occasions and your trusting me when you knew I just had to have my way. Thanks for teaching me to be an explorer and for allowing me to have my say and stand my ground. You are a damn good editor and I have learned quite a few things from you. It's a blessing I landed in your lap. Thanks for keeping your word with me regarding so many important matters and for keeping my secrets. I love the way you calm me when I am frazzled and the way you drive me on when I feel I have no more to give. Lastly, I know how busy you always are and I appreciate the extra time and effort you put into Connecting and me to insure we had a hit. We're going to the top, baby, I promise.

JOHN PAINE: *Capricorn.* Let me tell you something, people: Once you work with John Paine whom I have affectionately named "Editor in Chief," you realize you don't know everything. In fact, you start doubting whether you should be in this business or not. However, if an author shuts up and listens, sometimes she walks away with a well tailored blockbuster and hit novel. John, you cannot imagine how many times I hung up my phone or got off the E-mail and cursed you out. I actually gave up writing—twice, and cried my eyes out. I want to first thank Janete Scobie for hooking me up with your super editing butt and next I have to thank Kara Cesare for making sure I stayed put with you (even though I wasn't planning on ever being without you).

KAREN E. QUINONES MILLER: *Gemini*. Thank God for you, my sistah. Yep, gang, this is the abundantly talented author of an assortment of great novels. Karen, I'd like to thank you for such a warm friendship and for your support and advice on so many occasions. I appreciated your stopping your work and taking time to soothe and get me on the right track whenever I contacted you in a frenzy. Thanks for our late night consultations and for including me in your adventures toward your own successes. You're one in a million, girl, and such an inspiration to me. A week ago I curled up in bed after your launch party and got stuck on and into your newest release, Ida B. All I can say is, nothing got done in my house. It was a wreck for three days—but I was happy reading a dynamic piece of literature. Give me more—soon. Luv ya!!

CHERRY WEINER: *Cancer*. Thank you, my agent, for rescuing me in December 2003 when I was a basket case. I know you ordered a bottle of Prozac when you got me. Can we make enough money to get me some help? You need to know how much I appreciate all your efforts to perfect me. I love the fact that you are so very patient, smart, experienced, sensitive, and honest. I hate it when you ream me out. Thank you for always looking out for me. I love it when you check on me on personal matters like my kid being ill. I hate it when you boss me around. I love you because you always listen and give me what I need so many times in this business—your time to listen. I promise to make you very proud of me. Get the Prozac out—Illusions, Epiphany and Donations are headed your way. Now…what about my T.V. show? Did you get to that yet? Love you much. Adrienne.

ROSE HILLIARD: *Taurus*. Listen people, this executive at Penguin NAL responds quicker than 911 to a problem—and she fixes it every time. I'm in love with the girl. My publishers cannot ever get rid of her and she can't ever leave. I'll react and overreact if it ever happens. Can you just see the headlines "Author takes over big time publisher's building and is holding hostages." And, you people know there are a zillion authors in the world, but everyone would know as soon as they heard it that it was Adrienne Bellamy causing a ruckus. Thank you Rose, for being so quick to help and for trying to solve all my problems that come your way. Thank you for answering so many questions and having the patience to deal with my crazy butt. Thanks for making me laugh (me doing the James Brown) and letting me make you laugh. I may be a pain in the butt sometimes—but I'm always appreciative and grateful. Keep on running my show, baby—I'm always good to go with you.

KATHLEEN COPPOLA: *Pisces.* You're a smart one. Born right on the cusp of Aquarius and Pisces, I know I've got a dynamic publicist and she is as smart as can be. Thank you, Kathleen, for all your efforts to insure that the media finds all about Adrienne Bellamy and her work. Now…did you call Oprah yet?

MOMMY: *Sagittarius:* Last but not least, I'd like to introduce you all to my Mommy, Barbara Shannon. You're all gonna be jealous of me. I've got a best friend, a therapist, a confidant, a fantastic mother in law, a house hunting helper and someone to take my side—most of the time. I love her—and am so glad she's mine. Thank you, Mommy, for being proud of me, for all your support and encouragement and for listening to this brat of yours when that other brat of yours sends me crazy. Get some nerve pills—I'm on my way to Tulsa. Mommy, thank you for loving Anthony and I—separately.

See ya!!
Adrienne

Connecting

Chapter One

Paula

The early 1990s

H̲e was panting like a maniac and she was tired of waiting for him to come. Finally he blurted out those words, those corny words: "I am the King! I'm Mr. Whopper! I'm the Electric Man, and I light them up!" Same speech each time. Pitiful. Then he was silent. Thank God it was over. She just shook her head. His dick wasn't as big as the cigarette she was smoking, and it reminded her of a Newport because it got smaller and smaller each time she experienced him. She smoked and stared at him as he got dressed. They really could have done better with the uniforms. They were so drab and ordinary.

When he finished dressing, he reached up to the shelf stacked with clean laundry. He retrieved a brown paper bag and threw it at her. "Nice job, here's your reward," he said. Paula checked out the contents of the pouch—a hoagie, a pack of cigarettes and a can of beer. "You'd better hurry and get yourself dressed so I can walk you back to your cell." She looked at him, rolled her eyes and got dressed. Jesus, she had to fuck him three times a week for that one sack.

She'd been in over two years now and had a weekly clientele of three guards. This was Berman. Berman was a redneck from West Virginia. He was a closet Black-women freak.

As the two of them walked back to her cell, she had to listen to him brag about how smart his wife was and how much money she made. His thick southern accent was enough to make her vomit.

When Paula got back to her cell she sat on her bed and pulled out the hoagie and the can of beer.

"Hey, Josie," she said to her cellmate, "do you want half of my hoagie or a swig of beer?"

"No, thanks," Josie replied.

Paula sat there munching on the hoagie and gulping down the beer, thinking about Amber, Horace and that bitch Emily, who were the cause of her being in jail. She wished Emily had died when she crashed that statuette into her head three years ago. Amber, who always caused nothing but problems, had now managed to get out from under her grandmother Fannie, ending the county checks that Grandma could have been collecting. Had she been with Grandma, Fannie would have sent part of the money to Paula, who was sitting in jail because of the three assholes, Horace, Emily and Amber. "I should have hit Amber in the head, too," Paula thought. Horace was the father of Paula's youngest of three daughters, Renee. He and Grandma separately had brought her three children to see her nine times since she'd been there. Paula couldn't stand the sight of Amber, Sydni just cried when she saw her and Renee acted like she didn't know who she was. So Paula told them all to stay home for the rest of their lives.

Paula was having a pretty rough time dealing with prison life. She had to learn how to deal. She had to give sex for favors on a regular basis. The three guards she was playing hostess to were not only taking full advantage of the situation—they were wearing her out. Jake was a real tyrant. He was a big guy who reminded her of Paul Bunyan, sizewise. He had a shaven head with gorgeous green eyes like a cat's. Jake was a stone freak. He was an Aries, and Aries men are truly perverted. They like all kinds of crazy sex. Jake liked ice. Yep, he liked his stuff on the rocks. His spot for having sex with her was in the kitchen. He would get one of those giant silver salad bowls—the prison housed sixteen hundred and. the bowls were humongous. He would have her fill the bowl up with ice and sit in it. Jake wanted her ass frozen when he came through. He'd make her take everything off late at night and sit in that ice until she couldn't stand it. He'd start getting his private parts ready for the ordeal while she was freezing everything up for him. Then he'd make her get out and he would enter her first from the back, that lasting what seemed like forever. He'd grab some ice cubes and stuff them up her vagina while she had a mouth full of something else. Then, when it was time, he entered her the *natural* way. After it was over, he'd make her get dressed, wash him up with warm sudsy water while he was standing, dry him off and then clean the place up like they'd never been there. She received two packs of cigarettes and a homemade coconut cake once a week for that. Jake had his mother bake the cake, telling her one of the inmate's kids had cancer. He told Mom the inmate was a nice girl who had gotten caught up with the wrong people and gotten into trouble. He said the only time she ever stopped crying and smiled was when he came with the cake. So Mom kept baking cakes and Paula kept a frozen ass a few times a week.

Her other man was Carlos Camacho—a Puerto Rican pimp. He was single and twenty-seven years old, and she really didn't mind him too much. He was a lot more *normal* than the other two and treated her better. He'd get the keys to the library and that's where they would meet. She had a little control over him. He merely required a nice blow job and he would read to her while she did it. The only strange thing about him was that he had this quirk: He never kissed or touched her. When he was with her he kept one hand on his gun. The other hand held a book while she did her work. He gave her a bottle of bath gel twice a week for her trouble.

Josie, Paula's cellmate for the last fourteen months, was pretty cool. She was in for killing her husband, Larry. She shot him five times with a .38 for running around on her and making her life miserable.

Larry just liked to stay high off anything most of the time. He had a job working for the City of Philadelphia. He drank at happy hour at twelve noon, and happy hour at five p.m. He ran around with coworkers, she had caught him with one of her supposed "friends," and he also kept a main stash on the other side of town. He loved wine, women and song. She took a lot of shit from him. He lied like a rug, paid bills at their house—his share—and messed up every other dime of his money. He'd been married once before she and he got together. She should have known that "what goes around comes around." He'd been running around with her when he was married to the other wife. But she thought he'd change.

He stole money out of her purse, and her car—a stone thief. Josie said she would go to bed at night and hide her money. Sometimes in the freezer, the vacuum cleaner or anywhere she thought he wouldn't find it. Then he graduated to the ultimate—taking her ATM card and robbing her in the middle of the night while he was out getting coked up. She didn't even know it. She'd been so upset with everything she was going through that she started seeing a therapist. One day she explained to the therapist, Dr. Morrone, that she must be losing her mind because she couldn't keep the checkbook straight anymore. Checks were bouncing all over the place. He told her to bring it and the bank statement in on the next visit.

He took a look at the statement and said to Josie, "This is the work of a person who is on drugs."

"What do you mean? Nobody in my house is a drug addict. It's just me and Larry and our daughter Sherrie in the house. Now, Larry may be a drinker and may do a line or two of coke, but no way is he a drug addict."

"Look at this statement and the times that this money is being withdrawn from the machine. Look at the pattern. First a twenty-dollar withdrawal, then a forty-dollar one an hour later, then in the next forty-five minutes another thirty-dollar withdrawal. This is the way people on drugs operate. Have you been checking all your statements, and are you out at night at two, three, and four o'clock in the morning making withdrawals?"

"No," she answered.

"Well, this is the way it works, and I know because we counsel these people. They start out with a small amount of money. They feel that is all they'll need—just a little bit of drugs. Then they find they need more, so they get a little more money, and they tell themselves that this is the last hit—at the machine and with the drug man. Then they realize they need another hit. That's why they run back and forth this way. Your husband is on drugs." Josie was shocked. She couldn't imagine Larry really being a drug addict.

Larry didn't get in that night until about five a.m. He slept two hours and got up for work. She asked him about the money missing from the checkbook and he denied taking it.

So yes, she admitted to herself, she had a liar, a cheater and a thief. She knew the three things ran in succession. If you lie, you cheat and you steal. That's the way life is. So she informed him that she was going to the bank to explain that her money was missing and she was also going to demand to see videotapes of the ATM machines. He held to his story that he was never there. She went to the bank and explained. The bank required that she get a signed affidavit from Larry stating he had not made the withdrawals. They gave it to her to take back to him to sign. They would not replace her money or lift the bounced check fees unless she returned it signed.

She went home and waited for him to come home from work. He showed up about one thirty a.m. She explained the circumstances and he refused to sign the affidavit. She told him she wanted her money back from him and he told her he was not giving her shit. He went to bed and got up for work. She waited until he left and then took a shower. She gave four-year-old Sherrie her breakfast. This was Larry's payday.

Paula and Jake the tyrant—aka Paul Bunyan—had just finished having sex. She was pissed and her ass was still cold from the ice. "Listen, Paula, I'll be on vacation for two weeks."

She was thrilled, but kept it to herself. "Thank God," she thought. "Oh, you're going away—where are you going?"

"My girl and I are going down to South Beach, Florida, for a week and then on to Jamaica for another week. I'll be leaving in seven days and will be back around the sixteenth."

"Two whole weeks," Paula thought—she was delighted to hear that news. Jesus, she was sick of him and she was tired of being frozen in that kitchen.

He then said, "So, you know you won't be getting the cakes because I don't have anyone to deliver them. We'll pick up where we left off when I get back."

Paula was glad he was leaving but she surely would miss those cakes. One thing she hated about being in jail was not having those delicious baked goods. She thought about how she used to make all those treats when she was free. "Okay, I'll see you in a couple days for our regular meet."

"Well, while I'm away, you'll be servicing someone else for me."

"What?" she screamed. "You've got to be kidding. I'm not doing a damn thing."

"Listen, woman, you don't have a *contract* with me that I have to abide by. You need me—I don't need you, and don't you forget that!"

Paula was absolutely livid with Jake and not up for dealing with or having to screw a replacement while he was vacationing. "Jake, I don't want to be bothered with another person here. It's not even worth it to me."

"How do you know? You don't know what he may give you."

"I'm not interested."

"You sure?" he said, smiling coyly.

She hesitated, wondering who it was and what the person could do for her. "Damn," she thought. "Maybe it would be something good."

"Who is he?" she asked.

"I'm not telling you just yet. You just think about whether you want to do someone else and we'll talk about it on Tuesday."

Paula got the place clean, and Jake walked her back to her cell with the cake. On the way there she was wondering who this potential customer was and what he'd have to offer. She decided to give it some serious thought and think of something she would ask for. Maybe she could sell herself for something worthwhile.

They got to her cell and Josie, her cellmate, was "home" asleep. Paula went inside and unwrapped the cake. When she looked at it she thought about all the times she had made that same cake, and also how she had made it for Earl—but Horace screwed that up for her. She hated Horace. She reached over and got a pen and used it to cut a slice of cake. She lay back on the bed and looked up at the ceiling while she was eating it. "Damn, I'm really in a mess being in jail," she thought.

Half the time she wished she hadn't hit Emily in the head and gotten into this shit hole, and the other times she wished she had killed her. She lay on her bed eating the cake and fantasized about seeing that cop Terrance. Often she considered trying to call him at the station and asking him to come to see her. He sure was fine. She never forgot looking into his eyes that night he came to her apartment—and then stupid Floyd messed that up for her by showing up at her door. Damn, everybody was a pain in the ass. Whenever she got out of jail she planned to move as far away from Philadelphia as she could.

Her mother came to see her once a month, and all she did was complain about money, and how Grandpa Oscar, who never came home on time anymore, was out of her control. Floyd had hooked up with someone else and never came to visit Paula. Life was a bitch. She ate another piece of cake and drifted off to sleep in her uniform.

"Let's go meet your new client," Jake said as Paula was lying on her bed doing a crossword puzzle.

Paula got up and rolled her eyes at him. She couldn't stand his ass and couldn't wait until he left for vacation. She wondered who the hell she had to screw now. He'd never given her any information on the person. They took the stairs four flights up to some nicely furnished offices. Jake then pointed to a chair. "Sit down," he ordered. He went into an office, closed the door for a few minutes and came back for her.

"Paula Gray, meet Warden Walter Langley," he said.

Paula was stunned. Jake had arranged for the warden to be screwing her?

Chapter Two

Purdy

W hile preparing for a date with Maritza, Purdy sat in his office gazing at a picture of Stefana that was taken when he was last in Barbados. The sun was shining and the water was a perfect turquoise. The breeze that was blowing as Purdy drove the boat cooled him even more. He contemplated Stefana in the photo, leaning against the rail of the boat. She held a glass of chilled Grand Laurent, which was a little less white than her skin. Her blond hair was blowing in the wind and she looked stunning in those five-hundred-dollar sunglasses he'd brought back for her from Paris. She was a thirty-two-year-old beauty. She gazed at her man, operating this luxurious boat that he had rented to take her out to "catch" lunch. He sure was a handsome guy. Six-two and medium brown, a hint of gray at the temples, perfect teeth that he obsessively had cleaned twice a month, and those Denzel Washington kissable lips. Not an ounce of flab on his body.

Purdy, born Pierce Edwin Remington. Family rumor had it that he was such a beautiful child that everyone always cooed, "He's so pretty," and that's how he came to be called Purdy. Not only was he pretty, but he was bright. He emerged after fourteen years of college and medical school as a brilliant orthopedic surgeon. He was living the good life, just as he'd planned. He had a booming practice and a staff of forty. He loved Paris, fishing on the beaches of St. Martin, fine wines, squab, designer everything, and he showed up at his office dressed to kill *every* day.

Purdy met Stefana at her jewelry shop while he was vacationing in Barbados. He had stopped in to inquire about a Roger Dubuis watch. Seventeen grand. Yep, that was Purdy's style. He couldn't resist looking at her that afternoon as she explained the watch to him, and she turned him *way* on. He rarely went for White girls, but she was something special. Purdy found her charming and invited her to dinner. After Stefana played hard-to-get for a spin, she conceded to dinner. In an attempt to be modest as well as impressive, he gave her the wine list after they were settled in the restaurant. He was fully expecting her to decline to order, feeling she really wouldn't "understand" the wines. To his amazement, she eagerly accepted and spent a long time reading it. Finally, she ordered a fantastic bottle of Guy Larmandier Brut Rose champagne, and a half bottle of '92 Trimbach Cuvee Frederic Emile "for later." He was floored and captivated. This woman knew the juice. So they dated the entire trip and since then, for the past two years, she had visited him in Philadelphia and accompanied him on many Caribbean trips.

Purdy just couldn't seem to settle down with one woman. Something seemed to be wrong with every one of them when it came time to make a commitment. He got along well with Stefana because they weren't one-on-one. He was always a wonderful date, a generous guy and an excellent lay. He told great stories and had class. So—she could be "bothered." She could handle this.

As Purdy gazed at Stefana, his entire life started to replay in his mind. How he struggled through college and medical school, footing the bills by working, applying for grants and scholarships and accepting whatever his mother and father could do for him. It was a long haul, and seemed like an eternity. The *work* was cool with him. All those classes, all that work, no problem to him—he thrived on that.

Purdy got "drunk" on knowledge and kept his hangover. He loved to read and explore. It was all a challenge to him that he accepted and it did everything to benefit him. That was the easy part. Relationships were his downfall and weakness. He was selfish. Not selfish with money or gifts, not that kind of selfish. He was selfish with *himself.* He had a hard time really letting any female in. He was cautious and kept them all at arm's length. If anyone tried to get past that distance or he felt himself giving in, he managed to screw the relationship up in one way or another until the person didn't ever want to be bothered with him. He was definitely not a romantic. Valentine's Day meant nothing to the man. He hated it when a woman honeyed, babied, and sweetied him to death—he got bored with her. He required a woman to listen to him much of the time.

Purdy loved to talk and tell stories. Sometimes one could never shut him up. However, if people *could* listen, they learned a lot from him. He taught as much as he could along the way to everyone he met—not only in college and medical school, but also with people he encountered or interacted with on a daily basis, as well as his dates and patients. A visit with Dr. Remington left a patient walking out the door not only with the best medical care and advice, but with a couple of other things, such as a lesson on the exquisite floral arrangements throughout his lobby and private office. Or maybe he had the opera playing in a tone low enough that the two of them could also communicate, or maybe it was a day to "be spoiled and bad" and he introduced you to chocolate that he had brought back from his very favorite city in the world, Paris. Dr. Remington didn't just *hand* you things, he *explained* what he was giving you, and whether it was medication or chocolate, you came away knowing something.

Purdy's *local* hookup was Maritza, who lived in Philly, but she was a pain in the ass. Maritza was a twenty-three-year-old decorator. Purdy had met her when a friend referred her to redo a few rooms in his mansion in Center City, Philadelphia. This was a three-story loft with twelve rooms and four fireplaces. Maritza was one sassy, slender and well-educated Black woman, but she was young and crazy, which was part of his attraction to her. She reminded him of Jasmine Guy, even her mannerisms. He nicknamed her "Cousin Jazz." She was witty and flamboyant and worked for a design house in Philadelphia. Maritza, as well-educated as she was, knew nothing about fine wines or French restaurants and she was not trying to; she could snuggle up with a pizza and a bottle of beer in a minute and be in heaven. She liked crazy parties where you "had better watch your stuff" because the people were much less affluent than the likes of Purdy.

Once, when they arrived at a party she had "found," she immediately pulled out a Club from a bag she was carrying and attempted to place it on his steering wheel so his Ferrari wouldn't get stolen. He screeched, "What are you doing? Where did you get that thing?"

He continued to protest and refused to go into the party, and they started to argue in the car. "Look," she yelled, "I'm trying to help you, Purdy—save your car, man. You better let me put this thing on the steering wheel before we have to call a cab to get home."

He was casing the neighborhood as she was talking. "Look, Maritza," he said before she cut him off.

"Oh boy, here we go. Now I'm Maritza and not Jazz. I smell a lecture coming."

He continued. "Look, *Maritza Fleming,* first of all, where do you find these people and where do you find these neighborhoods? It would seem in your line of work, dealing with educated, well-mannered, articulate people, you could accumulate better friends. There is no way I am putting that damn gadget on my $150,000 automobile just so I can go into some wild party with some outlaws that you found God knows where. Anyway, I've lost my appetite for partying tonight." He quieted down. "Let's just change the scene, baby, and get some dinner at a respectable place. I'm not splitting chicken wings with you and your friends tonight."

Maritza had a snarl on her face and rolled her eyes at him. "You are *soo* uppity with all your degrees and all that stupid wine you drink and all those pigeons you eat. You can call them 'skawbs' if you want."

When she said "skawbs," he had to crack up laughing, and he was reminded of what turned him on about her. She was just so far away from his world, so common and down. She continued, "They are fucking *pigeons,* and if you sit out here until morning, you can get a few for free and stop paying damn near a hundred dollars a whop for them. Can't you ever relax and enjoy all classes of Black people like the rest of us? Just chill and quit judging people by their assets. Like, you're not 'all that'?"

"You know what, Jazz, you're not being fair. I'm just not judging anyone. I'm just not going in there. I can hear the music out here. I can't be bothered with a loud scene tonight. What's the deal, can we just split?"

"You know what, Purdy? When we hooked up, when you talked me into dating you, I explained everything about myself to you. I know you damn well understood it, too, as smart as you claim you are. You agreed that we like different things and you agreed to do some things I like and be around some people I like to be around. I didn't have to have your ass. I was fine doing what I was doing—which was nothing—but I was handling things and not out putting in applications for a man. Now it seems to me you're forgetting all about our agreement."

He said, "Do you know how many crazy situations I have been in with you because of what I promised? Don't forget about the last time you had me come to a party with you. When I got there the place was half lit up because they had an electricity problem or a blowout or something. At least I remember the house being half lit up. So, contrary to tonight's situation, there was no music playing because the DJ's equipment wouldn't work where it was situated. So I arrive there all dammit dressed up and you guys are trying to get things straightened out. Okay. Then the music is reduced to a battery-operated boom box and you start singing 'Last Night a DJ Saved My Life!' to the crowd. I had to listen to that, and by the way, you do have a nice voice—that wasn't the problem.

"Then you decide, while singing, to pick the damn boom box up, and you and all of your Jamaican friends elect to take the party down to the corner Jamaican bar. So the entire crowd exits the premises and boogies on down the street in a fucking line to this establishment. And, you, *my date*, lead the pack. *I* even ended up there after sitting in amazement in an empty and poorly decorated half unlit house for twenty minutes contemplating whether I should leave your ass.

"So, in an effort to support you, I go to the bar and you are *still* singing, and when you see me come in and finally find a seat in the place, you start chanting 'The bar, the bar, somebody run the bar.' Then you start pointing at me and the crowd starts chanting, too. So I run the damn bar for all those heathens. Then when things quiet down and you shut up and stop running the show, you introduce me to a friend of yours. I get engrossed in a conversation with him and he explains to me how for years he was a burglar. I learned everything about breaking into businesses and homes and how to break codes in security systems. So don't give me all this shit about my being too uppity. We're not going into that party tonight."

"Look, Purdy, the only reason I introduced you to Dredge is because he had gotten himself together and stopped being a criminal. I wanted you to meet him so you could help him get a job. You know *everybody*."

"Jazz," he said, "remember the last person you called me about requesting I get them a job? I went through my business phone book and finally came up with someone to consider your friend, who hadn't been able to find a job in over a year. Now, granted, you explained he had 'some problems.' Okay, I decide to try to help. I'm a nice guy—that's what I do sometimes. I try to help out. So I talk my ass off to a very affluent attorney friend of mine and damn near snag the job for your buddy. He gives the guy an interview—just because I asked him to. Your friend showed up not so dressed up, and with a Walkman on his head listening to music. Tony, my buddy, even goes along with that shit—just for Dr. Remington.

"Okay. Tony explains all the requirements to your friend. Now this was an easy position, and all your friend had to do was learn the system for delivering lawsuits and legal pleadings to the courthouse for filing with the court. Tony was even going to have him trained for four weeks and pay him while training. And speaking of pay—it would start at four hundred a week and he did not have to work weekends. Now that wasn't a bad deal at all considering the guy's resume, which was pitiful.

"Okay. During his extensive interview with my friend Tony—the deal is damn near nailed down for him to start the following Monday—your dizzy friend says, 'Now I can take this job and all that, but when Luther and Frankie come I won't be here.' Tony doesn't know who the hell Luther and Frankie are so he asks your friend. Tony actually thought they were his children. Your dizzy-ass friend then explains to Tony, head of the most prestigious law firm in suburban Philadelphia, Garcia and Russell, P.C., that Luther and Frankie are Luther Vandross and Frankie Beverly and Maze, and whenever they come to this area for concerts, he is unavailable to work because he has to get ready for the shows. Tony threw him out of his office and called me to curse me out."

Maritza burst out laughing, apologized and said, "Okay, point well taken. However, I promised my friends I was coming to the party and I am going to the party. Hell, I go a lot of places I hate going just to please your ass, specifically that opera. You and Mr. 'Pommerati' and all his singing friends get on my nerves. That's no fun for me. Jesus Christ, sometimes those 'operonians' scream so loud I think the roof is going to fly off the place. Then you make me wear those creepy glasses that make my eyeballs feel funny and then my head gets all confused with what's going on and I just get a headache. So, let's just put the pipe or Club or whatever this damn thing is on the car and go in, and if this music is too loud, you just deal with your headache like I do."

Maritza then resumed trying to put the Club on the steering wheel. "I must be crazy to be dating you," Purdy growled, snatching the Club from her hand. "Do you always carry these things around with you to put on people's cars? This is sick. I'm not interested in this shit. I'm leaving."

"I'm going to the party," she said.

Maritza opened the door, stepped out of the car and waited, tapping her foot. He hit the button and rolled down the passenger window. "I swear, Jazz, I'll leave your ass here." She gave him the finger. Purdy snarled at her, waved, and pulled off. She stomped her feet and marched up to the house as mad as hell. He couldn't stand her tonight and she was sick of him.

Chapter Three

Emily and Jared

Whe she first arrived on the compound, she said to the person stationed at the entrance, as tears rolled down her face, "I'd like to speak to the head man here. You know—the reverend? Is he here? I have a lot of problems and no direction. I know he helps everyone. I've heard about him. Someone has to save my life."

He felt sorry for this pretty young woman and said, "Sister, you want to speak with Dr. Yamaan. I can't let you through to him without permission. I have to ring him. What's your name?"

"Everybody calls me Cassy—you know—the people who care about me," she answered meekly.

"Okay, Cassy, hold tight and I'll see if I can get the doctor." She waited nervously as he spoke into the phone.

"He's sending someone to greet you and bring you to his quarters. That should take about ten minutes."

"Thanks so much. What's your name, brother?"

"Alvin Watts—or Al for short," he answered, knowing Dr. Yamaan would be thrilled to meet and help direct this beauty. There hadn't been one like this who came through in quite a while. She was pretty *and* mixed up and would require an abundance of the doctor's time and patience to "reroute" her. This was the doc's lucky day, Al thought.

"So, Cassy, what brings you to my haven?" Dr. Yamaan inquired as Emily sat down, placing her small amount of belongings next to her in his beautiful spacious office. She sized him up as she stared at him. This was a not-ugly, not-cute man—average looking. He had something done to his hair to straighten it out—some goop was in it. He wore it in a ponytail. He was medium brown–complexioned. His skin looked good and he had nice teeth.

He was dressed in an expensive suit, but she noticed what resembled Muslim garb—white and gold long clothing sort of like a dress—hanging on an expensive coatrack in his office. "Well, sir, I have been so very depressed and nothing seems to work out for me," she whined. "I'm well educated, a college graduate, and I taught school for a few years back east. I had a lot of savings and invested it in the stock market—I love the stock market. I'm really great at it. I got all sidetracked and crazy when my husband was killed. He was a fireman and died in a blaze. It happened nearly a year ago and I just can't seem to get myself together."

Dr. Yamaan was instantly attracted to Emily. "Your story is very unfortunate. Tell me more about how you found out about my organization," he said.

"I was at a retreat in Rhode Island about eight weeks ago and met a woman. She told me about you, I got on a plane at five o'clock this morning and here I am. I need help," Emily lied.

As she sat there, she wondered how Amber and the kids were doing. She had arranged for her best buddy Sheila, her brother Earl and sister Regina to take turns looking after them while her boss Horace worked nights. Emily was a fine nanny to those kids and she missed them already.

Dr. Yamaan interrupted her thoughts, distracting her as he moved from behind his desk toward her. He pulled Emily from her chair and into his arms and hugged her. "There, there, my sister, don't fret. I'm here. You've made it to the right place."

Emily hugged him back and whimpered, "You really think you can bring me back? I feel so lost."

He kissed her forehead and said, "I can make it better for you, sister. That's what I'm here for. I believe I can solve all your problems."

Emily despised his touch and wanted to move away from him, but didn't want him to get thoroughly discouraged because she had to find a way to become a resident on the compound, in order to get Jared out.

Dr. Yamaan pulled her over to the couch and sat her down. Sitting beside her, he kissed her on her ear. When she did not object to that gesture, he continued, kissing her face, moving toward her lips. He was testing her to see how far he could go. He gently kissed her lips. She gave no resistance. He then lifted her hand and placed it in his crotch. He murmured, "You are a very sexy young lady, my sister. Let me provide some comfort to you." By then he was guiding her hand up and down his erect penis.

"I would love that if only I could. However, I'm not so safe," she meekly lied.

He became nervous and abruptly moved her hand, held it and asked, "Is it AIDS, sister?"

"Oh, no sir—it's actually hepatitis C, which I contracted from my husband—you know—the fireman."

Dr. Yaaman quickly unleashed his hand and repositioned himself further away from Emily. He regained his composure and asked, "Don't you have some family, sister?"

"I do—but they can't seem to bring me around. I'm kind of lost. I need some guidance and sometimes family is just too close because they *know* you. They lose their patience or they have too many expectations. I need a new start."

"Are you poor now?"

"Oh, I'm not poor. Remember I said I have stocks and I did well in the market?"

"So, how long will you be here and how can I help you? Do you have any specific requests or any goals?"

Emily sniffled and said, "I just want some peace. I want to interact with your members. I can teach children if you have any around, and I'm willing to work while I'm here. I do need you to explain what goes on here and about housing. I mean, I can stay at a hotel or get an apartment if you have no space."

"We can accommodate you. There are classes that go on twice a day. One session begins in the morning, from six to seven, and one in the evening from eight to nine. The women have separate living quarters here and only interact with the men at meetings and mealtime."

"Oh, so there is absolutely no dating or fornicating on this reservation?" said Emily.

"You are correct," answered Dr. Yamaan, looking into her eyes.

"Well, I'm confused. A minute ago, you led me to believe differently."

Her candidness surprised him and made him uncomfortable. "Well, in some cases, exceptions are made, especially when I find a sister totally in distress or lonely, which is my opinion of you. I do believe sexual intercourse is a form of relaxation."

Emily was floored and wanted to interrogate him by asking him questions as to why his "relaxation technique" was prohibited outside the confines of his quarters. Instead, deliberately avoiding the subject of sex, she replied, "That's interesting. Can you tell me something about the classes? What will I learn?"

Dr. Yamaan moved back to his desk to continue the conversation. He also changed his lusting mind about ever getting in the sack with her. He felt it would be good to keep her for financial reasons.

"Cassy, you'll take lessons on self-preservation, you'll learn to give from your heart, and we teach spirituality. You'll also be required to work together with us and contribute funds. Since you have a profession, part of the day you'll spend earning money that is shared by all of us and is used to maintain our quarters and feed us all. We share everything on the compound. We also teach you to pray."

"To whom are we praying? I'm not being sarcastic, I really want to know. I'm Catholic and from looking around and listening to you, I don't think you want me praying to the Pope or to Jesus, do you?"

"We pray to Boosawa."

"Who's that?"

"An ancient African god who saved all his people. Are you still interested, Cassy?"

"Yes . . . I am. Can you get me set up?"

"Hi, Cassy, I'm Belinda. Welcome to the women's compound. Here's your bunk, and we have three bathrooms. Look around and get comfortable. You can put your stuff away in that dresser," the young woman said as she pointed across the sparsely furnished room. It reminded Emily of a ward in a hospital.

"Thanks—how long have you been here?" Emily asked.

"About four months."

"Do you like it? Have they helped you?"

"I feel better than when I came."

"Do you work?"

"I work at a restaurant in downtown LA during the day, four days a week. Most of the women are out working now, either on the compound or in the *other* world."

"Where are the men?"

"They have jobs, too, and if they don't, they work the buses and trains collecting money from the passengers. The women aren't allowed to do that."

"What do you guys do for fun—or shall I say recreation?"

"There's no outside life other than working in the other world, and we don't have any phones for our use on the compound. Phones are restricted to the guard's desk and Dr. Yamaan's quarters. The doctor doesn't approve of outsiders or even family calling in to us. He believes they will be distracting and therefore detrimental to our healing process. We do have group time where we get together and talk and occasionally we get to see a concert."

"Oh really," said Emily. "That seems like good recreational fun. Who have you gone to see?"

"We have our own singing group here and they get work in the area. They sometimes perform for us here on the compound. They're actually very good. They call themselves Reflections."

Later at mealtime Emily nabbed a seat in the dining hall and grabbed a tray. She got in line, got a platter and returned to her table, glancing about the room hunting for Jared along the way. No sign of him. She was conversing with the people at her table when she suddenly spotted Jared coming in the door. She took a deep breath. He got in line for his meal. She was cool and slowly removed herself from the table, taking her tray to the dirty dish bin across the room. Then she waited on the other side of the meal line for Jared to come through with his food. When he did she said, "You've got a package here." He was stunned.

"I can't believe it," he said.

"I can. Let me tell you something, goddammit, Jared Wells," she whispered as softly as she could. "You better find some fucking way to meet me, or I will forget my good manners and turn this plantation out. You got that? What the hell are you doing living in this crazy place? Now *I'm* signed up in it trying to save you. You meet me at the meeting tomorrow night—and my name is Cassy. There's no Emily here." She then walked out of the dining hall and returned to the women's quarters.

At the meeting the next night, Emily brushed up against Jared and he passed a note to her. The note asked her to meet him the following night at eight o'clock in back of the first group of men's huts, which were numbered one through four.

As soon as Emily saw Jared she rushed into his arms. "Did ya miss me?" she asked.

"Nope," Jared said.

"Liar liar, pants on fire—in due time," Emily seductively said.

Jared shook his head and smiled. "What are you doing on this compound?"

"Visiting," she replied, and kissed him.

"What's the matter—you scared someone is going to run away with me?"

"I don't trust you or your friends in California. My instincts tell me you're not in such good company. I'm going to get you out of here."

"Emily, I'm not being held prisoner. This is not a bad place, and I like it here."

"You must have been insane to hook up with these lunatics." She shook her head. "It is ironic you're wearing all these weird getups, worshipping the 'Ancient Boosawa of Africa' and collecting money on trains and buses and turning it over to that thieving Dr. Yamaan. I hope you know he tried to fuck me. You're so gung ho about thinking he's the greatest thing in the world. No fornication—yeah, right—that applies to everyone except himself."

"Well, if he did try to throw you in bed—at least I can say he had no idea you knew me."

"That's not the point—he doesn't practice what he preaches and he uses everyone. You're penniless after singing your heart out *and* working the Los Angeles Transportation System on a daily basis."

"Oh, it's not so bad, and it is a learning experience. I do get twenty-five dollars a day—remember?"

"Yeah, twenty-five dollars a day that you have to throw into the plate at the meetings. And what have you learned? Let's discuss what you learned. You learned to be satisfied eating bean sprouts while the doctor is probably having steak and lobster. You also learned to share—so you gave every dime to him. He certainly was dressed to kill. Let's just be glad and grateful I'm on the case now to get your ass back on track."

"Emily, I'm not ready to leave."

She was getting more frustrated by the minute. She shouted, "Why the hell did you come here, Jared? What was so wrong with your life?"

Jared sighed and explained, "I was tired of everything, Emily—the road, everyone fighting in the group, and all that royalty money we got swindled out of did me in."

"So that was reason enough to run away and leave us all?"

"Yes, at the time it was."

"Do you know you damn near gave your sweet mother a heart attack with all this madness? Jared, where in the world did you find that Dr. Yamaan?"

"He came to a show in New York just before I quit the Knightcaps. He gave me his card and we started talking on the phone a lot, and then he began introducing me to people, trying to get me a record deal doing a solo thing. He enlightened me about his organization, so when I got depressed and confused and needed an out, I joined his group."

Emily sighed and shook her head. "Jared, I'm tired."

"Do you need some sleep? Are you ready to go back to your quarters?"

"That's not what I'm really talking about. You know too much stuff happens between us. Sometimes it gets *too* weird, and often I feel responsible for you—and *us*."

"So I'm a real burden, huh?"

Emily took a deep breath and said, "I don't know."

"Listen, baby, I'd really like you to stay on here. Can't you give it a shot? It's really not that bad. At least we'd be together. Or did you just come all the way out here to get me home and then take back up with Jared Rooney?"

"Don't you dare start on Jared Rooney. That poor guy. I know he never wants to see me again."

"You were that rough on him, huh, baby?"

"No, *we* were that rough on him. You make me sick. I should have been able to make it with that guy. It was just too hard because the entire time I was seeing him I was dreaming about you every night. If I ignored the dreams and got through that, the radio would get me. It seemed like whenever I would get in the car with him, all your records would start shooting out. It was as if you were calling me—haunting me. It drove both of us crazy. He was a nice guy, too, Jared, and he treated me well. It's just a shame. I swear I thought you and I were through, especially when you decided to be a Holy Roller and join a cult."

Because Emily and Jared had a sound friendship that actually insulated their love affair, their relationship was composed of many facets. Emily was many different people to Jared all wrapped up in one package. She was totally comfortable expressing her true feelings to him. She had no fear of being honest with him. He was *the* person in her life she could relate to that way.

Emily continued. "Jared, to be perfectly honest with you—I just couldn't have a peaceful life without you and I drove Jared Rooney crazy."

Jared thought for a moment, took a deep breath and said, "Emily, did you ever give it any real thought when you met the other Jared and he had my name, brothers with the same names as my brothers, and my mom is Connie and his mom is Lonnie? Didn't you get an inkling that somebody or something was trying to trick you or tell you something? I mean, wasn't that spacey enough to at least make you *think* before you jumped into that? You should have known you were looking for me, baby."

"Maybe I was—hell, I don't know," Emily said, throwing her hands up in the air. "I do know that I'm tired of being on guard all the time. I feel like I'm being warned on an almost daily basis with you. This guardian angel thing has worn me out big-time and this cult shit has done it! I've been walking around looking like Raggedy Ann since I got here. That Dr. Yamaan plans to have me working outside the compound and at that kids' center, and I have to turn those checks over to him every two weeks and eat slop. I heard one woman left because she said she was starving."

Jared laughed and said, "Well, she weighed about two hundred and fifty pounds. She really didn't need anything else to eat, did she? I heard about her. You know what, Emily, I thought I would fall over when I saw you that first day in the dining hall. I swear I couldn't believe you actually found me. I really am glad you came, though. I have missed you *soo* much. Since we're talking about it all, what happened to Jared? Where exactly is he now? You never did tell me."

"He was so disgusted because of the way I was acting—waking up in the middle of the night and walking around looking at the walls—that he finally left. He knew he couldn't make me happy. He packed up and went down south where his parents live. He's done with me. Now I have a question for you."

"Shoot," said Jared.

"Just tell me one thing about this cult thing. Who the fuck is Boosawa? I swear I believe that doctor man made him up. He has us praying to a damn African god that none of us had ever heard of. I was even calling everybody in the 'other world' asking about him *and* went to the library trying to look him up. That ancient African god Boosawa doesn't exist and never did. I asked that crazy doctor to show me a picture in a book of Boosawa and he couldn't even come up with that. He ought to be ashamed of himself, having that giant bust of Boosawa on display at that temple and all of us kneeling to it every day. I know that damn thing is a piece of junk he probably picked up at a swap meet out here. I don't even like California anymore because of him. I should get Sheila to kick his ass or have Horace come out here with Killer. Horace and his pal Benny could make that dog mutilate the man. I swear I believe, as smart as you are, that you are stone loco for hooking up with him."

He laughed and kissed her. "Come on, baby—don't get violent on me. By the way, did you sleep with the doc?"

"Let me tell you how I got out of that one. First of all I gave him a phony name because I wasn't sure what you had told these people. I felt if they wanted to keep you there, if they knew who Emily was, they would feel threatened and not let me join. I told him a bunch of horse-shit when he interviewed me the day I arrived at the compound. Oh, I was a teacher and dabbled in the stock market, too. I told him I had money but I was all mixed up since my fireman husband got killed while he was working. Later, when he started approaching me about sex, I politely advised that the dead husband had hepatitis C and had passed it on to me through intercourse. Jared, you know many firemen end up getting that disease. So I explained that I had it and was still testing for *other* illnesses and had not yet learned what else I could have contracted. He never bothered me again." Jared fell back on the bed roaring with laughter. She was *soo* clever and he was thoroughly impressed.

"So, will you agree to stay on here for a month? Just one month, Emily. If you continue to hate it, I'll leave. I promise you I'll go back to Philly with you," he pleaded.

Emily put her face in her hands. Jared massaged her back and kissed her head. "Please, Emily, don't leave me right now and don't give me an ultimatum. Don't make me choose right now. I'm not ready."

Emily looked up at the man she loved and said, "I'm in." She kissed him good-bye and hurried back to her quarters.

Two nights later, Emily was awakened by Belinda, who was shaking her. "Get up! Cassy—get out of here! The place is on fire."

Emily jumped out of bed, glanced out of the window and saw thick smoke and flames coming from all of the nearby huts. "Oh my God! Oh shit!" she screamed as she ran out of her hut.

Belinda was trailing behind her. Emily was terrified and wondered if Jared would make it out. They ran across the grounds, and Emily darted over to the men's quarters searching for Jared. All of the huts were engulfed in flames. She didn't know which one he lived in. She was frantic.

"Cassy, come on, girl! What are you standing there for? We've got to make it across the field. Come on!" Belinda shouted as she grabbed Emily and yanked her.

Emily snatched her arm back and said, "I can't. I've got to find someone. I have a friend. I have to find him!"

"You're crazy! I'm leaving you," Belinda said before racing across the field.

Emily ran over to the men's quarters and began shouting for Jared. Guys were panicked, scurrying all over the place in pajamas, nightshirts and underwear. Fire was everywhere. Suddenly someone grabbed her around the waist and pulled her, saying, "I'm right here. Let's go!" It was Jared.

Emily threw her arms around Jared and said, "I was almost scared I had lost you. I should have known better. Let's get out of here."

They made it off the compound grounds and walked two blocks. They stopped at a house and rang the doorbell for help. A woman answered and they explained why they were in their nightclothes and asked to use her phone. It was Jared's mother, Connie, they called. The woman who owned the house had a wonderful family and they decided to let Emily and Jared stay at their house for a day and a half until money Connie overnighted reached them. The following day Emily and Jared got on a plane bound for Philadelphia.

"You'd better understand that I suspect they'll come after you to join up again," Emily said as they sat on the plane.

"Well, they won't be looking to bring anybody in for a while. They'll definitely have to rebuild. Someone had to have set fire to the place. You know anything about that? You've been known to set a fire or two."

Before Emily could answer, the captain interrupted on the PA system and announced that they would be landing in thirteen minutes.

"Saved by the bell," Emily said coyly as she looked Jared in the eye, fastened her seat belt and prepared for landing.

Chapter Four

The Luncheon

The crowd was all out there for Sheila at the Academy of Music for her graduation from Drexel University School of Nursing. Sheila had done it! Her husband, Leonard, and the kids were all there, too, and of course Sheila's favorite cousin, Terri, who had so long ago organized the graveyard dig-up of Sheila's former husband, Perry. Lucy had driven up from Norfolk and was as pregnant as she could be, expecting the baby in four months. Reba was all decked out and looking like a million dollars with all of her matching clothing. She was a far cry from the Raggedy Ann she used to resemble. She now hailed from the state of Maryland, city of Annapolis, and was loving every minute of being Mrs. Douglas Ransome.

Amber Alston, formerly just the daughter of the dreadful Paula Gray, was now living and loving life in the suburbs. Her daddy, Horace, had watched her grow up with a terrible mom since she was five years old, and once the wretched Paula was thrown in jail, he rescued Amber when she was fourteen. The proud adopted daughter of Horace Alston was now seventeen, her hair permed and her face lightly made up. She was sitting next to Emily, her nanny, who took very good care of Horace and her sisters.

The elegant Peggy Kinard remained the socialite of the neighborhood and was outfitted in a red silk suit and tan accessories, still running the fashion show. Sheila, their guest of honor, was down to one hundred twenty-two pounds and was seated with her classmates in the first ten rows. Everybody in the neighborhood was proud of Sheila, and this was going to be a real celebration.

The ceremony finally began, and the keynote speaker played, joked, got serious and gave a powerful speech to the graduating class. It was hilarious, inspiring and wonderful. When it ended, everyone met for a scrumptious lunch at Sheila's favorite restaurant, Founders, atop the Hyatt Bellevue.

At the lunch table, after congratulations were over, everyone decided to make a little speech about what was going on in their lives.

"All right," Sheila agreed. "Let's start with fat Lucy." Everyone laughed and coaxed Lucy to begin. She stood up, rubbed her stomach and started off.

"Well," she said, still rubbing her stomach, "Kevin and I are doing just fine. Little Anya or Dimitri will be here in a few months to run us around. Married life is just fantastic with the prince I caught thanks to Ms. Peggy Kinard over there looking like Halle Berry." Everyone laughed, and sixty-two-year old Peggy felt really flattered hearing that.

Lucy continued. "We bought a nice house, a three story, so we have enough room for all of you to come down and stay for a spell. I'm still working—I love it and will probably work until the minute I go into labor. Kevin, the prince, is the best husband ever and I'm sure will be a great daddy, too."

"Where are you working, Lucy?" asked Emily.

"Girl, I got a job as a receptionist at the radio station where our friend Sonja works. It is so wild there and a really fun place to work. I meet everybody, sometimes even celebrities. Food is always there, we order in all the time, I don't have to get dressed up because it is a relaxed place, and people make me laugh all the time. The anchors are really nice, and I just fit right in."

"How long are you going to stay home after you have the baby?" asked Sheila.

"I plan to stay home a year. I'm hoping they will have a lot of trouble with my replacement and hate him or her and let me come back."

"How is Sonja?" asked Peggy.

"Oh, she's fine—she and Dave are doing great."

"He's the doctor, right?" questioned Leonard.

"Yeah, the neurosurgeon that I call the astronaut." Everybody laughed. "Listen, let me tell you what happened at the station one day. You know Sonja does the marriage counseling stuff at night for the station. She is always jumping on people. Well, she started on this crazy woman one night after I got off. I heard about it."

"Let's hear it," said Reba. "I just love some good gossip."

Lucy looked at Sheila's kids and Amber and decided against it. "Uh-oh, I can't go into this with the minor children at the table. I'll have to save it for later." Amber protested with a sigh, but Lucy wouldn't budge. "Miss Amber, this stuff is X-rated and not for your young ears." Everyone was disappointed. Peggy ordered two bottles of wine; Sheila told her husband Leonard to go home and take the kids with him. It was party time.

"Who's next?" Reba immediately said,

Amber stood up and said, "Can I say my piece?" Everyone applauded and Emily put her head on the table before she could even start.

"Well, ladies," she said, "I am now a senior in high school, filling out all of my college applications, and I have a job. I go to church with Peggy every Sunday and I teach Sunday school. I've made honor roll each time."

The crowd applauded and whistled. "Okay, Amber, let's have it. You know I *really* know your butt," said Sheila. The crowd laughed and Sheila continued. "What do you have in that sharp purse of yours, some watches you're selling? Where are the cookies? Are they under the table or in Peggy's car with all your bottles you're probably getting a refund from to pay off somebody?"

Amber smirked and said, "Well . . . I do have a little dirt."

The bunch started hooting like owls. "Okay. Let's have it," said Sheila. "And I'll kick your ass later."

"Okay," Amber said. "Well, I got in trouble with a guy."

"Oh yeah?" said Peggy with her eyes lighting up.

"Yeah, but not that way."

"What way then, my love?" coyly responded Sheila.

"Well . . . see . . . my daddy is real strict and all, you know, about guys. So I met this guy and I liked him. He had a Beamer and a job and was in college."

"Whoa . . . ," said Reba. "Jesus Christ. A Beamer and a job? Humph. You go, girl."

"Yeah, his name was Dante. So, I told my daddy about him and I told him that he liked me and he was in college and he was nineteen. So, I asked Daddy if I could go on a date with him, and he said he had to meet him and all and talk to his parents. I knew that Dante would be embarrassed about Daddy calling his folks and all, so I asked Daddy if he could just meet Dante first and then talk to them after that. So Daddy reluctantly said okay. I knew Daddy would like him because he was a nerd with glasses, articulate, and dressed the weird way parents like guys to dress. And he went to a good college in Connecticut."

"What college, Amber?" asked Reba.

"Connecticut College."

"Okay," said Sheila. "Let's have the rest of it."

"So I made a date to go to the movies with Dante, and Daddy said it was okay. Dante showed up at our house at eight one Saturday night. When he came I introduced him to Daddy and ran upstairs to get ready. They went out on the porch to talk. Daddy liked him right off, just like I thought he would."

"So, Dante, what goes on in your life?" Horace said while they sat on the porch.

"Well, I'm working over the summer at a car dealership, and I am searching for a law school to attend."

"That's pretty impressive, and I'm glad Amber chose such a fine young man to begin dating."

"Thanks, Mr. Alston. What do you do for a living?"

"I'm a longshoreman down on the docks at the Navy Yard. I've been there for years."

"So, you have two other daughters."

"Yes, Sydni is almost twenty and in the military and Renee is almost five. They are all my pride and joy."

"Is Amber's mom around?"

"No, man, she's away right now. You'll probably meet Emily at some point, she takes care of them while I work."

"Oh, that's nice. I can't wait to meet her."

"Listen, Dante, why are you searching for a law school so soon? I mean you're only in your sophomore year of college. Why don't you just relax and concentrate on doing well, and wait until your last year to hit those applications. We're going through that right now with Amber, and they are a pain in the butt."

"Well, I just like getting a head start and researching the schools. I want to choose the perfect one."

"What type of law do you want to specialize in?"

"Corporate."

"Umm. That's great, young man. I'm pleased."

Horace really was pleased. He liked Dante, and he was relieved Amber wasn't going out with a bum headed nowhere. At that point Amber entered the porch looking gorgeous. She really was a pretty girl and her hair was lovely. Horace made sure she could afford Panache Hair Salon, a swanky shop in Center City Philadelphia, because her stylist Frank did wonders with her long, thick hair. Amber was wearing a denim miniskirt and a loose-fitting top.

"So, where are you guys headed for the evening?" asked Horace.

"Well," said Dante, "actually, we were going for a sandwich around the corner in that shopping plaza and we were going to rent some movies at Blockbuster and come back here to watch them. We should only be gone about an hour and will be right in the neighborhood."

"That sounds fine. Just let me get your information and your driver's license and registration before you take my baby out of here." Dante was surprised Horace requested the information. Amber was unhappy about this and made a face indicating so. She was staring at her father, pleading with her eyes for him not to take the information. Horace ignored her.

Horace went into the house and grabbed a pen and a piece of paper. Dante followed him in, handed Horace his license and registration and began writing down his address. Horace looked at the picture to make sure it was his. He then asked for his home telephone number and parents' number and address. Dante gave him the numbers and told Horace he resided with his parents, at the address on the license.

"Mr. Alston, we should be back by nine thirty."

"Okay," said Horace, kissing Amber good-bye. "I'll see you guys shortly."

Horace went upstairs, gave his mom and dad a call to check on Renee who was visiting with them in Florida, and took a shower. He soon got into bed and fell asleep. When he awakened at 1:20 in the morning he went into Amber's room. She was not there. He figured she and Dante were out on the porch and went there. Neither was in sight. He checked the house, including the basement, and couldn't find them. He frantically went to the paper where he had written down Dante's information and called his number. It was out of service. He was petrified and pissed. He jumped into his car and went to the address he had taken from the driver's license. The man who answered said he did not know Dante Evans. Horace then sped back to his house and paced the porch as he dialed the Philadelphia police department.

Just as the police answered, Dante's car came up the driveway. Horace hung up. Dante and Amber emerged from the vehicle and came in through the screen door of the porch. The phone rang, and Horace picked it up and told the police that he had no trouble and he didn't need them. He grabbed Dante with one hand and shoved Amber out of the way with the other. "I'm getting ready to kick your ass, motherfucker," he screamed at Dante, holding up a piece of paper, "Do you know what fucking time it is? You gave me this phony-ass information and took my daughter out of here."

"Don't hurt him, we only went to dinner!" Amber screamed.

"What the fuck have you been eating for five hours, motherfucker?" Horace shouted at Dante.

"I apologize, Mr. Alston. We got held up in traffic and the waitress took a long time."

"The waitress took a long time? Let's take a walk around the corner and ask the bitch what took her so long before I kill you."

Horace grabbed Amber by the collar with one hand and Dante by the collar with the other and dragged them down the steps and around the corner to the restaurant. The staff was cleaning up. He marched them both in and shoved them against the wall.

"I need some service," he shouted. "I need some service right now!"

A waiter ran over to them, and all eyes were on the four of them. "Tell me something," said Horace. "Have any of you seen these two people in here tonight?" He grabbed Dante by his ears and said, "Who waited on you? Goddammit, you better tell me who waited on you!"

"I don't see her," said Dante.

"Oh, you don't see her, let's search for her." Horace grabbed Dante by his collar and began dragging him all over the place, marching him up to everyone asking him if that was his server.

Finally Dante said, "We never made it here."

"Oh really?" said Horace. "So you're still lying. You just ought to be a lawyer, or you better know some, because when I get finished with your black, nerdy, preppy ass, you'll want to sue me."

"Mr. Alston, I am so very sorry. We were on South Street at a club and we had dinner and went to the comedy club and got caught in the traffic."

"The comedy club?" said Horace. "Oh yeah? Do they serve liquor at the comedy club? Let's go to the comedy club and let me ask all the comedians and staff if you ordered any liquor for my minor daughter. Wanna go there?"

By then Amber was on her knees in the front corner of the restaurant, crying over the seat of a chair. When Horace spotted her he said, "You better be praying, Amber, because you're next." Horace then grabbed her and marched the both of them back to his house.

"Amber, take your ass upstairs and get your pajamas on, and Mr. Dante, you give me your driver's license again. I'm writing everything on it down now." Dante handed the license over to Horace and he began checking it out. All of a sudden Horace screamed, "Twenty-four! Goddammit, your ass is twenty-four years old? What! You're going to jail. J-A-I-L—jail. Do not pass fucking go and do not collect my fucking daughter. I can't believe I missed this shit when I saw this license. You cradle robber! I'm calling the police again now!" Horace immediately called the police and they came and took Dante away. Then he went upstairs and cursed Amber out and forbade her ever to see Dante again.

She cried, "He's a perfect date and a nice guy. At least he goes to college."

"Oh, stop lying, that old motherfucker is out of college and has a degree in picking up seventeen-year-olds. What the hell happened with you and him tonight?"

"Nothing happened. I had fun at the club and didn't drink any alcohol."

"Let me tell you something, Amber. There is only one thing a twenty-four-year-old man wants from a seventeen-year-old girl, and we both know what that is. Now, if I ever catch you with him again or ever find him calling here or you calling him, I swear there will be trouble. You got that?"

Amber said nothing. Horace snatched her lamp off her night table and Amber flinched and said, "I understand, Daddy."

"Now go to bed," he said, and slammed her door.

Horace went into his room and sat on the end of his bed. He was royally pissed. He had never had any trouble with Amber other than the peer pressure thing at school with some of the White girls with the big houses and carriage houses on the property trying to get her to act a fool. He cooled that stuff out by threatening their parents. But this was the first time he had had this problem. She had never had a boyfriend or anybody like one. So he had to think. She goes and gets one with a sleek BMW and a college degree. Better than a drug dealer. Then he got mad at himself because he actually *liked* the guy. So at 3:10 in the morning he was livid with everyone—himself, Amber and Dante. He wasn't sure if smart-ass slick-ass honor student Amber would sneak and see him. He figured she would.

The next day Amber got up and went to church with the neighborhood socialite, Peggy Kinard. While she was gone, Horace went through her address book and everything else he could find in her room. He was searching for Dante's telephone number. Nothing. He pushed "star 69" on her phone, hoping it would ring Dante, and got a girlfriend's house. No luck again. Then he started going through her school things, composition books included. He did find a suburban train schedule for Conshohocken, Pennsylvania. He wondered what Amber was doing with that. Who lived there? He assumed it was one of her classmates. On a blank page in a composition book, he came across a number with no name. He called it and it rang to a car dealership. Bingo! It was closed, so he quickly jotted the number down and hid it in his bedroom. After that he started smelling, examining the underwear she had worn the night before and going through the dirty clothes in her hamper. He got every pair of dirty underwear she had and every pair of jeans and put them in a suitcase. He then took the suitcase over to his pal Benny's house and told him to keep it there until he heard back from him.

Amber returned home that afternoon, and Horace reiterated that she was not to see Dante. She smirked and said okay and left the kitchen headed for her room. He followed in a few minutes and noticed she was cleaning it up. He left the house and went out for a beer. When he returned home, he and Amber went to dinner and did not speak of the events of the night before.

Amber left for school the next morning promptly at nine. Horace called the car dealership and asked to speak with Dante Evans. He was informed that Dante was not in and got his voice mail. When the beep came on Horace said, "This is Horace Alston, Amber's father. I am calling to tell you that if I ever find you near Amber again, or calling her, I am going to put you in that BMW, doors locked, windows up, pour gasoline all over it and light a match. If you come out alive and tell anyone, I will pay someone to riddle you with bullets. You got that? And by the way, if you even mention to anyone that I left you this message, I'll pay somebody to cut your dick off—whether I'm in jail or not. Good-bye."

Horace hung up, then called right back and spoke with the receptionist. "I am looking to buy a BMW, and Mr. Evans is not in. Do you expect him today? I was referred to him by Henry Armsman—you know—he is the head man at IBM in Center City and has a really great BMW."

"I'm sorry, sir, Mr. Evans will not be in today. I can put you in his voice mail." Horace was glad that either she did not remember he had just called or they had two people operating the telephones.

"Well, let me think—you know, I really don't know Mr. Evans. I was just referred to him. What kind of a guy is he and how long has he been with your dealership? How much experience does he have making deals? What do you think of him?"

"Oh, Dante Evans is a good salesman. He has been here a little over six months. We're pretty fond of him here. He gets along with everyone, and his customers have all seemed pleased."

"Well, I don't know. Is he a family man? You know, does he have a wife, kids and all. I like dealing with family people."

"Well, sir, Mr. Evans is single and a graduate of Connecticut College and extremely bright; however, he is a single man."

"Well, I don't know—listen, who is in charge there, I mean, who heads up your organization?"

"That would be Steven Vizi—he owns the dealership."

"Can you put me through to him?"

"Yes, sir, I'll ring now for you."

Horace listened to the same high-class music before a voice came on: "Steven Vizi, may I help you?"

"Good morning, Mr. Vizi, my name is Horace Alston. I'm calling in reference to your employee Dante Evans."

"Are you calling to verify his employment, Mr. Alston? If so, you should be in our personnel department."

"Oh no, Mr. Vizi, I know he works there, I just need to discuss him with you."

"For what reason?"

"Well, Mr. Vizi, I have a seventeen-year-old daughter. I found a train schedule and train tickets in her belongings. Mr. Evans has been dating my daughter without my knowledge and meeting my minor child at your place of business. It is my understanding that he has been carrying on an affair with my daughter on your premises at night while he is working late." Horace knew nothing of the sort but he wanted the guy to listen. "I'm informing you of this because I have filed charges of statutory rape against Mr. Evans and am filing a restraining order in Montgomery County against Mr. Evans. I intend to name your company as an accessory because these sexual encounters have been occurring in your bathroom, on your premises, and in Mr. Evans' vehicle that you allow him to use. Your company will be liable, too, sir. I just wanted you to know that. I am sure that the Montgomery County Sheriff's Department will be there before Thursday of this week to serve Mr. Evans with the restraining order and other papers. I just thought you would like to know that your twenty-four-year-old employee is a child molester who has not only caused trouble for me and my family, but is causing trouble for your business."

"Oh my goodness, Mr.—what did you say your name was?"

"Alston."

"Look, Mr. Alston. I am very sorry. I really am. I assure you that I will have a talk with Evans as soon as I can. I promise this situation will be taken care of. I can't believe it. Please, can we settle this without going to the authorities?"

"How are you planning to fix it, Mr. Vizi?"

"I can't say for sure, but I assure you something will be done. Can I get back to you tomorrow?"

"Yes, Mr. Vizi, I'll give you until tomorrow. Here is my telephone number."

Horace gave Mr. Vizi the phone number and they hung up. Horace immediately called the main switchboard for the third time. This time he wanted to be put through to the employee directory. Nineteen people worked for that dealership and Horace left a message in every person's voice mail or told everyone who answered that Dante Evans was a child molester and had a seventeen-year-old girlfriend and was in deep shit with the law. After that, he checked on Renee in Florida and explained to his parents that he would pick her up on Saturday. Then he went food shopping, kept his doctor's appointment for his yearly physical, picked Amber up from school, picked Emily up from her sister Regina's, stopped by the post office and sent Sydni a jacket he had purchased for her, and hit the sack. He had to go to work at eleven o'clock that night.

The next morning when Amber got up to get ready for school, she couldn't find her jeans that had some of her tokens in the pocket. She wondered where in the world they were. She found something else to wear, got ten dollars out of the kitty Horace kept in the kitchen for emergencies and dashed off to school.

When Horace came home from working the night shift, the first thing he did was go to Amber's phone and hit "star 69." The person on the other end answered, "Dante Evans." Horace hung up.

Horace's phone rang at eleven a.m. It was Mr. Vizi from the dealership.

"Good morning, Mr. Alston. I wanted to let you know that Mr. Evans is no longer working for my company. I would also like to come to personally speak with you at your home, to formally apologize."

"I'll be home until two thirty and then I have to pick my daughter up from school."

"I'll see you at one thirty if that is convenient. May I have your address?"

"I live at 729 Prairie Lane, Rydal. See you at one thirty."

When he hung up, he called Jonita, whom he had been dating for the last eight months. She was a twenty-eight-year-old attorney whom he had met at the private school Amber attended. She had been there for Parents' Day filling in for her sister who had just delivered a new baby girl.

"What's up, Cancer with the attitude?" said Horace.

Jonita chuckled. "What do you want with me this morning? You got a case or something?"

"Oh, you hustling business this morning? Want me to lay down in front of a truck or something?"

"Not unless you've got plenty of insurance. I don't go for chump change," she said. "What's on your agenda today?"

"The norm, and I have a meeting at one thirty. Do you want to meet for dinner tonight?"

"Sounds great. Where to?"

"What do your taste buds say?"

"Seafood."

"Okay, let's do Dinardo's and I'll leave for work from your place."

"You got it, baby."

"I know it, baby. See you at Dinardo's at six, or do you want me to pick you up?"

"I want to be picked up."

"Okay—five thirty so the place is not too crowded."

"See ya, Sweetie."

"Bye," said Horace.

Horace made some breakfast, grabbed the morning paper to read and then took a shower. It was almost time for Mr. Vizi to come by. He wondered how long the man would beg him not to take Evans and his dealership to court. That damn Amber. He really was pissed with her, but he was going to protect her no matter what. He was not going for anyone messing up his plans for her. He'd scare the shit out of everyone if he had to. She really was a good kid and was doing so well in school. He had gotten rid of all the bad influences in her life. Fannie, Paula, and now Mr. Dante had to go. He hadn't had any trouble with Fannie since he told her off two years ago. He had even heard that Grandpa Oscar had another woman because he was so sick of her. That damn Muslim Hasson was still in that bakery, and every once in a while Horace would go by there and just look at him and leave. Then about once a month he'd make Benny go by there with Killer and stand outside the bakery for about a half hour and look in the window. Horace had all their asses in check.

Promptly at one thirty Mr. Vizi rang Horace's doorbell. Horace invited him in and they went out onto his lovely porch to talk.

"Mr. Alston, first of all, you have a lovely home. That is a fabulous piano you have. Do you play?"

"No, my daughters play—all three of them. I have a Russian instructor who comes to teach them."

"Wonderful. I can tell you are a good father."

"I do my best."

"Well, as I said, I have made some changes and cannot tell you enough times how sorry I am about your daughter and my *former* employee. I don't believe you'll have any more trouble with Mr. Evans. I am hoping you will change your mind about filing the charges, or if you do, about involving my dealership. We had no knowledge that your daughter was seeing him or meeting him at the dealership. So, again I say I am sorry. I hope you change your mind about the lawsuit."

"I believe you are sorry, Mr. Vizi, but you must understand that I have a daughter to protect."

"I understand, sympathize, and agree with you." Mr. Vizi then stood up to leave and shook Horace's hand.

Horace showed him to the door and when they walked toward the driveway, Horace noticed a BMW 395 parked in the driveway. "Nice car, Mr. Vizi. Maybe I need to come shopping there when I'm in the market."

"I hope you're in the market today—here are the keys. I know how to apologize." He placed the keys in Horace's hand and walked down the driveway. Horace was stunned. He believed he would be successful at frightening Dante to death and making him lose his job, but he never dreamed he'd end up with a car.

Mr. Vizi opened the door to another BMW and shouted back to Horace. "The papers are in the glove compartment, and send me the bill for the insurance. Call me if you need any information or details."

Amber was ready when Horace picked her up at school. She hopped in the car and said, "I didn't know we were getting a new car. It's sharp."

"You like BMWs, huh, miss?"

"Yeah."

"Make sure this is the only one you get in. You got that?"

"Yes, I got that. Hey, Daddy, I can't find my jeans. Did Emily put them somewhere?"

"*I* put them somewhere."

"You? For what? Where did you put them?"

"I've got something to tell you, Amber, and you'd better listen to me. I called the police department forensics laboratory. Do you know what that is?"

"Like that TV show *Quincy?*"

"Yeah, like that."

"So what do they have to do with my jeans?"

"They have your jeans and your underwear—all of your underwear that I could find."

"Why? Why in the world do they have it? What did you do, give it to them?"

"They are looking for DNA."

"DNA—whose DNA?"

"Who do you think?"

"Oh no—not Dante? Daddy, you are totally out of control. Are you crazy?"

"Yep—you guessed it. They are looking for his DNA, and if they find it his ass is going to the slammer for a long time. So they are testing not only your jeans, they are testing all your worn underwear—just like on *Quincy.* The rape unit has your underwear."

"Oh my God! You are crazy. You—I can't believe you—oh my God—

poor Dante—there's no DNA of his there. I only went to the comedy club."

"Well, we'll see when Dr. Quincy finds the results."

"This is so bad and so unfair—you are something else! This is not right," she said.

"Was it right for you to lie to me and stay out past curfew with a twenty-four-year-old man who gave me false information?"

Amber looked embarrassed and ashamed. She put her head down. "No, it wasn't right, but you would not have let me go out with him if I had told the truth."

"You're right."

"So that's why I lied. I like Dante and he was a gentlemen."

"Guess what else, Miss Amber?"

"What?" she hissed.

"Did you know he was married?"

"He is not. Stop lying."

"Oh yes he is. I had a private detective follow him."

"You don't know where he lives, so stop it."

"I know he works at the BMW dealership in Conshohocken and is a salesman. I know who his boss is and I talked to the boss and the other nineteen people that work there. I hired a private detective who followed him home, and his wifey-poo came out on the lawn to meet him after work yesterday, and their two little kids were out there playing on the lawn. That's what I know. Did you know that?"

"No way—oh, Daddy, you mean Dante is married?"

"Just as married as he can be."

"I can't believe it."

"Well, you'd better. And another thing. He doesn't have a job anymore, and we have a new BMW that his boss gave us to keep quiet and not throw everybody in jail."

"This is unbelievable," said Amber. "That nerd was married. I'm pissed."

"Know what else?" said Horace.

"What now? What else?"

"If I ever find out you called him or saw him, I am going to sic Killer on his ass and pay someone to cut his penis off. You got that, Amber? So if you get unpissed or change your mind about Mr. Dante or decide to try to be slick and see him—even when you go off to college or when you turn eighteen and think you can do anything you want because you are grown—I'm telling you if I find out, he will lose his private parts after Killer gets finished with him. Don't make me act crazy, Amber, you got that? He is history. *Comprende?*"

"*Comprende,* Daddy. I have a question."

"Shoot."

"When do I get my panties and jeans back? How long will it be?"

"The testing takes six weeks."

"They won't find any DNA, Johnnie Cochran."

Horace laughed and said, "They better not."

Everyone exploded with laughter, and Sheila had a linen napkin around Amber's neck threatening to strangle her. Lucy yelled, "All right, gang, we've been in here too long—one more person after I go to the bathroom and then we are out of here. We'll finish this mess at the slumber party tomorrow night."

"Can I come?" Amber asked.

"Oh no, little girl, that's X-rated, remember that? We'll see you in four years if Horace hasn't killed you by then."

~

Chapter Five

Paula

The next morning she and Josie awoke and headed for the showers and breakfast. The food was absolutely awful. Damn. Paula started thinking maybe she ought to just screw another guard and make him bring her breakfast from McDonald's a couple of times a week. Jesus, she missed her own cooking, and she missed the *good* home fries with onions in them—and Accent. After breakfast she and Josie separated for their work assignments. Josie worked in the mailroom sorting mail and Paula worked the laundry room assigned to sheets, towels and washcloths. She folded them every day for eight hours and it was driving her out of her mind. She got breaks for meals, exercise time and when Berman wanted to fuck her. She had to service him during the day. Two days ago she had been with Berman and had to listen to another one of his never-ending "wife so smart" stories.

Carlos, her gun-toting Puerto Rican, was an evening lay, and he worked the two-ten shift. Both of their asses were working today and Paula knew she'd be tired.

Josie sat sorting the mail, thinking about Sherrie, and went back to the events that put her behind bars. She had seven more years to go in the joint, but she could take it—at least that thieving, lying-ass Larry was dead. She had seen to that. After that bastard had refused to sign that affidavit, she got Sherrie dressed in mismatched clothes, pulled her hair out all over her head and wet it up so it would dry without combing or brushing and would look a wreck. She deliberately did not put shoes on the child. Josie then got herself dressed in purple Dr. Denton pajamas and leopard high-heeled boots and put on her six-year-old mink coat. They headed for Larry's office.

"May I speak with Larry Burgess? I'm his wife, Josephine," she said to the receptionist. She had carried Sherrie in and placed her on the floor. The receptionist eyed them, astonished at their appearance.

"Just one moment," she said as she paged Larry to the lobby.

Larry appeared and looked surprised to see Josie and Sherrie. Once he looked them over, he could not believe they were dressed as they were. He motioned her to the corner of the lobby.

"What in the world is wrong with you coming down here looking like this, Josie?" he whispered. "Why is Sherrie barefoot? Are you crazy, coming on my job looking this way? You are embarrassing me."

"I want the money back that you took out of my account."

"Don't you start any mess down here, woman, I mean it. You'd better get out of here. We'll talk about this when I get home."

Josie marched past him and the receptionist and headed for the cubicles. He immediately followed her, and Sherrie started running trying to keep up with them. Josie stopped at the first cubicle, where a woman was sitting with a lot of papers.

"Hi, I'm Josie Burgess, Larry's wife. It is a pleasure to meet you. Let me introduce you to our daughter, Sherrie." Josie then picked Sherrie up and told Sherrie to say hello to the woman. Josie extended her hand to shake the woman's hand.

"Hello, Mrs. Burgess, I'm Amanda Corman, it's nice to meet you," she said, staring strangely at Josie's attire.

"Well, it's nice to meet you, too, but we can't stay long, we have to move on to meet the rest of my husband's coworkers. I just like getting to know everyone."

Josie quickly moved on to the next cubicle and introduced herself to Lynette Braman. Then Larry grabbed her by the hand and led her back out to the lobby. He handed her his paycheck that he hadn't had a chance to cash and said, "Take this damn money and do whatever you want with it, but do not under any circumstances come here again." Josie sashayed out of the office. He followed her to her car and said, "I'll talk to you when I get home!"

She went straight to the bank and deposited the check into their account and returned home. She was pissed with him as she waited for his return. She had been doing laundry, trying to stay up until he came in. She had been crying. The clothes were folded on the dining room table. When he came in she asked, "Can I talk to you? I'm upset."

He looked at her and rolled his eyes, walking past her into the kitchen. "Leave me alone, bitch," he said.

"Don't call me that."

"I'll call you anything I damn well please, *bitch.*"

"Listen, Larry, I can't take much more of us. Everything is all messed up all the time. You need to leave."

"I plan on going nowhere, *bitch.*"

"Listen—it's bad with me, Larry. I'm on medication, my nerves are shot, my health is at stake and I have Sherrie to raise. This just won't work. You need to go." He continued to ignore her and began heating up the dinner she had cooked.

She sat at the kitchen table and tears streamed down her face. She said, "Okay, if you won't move out, why don't you leave for a few days— just give me some space. I've washed up all the clothes." She then walked into the dining room and gathered some of his things and went back into the kitchen and meekly handed them to him. "Take these things, and wherever you spend most of your time—go there for a few days." His eyes pierced her.

"*Bitch,* didn't I tell you not to touch my clothes?" He then grabbed her and punched her in the face. He dragged her into the dining room and pointed to the clothes, saying, "Do not ever touch my clothes."

"Let me go!" she screamed. He then pushed her down to the floor and they wrestled with each other until they were under the dining room table. He was choking her with one hand and hitting her in the head with the other. She screamed and cried but could not defend herself. When he was through, he stood up and headed to their basement.

Josie lay there for a few moments sobbing, but grateful that they had not awakened Sherrie. She got up and stared at the fireplace. It contained a revolver that she had purchased a year ago due to break-ins in their neighborhood. She was often at home alone and purchased it to protect herself and Sherrie.

Josie reached into the fireplace and retrieved the gun. She slowly crept down the stairs and walked over to Larry, who was flipping channels with the remote control for the TV. She fired three times, landing bullets in him each time. He was bleeding profusely. She then stood over him and said, "Do you wanna fight now, motherfucker? Get up and fight like a man! Do you need some Band-Aids, the cops or the hospital? Want me to take you to the hospital?" He was scared to death looking up at her.

"I *said* do you want some *Band-Aids?*" she shouted.

"No, hospital, hospital," he said.

"Then get your ass up. The *bitch* is driving you there." He tried to get up, but it was too hard for him.

"Get your ass up or you'll die on this carpet," she said with fire in her eyes. She was still pointing the gun at him. He managed to get up, fearing she would shoot him again.

"Now, get your jacket on so you don't catch a cold," she said as he was trying to make it up the stairs. He entered the dining room and she pointed to the kitchen where his jacket was. "Get in there and get it and get some clean underwear to take with you. You advised me never to touch your clothes." He retrieved the underwear and jacket, holding it in his hand.

"Put the jacket on," she yelled, still holding the gun on him. He put the underwear down and struggled to put the jacket on. Then he retrieved the underwear and waited for her. "Sherrie," he mumbled with a questioning look.

"I have her covered," Josie said as she picked up the kitchen telephone and dialed a number.

"Hi, Elaine, it's Josie next door. Larry isn't feeling well and I have to run him to the hospital. I need to leave right now and Sherrie is upstairs asleep. Can you come over here and take her to your house? I might be all night in that emergency room. You know how they are. You've got to be damn near dead to get waited on quickly at Lankenau." Larry looked at her like she was crazy. He was truly petrified to get in the car with her.

"I'll be right over, go on—leave the door unlocked," Elaine said. "Look, Josie, when you get over to Lankenau Hospital, just pretend Larry is a lot sicker than he really is and they'll take you sooner. I do it all the time."

"Okay, good neighbor, we're out of here. I'll call you."

Josie cursed him out all the way to the hospital, keeping the gun in one hand.

"Now if you touch me or try to touch this gun, I'll use the last two bullets on your ass before we get there. Then I won't have to drive so far. You got that?" He nodded his head yes in between moans.

"Now, Larry—let's get something straight. You know you were wrong, always have been, and I *had* to shoot you. You understand that, don't you?" He didn't answer. She slammed on the brakes, looked into his eyes, pointed the gun in his face and growled, "Did you hear me ask you a question?"

"Yes," he replied.

"Well, answer me."

"I understand, Josie."

She then continued to drive. "Good, Larry," she said. "Now you know you *needed* to be shot, right?"

"Right," he said, praying to see the hospital any second.

"Now you better tell all those doctors and nurses there what you did and what you've been doing to me, okay? And you tell them that you needed to be shot. Okay, Larry?"

"Okay," he muttered.

"Are you hungry?" she asked. "You never did eat your dinner. Want me to stop over there at McDonald's? You may get hungry waiting for the doctors."

"I'm not hungry, Josie."

"Do you want a Xanax? I have mine in the glove compartment and there is a bottle of water in the back seat. Are your nerves bad?"

"No, thanks, Josie," he stammered, holding his stomach with one hand as blood oozed from it. He used the other hand to pull his pant leg tightly around his leg in an effort to create a tourniquet for the leg wound. She had also shot him in the behind, and he was sitting in a pool of blood. He thought he would bleed to death before they reached the hospital. Finally, they arrived at Lankenau. When they got there she exited the car and stood in front of the vehicle. "Okay, let's go, get out, we're here."

*   *   *

Warden Walter Langley was short, fat and round. He was almost bald with a little hair on the sides and in the back. He had little beady eyes. He had on a cheap suit and black leather shoes that strung up and were shining. "How are you, Ms. Gray?"

"I'm okay," she answered.

"Jake, could you leave Ms. Gray and me alone for a while? I will ring you to pick her up when we have finished our discussion." Jake left the room, closing the door.

"Now, Ms. Gray, it is my understanding that you have been an exemplary inmate, and that pleases me. Jake also tells me you have an amazing personality and are quite friendly. That pleases me also," he said with a gleaming smile.

"I do what I have to do to get along," she answered.

"Well, Ms. Gray, it gets a bit chilly here sometimes—for me." He hesitated for a moment to watch her reaction. Paula was looking him in the eye. He continued and said, "I was wondering if you wouldn't mind keeping me company when you aren't busy with other things. Are you being treated okay by your friends, and the supervisory personnel?"

"I'm making out okay. It's all right," she said, looking him up and down. Then she glanced over at the family pictures of him with his wife and children on his desk and on shelves throughout the room.

Paula wondered exactly what and how much of it she could get out of him.

"Since you have agreed to spend some time with me, is there anything I can do to make life easier for you while you are with us? Any special requests, Paula?"

"Well, if you really would like to give me something, I'd like it to be something I could use to make you have a good time with me."

Walt was surprised, curious and intrigued, and it showed on his face as he raised his eyebrows and asked, "And what would that be?"

"Lingerie," she said.

"Umm, that's quite a request. I don't know," he said.

"Well, I don't see what's so hard about it, and having nice lingerie helps the performance. Seems to me you could just go and buy a few things or take some from your wife's drawer if you can get away with it. Or maybe you could get a friend to keep her mouth shut and go shopping for it," she said, looking directly into his eyes.

"Oh, I don't know, Paula. I don't know. I'll have to think this over."

She stood up and slowly walked over to him and pinched his cheek. "You think it over, Walt, baby, and let me know. I'll bet you one thing, you'll love snatching some leopard underwear off my ass. Take a look at it." She pulled her pants down to expose her butt. She then slowly and seductively turned around in a circle for him with her white panties on. Then she pushed her uniform pants all the way down and stepped out of them and pranced around his office in her underwear. She put one foot on the chair behind his desk and then reached over and picked up a picture of his wife and said, "She looks like my size. How much trouble can this be—I mean for you to take care of this ass of mine?"

Walter could feel an erection coming on and he was quite nervous, too. Paula slowly put her pants on and walked back to the other side of his office and sat down. She folded her hands and said, "Can you call for me to be returned to my cell?"

Walter composed himself and made the call. When he hung up he said, "What size is your ass? Write it down."

In Lankenau Hospital's emergency room, Josie listened to them ask Larry questions about his wounds. "Now tell us, sir," the nurse said, "how is it you were wounded?"

Larry looked up at Josie and thought about her instructions to him.

"My wife shot me. That's my wife," he said, pointing at her.

The nurse quickly called 911 to advise they had to report a gunshot wound. Josie started getting nervous.

"Larry, tell these people how you got shot, I mean *why* I shot you."

"She shot me because I was late getting home from work. She's crazy. She's been threatening to kill me for a long time."

Josie looked at him and growled, "Tell her the goddamn truth, Larry. Tell them all the stuff you did to me!"

"I have no idea what she is talking about. She is loco! I told you that a minute ago. She tried to stop for dinner on the way here while I was bleeding to death. She's out to kill me."

The two of them began arguing back and forth, and the doctor attempted to remove Josie from the emergency room until the police arrived. Then Larry stood up and said, "I'm gonna make sure you get what you deserve, you bitch. I got people with me now to take care of me. You know you had no business shooting me. I think you've been lying and running around since we've been married, bitch."

"I can't believe you have the unmitigated gall to make a statement like that about me. You are a lowdown son of a bitch—that's what you are," she growled as she lunged toward Larry. She was held back by two nurses.

"Go ahead, bitch—yeah, that's what you are, a bitch. Try some shit now in front of these people. Wanna shoot me again? Go on, you punk. Try it again and they'll cart your ass away for sure! Then I'll really be rid of you."

Fuming, Josie reached in her pocket, grabbed her gun and shot Larry twice in the head and stuck the gun in his mouth when she was done to make sure he couldn't call her another bitch.

Josie went to jail right away. Her lawyers explained to her that had she not shot Larry at the hospital she would have gotten off for shooting him in the house because she had marks on her from their fight. Also, she would have looked good because she had taken him to the hospital in an effort to save his life. She blew that with murder in front of a half dozen witnesses.

In two days Paula and Walter the Warden were rocking steady on the couch of his office. She looked marvelous in the sexy nighties he'd had his best friend's wife pick up for her in Victoria's Secret. He told the friend they were for his wife. Walt had also stolen two items from his wife's personal collection.

"You're right, Paula," Walt said as they were about to have sex. She was standing clad in a sheer leopard camisole with matching undies. "You look delicious."

Paula had him naked as a jaybird at eleven thirty in the morning, and she went down on him, telling him his dick was her own Häagen-Dazs ice cream bar. He was loving it. When she was done, he went to put a condom on. "Oh no, Walt baby—let's do the real deal. Go bareback, baby. You don't have to worry. Jake uses them all the time, so we have no problem—not unless you or your wife have some mean thing that will infect us. And I know you've examined my medical records and know I've had my tubes tied and can't have any more kids. Give me that big whopper straight up—raw, baby," she begged.

He shoved it in her, moaning with joy. She wrapped her legs around the base of his back and used every ounce of strength she had to keep moving. First she moved in circles, then she fanned her ass up and down, bucking like a horse. He was screaming, dying and going to heaven all at the same time. She shouted at him, "Faster, goddammit! Give it all to me, motherfucker, don't you dare come! I'm opening it up more—come on, Walt, move your ass!"

"I got it, baby!" he screamed. "Oh shit, I got it! Come on, Paula— cream for me, girl—I'm in it, I'm in it!" Paula began imagining her ass was a windmill and twirled it as fast as she could. She came, and then she allowed him to have his share of the action. When it was over, she lay in his arms, and he said, "Never, never in my life have I had it like that. I can go shopping again if you want me to."

Chapter Six

Purdy

*P*urdy picked up the ringing private line as he was consulting with a patient. "Hello."

"Hey, Mr. Doctor . . . right? You are a physician, correct? How are you this afternoon?" Stefana said.

He chuckled, delighted to hear her voice. "I'm good. How are you?"

"I'm fine—missing you just a tinge. I was thinking of coming for about four days. You game?" she said.

"That could be a possibility," Purdy said, looking at sixty-two-year-old Wally Noonan sitting across from him impatiently awaiting his test results. "Can I call you later? I'm with a patient."

"I've got a meeting from four to six this afternoon. Get me at home tonight after eight," she said.

"Okay—you got it."

Purdy finished up with his patient and thought about the evening to come. He and Jazz had made up since they told each other off a month ago outside the Jamaican party. He was having a light dinner with her at a restaurant and intended to break the news to her that he was going on a trip to Paris and China without her.

He knew she was going to have a fit, but he knew he couldn't take Maritza abroad for that length of time. God knows what organization or who she'd befriend in those countries. He knew he could not take Stefana because she'd never leave her business for two weeks straight. She was basically a one-woman show and just had help covering for her in short intervals. She had explained that to him when they first began dating. He'd be glad to call her later, though. It would be nice to spend a few days with her before he departed to Europe and the Orient.

* * *

He was still thinking about Stefana as he pulled into the Cuban restaurant parking lot. He saw Maritza's car and was glad she was on time. He found her in the lounge. "Hey, Cousin Jazz," he said, bending over and kissing her. She smiled and returned the kiss.

"No fighting tonight, Dr. Remington," she said. He smiled and the hostess escorted them to a table. He ordered a glass of Pinot Noir and she ordered a Bud Light. They chatted a while about the events of each other's day. He said, "Listen, Jazz, I'll be away for about sixteen days, I'm leaving in three weeks."

"Where are you going? Are you taking me?"

"Well, that won't be possible. I have some meetings and wouldn't be a good date."

"Where are you going?"

"Paris for seven days and China for the remainder of the time."

"You know I can amuse myself while you are at meetings." Maritza rolled her eyes at Purdy and began to pout. "Why don't you just come on out and say you don't want to take me?"

"Maritza—don't start. I'm trying to make this a nice evening," he said.

Maritza slugged back some of her Bud before she said, "You're selfish—you know that. But that's okay—go on to La Paree and Chinatown without me."

He knew a fight was brewing and tried to soften her up by saying, "Why don't I get a chance to miss you a lot while I'm gone and bring you something special back?"

"Whatever," she replied.

After dinner as they were leaving she said, "Am I following you home or what?"

"No, baby, not tonight. I have some work to do at home and some calls to make. I'll call you tomorrow and if Dr. Gelding can cover for me over the weekend, we can hang out."

"You're awfully busy these days, Purdy," she said suspiciously as he kissed her and said good-bye.

Purdy was not up for any run-ins with Maritza. He really did wish he could drop her, but he liked spending some time with her. It bothered him when he was away from her too long—even though most of their time together, they disagreed about almost everything. She was just so damn crazy and unpredictable—and he loved and hated it.

About two weeks ago, she'd gotten pissed off because he was a doctor. Unbelievable. They had gotten into this discussion and she started the "snob" stuff again. She was making fun of the fact that he had purchased a gold stethoscope, because he kept going on and on about it. She got tired of his showing it off and of listening to him teach her the quality of the thing. To change the subject she suggested she had a taste for fried chicken and wanted to go to Popeye's. He kept complaining about it being a fast-food restaurant—contrary to healthy food and the places he was accustomed to. He kept on until she told him to go to the butcher and get some chicken and fry it himself for her. He was a great cook. They picked the chicken up and went to his house.

As soon as they got there, the phone rang. She was starving, and he became engrossed in a conversation and ignored her. He was still on the phone, talking and smiling at that stethoscope, when she marched out of his bedroom and began washing and seasoning the chicken while the oil was getting hot. When she returned to the bedroom, he was still on the phone. He held his finger up to let her know he was coming. She went over to him and gently took the stethoscope from him, smiling at it in approval. He smiled up at her, happy she had accepted it.

In five minutes he still had not made it to the kitchen and she dropped the poultry into the hot oil. Fuming, she thought, "Fuck it— I'll cook my own damn chicken. I knew I should have gotten it at Popeye's anyway, instead of listening to him."

Purdy smelled the wonderful aroma of the chicken and came down to his kitchen. There he saw Maritza turning it over with the bars of his exquisite stethoscope. She had flour spots not only on her clothing, but also all over his counters. He screamed and ran over to her. "Are you crazy! Are you out of your mind using my stethoscope to fry some damn chicken!" He began trying to grab it from her.

"Shut the hell up!" she yelled. "You should have had better manners knowing you had company in the house. You stayed on the phone too long. This damn thing is turning the chicken just fine for me. It serves two purposes now. It's a perfect chicken turner overer." Many times Maritza would deliberately make up a word merely to aggravate the articulate Dr. Pierce Remington.

He was absolutely livid and finally got it away from her. "You are a pain in the ass and have no regard for my good things." He wanted to cry as he observed the grease dripping from his stethoscope. She looked into his eyes and didn't say a word.

"Do you have anything to say for yourself about misusing this valuable item?" he said.

"Buy another one for the kitchen, Mr. Rich Guy, and finish cooking my chicken." She then pranced out of the kitchen and stomped upstairs; she got into his bed and turned his television set on. She suddenly thought about how mad he was and knew she needed ammunition to fight him when he returned. She jumped out of the bed, let her gorgeous mane of hair down, got naked and put on her leopard pumps. She returned to the kitchen, walked past him and opened the refrigerator door. She grabbed a Popsicle from the freezer and slowly removed the wrapping while standing in front of him. She sucked on it and looked up at him and said sweetly, "Is dinner ready yet?"

He looked at this beautiful creature with every curve in place, and he was mesmerized. He turned the stove off, picked her up, carried her to his oval dining room table, gently placed her body in between two gorgeous statuettes and made love to her. After it was over, he went to Popeye's and brought her dinner back to her.

Purdy sped home and called Stefana. "Hey, miss, it's the Philly connection. How are you?" he said.

"Just a little restless and wondering when I could get there. I could be there next Monday if you have some time," she said.

"That'll work, but I'll be leaving here on the fourteenth for Europe and the Orient. We need to get you in and out by the time I leave."

"That's fine—I'll make all my arrangements and call you. Look to hear from me in two days with the details."

"Okay."

The next day at his office Purdy was feeling pretty low, despite prepar-

ing for his trip to Paris and China. He was excited about the trip; however, he was doing some pouting as he thought about his empty life. He
often had moments like this, thinking of growing old without a family,
and today those feelings had seeped into the front of his brain. He still
didn't want to give in and settle down with any of the women he knew.

The preceding week a patient had come in to see him. She had a gorgeous infant boy, and he envied her as he watched her coo with the baby
in his office. That scene had been playing in his mind over and over. The
baby was so cute.

His office manager came into his office to talk to him about a staff
member. After their conversation, he shared with her how he was feeling
about his life.

"I swear I am considering adopting a child," he said to Jillian.

She laughed and said, "You—Mr. Christian Dior, who flies all the
time and has no time for anything and no experience with children?" She
assessed him with a sharp look. "You've got to be drunk or kidding."

"Oh no, it has really been on my mind. I am seriously thinking about
it."

"You know there is a gigantic procedure for that, lawyers and all, and
you know the problems associated with it," Jillian said.

"What problems?"

"Well—all kinds of problems. If you go the surrogate route sometimes the mothers don't want to turn the child over. If you legally adopt
and get the child, there are different laws in different states, and you
could be forced to give the child back if the mom changes her mind. Oh,
it's just a bunch of mess with that," Jillian said.

Purdy could imagine all the rigmarole, too, and was losing his appetite
for it by the minute. He didn't have time for all that shit.

"Listen, Purdy," his longtime friend and employee said, "first of all,
let's face it—you're just not the daddy type. You're into everything *but*
kids. You like the nightlife and the fast lane when you're not in here
working yourself to death. Even if you did do a crazy thing like adopt,
you'd be better off adopting a kid who was at least twelve years old who
could do for themselves. Why don't you call Philadelphia Family Services
and run it all by them? They can probably find you a kid. That would be

a nice thing if you could handle it. There are so many Black kids out there who need a parent. There are loads of them in foster care. So listen to me. If you make up your mind that this is what you intend to do, then get an older kid and help him or her. You'll still have the benefit of being a parent and having something else in your life. It's either that or letting Maritza get pregnant." Purdy's eyes lit up in disbelief at her statement and his forehead hit his desk.

Jillian laughed and said, "Now that would be a trip, wouldn't it? Talk about a mess—we would never have a minute's peace around here pulling the two of you off each other as you fought over that child. And you know that crazy Maritza wouldn't take any shit from you."

"Jillian, I may be contemplating this thing. However, I'm not desperate or insane—Maritza is out."

Jillian laughed and said, "You know what else—I don't know if you would be a good parent."

He looked up at her angrily and said, "Why would you say something like that?"

"Because of the way you handle staff. They get away with everything. If I weren't here to run the place, it would go down the drain. There's entirely no discipline from you. They put reports and information in the wrong charts, they're late for work, they take advantage, too many personal phone calls—you name it and they get away with it with you. That's why they cannot stand me. I don't allow all that madness. They know I'll have their asses out of here if they aren't doing their jobs. That's why I'll quit this place if you ever step in and go over my head in a decision I make with regard to staff and hiring and firing. If you get a kid, you'll just let him run over you. I'm not sure if you are organized enough to run a kid's life and do the daddy thing right. It's not an easy job. I don't know, Purdy." She shook her head looking at him.

"I could do it, Jillian," he said feverishly. "I'm a doctor. I'm bright. I'm organized with my patients, too. I simply don't have time to be policing staff. When I find the things in the wrong place in a chart or in the wrong chart, I just find the right chart myself and put it there or tell them to do it." Jillian continued to shake her head.

"You need to leave this baby stuff alone—you're not ready. It's too involved. Go on off to the other side of the world and do the other things you do best. Eat fine food, drink fine wine, chase the beauties, shop and go fishing. That's your thing, Dr. Remington."

Purdy wondered if it was all worth the trouble. He decided to end the conversation. "Good night, Jillian—I'm through for the day. See you tomorrow," he said, walking out of the office.

Chapter Seven

The Slumber Party

Everyone was at Peggy's house putting their things away and setting up for the party. It was lightweight food and hors d'oeuvres and Peggy was steaming crab legs in Old Bay Seasoning, crab seasoning and garlic. The entire lunch crowd was there with the exception of Leonard, the kids and Amber.

"Okay," said Peggy, "does anyone have to make any calls or anything before we start the party? Do you have to call Doug or the kids, Reba? Lucy, what about Kevin? I've got two phone lines and you guys can go up and make calls upstairs if you like. Emily, Terri—do you need anything?"

Sixty-two-year-old fashion plate Peggy Kinard was so sweet and so immensely enjoyed having the "kids" around. She took pleasure in her work as a seamstress and her life dating Howard, but she missed Lucy, her godchild, and Reba, and was happy she had decided to throw this party. They made her feel young again and filled a void in her life of never having any children of her own.

She was so proud of Reba, who had emerged such a confident woman after all her trials and tribulations living the life of Mrs. Johnny Penster. Now Reba was the affluent, well-dressed and connected Mrs. Douglas Ransome. That was quite an achievement.

Lucy, now five and a half months pregnant, loving her husband and her new life, convinced Peggy she couldn't have done better for Lucy with Kevin even if she had handpicked him herself. He was a great guy, and his being head over heels in love with Lucy actually relieved Peggy. She felt she had a grandchild on the way. Yep, Lucy's baby was going to have three grandmas. Peggy had already started shopping for the baby. Many times over the past two years Peggy said, "Thank God I took them to Norfolk and had them do that fashion show." Doug and Kevin were there, and her girls met and captured extraordinary prizes and new lives.

"Peggy, we called everybody before we left to come here. No more phone calls to be made," said Reba. "Let's get our spots and some wine and a little stuff to eat. I'm not really hungry."

"Well," said Lucy, as she stood in front of the pot containing the crab legs, guarding it, "everybody get what they want to eat. I'm getting me a big giant bowl or a pot and put my crab legs in it and get me a spot. I'm not telling my story for a while, I'm eating."

"You are such a pig," said Emily. "You have been eating all day long. Jesus, that baby is going to come out as big as one of those sumo wrestlers on TV."

"Oh, leave her alone, Emily—you know she loves them," said Reba. "She's going home in two days and she'll be okay. You know how people pig out when they go on vacation. Anyway, crab legs aren't fattening."

Lucy paid absolutely no attention to what they were discussing and just piled the legs into a roasting pan and waddled into the living room with a jug of lemonade and an entire roll of paper towels.

"You know you're not getting on that couch with all that junk taking up all the space," said Sheila to Lucy.

"Well, I need a table. Peggy, do you have a card table or something I can set my stuff up on? I don't want to be away from you guys and I'm not putting the crab legs back."

Peggy went down the basement and came up with a table that opened up and a vinyl tablecloth. They set Lucy up.

"All right, ladies, I'm up," said Peggy. "Now you know I don't do the devilish sex things, so my story may be a bit boring. But here it is. To be honest with you, I have a problem. I'm in rehabilitation and I go to therapy twice a week."

"Oh shit," cried Sheila. "Are you an alcoholic, Peggy?"

"No, Sheila, it's not that kind of problem."

"Well, what's going on?" a concerned Reba asked.

"I've become a compulsive shopper. It's really bad." Everybody laughed.

"What!" screamed Lucy, who had been engrossed in eating what looked like a million Alaskan king crab legs.

"I'm serious," said Peggy. "I've got a real problem."

"What are you buying? Hell, you *make* enough clothes. Are you sewing and just buying more stuff already made?" asked Reba.

"Well, it's not clothing I'm buying . . . well, I take that back, I do get some clothes, but it's mostly other stuff I get."

"Like what?" asked Sheila.

"Everything. Pots and pans, candles, a fish tank with fake fish so you don't have to clean it, cleaning solvents, jewelry, mops and brooms, books, you name it."

"You must go out shopping every day," said Terri.

"No, I don't go *out* shopping. I'm purchasing the stuff off the TV—on QVC."

"Holy Jesus Christ!" exclaimed Lucy, coming up for air from the crab legs. "That show is deadly. Oh my God. Listen, I bought a couple of things off there and loved them. Then I started watching it a lot. I quit when I got my credit card bill. They make it too damn easy for you on there."

"Yes," said Peggy. "I got a Q card. They always have a Today's Special Value, Easy Pay, use your own credit card, send a check—you name it, they can accommodate you."

"How did you get hooked on that?" asked Reba.

"Well, Esther bought me a nice watch for my birthday and told me where she got it. So I started looking at the show. Then I started purchasing a few household items I really needed and they were good. They had that line of pots and pans—you know, the nonstick ones, Cook's Essentials—and I started on them. Before I knew it I had twenty-six pots and pans. They are really good, too, and you know how I love to cook. Then I started sending friends gifts from off the show."

"Yeah," said Reba. "I love those pans you sent Doug and me for Christmas."

"Thanks, sweetie." Peggy continued. "Then I started buying things like silverware and cake cutters and books. I went from there to the Northern Nights linens, which are superb. The next thing I knew I had all kinds of cleaning fluids, mops, and a swimming pool so the kids in the neighborhood could have fun when they came over. You know, the pool has a battery that blows it up and it is really safe. I kept on with the jewelry and I also bought some food."

"Food? What kind of food?" asked Lucy.

"Well, for instance, those crab legs you are totally taking advantage of—they sell them, too. They sell all kinds of cheesecakes, steaks, hamburgers—even potato chips. They've got everything. It's a wonder I'm not bankrupt. I just couldn't stop. You know, it stays on twenty-four hours a day and I had it on all day while I was here working. I even taped it when I went out so I wouldn't miss anything. I started staying up most of the night, too. If I turned the TV off, I couldn't sleep. Let me show you something. Come with me—all of you."

Peggy led them all down into her basement. It was filled with boxes. Almost every inch of it had items in it. It resembled a warehouse—shelves were built in and items were also placed on them.

"Holy shit!" screamed Sheila. "Peggy, you are in deep trouble. Have you gone crazy?"

"I know," Peggy said, shaking her head.

They all started going through the boxes and examining the stuff and checking out what was on the shelves. The majority of the things had never been used. It seemed to be great stuff and they had a ball down there. It was like Christmas, the way they were opening boxes and looking through things.

"What are these little lights, Peggy?" Lucy asked, holding them up for everyone to see.

"Oh, they're tire lights," said Peggy.

"Tire lights? What the heck do you do with them?"

"You put them on your tires and they check your tire pressure. They tell you when you need air or have too much air in them. The lights blink. If the lights blink green, you are safe and have adequate air. If they blink yellow, that is 'caution'—telling you the air is dropping. If the red light comes on, that's 'danger' and you need air. The light fits over and replaces your old valve cap."

"Unbelievable. Let me check them out," said Terri, taking the lights from Lucy.

"So, Peggy," asked Sheila, "why aren't they on your car—helping you?"

"Oh, I have a set on my car, I bought those for extra. I bought three sets, just in case Howard or Donald needed them. You know, when you find something good on QVC, you have to hurry and act right away. You see, many people stay up all night waiting for the things and they are so selfish sometimes and buy up everything before the others can get to it. So I always stock up. Also, many times QVC either runs out or an item is discontinued, so I have to move fast and get plenty in case something happens like that."

"Peggy, why did you buy a knife with two handles?" asked Sheila, walking over to Peggy with a gadget.

"That's a cake cutter. It cuts a perfect slice of cake each time. You hold on to the handles and insert the cutter into the cake and you've got a perfect slice. If you want the slice bigger or smaller, you squeeze or open the handles. Then the piece of cake also stays inside the cutter until you get it to a plate and you never have to touch the slice of cake. It's perfect for parties. We'll be using the one I have upstairs later when we cut your graduation cake."

"What does the doctor say, Peggy?" Reba asked sternly.

"Well, they just talk to me. Once a week they discuss how I feel and what I bought, with me alone, and the other day I have group therapy."

"You mean, there are some more of y'all with this QVC problem?" asked Sheila.

"Well, I'm in the Shopaholic Group, you know, of the Compulsive Shoppers, but a lot of them go to the malls and stores—they buy everywhere. I'm the only one who is a QVC addict."

"What do the others in the group buy?" asked Emily.

"Well, one guy buys ties all the time. He has about four hundred beautiful ties. He goes to Bloomingdale's for them, and all the good stores. He changes his ties three and four times a day at work, according to how he is feeling. If he is happy, he puts a real colorful one on. If he starts having a bad day, he switches to a dull color like brown or gray. If he is really lively, he puts one on with a lot of red, purple or yellow in it. He bought one of those portable safes and he keeps ties on the job in it, just in case someone tries to steal them. He also keeps ties in his car. He said that sometimes his moods change while driving—you know, for instance, if he gets in a traffic jam or something or somebody in another car makes him mad. He keeps a box of ties in the car because he pulls over and changes his tie. He said his personality changes with the music being played on the radio and he gets happy or sad or lonely or whatever—so then he has to change his tie."

"You know what, Peggy, that guy should be attending an additional group because he has another set of problems, too," Emily said. "The plain and simple truth about him is, he is a fucking nut." The group was laughing hysterically and Peggy continued.

"We also have a girl in our group who is about thirty-two years old and all she buys is earrings. She can't stop buying them. She only has one hole in each ear, but she has over three hundred pairs of earrings and keeps going strong. She almost lost her house and that's how she ended up in the therapy group. She buys good stuff."

"Why don't you cancel the cable? Won't that help you?" asked Terri.

"I can't. I'm not ready for that yet. I'm having trouble withdrawing from the show."

"Why?" asked Emily.

"I like everything about it. The hosts are like my friends, kind of like family because I see them so much. I call in and talk to them sometimes, you know, on air, and I like the products and new inventions. I love the prices and I use QVC because I don't have to go out running around to purchase things. If I get something I'm not happy with, I just send it back and they credit me. My items come right to my door. I enjoy watching them cook and I've learned to make a lot of new dishes. You know, Bob's in the kitchen every weekend cooking. I like Bob and he teaches me things."

The girls continued to look at the merchandise and started offering to buy some of it. Lucy got up and left to continue eating the crab legs.

"Peggy, is there anything I can do to help?" asked Reba. "This is serious. Send this shit back. You can do that."

"I want my stuff. I may not need it all, but I want it—just in case."

"Just in case what? Just in case a hundred people come to dinner and you'll have thirty pots to cook food for them? I say send this shit back. I ought to pack it up myself and take it all to the post office. You need to get your money back," Reba said.

"I got my money back once, but it didn't work. I bought the stuff all over again," said Peggy.

"You mean you sent all this crap back once and bought it all over again? Jesus, I'm really worried about you now," said Sheila.

"Well, I didn't send it back."

"What are you talking about?" asked Terri.

"Let's go upstairs and hear the rest," said Emily. "I want some wine."

They all went back to the living room, passing Lucy. She was still at it. They passed the wine around. "Okay, Peggy, let's hear the rest," said Reba.

Terri said, "What's the doctor saying, Peggy?"

"The *doctor?*" said Reba. "What is *Howard* saying? He comes here, so he's got to know about this. What is *he* doing to help?"

"He tried to do a lot of things in the beginning. You see, when he would stay over, I would tape the show until he went to sleep. Then I wouldn't be able to go to sleep and I'd get up and turn the TV on to watch and buy. Howard would turn over in the bed and find me missing and get up to look for me. He'd make me go back to bed and I'd tell him I wasn't tired. After that Howard tried to help by going to the sex store."

"The sex store?" asked Sheila, intrigued.

"Well, he had this theory that if he could tire me out . . . you know . . . that I would stay asleep during the night. So he went and bought a sex toy and he got some Viagra, too, from his doctor. So we would . . . you know . . . have longer sex and he felt I'd fall out and not wake up to shop."

The room was quiet. All the girls were in amazement listening to this story because Peggy was so refined, levelheaded and classy. They couldn't imagine her being involved in any of this.

"What kind of toy did he get?" inquired Emily.

"Oh, honey, please don't make me get into that. This is already embarrassing enough for me."

"Go on, Peggy," said Terri. "I want to hear the rest of this."

"Well, that didn't work, so Howard went back to the sex store and purchased another device, and I'd still get up and shop afterward."

"Damn," said Sheila. "You are something else, Peggy. Do you still have the toys? I'll buy them off you if they were any good. Were they things you stick up you or what? If they weren't that personal, you may have a sale."

"Sheila, shut up!" cried Reba. "You are going to make Peggy feel bad. Go down to the Pleasure Chest and buy your own shit. Come on, Peggy, finish explaining."

"All right, since the first two things were not doing the job to make me fall out and stay out, Howard kept going to the sex store looking for the right thing and paying for the Viagra prescriptions, which was running almost three hundred dollars a month for thirty pills. Pretty soon he had spent a heap of money and was afraid he would end up with the same problem I have—only at the sex store." Everybody cracked up.

Peggy, feeling a little more relaxed and less ashamed, invited the girls up to her guest room and they followed her. She opened the bottom drawer of the beautiful oak chest of drawers and pulled out a vinyl zip-up bag. She sat on the bed and unzipped the bag. One by one she took out the items, which included an Eager Beaver vibrator which had a clitoral stimulator with the face of a beaver and Fundies underwear made for two, which had four holes for both partners to get into and stretch space for their rear ends. They could both fit into it together. Then came a purple feather tickler, a set of dirty dice with instruction words on each side of the dice, giant jelly boobs and a flashlight massager so you could find all the right places, even in the dark. She had a purple five-function butterfly vibrator that strapped on like underwear, and it had extra long straps that reached different places. It was a pulsating device, and you could keep it turned on while wearing it around the house.

Her guests were floored. They went through the stuff like it was a pile of candy and they hadn't had sugar in months. After they examined the things, Terri said, "Since all these goodies didn't do the trick, what's Howard got in mind now?"

"He's helping me pay my bills and he made me go to the therapist."

"Peggy, you need to be going there more than twice a week," Emily said. "Maybe you need to be an inpatient." Everybody cracked up.

"Let's get back to your getting your money back for the stuff and you still have it. I want to understand that," said Reba.

"Well," said Peggy, "about five months ago, it was turning cold here in the house. Howard was away on a trip with his son, Donald. I needed the radiators bled so the heat would come on. I called a plumber—like a handyman in the neighborhood. He came and serviced me and the heat came on, but the hot water went off after he left. So I called him and he said he couldn't come back for two days, he said he was busy. So I just bore with the cold water. Well, the weather was really getting too cold and I needed my fall things, so I finally went into the basement to get them off the hanging racks.

"When I opened the basement door and headed down the stairs, the place was full of water. It was up to my thighs. Everything was floating. You know, I've stored things in the basement since I have lived here. Everything except the washer and dryer and hot water heater were floating including all of my clothes and boxes of shoes from over the years. I never threw much away because styles come back, you know.

"I started screaming when I saw all this mess and stuff floating. All my QVC things were there, too. I called the plumber and asked him what he had done. I hadn't been in the basement since he had come to bleed the radiators. I told him to come right away. He got mad and said he didn't know anything about any water and he was not coming.

"By then Howard had returned and he came. There was so much water he called the water department and they came and shut it off. Then I called another plumber that someone referred me to—he was also a fireman. To make a long story short, I had to be evacuated from the house because there were wires in the water from the humidifier and the electric company got involved. It was a mess. They found out that the plumber guy had turned a valve and he forgot to turn it back and water went everywhere."

"Where did you go, Peggy?" Terri asked.

"Well, I had homeowner's coverage and I called them. I ended up going to the Hyatt downtown."

"The freaking Hyatt! They put you in the Hyatt? Shit, give me that jackleg plumber's name and number so he can come bleed my radiators," shouted Sheila. "That Hyatt is my spot!"

Everyone laughed as Peggy continued. "Well, they didn't want to put me in the Hyatt, but I had to be moved right away and I don't have any family here and I really didn't want to move in with Howard. They tried all day until dark to find me a place with a kitchen and laundry, but they couldn't find a place. I went to the Hyatt and they had to pay the bill. I offered for them to move me the next day, but the insurance company felt they would have it cleaned up the next day so I stayed there."

"Well, I see they cleaned it up," said Reba. "It's not wet."

"Yes, they cleaned it up and redid the walls and all and they paid me for my stuff. It took them three weeks. They ended up paying me over fifty-five thousand dollars."

"What!" screamed Sheila. "Now I know I want the number. You had fifty-five thousand dollars worth of QVC shit down there? Reba, give me that wine bottle!"

"Well, I had ninety-seven pairs of shoes in the basement," Peggy said.

"How do you know how many if they were floating?" asked Emily.

"They sent a crew out here and they counted each and every item in the basement and replaced all of it, and they also gave me a new Maytag washer and dryer and paid for all of the old clothes I had down there plus what was hanging—even underwear and all the QVC stuff. There were stereos and a couple of old TVs down there, too. They paid me for everything. I had replacement coverage. The hotel bill was three thousand seven hundred dollars because I had my meals there and they paid for my parking. They also gave me a special rate because I stayed so long."

"Peggy, how much money do you have left?" Reba sternly asked.

"You mean from what they gave me or my regular income?"

"From what they gave you, Peggy."

"Nothing."

"Does QVC have the money, Peggy—all of it?"

"No. Reba, I have the new washer, dryer, and heater and paid the contractors to fix the walls. I got a new wardrobe for what was lost in the flood. I replaced all my QVC stuff and bought some extra things. I paid the hotel bill and sent out some gifts. I paid my bills up, put ten thousand dollars away in case I get married and I bought some stocks. I'm broke."

"And you are still shopping on QVC?" asked Reba.

"Only on the weekends."

Reba looked at Sheila and said, "Sheila, help me get every last damn TV out of this house." Everyone cracked up.

"Okay, Reba the Diva. Let's go, girl. I want to hear your story. Come on, Reba baby, tell us the news," Lucy said.

Reba stood up. She was as fine as she could be. She had a short haircut, an olive green silk dress that went to her ankles with slits on each side, leopard shoes and bag, and there wasn't a bottle of ketchup in sight. She was off that sauce that her ex-husband had trained her to cook with and eat every meal doused in. Dangling from her ears were beautiful gold hoop earrings; she had three gold bangles on her right wrist, and her wedding ring sparkled with diamonds. Reba had made a remarkable transformation from the dull, drab, colorless person she used to be when she lived in Philadelphia with that rotten ex-husband of hers, Johnny Penster.

"Hello, folks," she said, waving her hands. "First of all, I love my life—thank God and Peggy. Doug is still a dream. My six brats are happy. I love the house. I'm no longer a librarian—I work for an insurance company."

"What, Reba?" asked Emily. "What do you do at the insurance company?"

"I work in the investigation department, you know, like the fraud department. I investigate claims. Marlene Prescott from Ryers got me the job after I did Johnny in when he tried to scam her company for all that money. Her company has a branch in Baltimore. They like my work."

Peggy started laughing and said, "Yes, Reba, you do nice 'work' for insurance companies. I can see why they hired you." Everyone started laughing.

"Well, Reba," said Sheila, "just fill us in on something else, you know, since your husband Doug is not here and all and we can *talk*."

"Yeah," said Emily. "What's going on with Johnny the man, you know—the trash bag loser?" Everyone cracked up.

"Well," said Reba, "he calls and writes to the kids and I think that is a good thing, and he also came down about eight weekends over the last two years to see them. He gets a hotel room when he comes and they have fun. He's having money problems so he doesn't get down often." Lucy started laughing and Peggy put her head down.

"Let me tell you!" Reba cried. "He is having a rough time, and that Tamara cannot stand him. The kids tell me everything. They are always strapped for money because he is paying all that child support. Oh my God. They have one problem after another. Shut-off notices, cars breaking down, Geraldine, the ex-girlfriend, dropping her kids off there—the works. He is catching hell. The kids went there last Thanksgiving and when they got there that Wednesday the water had been turned off that day. You know the water department wasn't coming back out there to turn it back on late Thanksgiving Eve—you know city workers start getting drunk around then. Hell, half the time you can't even find the mailman the day before a holiday. They all ended up having to drive to Trenton to stay at his parents' house for two and a half days. Nina is in college, and he has to help pay for that, and she calls him every five minutes and every time me and Doug say 'no' to something. He's paying support for two other kids not including my six, and crying the blues like no tomorrow. For Christmas we sent Tamara a pack of blank tapes and a cheap tape recorder to remind her of how I caught their asses before I left Johnny's ass. Girl, I know she was pissed."

She looked around and saw everyone was paying close attention. "He called me one day and asked me to come to Philly to talk to him. He said he needed to say some things and needed me to come. I said no. He begged. Started crying on the phone. I finally agreed and decided to talk to the thing. I told Doug and went. I was scared the fool, Johnny, might kill himself or something and then my kids would be all upset. His parents won't give him a dime because of everything he did, but they send the kids stuff and help out with Nina's college. So, listen, I told him I would meet him in Delaware at that casino because I knew my way there and I wasn't meeting him at any hotel or any place like that. So I go to

Delaware and he shows up. He looks bad, too, like he is going through something. He looks sad—sort of depressed."

"Hi, Reba, I am so glad you came." She didn't say a word. He observed how good she looked. *Damn,* he thought. She looked like a model. Every hair was in place, she was wearing a gorgeous fuchsia-colored pantsuit, with silver jewelry, and he noticed an exquisite silver watch on her wrist. As he looked her over, he was convinced that his paying all that child support, and his not getting a dime from the sale of their house, bought this new look for her. She had to be loaded, or else her husband had to be. Shit, somebody had the bucks. This was not the Reba he'd had for fourteen years. He was impressed and even more damn sorry he'd fucked up. They walked over to the restaurant of the casino, were seated, looked over the menu and ordered.

"Hi, Johnny, what can I do for you today?" she finally said.

"First of all, I want to apologize for everything I did," Johnny said, looking pitiful.

"Do you really know what you 'did' for fourteen years? Do you know the extent of the damage?"

"I know I did you wrong and I just wasn't acting like a man, a husband and a father. I just wanted to meet with you to apologize and hope you can forgive me and we can be friends."

"I've got enough friends, Mr. Penster, but I accept your apology."

"I want to do more for the kids, Reba, especially with Nina being in college and all."

"That's extremely generous of you, Mr. Penster."

"I was wondering if you could help me to do that."

"I don't say anything bad about you to the kids, Johnny."

"I don't mean in that way, Reba. I mean, well, I just want . . ."

"What are you trying to say, Johnny, what *do* you want?"

"Well . . . ," said Johnny.

"Well, what? What did you have me drive all the way up here for?"

"Well, I just figure things are going so good for you and all. And you look so good and well provided for, and you did make out like a bandit in the end and all, and, well . . ."

"Well what?" Reba tapped her foot.

"The child support—you know all the child support I'm paying?"

"You mean the support you pay for the kids you got out in the street while we were together and I was working hard and taking care of all of you and cleaning and cooking and doing all the laundry and eating ketchup and wearing mismatched clothes and staying home and not going to the movies and answering the door for women and getting infected with *Trichomonas*. You mean *that* child support, related to all *those* events?"

Johnny was floored as she reeled off all that stuff. This was going to be tough. "Listen, Reba, I still have a lot of feelings for you, but you won't take me back."

"You're getting smarter by the minute, Johnny. That was a good interpretation of the facts."

"I understand that, Reba—your feelings and all—but I wanted to meet with you to ask you, since we never will be back together and I have lost you . . ."

She cut him off by saying, "You did not *lose* me, you *gave* me to a man. Don't start getting amnesia. Don't piss on me and tell me it's raining."

"Okay, Reba, let me say this the best I can." Reba impatiently continued to tap her foot as he stuttered on to say, "I'd like to know if you could work it out so that I can take a break from or discontinue the child support payments for a minute, until I get myself together and get my feet on the ground. I want to accumulate some things—like you have."

Reba couldn't believe it. She just stared at him. He had to be crazy. She stood up over him and shouted as the waitress brought the food to the table. "Are you crazy? I have six kids by your thieving ass. Have you forgotten Nina is in college costing me more money? You made me waste my gas driving all the way up here to listen to you piss and moan about *your* life after you *robbed* me of mine? You mean you dragged me all the way up here to ask me for *money?*"

"I haven't asked you for any money, Reba," he said.

"Oh yes the hell you have! You just asked me to discontinue your child support payments, didn't you?"

"Yes, but that's different. I mean . . ."

She cut him off and said, "That *means* you are asking me to take something away from myself and our children and give it to you. It's *money.* So you are *asking* me for *money.* It's plain as day to me—don't act like you don't understand."

"Reba, I just need to get myself together for a while, you know, just regroup."

"Regroup?" she asked sarcastically.

"Yeah, regroup. Just get myself on a better footing, and the money . . . I wouldn't have to give you would put me in position to do that."

Reba was pissed off big-time by then. "Let me tell you something, goddammit, Johnny Penster," she growled. This was a familiar tone of voice to Johnny, and all he could see in his mind was her standing outside her job that day ranting and raving when his clothes were missing, three years ago when he was still married to her. He knew he had trouble then and he had trouble now.

Reba continued, "You robbed me of fourteen years of my life and I'll just be damned if I'll help you *regroup,* get yourself together, get on a stable footing, get on your feet or whatever else you want to do. And the last thing you'll get from me is *money.* In fact, give me my goddamn gas money back that I used to get here before I file a Petition to Modify Support with the court and collect some more damn *money* from *you.*"

He looked up at her in astonishment. "Look, Reba, things are really tough for me and it would just be for a short time."

"Oh no, goddammit, it won't be for a short time—it won't be at all. Give me my damn gas money or I swear I'll have your ass back in court. Whatever situation your life or your wallet is in, your dick put you in it. Get some *regroup money* from that tired dick of yours and stop trying to continue to rob me." Reba then picked up the butter knife from the place setting, stood up and bent over the table. She touched Johnny's penis lightly with the knife, and then again as if to wake it up. "Get up, Dickie, and go make Johnny some money. He's having a hard time." She then said with the look that was so recognizable to Johnny, "Now, I am telling you for the last time, I want forty dollars right now for gas and tolls. If you don't hand it over, I'll get in my car and drive to Philly and go to the courthouse." Johnny took out his wallet and handed her forty dollars and headed toward the exit of the restaurant.

Reba called him back and said, "Didn't you forget something?"

"What, Reba?" he responded.

Reba pointed to the two plates of food on the table. "*You* invited *me* to lunch. You need to leave me another fifty dollars." He went back into his wallet, took out two twenties and a ten, threw them on the table and walked out. Reba finished her lunch, walked to the casino, put a twenty in the slot machine and began playing.

It was eight o'clock in the evening and the party was going strong with everybody telling their story. The doorbell rang and Peggy went to the door. She was shocked to see two faces in the porch light. Angie immediately put her fingers up to her mouth and whispered, "Shh." Peggy walked back into the living room and Angie and Bridgette followed.

Lucy screamed as soon as she saw Angie. "What the hell. Oh my God!" Everyone else started crowding around Angie and hugging her.

"Angie, I'm so glad to see you!" Peggy exclaimed. "This is such a pleasant surprise. And who might this young lady be?"

"Peggy—this is Bridgette."

Before Angie could go on, Lucy shouted, "We met her the night I met my hubby, Kevin. She did an astrology reading on him and read his cards. She's great! Hey, Bridgette! I am so glad to see you. We're really going to have a wild time now!"

"Hi, everyone. It's nice to meet all of you. I'll do my thing later," Bridgette said.

"Angie, girl, how have you been?" Reba asked, hugging her.

"I've been fine, still as crazy as hell."

"Angie, how did you find out about this? How did you get up here?" Peggy asked.

"Kevin told me everything and we took the train up. He knew we were surprising you guys. I really am welcome, aren't I?"

"Girl, welcome ain't the word," said Sheila. "I'm *honored* you came through. Give me a hug and a kiss." Angie moved over to Sheila for a hug.

"So, Sheila, you're a real nurse now, degree and all?"

"Yeah, Angie, I made it through. Let me introduce you to Terri, she's my cousin. Terri, meet Angie, Miss Wildwoman."

"Welcome to the club," said Terri. "I've heard some stories about you—all bad." They laughed.

"I heard you were part of the Graveyard Dig Up Crew, Terri. Lucy and Reba gave me the scoop a long time ago," said Angie. Everybody laughed.

"Yep, Angie, that was me doing my duty and looking after my baby cousin. She ought to split that diploma with me," Terri said.

"Jesus, Lucy, you're getting big, child," said Angie.

"Yeah," said Reba. "And you should see how many crab legs she's eaten tonight and is still at it."

"I'm ready for some food myself, but I've got a taste for pizza. Can we order in? I'll buy."

"Reba, look in the kitchen drawer near the knives and get the folder out that has the menus in it. Let's get Angie some pizza," said Peggy.

As Reba walked back out of the kitchen, Sheila said to Angie, "What's been going on with *you*? We've been telling stories all night. What's yours?"

"I've got to think of which one to tell. I've got so many," Angie said.

"Okay, I've got the menus. Who's getting what? I'm the waitress," Reba said.

"I want ground beef and mushrooms," said Terri.

"Cheese only, oregano and seed peppers for me," said Emily.

"No cheese—just a tomato pie," said Sheila. "I didn't go to all that trouble to lose weight to gain it back."

"Okay, who else?" said Reba.

"I'll pass. I'm eating crab legs all night," said Lucy.

"Lucy, you need to stop, child, you're going to make you and that baby sick," said Peggy.

"Yeah, Luce, lay off," said Reba. "You've been eating those things for almost three hours now. That may not be good."

"Oh, I'm okay—I'm having fun."

"Okay," said Angie. "Let's call the order in. I want a veggie with oregano. Where can I put my stuff?"

Peggy said, "Let's get it upstairs. We're all telling stories. Get settled and then you can tell yours."

Peggy and Angie headed to the second floor and Reba called in the pizza order.

When they returned, Angie got a bottle of wine, poured a glass and said, "I'm not ready to start yet. Can someone else go?"

"Come on, Angie, Miss Exotic Dancer," said Lucy. "Have you been in any strip joints lately?" Everybody laughed as they remembered Angie making everyone go to the hoochie bar to watch the female dancers when they were in Norfolk for the fashion show.

"Nope—I do have something for you but it's got to wait."

Sheila said, "What about you, Emily, Miss Knightcap? What the heck is going on with you and Jared the crooner?"

"Well," said Emily, "not now. Sheila, let's hear your story."

"Okay," said Sheila, "here comes the guest of honor."

"You're on," said Terri, pouring wine for herself and Sheila. Terri handed the glass to Sheila and said, "Drink half of that straight down and start. I can't wait to hear this."

The eight of them got into their seats. They were ready.

"Well," said Sheila, "you remember I had a considerable amount of trouble with that Bea woman that Leonard had dated before he met me. You know, the one I had to snap into reality that night she came to his house when I was there?"

"Yeah, I remember her," said Terri, chuckling before Sheila could begin.

"Well, listen, she was writing Leonard letters way after we got married— begging him to come back. She was also calling his job trying to get him to visit her. Leonard told me about it, and that she was sending him mail by FedEx to his job. He brought the letters home to me. He was on the up-and-up with it, I guess so I wouldn't act a fool with him if I ever found out. He kept refusing to see her, and she was getting all bent out of shape and started using drugs and drinking. Leonard kept telling me things and bringing the letters home. So I was really pissed, but I didn't get on him about it because he was being up-front and never *missing* or anything, so I knew he wasn't cheating. But it was bothering me, so I started going to this tarot card reader for advice."

"Oh man," said Lucy, "I love this story already! What did she tell you, Sheila?"

"Well, the woman was really accurate about my life and all, and she said Leonard was really a good man. She also told me at one reading that something was going to happen in about ten days—that it would be an unexpected feeling I would get, and to just act on it, follow my instincts. I couldn't figure out what would happen, so I just waited. Nothing happened in six days and I was getting impatient. I was starting to think that Leonard just might be up to something—or maybe Bea. So on the seventh day I took the kids over to Perry's mom and dad's house and told Leonard I was going to Maine to the correctional facility to see Lenora."

"Lenora, Jesus Christ," said Reba. "How is she doing? I meant to ask."

"She's doing well, but let me go on."

"Okay," said Reba. "Let's hear the rest."

"Okay, I go over to Maritza's to hide. I didn't know why in the world I was doing all this, but something just made me do it. You see, everything that tarot woman ever told me was the truth about my past life experiences, and when I started going to her she had told me a few things about the future that came true."

"Like what?" asked Emily.

"Well, one time she told me that there would be a knock on my door and it would be detectives. She said they would be questioning me about something that happened in the neighborhood. That happened. There was a big fight in the neighborhood with some teenage boys who had come around and beat up another boy. The boy was pretty badly hurt and the detectives knocked at my door and were questioning me as to whether or not I had seen anything.

She also told me that a petty thief was around me and was stealing small amounts of money from me. That rang true because I had hired a housekeeper and babysitter after Lenora went away and she was stealing money out of the jar I kept in the house for emergencies. A couple of times we missed twenty-dollar bills. I would always keep a twenty on the mantel in case the kids needed to get a cab in an emergency. She didn't last very long, telling me she didn't know what happened to twenty-dollar bills twice in a row and that maybe the kids took them.

"Then once the tarot card reader told me that my girlfriend was going to have an accident—the one with the white car. Well, I told her that I had two girlfriends and both had white cars. You know, I have some friends at school, and Maritza has a white car. So I was trying to figure that one out and I told them both. My girlfriend Sasha from school had a terrible accident near Bucks County and the car was to-taled. So I just knew, when that woman told me something weird was going to happen and for me to just act on what I felt, that it would hap-pen. I've only told you three stories about what she'd told me, but I have a long list of stuff."

"Okay, come on, so what happened?" asked Peggy.

"Well, I stayed at Maritza's two nights and I'd use her car to go by the house and watch."

"Watch for what?" asked Lucy.

"Shit, I don't know, Lucy. I don't know what I was watching or wait-ing for, but I thought maybe that Bea was going to come to my house or something."

"Oh, now you know Leonard wouldn't bring that woman there," said Reba.

"Well, I wasn't sure of anything, so I went to the house. Nothing. On the ninth night, I went to the house about seven o'clock. I used Maritza's car so Leonard wouldn't see mine. I parked it and went into the house and went in my back room and got under the bed and I kept all the lights off."

"Sheila, you *are* crazy!" said Peggy.

"Yeah, I know I am, but I couldn't help it."

"Damn, Sheila," said Lucy, "you were just going to *make* something happen, weren't you? Poor Leonard."

"So, I stayed under that bed until about ten thirty. Leonard wasn't home from work yet. Something told me to get up and go down to the Rockaway bar. You know I never go in that place. I don't know why, but something just told me to do it and I went there. Girl, I found Leonard and Bea sitting in the bar with drinks in front of them."

"No—no way—you mean he was in there with her? Oh shit, I'm going to the lady, where is she? She's good!" screamed Reba.

"Is Bea still alive?" Emily asked after being quiet for a while.

"Oh yeah, she's around. Let me finish. They were at the end of the bar. I just stood there for a minute in shock. Leonard looked up and saw me. He looked at me like I was a ghost. I walked real slowly to the end of the bar where they were sitting. I looked deep into his eyes and then hers. I didn't say a word to him. I had on a green sweat suit that was too big for me because of the weight loss. Leonard grabbed me before I could grab her. He had the back of the sweatshirt twisted to hold me. I was like Gumby—all rubberized in that thing trying to get away from him. I couldn't get away. She started to run toward the end of the bar. I was trying to chase her and he wouldn't let me go. Guess who was in the bar at the other end and saw everything?"

"Who, girl?" asked Emily.

"Wesley. Remember Wesley, the one that went to the graveyard with me. Now you *know* Leonard did not want to fuck with Wesley and me at the same time. Wesley is a stone thug, from the neighborhood big-time, and is always into cousin Terri for something, so I'm like family. Terri's always lending him money for one thing or another. Wesley jumped up from the stool and got to the door before Bea could. He held her and told Leonard to let me go. Leonard started giving him some talk about my being his wife and minding his business and all this stuff, and then two of Wesley's boys just stood up and came over and got me away from Leonard. Girl, while I was whipping her ass they were fucking up her car. They made Leonard point out the car. It was a trip. Everybody ran out of the bar and was watching the fight like they were in Las Vegas and it was Ali and Frazier. It was something. After that, I cursed Leonard's ass out and we went into our house. I looked in the freezer and got two packs of frozen ribs and beat the shit out of him with them. He loves ribs and I was planning to cook them over the weekend. You know

I believe in giving my men what they enjoy—just like I gave Perry those five decks of cards at that graveyard.

"After that we talked. He told me he had agreed to see her because she said she needed someone to talk to because her life was all messed up. It seems she got some money from an accident. Apparently she had gone out two New Year's Eves ago to a party at a fancy hotel. She got coked up and was also drinking too much. It was one of those hotel parties where you pay a fee that includes a room and dinner and open bar. A package type thing. Well, she stayed at the open bar and got too wasted and fell off a balcony while hallucinating or thinking she could fly or something."

At that point Emily interrupted Sheila and started waving her arms up and down as if she were flying. Then she started singing that song that goes "I believe I can fly, I believe I can touch the sky." The whole crowd was roaring laughing. Sheila calmed them down and continued.

"In any case, Bea jumped off the second-floor balcony. Leonard said she told him her friends were standing in the lobby when she did it, so I guess she was in a hurry to get down there to them and figured it was best to fly. Hell, I don't know. The bottom line is she collected this money in a lawsuit. The hotel was negligent because they should have flagged her and didn't. So when she got hurt, even though it was her fault, they had to pay.

"So she gets this lump sum of money and she wants to buy a house, but her credit is so bad that she couldn't get the loan. So she gets a friend of hers, a guy with excellent credit, to go thirty percent 'no doc' with *her* settlement money and get the loan in *his* name. Apparently they had been platonic friends forever—or something. Well, lo and behold, thirteen months down the road after she gets the house, they have a fall-out. Bottom line is she was making all the payments, paying all the utilities, had homeowner's insurance in his name and renter's insurance in her name—the works—and he was putting her ass out anyway. He didn't even live there—he had his own place. So she was in deep shit after running around nearly a year and a half trying to stop him. She got depressed and wanted to talk to Leonard, and that's why she was at the bar. She asked him to meet her there. She had called him on his job."

"Don't you think you were pretty hard on Leonard, Sheila?" asked Peggy.

"Well, I had to respond that way so I wouldn't have that problem again. Leonard is a good guy. I wanted to make sure he knew better than to get involved with that nut again for any reason. I love Leonard, don't get me wrong—and I do trust him—but he is a man, let us not forget that. So I keep a couple of slabs of frozen ribs in the freezer and I make sure Leonard knows how tight Terri and Wesley are. We get along fine and I never bring up what happened."

"Can the guy really put her out?" asked Emily. "I mean, doesn't she have cancelled checks and papers that can verify that she gave her settlement money for the house? That's a shame."

"Well, it's a big thing and lawyers are involved now. I don't know what is going to happen, but I know Leonard better stay the hell out of it. I'm not going through any more bullshit with anyone."

"So how is Leonard acting now?" asked Angie.

"Just fine, and she stopped sending the letters, too. Wesley and his boys scared her, and she probably thinks they'll do something to her *and* Leonard if she doesn't stay away."

The doorbell rang and the pizza delivery guy had the goods. Peggy invited him in and Angie came over to pay him.

"Look at this fine Philly brother I found here," Angie exclaimed.

"Oh God," said Lucy, "here we go." She got up from the couch and waddled over to the dining room table where Angie, Peggy and the deliveryman were. "Listen, mister, try to get out of here quick. This one is a maniac," she said, pointing to Angie. The guy smiled.

"I'm not afraid," he said. Lucy starting hooting like an owl and Reba and the others joined in.

"You got a girlfriend?" Angie asked the man.

"I'm looking at her," he answered.

Angie turned around in a circle and did a little dance, and the crowd started hooting big-time.

"Is he my type or what?" Angie asked. "What's your name, brother?"

"Dorsey, Dorsey Grimes."

"I'm Angie Sayer. I just got in from DC."

"Looks like a nice party you have going on here."

Angie handed him twenty-five dollars and said, "Why don't you keep the change and stay? I've got a real job for you."

Everybody started hooting again and then fell silent because they had no idea what was going to happen next.

Chapter Eight

Emily and Jared

One Tuesday night Jared told Emily that he was leaving to work out of town. He explained that he'd be back in a week. The weekend rolled around to Saturday night. Emily became bored and kind of lonely. She had gone over to Maritza Fleming's house for the weekend to pass the time. Good friend Maritza said to Emily, "Look, there is this party happening at this bar at Fifth and Columbia. Wanna go? I know the barmaids down there and it's a birthday party for one of them, so let's check it out. You need to do something besides sit around thinking about Jared."

Emily didn't usually go *out* out when wonderful Jared was at work, but she decided to do it. Maritza called up a girlfriend of hers, Valerie, and she decided she'd come along, too.

It really was happening and the place was packed. They met some nice guys there and they were sporting them. This one particular guy named Leo started paying a lot of attention to Emily, spending big cash, and he really was kind of nice. Not attractive, but a great guy. They were soon talking up a storm. Emily asked him what sign he was and he said Leo. Emily thought he was lying but checked the driver's license out and indeed he was a Leo. They were all having such a good time with him and his friends that she was surprised when he said, "Wanna split and check out another spot?"

"What spot, where?" Emily asked.

"A place downtown called Hippopotamus. It's a pretty nice club. I've got you and your friends covered." Emily ran it by Val and Maritza, and they split with Leo and his friends. Emily rode with Leo, and the others were in Maritza's car. As Leo was driving he began chatting with Emily.

"You're pretty cool. Are you married or hooked up with anyone?" he asked.

Emily didn't know whether to lie or tell the truth about her and Jared.

She didn't want to scare him off because she had an attraction for him and was having fun. She decided to be vague and said, "I've got a boyfriend, he's working this weekend. What's the story with you?"

"I do construction work, have a lot of fun when I can. I'm presently not dealing with anyone. I'm free. What does your man do?"

"He's a salesman and works a lot of weekends out of town."

Emily was smart, and she had made up her mind a long time ago that no one other than her close friends would know what Jared did for a living now that he was back with the group. She used this precaution because she couldn't trust people. She worried about some crazy person trying to kidnap Renee or her niece or nephew thinking Jared had money. Also, she was being careful with her and Jared's relationship. She didn't ever want some guy who liked her and couldn't have an affair with her to know that Jared was in the Knightcaps. He could get pissed and appear at a concert to have a little "chat" with Jared during an intermission, just like she had the night she met him. Jared's life was simply too open and public and people had access to him, so Emily kept that part of her life pretty private.

They continued talking, finding out where each other lived and where he liked to party until they arrived at the club. They went in for a few dances, had a great time and left. They were standing outside the club talking and decided to go out to breakfast at the Marriott on City Line. When breakfast was over, Leo asked if he could come home with Emily. Emily explained that she was staying at Maritza's.

She really did like him a little. She'd had a good time and she was interested in him. Maritza gave her "the look" and said okay. So they left to go back to the bar where his friend left his car so he could pick it up. Then they all went back to Maritza's house.

When Maritza went to bed, Emily and Leo got it on. Jesus, it was good. The boy had a lot of imagination. But what she liked about him, what attracted her to him, was that he was real normal and homely-like. She couldn't explain it. Just real natural, like she had known him all her life. She trusted him. He was generous and fun, and the sex was definitely an asset. So he spent the night with her. The next morning he got up and dragged her into the shower with him.

There were no words for what went on in there with that water going. Honest to God in heaven, he put it on her. When they got out, he dried off, got dressed and said he was leaving. Didn't give her a number or anything. Just left. She thought, "Oh boy, that was certainly a one-night stand."

About an hour later he returned. He entered the house loaded with groceries. All this food: bacon, ham, sugar, coffee, pancake mix, eggs, steak, napkins, all kinds of stuff. Then he started cooking breakfast for Emily and Maritza. Everything he bought was in large quantities, like five pounds of sugar and three pounds of bacon. He told Maritza that he wanted to make sure some things were left over in case she hadn't gone shopping for the week. Emily was impressed that he could cook. Then they sat around stuffed from all the food they ate. Maritza decided to take a shower and get dressed, leaving Leo and Emily alone. Leo said to Emily, "I wasn't playing with you last night. I really dig you. I'm serious. Talk to me."

"Listen, Leo, I have to be honest. I'm involved with someone. This thing was nice—last night and right now—but I'm hooked up."

"How long hooked up?"

"Over a year."

"How does he treat you—you happy?"

"Yeah, I'm happy."

"Then what were you yelling about in the shower?"

"Extra passion."

"So you need extra passion?"

"Apparently so last night and today, or I'm a bit lonely and confused."

"Do you love him, baby?"

"Madly."

"When's he coming home?"

"Tuesday."

"Wanna hang out with me tonight?"

She looked at him and she could not say no. She really wanted to be with him. It had nothing to do with Jared doing or not doing anything. She wanted to be with this guy. He was so ordinary and so unlike what she had with Jared—all the lights, the egos, the drama and the screaming females. There was no noise, glamour, room service or abundance of money. No traveling around from here to there. Also, with Jared in her life she had to watch everything, everybody and herself. She had to be so many people, wear so many different hats: the girlfriend when appropriate because of Stephanie, who was still his wife; the police, because often she felt Jared was in danger out there in the fast lane of the "exciting" world; the confidante, because they were so tight; the secretary when he was in business discussions; *and* his love companion. Then she meets this guy and he is a construction worker—blue collar—no glamour, glitter or lights. He wasn't singing anything. He was relaxed. She looked at him and thought about him coming home from a hard day's work all dirty in construction boots. She thought about meat loaf and mashed potatoes for dinner and not lobster, and the diversion appealed to her. She thought about having Kool-Aid instead of wine and somehow that turned her on. She imagined his paycheck being five hundred a week instead of five grand and them having to do *normal* things. For the moment, all that looked damn good—the change in scenery—the low-key life.

So Emily agreed to see him on Sunday night, and they decided to hit some spots to party and grab some light dinner somewhere. He would pick her up at seven. She was happy to be going on this date. At about four o'clock a delivery guy came with a beautiful bouquet of pink tulips. The card read, "If you think you know me now, wait until tonight." She screamed with delight.

She gave Maritza the entire scoop and spent the day there. Leo arrived around six o'clock and parked on the couch while she was ironing jeans and a blouse to go out. She put the ironing board up in the living room to keep him company while he watched television and waited for her to get dressed. Maritza was in the kitchen making some food.

About six thirty the doorbell rang. She was still in the living room talking to Leo. Maritza was still in the kitchen. Emily answered the door. Jared was standing there with Lee and Kelly. He walked in and said, "I'm home early." She looked at him like he was crazy. She rushed into the living room ahead of them and looked at Leo and put her finger to her mouth to say, "Shh."

They came in behind her and she introduced them to Leo. "Hey, everybody, this is Leo, a friend of ours."

Jared saw the ironing board up and started scoping out the place. The Knightcaps proceeded into the kitchen. She stayed in the living room ironing. She was scared to go in there. She didn't need to be interrogated.

"Hey, Maritza, what's up, baby, what are you cooking?" asked Lee.

"I'm baking some fish and making a salad."

"Good, we're starved. Do you have enough for us?" Kelly asked.

"Uh . . . well . . . yeah, yeah, I've got some more food. I thought Emily said you guys were coming back in town Tuesday."

"We got off early. Who's that in the living room?" asked Jared.

"Somebody I need to try to marry." Maritza gave that answer because she had a feeling some shit might hit the fan and didn't want to get involved. She had enough drama with Dr. Pierce Remington and wasn't up for anything that night. This was Emily's problem, and she was definitely staying out of it.

Emily used her little bit of time in the living room wisely while the Knightcaps were in the kitchen.

"Listen, Leo, that's my man in there. Just listen to what I say." She immediately called her sister Regina's house and thanked God she answered.

"Regina, listen to me and do not say a word. I have a guy at Maritza's. Jared just walked in unexpectedly. I had a date with this guy. Talk to him and whatever he says about the two of you going out tonight, you go along with it. He'll be leaving here soon." She then handed the phone to Leo. He and Regina began talking.

Emily then walked into the kitchen. Everyone was quiet when she walked in. "Hey, so how was work? I thought the gig was over Tuesday. How did you all manage to get away so soon?"

"Who's in the living room?" Jared asked.

Emily immediately developed the jitters and it showed in her face. "Leo, remember . . . I just introduced you to him."

"Who the hell is Leo? I never heard of him."

Maritza continued washing fish and never said a word. Emily wanted to kill her.

"Leo is a friend of Regina's, my sister. He's going by there tonight and stopped here to pick up those jeans I'm ironing. She wanted to borrow them."

"Oh yeah?" said Jared. Everybody else remained silent.

"Oh yeah, Mr. Detective."

"You know what, Emily? You are one busted ass this evening. You must think I'm stupid. Now, if I go in there and ask that guy to describe Regina and tell me where she lives, you'll be fucked. Won't you? Why don't you come clean—you know I caught you." Everybody started laughing, even Emily.

Jared walked back into the living room and sat down on the couch next to Leo. He wanted to be smart and *really* rub it in.

"So, Leo, how long have you been dating Regina?"

"Well, actually, this is our first date tonight."

"How did you meet her?"

"I met her at a club last night."

"She really is an attractive girl, Regina, and nice, too. That was a good catch," Jared said.

"I hope so. I'm really attracted to her."

"What does her husband think about that?" Jared asked.

At that point Emily walked into the living room and said to Jared, "You know what, stop it. Leo, listen, I have to ask you to leave. Jared and I have a situation here and it really isn't your fault. Thanks for coming by and I'll talk to you soon."

Leo walked to the door. Jared picked the jeans and the blouse up off the ironing board and gave them to Leo. "Don't forget Regina's outfit," he said. Leo walked out of the door without the clothing.

"Let's take a walk out to the porch," Jared said.

Emily looked him up and down and was thinking, "Here comes the shit."

This was the first time he had ever caught her at anything, and she didn't know how she'd handle him or what he was going to say. She did know one thing. Jared was a calm guy and he had never even raised his voice to her. This was different, though, and she wasn't sure what would go down. She remembered when she caught him.

* * *

She showed up at his office unexpectedly one afternoon and was standing at Astrid's desk talking to her while waiting for the Knightcaps to get in from a meeting with Norman Harris, a songwriter and producer. The Knightcaps had been on the road for four days and had this emergency meeting, and Emily had not talked to Jared in two days.

Two White girls walked into the lobby and up to Astrid's desk. They were giggling and as happy as could be. Two dumb blondes. One of them announced, "Hi, I'm Wendi and this is Lynne." Emily noticed they had southern accents. The Knightcaps had been working in Florida over the last four days.

"Hi," Astrid said. "What can I do for you?"

"Well," said Wendi, "we're here from Florida. We just love the Knightcaps. They are so great. We had a ball with them in Tampa. I belong to Jared and Lynne is in love with Damon. We flew up today. Are they around?"

Astrid shot a look at Emily, not knowing what the hell she was going to do. Serena, their administrative manager, who had walked by and heard the conversation, quickly approached the desk. She figured Emily was going to go ballistic. "Those damn Knightcaps," thought Serena. "At it again." Every time she turned around women were at the office looking for them, causing confusion.

"We had so much fun in Tampa with them," Wendi babbled on. Emily was quiet, taking it all in. Astrid was scared to death and Serena was pissed.

"Yeah," said Lynne. "Things went so well and we enjoyed them so much that we took off work for a few days to go romping with them in Philadelphia. We got time off when we explained to our boss what great guys we met."

"So, you guys work for the stars, huh?" asked Wendi. "That must be *soo* exciting. Jesus Christ, you get to see and talk to them all the time. You've got the best jobs in the world, especially looking at those gorgeous guys. Every time I see Jared's dimples, I melt."

"What are your names? Let's get to know each other. What do you do for our Philly boys?" Lynne asked.

Emily cut in, "I'm Emily Frazier, the Knightcaps' managing secretary."

"For real?" screeched Wendi. "Just what do you do?"

"I set up their contracts, review them, and watch their money."

"Oh, so you'll be getting the hotel and restaurant bills? We're sorry we ate and drank like pigs with them," said Lynne.

"Yes, darling, I'll get them, but don't worry about that. So, how long are you two in town?" asked Emily.

"We don't know yet. They don't know we're here. We're surprising them. Are they around?" asked Wendi.

"No, but we do expect them. Where are you staying?" inquired Emily.

"Well, we just got in and haven't found a hotel yet. We're going to wait to see what the guys tell us about that," said Lynne.

"Okay, you two wait over there on the couch. They'll be here soon, they had a meeting."

"Thanks, Emily, but before we do that, we want to get the names straight so we can let Damon and Jared know how nice their staff was to us. Maybe we'll get you all a raise," said Lynne.

"This is Serena and this is Astrid," said Emily. "Now you two make yourselves comfortable. Do you need anything, food, something to drink?"

"I'm starving," said Wendi. "Where can we get something?"

"Well," said Emily, "I can order up for you from a local restaurant or I can tell you where some places are."

"Tell us where to go and we'll eat there and come back. Then maybe the guys will be here by then," said Lynne.

"Okay," said Emily, "I'll call you guys a cab and write down where you are going. Then I'll see you back here later."

"You are a dream," said Wendi. "I'm going to make Jared do something for you. You are such a good worker."

"Yes, I do my best to take care of the Knightcaps, and *Jared*."

Emily got the girls the information, called a cab and sent them on their way. Once they left, she, Serena and Astrid started laughing and shaking their heads.

"Emily, I've got to hand it to you, you are smooth. What are you going to do to Jared?" asked Serena. Astrid sat there with a blank expression on her face because she was wondering, too, what the hell was going to happen when Jared got to the office.

"I'm not going to do anything to Jared—in fact, I'm leaving here."

"What!" yelled Serena. "You mean you're going to let him get away with this? You mean you are *really* on 'calm mode'?"

"Yep, 'calm mode' is what the deal is." Emily got her purse and switched out of the office.

Now that Jared had caught her, she was getting ready to bring up the dirt on Wendi if she had to. She'd definitely go for it if necessary.

They proceeded to Maritza's porch. It was enclosed and had plants everywhere, small trees in pots, a couch, phone, cable, and the walls boasted a beautiful shade of paint like a deep peach. Maritza was quite the decorator. The ceramic floor looked like marble, and to add warmth, she added a beautiful Oriental rug of mint, black, peach and beige.

Jared sat Emily down on the couch and picked up her hand. "Now, you know I'm about teaching you a few things when I can," he said. "So this conversation is going to go in three segments. I say my piece, you don't interrupt, and then you go. Agreed?"

"Agreed . . . I guess, but I reserve the right to interject if I have to. Agreed?"

"Maybe. Let's see what happens. Just listen first, okay? First of all," said Jared, "I'm not going to ask you what you've been doing all weekend because I already know. I'm going to let you know *how* I know so you won't make the same mistakes again. This Leo, you know . . . the one who just left here . . . your sister's 'date' . . . well, we both know he was *your* date and probably your date all weekend. I knew something was up this morning when I woke up, so seeing you was the first thing on my agenda when my plane landed. I came home early just for you. We left Rodney and Damon in Atlanta. I called Horace's and he said you had been gone since Friday, so I figured Maritza knew where you were. That's why I came here. When you answered the door, you gave yourself away because you always greet me like you really missed me, but tonight you were nervous and your tongue didn't go down my throat. We both know that you don't give a damn who shows up with me when I come to you. You lay it on me no matter who is watching.

"Also, you smelled too good, baby. Showered and perfumed for Maritza? Nah . . . I surmised. You're wearing the good stuff, baby, the stuff you wear for me. My antennas really went up then. I walk into the living room and you're ironing? You don't iron unless you're going out. I know you. And, *Leo* is sitting there. Leo is really relaxed, like he is at home. Comfortable. Okay. Then we take a walk into the kitchen and Maritza doesn't know anything. The least she could have done was cover for you. I mean if she had *talked,* it would have brought suspicion down, but Maritza didn't want to touch that living room with a ten-foot pole. Then I knew it was a little serious because she didn't want to get involved.

"You stayed in the living room too long, baby . . . giving yourself away even more. Then Leo turns out to be a friend of the family that I never heard of and came to pick up clothes. Okay. So, Emily, you got busted and I know something happened between the two of you. Let's proceed on to segment two of this conversation." Emily held her hand up for permission to speak. He ignored her and continued.

"I know you . . . always remember that. So I know the interjecting you want to do is about Stephanie and Wendi. You want to play those two cards right now so badly you can't stand it. Don't you?" Emily took a deep breath and attempted to speak again, and before she could respond, he cut her off.

"Now, to be fair I must admit, I've given you a run for your feelings for me. Yeah, you've gone along with Stephanie big-time—for a long time—and you caught me red-handed with Wendi, but you know I did not bring that birdbrained blonde up here. I admit something went down in Florida and I explained all that to you after she told me how sweet and efficient you were when she showed up at my office. You know I haven't seen Wendi since then. I had Astrid *personally* put her and her friend on a plane that same night. To apologize, I did give you a nice 'raise' in Aruba for seven days and literally kissed your ass for three months because I fucked up. And that is exactly what I did. I fucked up.

"Now, Stephanie. You knew about that from jump street. When Stephanie showed up in Chicago and caught you and me and went crazy, was pregnant and about to kill herself, I thought the whole thing over. I decided to go straight, do the right thing and marry the girl. I know what that must have done to you, but I came to you and I explained it all. You know how distraught I was and how guilty I felt about everything. Okay. So, I break your heart and become a husband—all in the same day. Nine days later I'm back in bed with you. Okay, my life is at the point where I'm still trying to keep all three of us happy. No doubt, I couldn't live without you in peace . . . and vice versa.

"Okay, here comes my son popping out. You see him and you've got a problem. My mom sees him and she's got a problem. So, yes, we all realize he's not my son. So, since I had cheated on Steff, too, I thought it over and stayed with her and never let her know I knew the kid wasn't mine. I felt guilty again and felt that maybe she wouldn't have been screwing around with the real father if I hadn't been doing the same thing with you. I felt I owed her and she wasn't stable enough for me to walk. And I couldn't give you up. I couldn't let you walk. So I became a madman for a while, running here and there trying to keep everybody happy.

"Steff knew I was with you while I was in the marriage. Then she gets tired and you get tired, too. And I'm *thoroughly* exhausted. So she and I split up. Now here you and I are, alone at last . . . together . . . and now we have *Leo*. Here comes the third segment.

"I know I expect too much from you. I always have. I depend on you too much to *understand* everything. It never really was fair. I'm crazy about you and you know it. I understand the pressures that you have been under with me for the past three years. I know my job is a pain in the ass with the traveling and the traffic. I know how much you care for me. You proved that in California. I can't say I'll never make a mistake or fuck up again, but what I do adore about us is the honesty we have always shared—the solid friendship and the omission of jealousy in our relationship. You and me can deal. You know that. I can tell you *anything* about *anybody.* That creates a blanket of trust in our relationship.

"Now, Leo said or did something to move you. Knowing you, it was more than a few things because you're not a whore. Something was there, and you haven't been ironing all weekend. I'm not going to give you any ultimatums, tell you what you'd better or better not do. I'm not going to leave you and I'm not going to ask you not to see this guy again. In fact, I'm going to give you some space, baby. I'm not leaving you because I can't, I love you, but I want you to be a *whole* Emily. I can't use you mixed up and in pieces, baby. I need you clear and focused. I'm just buying us some condoms in case you call me. You got that?

"Maybe you need to do some exploring and you'll learn something. You have intrigued me from the second I met you. I am not a stupid man. I plan on keeping you—in any capacity—because you are real, even sort of *sacred* to me. I trust you. I need you. I can take my armor off with you, Emily. I can take it all off knowing I can relax. Don't think I'm being overly generous with you or anything like that because I'm not. And I do suspect one thing—I suspect that the two of us will never be overcome or completely separated by another person—no matter how thick they lay it on us. I can wait, baby—do your thing. One thing you do not have is an insecure Jared. Now, where's my kiss?"

Chapter Nine

Paula

For the last seven days, Paula had been in Walt's office banging his brains out. He had even come in on the weekends to 'work.' She was being worn out and he couldn't get enough of her. She felt she was getting some control with him; however, she was taking it slowly. The ninth day they were together, after she got 'dressed,' she looked so good he smacked his lips and said, "I really have to have some of that my way today, Paula." He got on his knees and began nuzzling and kissing her crotch, around the edge of her red lace panties. She moved his face away and looked down at him and said, "No."

"Why?" he asked softly.

"You see, oral sex from a man to a woman is a very special and private thing—so very, very personal, Walt. You just can't do that with everyone. You have to truly care for the person. You have a wife, Walt, and that is something you only share with her. I'm your play toy. Just some dessert you have. Your wife—that wonderful woman whose pictures sit about this office, with your loving children—she is the only one worthy of that from you. I am not." She bowed her head. Paula should have gotten the Academy Award for that performance.

He was stunned. He felt so sorry for her and he was truly moved by her compassion for his wife. He wondered how such a decent person could end up in her situation.

"It's okay with me, Paula. I care about you. I want to do that with you. I want to please you like you please me," he said.

"Oh no, Walt. I cannot allow you to do it. Lie down, let me give *you* pleasure. That's what I'm here for. I'm here to serve you—to keep you warm and safe," she said. She then gently pushed him down on the couch and went down on him. He had tears in his eyes.

After that she fucked his brains out again, and as they lay on his couch talking, she said, "Can you get something for us?"

"What, sweetie?" he asked, stroking her face.

"Depends," she said.

"Depends on what?" he asked.

"The diapers—you know, silly," she answered.

"What? You really mean those diaper things? What do you need them for?"

She got on top of him and rolled her ass around grinding on him, causing another erection. " 'Cause you're my baby, Walt, and I'm going to put my baby in a diaper and fuck him wild next time we meet." He screamed with delight and said, "Sure thing, Paula—I'll have them here for you."

Paula sat in her cell telling Josie all about Walt. Josie was dying laughing. In a few minutes Carlos, her Puerto Rican pimp, came for her. It was time to go to the library to 'read.' After they finished, she said, "Hey, Carlos, I just love it when you read to me. You have such a gentle and soft voice, and it's so calming. Many times I sit in my cell and think about the great books you read and wish I could have you read to me there. I know that is impossible, but I was wondering if you could get me a Dictaphone and some tapes and record our sessions. We could do it if you can control yourself and not make any sounds when I'm doing my job for you."

He was startled at the request and a little suspicious, but said, "I'll think about it. We'll see."

"Is it that you want me to pay you money for the things?" she asked.

"No, it's not the money—I just don't know if I would be comfortable doing that. Let me check it out first to see if it is okay for you to have it. I'll let you know."

"If the cost is too much for you, you can stop giving me the bath gel and I could also give you something toward it. I'd really like having the relaxation of your reading to me in my cell. You know it's hard for me to concentrate when I'm here with you during the reading because I'm try-ing so hard to please you."

"All right, Paula—I said I'd work on it. Come on, let's get out of here."

"Hey, Carlos," she said.

"What, Paula?"

"My birthday is coming up."

That damn Jake the Ice Man was coming back in four more days. "Shit," Paula said. Jesus Christ, she wished he would stay where he was. She knew she'd have four men to do once he got back. She didn't know how she would hold up. Walt was supposed to be just while Jake was on va-cation but she knew he wasn't about to end it with her. Tomorrow she had to meet Berman for lunch. Every time she saw him she wanted to vomit. When he opened his mouth with that southern drawl, it was hard for her not to grab his gun and shoot his rednecked henpecked ass.

As soon as Paula walked into his office, Walt pulled the Depends diapers out of the bag and held them up, smiling. "I've got 'em, cupcake—just what you wanted," he said. Paula looked at him blankly and sat on the couch, sulking. He rushed over to her and said, "What's the matter? You asked for these and I got them."

"I miss having something real. You know—like other people have."

"I don't understand, Paula, I really am nice to you," Walt said.

"I know you are, but it's not like a real relationship. I never have any memories to look at, like pictures of us and stuff. You know?"

"Well, what do you want me to do? I try to make you happy. It's not like I can take you out and do things like real couples do," he said.

"Why can't you take some pictures of us, or let me take some of you so I have them to look at when I am alone—when I am without you? Also, you know Jake will be back in a couple of days and then it will be all over. I have no memories of our good times together. That is bother-ing me."

She then got up from the couch and approached his family pictures.

She picked up the one of him and his wife and stared at it. A tear fell from her eye. She put the picture down and returned to the couch. "I'd like to go back to my cell. I'm not in the mood today. I'm sad and depressed," she said.

Walt sat down on the couch next to her and sighed. "Paula, what do you want me to do?"

"Can I take some pictures of you? I promise to hide them and not let anyone see them. I'll sneak and look at them when no one is around."

Walt pondered her request for a few minutes. He then went to his desk, unlocked it, and took out a Polaroid camera that he used to take pictures of contraband such as weapons and drugs that were taken from inmates. "Here's a camera," he said. Paula looked relieved and then smiled and jumped up and hugged him.

"I love you. I just love you to death," she whispered, and she did a little dance.

"Okay, calm down. What are we going to do?" he said.

"Well, let's get my baby into his diaper and I'm going to take the cutest pictures of your sexy ass, and I'll look at them every night before I go to sleep so I can dream about you, my sex maniac," she said.

Walt snatched his clothing off immediately. Paula said, "Come here, handsome." He walked over to the couch where she was.

"Go get the lotion and the Vaseline out of your drawer and bring your ass back over here," she ordered. He obeyed, going over to his desk. She watched the blubber on his fat ass and thighs jiggle as he skipped. He retrieved the two items and returned to her.

"All right, little baby. Lay your booty down so Mommy can put your diaper on."

Walt lay down. Paula reached into her uniform pocket and pulled out a pacifier she had "ordered" from a fellow inmate and stuck it into his mouth.

"Suck on this for now, and if you're good, I'll give you something else to suck on later." She then proceeded to apply lotion to his stomach. Then she had him turn over and she massaged his ass and inserted a little Vaseline into his asshole. He was moaning with delight. She had him turn over onto his back and lift his fat ass up, and she grabbed a diaper out of the box and placed it under him. She put a little Vaseline on his crotch and penis, then taped the diaper to his waist. When all was done she had him stand up and strut around the room as she purred sexual obscenities at him.

"Skip for Mommy, Walt. Just skip around the room, baby." He carried out her wishes with his pacifier still in his mouth. He was loving it.

"Now, do a little dance for Mommy, my little baby," she requested. Walt began dancing to no music and clapping his hands.

"Get over by the wall, baby. Face the wall and shake that cute ass— just shake it for Mommy. Move it around in circles, baby." Walt was moving his butt around, and she got up and stood to the side of him.

"Now I want you to imagine I am against the wall, but don't touch the wall. Move your ass real slow in circles, baby," she directed him. "Pretend that big whopper of yours is in me. I *need* it. That's it, baby," she said as he moved his ass.

"Move to the left and then to the right. Yeah, you've got it, baby. You are *sooo* smart, Walt. You're Walt the Worm and you're in me. Oh shit, goddammit—it feels *sooo* good. Oh baby—you are the fucking best— you are the man! Work it, Walt. Now, make pretend you are a beater on an electric mixer—you know, like you use to make a cake. You've got to go around and around to the left and then to the right—but on low speed. You're allowed to hold on to the wall now. Don't fall, baby. Yeah, baby, you've got it. Now, stop. Stop, Walt. Now, push your butt out and freeze. Poke that ass out, Walt the Worm. Freeze! Now go back into me hard! Hunch your ass in. Bend, Walt, bend your cuddly butt—I love that butt. You know that's *my* butt, don't you? All mine. Now vibrate your ass, baby. Go fast now, Walt—shake it!" Walt adhered to each and every command, panting like a maniac.

"I'm gonna come! I'm gonna come! What should I do?" he screamed. The pacifier hit the floor.

"Hold it, Walt, baby—don't you blow this," she yelled. "Stop. You don't want to have to start all over again." She moved away from him and went to the couch.

"Come here, Walt the Worm," she ordered. He inched over to her.

"Stand there while I take a couple of pictures for us," she said. He was a nervous wreck standing there sweating, and he was red as a beet, but he stayed still. Paula grabbed the camera and he tried to regain his composure, fumbling, as he showed her how to operate it.

She took three pictures of him and put the camera on the floor after she snatched out each picture. They looked at them in awe. She put the snapshots in her pocket and quickly removed her clothing. When she was butt naked she lay on the couch. He was standing over her and his mouth was watering. With her index finger she pointed at her vagina and said, "Finally, my love—it is lunch time for you. Go at it, man, and remember you are not on a diet. Don't leave anything for anyone else."

As he was engrossed in going down on her, she snapped two more pictures.

Chapter Ten

Purdy

Stefana was lying on the chaise lounge in the library when Purdy walked into his house. She heard him come in and strolled to the foyer. "You must be my date," she said seductively as he stood holding two bags that contained dinner.

He dropped the bags, took the box of vanilla wafers out of her hand and let it fall to the floor. He took her into his arms and hugged her tightly, then passionately kissed her. He moved away and they held hands, looking at each other. "The scenery is captivating," he said.

"I've got a job for you," she whispered sweetly, as she picked up the box of Nabisco Nilla Wafers.

"What would that be?" he said, whispering between kisses.

"I want you to make me a banana pudding, meringue and all, before I leave here."

He laughed and said, "What are you trying to do, get fat on me?"

"No—not at all. It just looks *sooo* scrumptious, like you. I want some."

"You want some? You *really* want some? Let's take a walk and get some quickly," he said. He led her upstairs to a door that was locked. He opened it and said, "This is your playroom." Stefana squealed with delight as she viewed the room, which contained a hammock that hung from the ceiling and had thick vibrantly colored pillows, a huge trampoline, an adult-size sliding board and video arcade games.

"This is amazing! When did you have this done? I absolutely love it!"

"It was completed last week. Watch this," Purdy said as he turned all the lights off. The tiny silver stars on the beautiful purple walls and in the ceiling were sparkling. Stefana was spellbound. "Take your pick on where we begin," said Purdy.

Stefana walked over to the arcade game and started to play Pac-Man.

As she was standing, he leaned up against her and began gently massaging her from the neck down as he undressed her. She was aroused and it became impossible for her to continue the game. She turned her body around to face him and completely disrobed him. She teasingly backed up to the sliding board and then climbed the stairs to slide down. When she was at the end of the slide, he was there on his knees to greet her. He placed his palms on her knees and his mouth entered every crevice of her vagina. He then picked her up and laid her in the hammock. As he made love to her, in between kissing her and catching his breath, he was saying, "How was your flight? Are you hungry?" Any problems with the limo? I'm so glad you're here." They swung into ecstasy.

When it was over, they entered his bedroom. He retrieved his address book and dialed a number while she lay in his arms and he stroked her face.

"Hi, Mrs. Charleston, it's Dr. Remington. I was wondering if you could prepare a banana pudding for me. How soon could that be done? I also need it delivered to my home. Can you swing all that? I know this is short notice, but I have a dinner guest who's craving it." Stefana giggled, kissing him on the cheek.

"It's nice to hear from you, Dr. Remington. I don't have all the ingredients I need to make it and will have to shop a bit. Can I have it for you first thing in the morning?" she asked.

"First thing in the morning?" Purdy asked as he looked in Stefana's eyes for approval. She pouted.

"No, that won't do. I really need it tonight. A midnight snack of it is what we're aiming for. Let me see if I can make some calls and get someone who could have it ready sooner."

"I'm sorry, Dr. Remington," she said. They hung up.

"Okay, baby, we have to work on that one. Get up and let's shower. I've got dinner downstairs. I'm cooking for you tonight."

"Are you sure you're up to it?" she asked, running her index finger across his penis, causing an erection. They made love again and afterward he went down to the foyer to put the bags away. On his way back to Stefana he stopped in the playroom and retrieved the box of vanilla wafers.

He returned to the bedroom and said, "You've blown dinner here, baby—either eat these or let's head to a restaurant." He picked up the phone and called Mrs. Charleston back, requesting she deliver the banana pudding in the morning, preferably before noon.

Purdy arrived at his office. As soon as he heard his private line ring, he figured it was Maritza, and it was.

"Hi, what's up?" she asked.

"Hey, Jazz, how are you, baby?"

"I'm good. I was thinking about coming by for lunch."

Purdy knew he couldn't get tied up with Jazz at the office. He felt he wouldn't be able to get rid of her. "I'm only here two hours today, Jazz. I have to go up to New York for a conference for three days. I'm seeing a few patients and I'm out of here. You know I have to get a lot of things done before I leave for Europe and China. You'll have to sit tight. I plan to spend a couple of days with you before I leave for the big trip. Will that work?"

"I want you to do better than that. Find some time for me before that," she demanded.

"Can I go through my schedule and the list of things I have to do and call you back?"

"Call me back when—today?"

"Yes, today," he said.

"Well, what time are you leaving for New York?"

"I'm trying to be on the train by two, Maritza," he said.

"I'm Maritza now—I know what that means."

"Look, Jazz, just let me breathe a moment and get some things done. I can look over my schedule while on the train and try to do what you want me to do. Okay? Just let me get my work done here and get out. I'll call you later." He hung up.

Maritza sat staring at her phone. It was nine fifteen and she had to see a client at ten for two hours. She missed Purdy. No one knew that she loved this man to death. He was the man of her dreams, and she was trying to hold on to him. She fantasized many times about their wedding and her and his enormous family. Even though they fought like cats and dogs, this was her man and she adored him. She just couldn't let *him* know it.

Stefana scooped three heaping tablespoons of the banana pudding into a saucer and went up to the playroom and lay in the hammock. She thought about Purdy and smiled as she ate the wonderful pudding. She knew she'd better not go near any more of the scrumptious stuff, for it would surely ruin her figure. She oozed down into the hammock, thrilled with her life, which was working out perfectly. After a few games of Pac-Man, Purdy arrived around noon and they headed for Manhattan. She loved that town, and he'd gotten theater tickets for two shows— *Smokey Joe's Café* and *Miss Saigon*. Stefana loved spending time with him and enjoyed his attentiveness and the way he pampered her. He also provided the best sex she'd ever had in her life.

It was six o'clock when they pulled into Purdy's driveway. His car was gone so Maritza knew he had left for New York. "Okay, come on, Dredge," she said.

He began fumbling around with the alarm system as she watched to see if they were being observed by anyone. It took him about eight minutes before he had blocked the system. He then reached into his pocket and retrieved an object. He jimmied the lock, and in another two minutes, they slipped inside the elaborate residence of Dr. Pierce Remington. Dredge was stunned at the beauty of this home. He started walking around and shouted, "Damn! The doc is living large."

Maritza was busy checking the place out, hunting for some signs of a woman. She checked the bathrooms, cabinets and drawers. Then she went into his bedroom and took the neatly made bed apart and checked the chocolate-colored sheets for semen. Yep. It was there, and she hadn't been on those sheets with him. She went back into the bathroom and looked in the shower, finding two wet washcloths hanging—one was a beautiful shade of pink with an embroidered rose on it. After checking his bureau drawers for more evidence and finding nothing, she remade the bed and exited the bedroom.

She then noticed the playroom door ajar and walked in, finding the surprise that she'd never been introduced to. She returned downstairs and told Dredge it was time to go. She was pissed—she knew that bastard Purdy had probably taken the bitch with him to New York and also hired another decorator to do that room. "Business meetings," she muttered as she and Dredge left the house. She didn't hear from him over the next two days.

After their fabulous night in Manhattan, they returned to Philadelphia and Stefana spent the last night in Purdy's bed having multiple orgasms. A limo picked her up at six in the morning and she was one happy camper on her way back to Barbados.

Purdy called Maritza before he left for his office. "Hey, girl, I got back late last night. How are you?"

"I'm fine, Dr. Remington. Have you missed me?" she asked. While talking to him she envisioned him with another woman in Manhattan. She was still pissed.

"A little, I think," he said smoothly. "I apologize for not getting back to you. I've been terribly busy. Do you want to have dinner with me tonight? You can pick the place and I'll spoil you a little, too."

"How about the Striped Bass? I'm in a fish mood." She knew he'd go for that because he loved the elite establishment. It used to be a full-service old-fashioned bank, full of history, and was renovated into an elegant restaurant.

"That's a great choice. Meet me there at six o'clock. Do you want to make the reservation?" he asked.

"I'll take care of it. See you at six."

Purdy entered his office and, after settling down with coffee, checked the list of appointments. Ramona Cashman was coming in again, and that brought thoughts of loneliness and fear of growing old. He knew she was probably bringing that cute baby boy with her. He again started considering adopting a child. He eased back in his chair, remembering his chat with his office manager, Jillian, and her advice. While sipping his coffee, he made a list of all the things he would have to do to be a good father:

1. Get some books on parenting.
2. Find the right schools.
3. Be available for everything.
4. Find adequate nanny and help.
5. Not too much dating.
6. Keep up with child's medical care.
7. Go to the zoo.
8. Child has to have right diet—no junk.
9. No long vacations.
10. Parent-teacher meetings are a must to attend.
11. Music lessons.
12. Read to child as much as possible.
13. Childproof the house unless child is of an age to understand.
14. Take off from work when child is sick.
15. Maybe get a nanny who speaks another language so baby does, too.
16. Child should have a pet.
17. Teach child good manners and child not allowed to chew gum.

By then he got tired and put the list in his drawer. "Jesus," he thought. "Kids are a lot of responsibility." But Purdy knew he was getting older and wanted someone in his life. He thought a child would be perfect.

"So," Maritza said, "how was the Big Apple? Did you meet anyone interesting who might try to take my place in your unbelievably big heart?" Purdy chuckled.

"A lot of work, a little fun, and a tinge of shopping is how it went."

"Shopping?" she asked with her eyes lighting up.

"Yes, Jazz, here it is—just for you." He handed her a beautifully gift-wrapped package that he'd had FedExed from the store to his office so he wasn't carrying it back and Stefana would not see it.

She smiled at the diamond bracelet, which had matching hoop earrings. She leaned over and kissed him.

"You are such a sweet man. It's amazing, with all you had to do to get off in time and then work up there, too, to find the time to pick this out for me. Don't make me fall in love with you, Dr. Remington."

"You're much too smart to fall in love with a pain in the ass like me, but I'm glad you like it and I hope you forgive me for not calling you before I left. Since you adore the slots, I can arrange to take you down to Atlantic City for a night and half a day before I leave for my next trip. How does that sound?" he asked.

"That will be fine."

"Okay, we're leaving in three days. Get your schedule together."

"Yes, sir," she said. "Am I invited to your home tonight?"

"No, baby—I've got to get some rest and get my stuff together. Let's save everything for Thursday."

"Okay," she said.

Purdy was glad she didn't give him a hard time about not going home with him. Maritza surmised he was fucked out from whomever he had been with and she let him off easy. She also had other reasons for being cool for the moment.

Purdy had serious jet lag when he reached Paris—his favorite city in the world. He couldn't wait to rest up in his favorite Saint Germain haunts and tended to stay at Leticia, except when he got pissed off because they made him wait for his room and didn't even offer him a cup of coffee after he had been flying seven hours. On these occasions he would stay at what the French refer to as "a charming little hotel on the rue des Saints-Pères." Since he didn't want any snags in the pleasure of his trip, he'd booked his charming little "no problem spot." Saturday in Paris for him was always lunch at Tan Dinh, a Vietnamese restaurant. Robert and Noelle Vifian, the owners, would eventually join him for lunch—that lasted about four hours and consisted mostly of drinking old clarets and burgundy wines. He couldn't wait to see them. After six days, which included two meetings with clothing designers and a medical seminar, he was off to China.

United Airlines delivered Purdy safely to the airport in Beijing. This was his first time in China. He was immediately intrigued but a little worried because Chinese, he couldn't speak a word of. Before he left the States he had arranged for a guide throughout his stay. When settled into the State Guest Hotel at Presidential Plaza, he had dinner in the hotel and went to bed exhausted.

The following day, Chinese- and English-speaking Ling-Ani, a twenty-five-year-old beauty assigned to escort him in and about the city, came to his hotel to meet him. For a hefty fee, she would show and tell him everything about her country for the next seven days. He was willing to let her plan his trip, but had a few suggestions as to what he wanted to do. They started out by catching the shows at Tiananmen Square and also toured the Forbidden City's Imperial Palace, seeing living quarters, jewelry areas and museums. Later that evening, Ling-Ani took him on a cruise on Lake Kunming.

When the evening was over she explained the agenda for the next day, which would include a walk to the Great Wall at Mutinyu, located in an ancient, well-preserved section. She told Purdy he would love the gondola ride as well as a visit to the Temple of Heaven. They'd finish up the evening at the Beijing Opera and learn lessons on face painting and makeup. He was excited as she drove him back to the hotel.

"This all sounds marvelous," he complimented Ling-Ani. "However, I'd also like to see where common people such as yourself live. Can you take me to where you live, and can I perhaps meet your family?"

Her face turned down with shame. "I live in a rural part of the city of Beijing and my family is basically poor. You know, I don't make much money."

He had a slight attraction for her and thought she was really cute. He felt by being a bit more personal with her, he'd manage to get to know her on a more nonbusiness level, so he asked to meet her family. After all, he thought, Ling-Ani could become great to hook up with in the future, and she was real long distance and wouldn't pose a problem.

"I'd like to see where you live, if you don't mind," he said. "You don't have to be embarrassed with me. I was not always a doctor. I know about struggle."

She was relieved to hear that. More comfortable, she said, "Okay, we can fit it in, but my family is not too happy these days. We have some problems."

"What kind of problems?" he asked.

"Well, my cousin Chung Soo is seventeen years old. She got pregnant and had a baby girl. Are you familiar with what goes on here with infant females?" she asked.

Purdy found himself suddenly very interested in this conversation and admitted, "I have no idea what you are talking about. Explain it to me."

"Female babies go through terrible abuse. Daughters are basically worthless to the Chinese Communist Party, unlike the male infants. There are laws requiring couples to produce only one child and the preference is a boy. That keeps the country from becoming overpopulated. So, married couples can have one child. If they have any more, they are fined, and the second child is not allowed to be educated or to receive medical services. Sometimes women pregnant for a second time are jailed, and if they give birth to a female, the baby is killed or placed in an orphanage. The girls are treated badly there and are not able to have toys. They are often strapped to potty chairs for entire days. The orphanages are filled with disease because the children get no medical care. There has also been talk that some infant girls are drowned at birth."

Purdy was flabbergasted hearing this information. Ling-Ani continued. "Chung Soo has no husband and therefore has no rights. We are afraid the baby is going to be killed. Chung Soo hid the entire pregnancy." Ling-Ani looked forlorn and frightened. "She had the baby at home and we've been hiding her. The baby has never even had a checkup. We cannot hide her forever. My family is terrified."

Purdy was sad and stunned. "Unbelievable," he said, shaking his head. He could picture Ramona Cashman sitting in his office, playing with her infant son while he consulted with her. "That is a sad story. How old is the child?"

"She is two weeks old."

Purdy had a wild thought: He could adopt the child. No, that was crazy—but tempting. "Let's make your home the first stop we make tomorrow. Can you take me there tomorrow? Can you find out if I can meet the baby's mother then?"

"Why?"

"It's a long story, but lately I have been thinking of adopting a baby. I'm a single man and a doctor, and that's hard adoption material in the States. Do you think your cousin may want to give the baby up for adoption in order to save her life? I can pay for the child."

Ling-Ani was shocked at the proposal. Then she began considering it. It would indeed solve a lot of problems, and her family was in need of money. Dr. Remington just might be a blessing in disguise.

"Let me talk to my family tonight. I can call you at your hotel."

"Please do," he said, giving her a card for the hotel, one of his business cards and a fifty-dollar bill.

They proceeded to do some sightseeing, and he treated her to an early dinner.

She returned him to the hotel at seven thirty and said, "I'll talk to you later."

With the thirteen-hour time difference, it was now ten thirty in the morning in Philly. "Tony Garcia please, this is Dr. Pierce Remington calling." He held on.

"I'm sorry, Dr. Remington, but Mr. Garcia is in a meeting. He said to tell you he can return your call around noon."

"Please ring him right back. Tell him I'm in China and I need him right now. I'll continue holding."

Soon his old friend's familiar voice filled his ear. "Tony Garcia at your service, Pierce. What's up, man?"

"Listen, Tony, listen fast. I'm in China and I need you to get in touch with whomever you have to in order to pull strings for an immediate adoption of a Chinese baby girl. She is two weeks old and the mother is seventeen. There is a strong possibility the child will be killed. Don't ask me the particulars, but the Chinese government is not so hot on female babies. In case the family lets me do a quick adoption, I need you to do the legwork and get the right adoption attorneys in place in Philly, New York, or wherever it has to be done. I can't explain much more. Just get the ball rolling. I can get whatever money is necessary by wire transfers. Take down the information as to where I'm staying. I believe I'll be meeting with the baby's mom tomorrow. I had planned to be here about seven days. I may be bringing the baby back with me if money talks. You got me?"

"I've got you, and I don't know a damn thing about this shit. Nothing. I'm strictly a personal injury and criminal attorney. Let me start on it and get my secretary on it. I'm going to put you back on with Alexa, and you give her all your info so we can reach you. I've gotta run. I'll call you to get more questions answered tomorrow. If you get any strange calls from anyone here or in Philly, take the calls because it could be the attorney who handles this stuff."

"Okay, Tony. Thanks, man—I'll owe you one."

"Just don't pay me by finding someone to work for me."

"See ya," Purdy said, laughing.

Purdy then went down to the concierge desk. He was grateful someone was still on duty. "Would you be able to tell me the name of a pediatric physician—someone very good? I'm Dr. Pierce Remington, an American physician, and would like to consult with one while I'm here. I would prefer an American physician if you know of one. If not, a Chinese doctor will be okay."

"Let me call you in your room, Dr. Remington. If I cannot find an American doctor, the embassy may know of one. They are closed at the present time but will reopen in the morning. I'll see what I can do."

Purdy thanked him and gave him a twenty-dollar bill to encourage him. He headed back to his room to wait for Ling-Ani's call. He waited and waited, but she didn't call. He showered and got into bed. He was tired and his brain was sailing. He was just about to take a Xanax and pass out when the front desk called to say he had a visitor named Ling-Ani in the lobby who wanted permission to come up to his room.

He quickly threw pants and a shirt on and opened the door to find not only Ling-Ani, but also a girl and a baby. As he let them in, the phone rang.

"Dr. Remington, this is Maitan at the concierge desk. I have a name of an American doctor who treats children for you, and I have a number and address. Do you want it now?"

"Thank you, Maitan," Purdy said, looking bewilderedly at the two women and the baby who were sitting in the chairs across the room. "Can you just keep that information there for me in an envelope and I will come for it later?"

"Of course, sir."

Chapter Eleven

The Slumber Party

*a*ngie removed the pizza from Dorsey's hands and introduced him seductively to all of the women. "Do not touch him—any of you," she said.

"Oh God—here we go," said Reba.

"Dorsey, are you hungry? Can I get you something to eat or drink?" asked Peggy.

"No, I'm fine, but I have to get back to work. I'm still making deliveries."

"What time do you get off? Wanna come to a party?" Angie asked. Lucy and Reba started hooting like owls. Dorsey really was cute and all kinds of things were going through Angie's mind.

"I'm done at eleven."

"That's late—that's two hours away," Angie said, looking him up and down.

"Angie, will you let that man out of here and permit him to do his job?" yelled Lucy as she picked over the crab legs.

"Look, Dorsey," said Reba, "you just met a maniac. That girl is crazy. Don't you lose your job messing around with Angie. Come on, let me walk you to the door—you have your money, right?"

"Yes," he said, smiling, "I'm paid." He walked toward the door. Angie followed him.

"I've got a plan, Mr. Dorsey. How about a couple of us riding with you to deliver the pizzas real quick so you don't keep those people waiting and you don't get into trouble? That's the first part. Can we work that?"

"I don't mind that."

"Okay, so that's a deal. Here's the next part. Do they have another delivery guy at your store?"

"Yeah."

"Okay, before you leave here, let us call there and order another pizza. What's the guy's name who delivers?"

"Steve."

"Okay, we're making progress. Emily, get the shop on the phone. Dorsey, what's the number real quick? Hurry up, the pizzas are getting cold in the car!"

"555-7532," Dorsey called out to Emily. She dialed the number and Angie took the phone from her.

"Hi, I'm calling with another order of two extra cheese pizzas to be delivered to 2240 Marshall Street; the telephone number is 555-4118. I'd also like to talk to the delivery person if he is there. I have to make sure he knows how to handle my pizzas."

"Was there a problem with your first order tonight? Did you get your pies?" the gentleman asked.

"Oh yes," said Angie, "they were delivered with no problem. I just like talking to people who are coming to my house. He needs to know all the entrances because we are entertaining in different parts of the house and we want to make sure he knows we're here. We could be in the basement or something—you know?"

"Oh—fine, ma'am, I'll get him."

"Hello," the voice answered on the other end.

"Hi, Steve," Angie said sexily. "I'm a friend of Dorsey's and we just got pizza from him. We ordered some more and you'll be bringing them here. We're having a little party and some fine women want to meet you. Can you make this your next and final delivery and plan to be off for the night? Are you game or are you chicken?" The crowd roared.

"Is it safe over there?" he facetiously asked.

"One of the ladies here works for an insurance company—you're in good hands with Allstate, baby."

He laughed. "I'll see you in forty minutes." Angie hung up and everybody was laughing.

She snatched Emily and they dashed out the door with Dorsey. When the three of them arrived back at Peggy's, Steve was there.

"Hi, Steve, glad you made it. I'm Angie and this is Emily."

"Nice to meet you both," he said as he looked at Dorsey for some explanation.

Angie opened her handbag and put two hundred dollars on the coffee table. "Here's your pay for the night." The two glanced at the cash and their eyes lit up.

"That's a lot of dough—even for pizza men," said Dorsey. "What are the requirements for this job and exactly what is the job description?" At that point Lucy got up from the table and walked her fat self into the room. The guys looked at her and many things began to run through their minds.

"Welcome to the party. I'm Lucy."

"Okay, guys, I've got some equipment to help with your duties. Let me bring it down." Angie headed upstairs. All were baffled.

"Okay, here they are," she said when she returned. "I have four of them. What do you think?" She looked at Sheila and said, "Congratulations, Miss Registered Nurse, these fine gentlemen are going to put on a show in your honor," she said as she held up four male G-strings.

The crowd was astonished, and everybody started grinning and screaming. Peggy, the refined socialite and respectable sixty-two-year-old surrogate mom with all the class, actually lay on the floor kicking and screaming with laughter. Lucy started hooting. Emily pulled out some CDs from her bag and put on "Keep on Lovin' Me" by the Whispers, blasting the music. Sheila snatched the G-strings from Angie and gave two to each of the guys and said, "Get dressed, fellas, and make sure you earn your money—the party is on!"

Everybody gave Angie a high five, complimenting her on a job well done. The women then began dancing and waiting for the show to begin.

The next record was "Ladies Night" by Kool and the Gang and Dorsey and Steve entered in their "uniforms." Dorsey was in a turquoise sequined thong and Steve was in leopard. The crowd roared. The men not only danced seductively for the ladies, but were even on and off the furniture, arousing everybody. They laid Sheila down on the floor and picked her up, gently swinging her body. Dorsey had her feet and Steve had her hands, rocking her. Reba and Terri were dancing on chairs, claiming they were go-go girls. After that Peggy insisted on the limbo, and the guys obliged her by inching under the broom being held by Angie and Emily. When they made it through and under the broom, Lucy was there holding a slice of pizza in one hand and a bunch of grapes in the other, feeding them. Then the guys came around and started over again for the snack. The refined socialite and grand duchess of the neighborhood, Peggy, was standing next to Lucy armed with the blow-dryer set on "cool" to comfort their sweating bodies. Sheila had run upstairs and gotten Peggy's sex toys and had successfully fitted the "all-in-one belted vibrator" on Steve. They all carried on until after one o'clock in the morning, at which time no one could eat another thing or dance another step.

"Okay, gang, Bridgette the astrologer is about to do her thing. I've been waiting all night for this," Lucy said.

"Okay, I'm going for the Scorps today," said Bridgette. "Are there any in the house? Can you take it?"

Angie stood up and said, "Why do you have to start picking on me?"

"Oh shut up, Angie, and stop crying. Come on and take your medicine. I've got to hear this mess. I've been waiting a long time for this. Let's go, Bridgette—don't pay her any mind. Angie, just get a bottle of wine and start getting drunk. As good as I hear Bridgette is, you're gonna need it," Sheila said. Everybody started hooting.

Angie gave Sheila a dirty look. She went to the table where the beverages were and got a glass and a bottle and plopped down on the floor. "Okay," she said, "bash me, girl."

Bridgette announced, "Is Angie is the only one in this crowd who is a Scorpio? I guess the rest of you are scared to death to admit it and you're hiding out there somewhere and not going to own up to it. Come out, come out, wherever you are," she said.

There was no response. The other guests starting hooting at Angie. Once everyone got settled, Bridgette began.

"Okay," said Bridgette, "I'll start out with the good stuff and work my way down." She had everyone's attention as she pulled a stool over to the center of the room and sat down. She looked directly at Angie when she started. "You are the sexiest sign in the zodiac," she purred. "Pure passion and lots of imagination. You've got it, baby. A Scorpio can really give it to you. Most of them are excellent cooks, too. Even the men. Their food is just scrumptious. They are organized. They are great parents, if they are not too rigid. They are great concentrators and calculators. They are not impatient. They have terrific basic personalities if you are not dealing with them one on one. They are the most complex sign in the zodiac and the hardest sign to have a relationship with—I mean *close* relationship. They are water signs, full of emotion.

"They are suspicious people by nature—they can't help it. They are also extremely possessive. Because of their insecurities, they are stone control freaks. They *have* to be in control and they can't relax because they are carrying too much. You know—they are strapped with the burden of insecurity, which makes them jealous. So they are on guard all the time. They aren't good at relationships because of those shortcomings, which make them unable to relax.

"When I say 'relationship,' I don't just mean *intimate* relationships, I mean relationships *period*. Working ones, family ones—any kind of relationship, they usually screw up because they are just plain not good at them. Scorps are fun people from afar, and you can have a lot of good times with them if you don't get too close. *Close* gets you the negative adjectives I described. *Close* buys you problems. These people are so insecure they are basically scared to death. They are also truly vindictive people. Oh my God, the last everything they have to acquire. The last word, the last hit, the last everything, and a Scorp in a relationship will suspect you of *everything*. Even though their imagination is a positive attribute, it is often their mate's worst enemy.

"They are unlike the Pisces who just sets out to do some dirt from jump street. They don't have the self-confidence that the Pisces people have, because Scorpios are drowning in insecurity. The other water sign is Cancer, who are also emotional and jealous, but they aren't *vindictive* like the Scorps unless they have a moon or a rising in Scorpio. Cancers are mainly frugal, moody, jealous and supersensitive. Cancer people drive you crazy in other ways that I won't even start on, but *all* the water signs have a certain degree of that backstabbing capability. You know they are crabs, fish and scorpions. They've got claws, they are slick, and two-faced by nature unless they have planets in their astrological charts that alter the typical and normal behavior of the sign. For instance, Cancers are nailed as being frugal and thrifty—but not a Cancer Snake. In Chinese astrology, people born in the Year of the Snake are quite different and the Snake is a sign of beauty and extravagance. I'll explain all that to you next time—but each and every one of you is an *animal* in Chinese astrology, according to the year you were born. I love Pisces Monkeys, even though I warn people about Pisces people. Look yourselves up when you get home. You'll learn something. Let's get back to business.

"I have Scorpio friends whom I love. I'd never break my friendships with them. They are fun. I just know not to cross them and to keep them at arm's length. I feed them with a long-handled spoon—big time. I know how to handle them. I know they can't take criticism well and you can't go anywhere near telling them they didn't do a good job on something. They can't take it, and believe me, they do things well, but they are not perfect or infallible. Nonetheless, you can't discuss that with them. That's a no-no.

"I give the Scorps a lot of credit for having excellent parenting skills, and if you give them a project to work on, they can do it, and they are able to charm you their way—every time. They can lie with a straight face all day long and smile, and you're not on to them if you don't know what I know. People won't even realize they are headed into their corner until they've been there a while and started to get comfortable. They make excellent attorneys—especially in criminal law. They are extremely manipulative people and they want you to *need* them. Believe me, they don't want you totally independent by any means. Another thing about the Scorpio is when you have found them wrong, they are going to turn it all around until it's your fault. It will be like you are talking to a wall when you are trying to get your point across. In the end they will find *you* guilty of whatever the problem was—never them.

"You can become addicted to their food and their sexiness. They *think* about what they're going to put on you. They've studied you and concentrated on you so they know how to woo and move you. They won't rush you—they're going to take their time and *really* fuck you up—in the sack or on the floor by the fireplace. Now, a Scorpio hooked up with an

Aries, Leo or Pisces is going to enjoy sex like they've never had it before. Let's hope they don't kill each other in bed because these are *the* sex signs—but the Scorps *really* have the power. All these signs have a freakish nature about them—no holds barred.

"Remember you are a *project* to the Scorpio—an *investment*. Just like people watch their stocks—whether they are going up or down—they are watching you—whether you are up to something or not. And if you are, they will be the first to know it, and if you betray or cross them, you will truly pay in the end.

"So, ladies, remember this, this Sunday afternoon at—what time is it?—precisely 4:48—a Scorpion stings your ass. They are born late October and run into late November. If you've got one you better hope to God they have some Libra, Aquarius or Sagittarius planets in their astrological charts, or you'll pay dearly. This is a wrap, ladies—let's close the astrology corner for today."

"I swear I've got to go to bed," moaned Lucy.

"Yeah, me, too," Reba listlessly added.

"Okay—where are we sleeping, Peggy?" asked Terri.

"Anywhere you want—I've had it. There are some blow-up AeroBeds in the basement from QVC. I put them by the stairs. Just plug them in anywhere. There are three bedrooms upstairs and the beds are made up. You can find the bathrooms, the couch is available and blankets and sheets are in the linen closet upstairs. Find your stuff and your way around."

"What about our 'employees'?" Angie meekly asked.

Peggy glanced over at Steve and Dorsey, who were lying on the living room floor in separate corners. Peggy waved her hand at everyone and said, "Find them somewhere to sleep and give them some pillows and covers. I'm going to bed." She headed for her bedroom.

Angie walked over to the guys and said, "You've done a bang-up job. Thanks, and we'll make you comfortable. I'll see you both at breakfast later on." Then she winked at Dorsey and said "Remember, I live in DC, but I'll be back. How about me and you going on a date? I promise to let you keep your clothes on. Sleep tight, baby." She switched out of the room. Reba watched her walk away and hustled up four sheets and two blankets and dropped them on the couch.

"Hey, dancing men—the basement is that way," she said, pointing across the room. "Find the beds and I'll see you in the morning."

It was after four a.m. when Lucy waddled out of the bed and went into the bathroom to pee. Her stomach felt funny. She got back into the bed with Reba, who was out like a light. She tossed and turned, trying to get in a position to go back to sleep. She began having cramps and tried to relax, but the pain was worsening. She was quite uncomfortable. "Wake up," she said as she shook Reba. Reba didn't respond. Lucy gave her another good shake and whispered right into her ear, "Get up, Reba, I'm having pains." Reba sat up and began rubbing her eyes.

"What's going on? I'm tired. What's wrong?"

"I don't know what's wrong—I'm sick or something, or going into labor. I'm having some pains. I feel creepy, too."

"Oh shit—get up! We're getting out of here!"

Reba got out of the bed and helped Lucy up. "Just sit here until I get everybody up. We're going to the hospital. You're getting out of here, girl. How long has this been going on?"

"About an hour and a half."

Reba went into the second floor hall and shouted, "Everybody get up! Lucy may be having the baby!" Nobody answered or moved. She went into Peggy's room and began shaking her. "Get up, Peggy, we have to take Lucy to the hospital."

She ran out and entered the bedroom where Emily and Angie were sleeping. She turned on the light and yelled, "Get up! We've got to get out of here! Lucy is in labor!"

The next stop was the living room, where she found Terri knocked out in the recliner and Sheila in a coma on the couch. She immediately started yelling about Lucy's pains and they started stirring. Within fifteen minutes everybody was ready to go.

Soon they were all at the hospital. Lucy was being examined, her parents were on their way there and Angie was on the phone calling Lucy's husband, Kevin.

"Listen, Kevin, we're at the hospital with Lucy," she said.

"At the hospital? She's not due for four months. What happened, did she fall down or something?"

"No, she didn't have any accidents. She ate a bunch of crab legs. She just wouldn't stop eating them during the party. We went to bed and she woke us up because she started having pains."

"What? Let me get out of here! What exactly is going on with her now? How far apart are they?"

"I don't know. She's with the doctor."

"Who else is there? Did you call her mom and dad?"

"Yes, Kevin, and they are on their way."

"Okay, Angie, let me get myself together and get there. I have to figure out exactly how to get there. If I get a flight it will have to be first thing in the morning. It'll take me six hours to drive. Oh shit—this is something."

"Look, Kevin, why don't you stay put until the doctor comes out and tells us something? I'll have the doctor call you," Angie said.

"Okay, Angie—don't take too long."

The nurse returned as Lucy's parents were rushing into the waiting room asking questions. Peggy was filling them in. Mr. and Mrs. Noble were amazed at how many people were there.

"Who are those two, Peggy?" Mr. Noble inquired.

"The pizza delivery boys."

The bewildered look still appeared on their faces and Peggy said, "It's a long story, but they're nice young men, and very concerned about Lucy."

The nurse then announced that Lucy was doing fine and they were planning to keep her for a couple of hours to watch her. They gave her something to stop the contractions. The nurse let everyone know that the doctor was on the phone with Kevin, and in a few minutes two members of her family would be able to see her briefly. Shortly thereafter, Mr. and Mrs. Noble went in to see Lucy and the rest of the gang decided to wait the entire thing out and bring Lucy back. In fifteen minutes the Nobles returned to the waiting room.

"Okay," Myra Noble sternly said. "My daughter will be fine and should not have another crab leg while she is pregnant. We'll wait here until she is discharged. You guys can go on back to Peggy's. I'll call when we're settled at my house. I told Kevin to stay in Norfolk."

"Okay, Myra. We're heading back to my house. Looks like the slumber party is over," Peggy said.

Chapter Twelve

Emily and Jared

Emily was sitting in the park with Renee. A White woman who looked to be around seventy-five years old sat down next to her.

"Hi," she said to Emily.

"Hi, how are you?"

"I'm not so good. I'm pretty sad." Tears began rolling down the woman's face.

"Oh, what's the matter? Don't cry," Emily said as she began to hug her. The woman cried in her arms.

"My husband died a month ago. I miss him so much. We were married fifty-two years."

"Oh, I'm so sorry. I hope things get better for you. Please don't cry. Is there anything I can do for you? Do you have any family?"

"I have a son who lives in Center City, and a grandson. I go there sometimes on the weekends."

"Where do you live?" Emily inquired.

"I live in Abington."

"Do you have someone who lives with you?"

"No, it's just me. I'm pretty lonely most of the time."

"Well, I live in Rydal, not far from you. I'm a nanny and I'm here with Renee; I keep her and she is five. See her over there in the pink jacket on the sliding board?"

"Yes, I see her. She's cute."

"Well, I come here on nice days with her. I'll be here on Friday if you'd like to come by and we could get some lunch together at a nearby restaurant if you like."

"That would be nice."

"My name is Emily Frazier. What's yours?"

"Rachael Feiner."

"Well, it's a pleasure to meet you, Mrs. Feiner. I'm going to write down my name and telephone number and whenever you get sad or if you'd like to see Renee and me sometime, you call me. I do work a lot, but if I can make some time for you, I certainly will try to do so. I'll be back here on Friday. Cheer up, things will get better."

"That's so nice of you. Let me write down my information for you, too. I'd like it if you could call me sometime just to chat—even if you don't have time to meet me. What time are you planning to come here on Friday?" Rachael asked.

"I'll be here at three o'clock in the afternoon. You're welcome to visit with us. I have to leave now."

"Okay, Emily, I'll probably see you on Friday—you and Renee."

Rachael never showed up. Two weeks later Emily's phone rang.

"Hello, may I speak with Emily?" the voice on the other end asked.

"This is Emily."

"Hello, Emily, this is Rachael Feiner. We met in the park. Do you remember me?"

"Hi, Rachael, of course I remember you. How are you? I'm sorry I never got a chance to call you. I've been really busy. Why haven't you been back to the park?"

"Well, I've still been sad. It's hard for me. I've been crying a lot today. Do you think you and I could get together?"

"I'm working two jobs, Rachael, and I'm very busy, but we could set up a lunch date."

"I have a doctor's appointment tomorrow in the morning," Rachael said.

"Okay, why don't we set up a date for next week?" asked Emily.

Rachael seemed anxious and began weeping. "Can you meet me tomorrow after my appointment? I really need someone to talk to."

Emily hesitated, knowing she had plans the following day. Then she felt Rachael must really be desperate. "All right, Rachael, I can meet you around twelve thirty. Where would you like to go for lunch?"

"I like the sandwiches at the Scoreboard on Old York Road. It's also quiet there during the day. Do you know that place?"

"Yes, I know the place. I'll be there."

"Do you promise? Will you remember my name? It's been a long time. Will you remember what I look like?" Rachael asked.

"Don't worry, Rachael, just sit at the bar and I'll find you. Twelve thirty tomorrow, okay?"

"I want you to write my name and telephone number down right now," Rachael said.

Emily took the information down and hung up. She genuinely felt sorry for Rachael and was worried about her. She was glad to take her out. She thought about her own mother and how maybe that would be her one day—needing someone to talk to if her dad had passed away. She fretted about her parents all the time and wished they would move from Detroit to Philly. Emily had completely forgotten what Rachael looked like but knew she'd find her. There couldn't be too many seventyish women sitting at the Scoreboard bar at twelve thirty. She immediately called the boutique and told them she couldn't make it to work the next afternoon. Now her phone was ringing again.

"Hello," she answered.

"Hey, cutie, you miss me?"

"Where the hell have you been?" she asked.

"Working like a slave. How come my question hasn't been answered?" he asked.

"Okay, I do miss you. I haven't had any real fun lately—you know—the kind you provide so well."

He laughed. "Wanna get together over the weekend?" he asked.

"That may work—which night?" she replied.

"You can choose—I'm at your disposal."

"Let's do Saturday and start in the afternoon."

"Is there anything special you want to do?" he asked.

"I'd love to go shopping and have lunch in Rehoboth Beach. Is that too far?"

"Don't I always go too far with you, Emily?" he said, laughing. She started chuckling, too.

"I'll be ready at noon and I'll meet you at my sister Gina's. I have to watch my niece and nephew while she and my brother-in-law go to some time-share meeting. Their appointment is at nine so they'll be back by the time we're ready to leave."

"Okay, sweetie—I'll meet you there."

When Emily arrived at the Scoreboard, she spotted a little old lady at the bar and walked up to her. "Hey, Rachael, here I am. Let's go to a booth." As Rachael stood up, Emily noticed how short she was. Her gray hair was chin length and she had on sunglasses. Emily figured since there was no sun outside, she must have been crying again.

During the drive there, Emily had decided to make time for Rachael in her life. She would try to see her at least a few hours a week, taking her to a movie or out to lunch. Emily's schedule was pretty full, but she was going to deal with Rachael and find some fun activities for her. She presumed Rachael would love Renee coming along sometimes because she probably missed her grandchildren. She felt good about doing this. Maybe they could even do a pottery class sometime, she thought. The two got situated in a booth.

"I'm so glad you came, thank you," Rachael said.

"You're welcome and the pleasure is mine. I'm really glad you called me and I apologize again for not getting back to you in all this time. What have you been doing? I see you've been shopping today, too," Emily said as she noticed a bag.

"I purchased some books from Barnes and Noble. I walked there from the doctor's office. I walk all over the place. I'm too old to drive anymore and I gave my car to my daughter who lives in New Jersey."

"What books did you buy? Let me see them," asked Emily. The waitress then approached the table and they ordered soup and sandwiches. Rachael removed two books and a magazine from the bag.

"I like poetry, so I got this one, and I got this other book which tells about the Holocaust. I lost a lot of my family there. I also got this magazine that tells about royalty in Britain. I love all that stuff, especially Princess Diana."

Emily picked up the books one by one, reading the backs of the cov-

ers, and then flipped through the magazine. "These are interesting topics. You should have fun with them," she said.

"I like you, Emily, and I want us to be friends. Can we do some things
together sometimes? Where do you work? Can we talk on the phone
sometimes, too?"

"I work at a boutique near Neshamany a couple of days a week during the day, and you know I babysit at night. Yes, of course we can do
some things together—we just have to make a schedule. Okay?"

"That will be fine. You can also come to my house sometimes if you
like. You know I'm right here in Abington. You'll see where I live when
you take me home. I need you to take me home when we leave."

"Okay, Rachael, I'll do that. I also have some things in mind that we
can do next time we get together. I'll tell you about them and you can
let me know some of the things you like to do."

The waitress then delivered the soups. Emily stirred the salmon chow-
der as Rachael started explaining how close she and her husband had
been and the things they used to do. She explained how much she missed
his companionship.

"Listen, Rachael, things will get better, sweetie. How long has it been
since he passed away?"

"Five months."

"Yeah, that's a short time. Give yourself some time and try to stay
busy. Things will lighten up."

"Emily, maybe I shouldn't be telling you this, but I want to anyway. I
need to tell you some things. Can I?"

Emily figured Rachael was so lonely that she may have been contemplating a move in with one of her children. It also ran through Emily's
mind that she was going to ask Emily to move in with her. "Sure you can,
I'm listening."

"There was a gentleman who was coming to our house and taking
care of my husband the six months before he died. My husband died of
cancer. The gentleman came from an agency and had an eight-hour-a-
day shift taking care of Jacob."

Emily listened and surmised the guy had stolen things from them or done something wrong. Instead of indicating her true feelings, Emily asked, "Was he nice, and did he take good care of Jacob?"

"Yes, he did," Rachael said and then paused, looking into Emily's eyes. She had never removed her sunglasses. "He also took care of some other things for me after Jacob passed away."

"Oh, that was nice of him," Emily said, feeling ashamed. She had figured the guy was a thief. "It's nice when people go above and beyond the call of duty."

"Emily, I've been having an affair with him since my husband died. He is twenty-seven years old."

Emily's face nearly fell into her soup bowl. She was speechless! She lifted her head and looked into Rachael's eyes, not knowing what to say. Finally she laughed and said, "You go, girl! You're something else, aren't you?" Rachael looked at her and smiled.

"There's more," she said.

By this time Emily was thinking, "I'm not ready for this. Oh boy." Emily was embarrassed, intrigued, and downright nosy all at the same time.

"What's the story, Rachel?" she asked.

"Well, I am having some problems with him."

"What kind of problems?"

"Well, I have to pay."

"Excuse me?" Emily said, startled. For a moment she hoped Rachael was talking about the check for the lunch. "Pay for what?"

"Sex. He calls it 'companionship,'" answered Rachael.

Emily was floored and really getting interested now because she had never been exposed to anything near prostitution. "How much do you have to pay?"

"Well, it varies. I paid the tuition for him to go to Temple University. He said he needed to go to college in order to get a better job because he only makes eight dollars an hour working for the agency."

"What!" Emily shrieked. "You paid for him to go to college? Did you make the check out to Temple or to him?"

"I made it out to him."

Emily was astonished. "Did you at least call Temple to see if he was enrolled there?"

"No, I didn't want to check up on him like that."

"Jesus Christ, Rachael! Give me his telephone number; I'm calling him up. What's his name? Do your kids know about this?"

"My youngest daughter knows and she is mad. I won't tell her his name or anything. She'll go berserk on him."

"Tell me his name," Emily demanded.

"No, I can't."

Emily fell silent for a moment in order to gather her thoughts. "Rachael, take those glasses off so I can look into your eyes and talk to you."

Rachael removed the glasses, exposing her swollen and red eyes. Emily looked at her and shook her head. "Rachael, this guy is probably going to try to take you for everything you've got. Are you crazy? How much was the check for?"

"Well, a few thousand dollars for that."

"What do you mean 'for that'? What other money have you given him? Tell me something—is this guy Black?" Emily figured the guy might be Black because of the low salary, and she remembered her aunt in Detroit had needed care a few years ago. Most of the workers from the agency who came to take care of her aunt were Black.

"Yes, he's Black. I also gave him money to take other classes somewhere else. He said he had to take a separate set of classes in order to enroll in Temple. That was eight hundred dollars. Then he needed money to get his driver's license restored by the state so he could drive to and from school. Then he said I had to keep him in cigarettes—he *had* to have the cigarettes because he needed to take some tests to get into school. He told me there would be many exams and he'd be nervous if he didn't have the cigarettes."

"You know what, Rachael, I need a cigarette myself." Emily reached in her handbag in a state of total shock. She was pissed. "Rachael," she growled, "how much money have you given this gigolo? What's the total amount?"

"Well, with all that and the car—" Emily screamed again, cutting her off.

"Car!" Emily screamed. "Are you completely loco?"

Emily sat and shook her head. She absolutely could not believe this story. She calmed down and gently said, "Rachael, you cannot be this lonely—or is it the sex that makes you do this? How old are you?"

"Well, I don't want to say my age, and the sex I need to talk to you about."

Emily quickly summoned the waitress and ordered a bottle of wine and two glasses. "I need a drink," she said. "And so do you."

As the waitress was getting the wine, Rachael said, "The trouble with the sex is that he doesn't always take care of me. At first he used to—you know—in the beginning. Then he made up this rule that I have to go first. You know—we have to start with him. I have to give oral sex to him. So I started doing that to appease him, and then I found that he would get finished and there would be nothing left for me. It would be over."

Emily shut her eyes for a second and then walked over to the bar and demanded, "Miss, please give me that bottle *right now*—*and* those glasses." She marched back to the booth and poured two full glasses of wine. "Drink it," she ordered, handing Rachael a glass.

"Now, I'll shut up for a while, Rachael. I want the entire story."

"I've told you most of it. I really like him. I like having someone come around. I'm lonely. He takes me to the movies and he is always complimenting me about my boobs—you know, jollying me up. He is fun to be with, but I like oral sex, too, and now I get nothing. I think he should at least let us take turns starting off on each other. You know, some days I'll do him first and then the next time he should go first. I think that's fair."

Emily drank the entire glass of wine and refilled her glass. "Go on," she said to Rachael.

"Well, I've been trying to get him to do better with the sex, but he is being selfish. I miss having someone to sleep with, you know, just sleeping next to me. I like someone in my bed. He now tells me that since his girlfriend came back and they are living together, he can't sleep over. Now they are having all these problems, like the heater in their apartment broke and they were cold and it had to be replaced and he wanted me to pay for that."

"You bought a heater for an apartment, Rachael? How dumb can you be? If he rents an apartment, he's not responsible for replacing a heater. A landlord has to do that. Jesus Christ," Emily shouted.

"I didn't buy the heater, Emily."

"Good. Why not?"

"Well, yesterday he stood me up. He was supposed to take me to the movies, and I waited all day and up to nine o'clock last night. He never called either. I started crying and I was sad. I missed him. I missed my husband, too. I felt so bad because I do everything for him. It's not fair the way he treats me. I don't deserve that. So I called you."

"Rachael, do you want to get another boyfriend, and did you call me after all this time because you want me to introduce you to a Black man? You can tell me the truth; I'll still be your friend. You know there is this saying, 'Once you go Black, you never go back.' Is that the case here?" Emily asked.

"Well, if you know any men you can introduce me to, I'd consider getting another companion. He doesn't have to be Black and I don't care about age. However, since I have to pay anyway—and I know I will—I want the person to spend the night, all night. It's a comfort to me to have a warm body in the bed, even if there is no sex. I just want someone to talk to and go out with to do fun things and sleep over."

"The first thing you have to do is get rid of Mr. Noname. What's his name? You'd better tell me, girl." Emily thought Rachael was cute and that she'd get a kick out of being called "girl."

Rachael had a worried look on her face and had the jitters. "I won't tell you his name, you'll do something."

"All right, have it your way. Let's get out of here. I'd better get you home. This has been a day."

As the two women got up from the booth, Rachael stopped to put her snazzy sunglasses back on. Emily watched her and shook her head. She smiled and said, "Honest to God, you are quite a surprise—and something else. You rocked my world today. I thought I had an exciting life. You've got me beat."

Rachael blushed and asked, "Are you still going to be my friend? Can we still do some things together?"

"Yes. I will be your friend. I'm paying the check and you leave the tip. Let's go."

They arrived at her home, a magnificent house full of antiques with a marvelous kitchen. The property sat on an acre of land. Emily thought, "That gigolo is pretty smart."

He pulled up to Regina's house precisely at noon carrying two bottles of Mike's Hard Lemonade and a rose for his sweetie, Emily, and rang the doorbell. "Hey, baby," he said, reaching for her when she opened the door.

"Hi, I sure am glad to see you. Brought me something, huh?"

"Of course."

They walked out of the house and she didn't see his car. "Where are you parked?"

"Come see, just follow me," he said.

He led her to a beautiful green Chrysler LeBaron convertible. The top was down. She screamed with delight, "This car is gorgeous! When did you get it, Leo?"

Chapter Thirteen

Angie

Dear Lucy:

How are you, Baby Cakes? I hope that you are fine and that those two gorgeous men in your life are healthy and happy as clams. I'm doing fine, still crazy as hell. Listen to this shit, girl, everybody is going off the deep end.

I met this girl in the nailery. Her name is Daphne. She started getting friendly with me. She lived in the apartments around the corner from me. She and her man, Wendell, live together. I eventually had the two of them over for a late lunch one Sunday afternoon. I forgot where he works now, but she works at the all-night Laundromat not far from me. Wendell was pretty sharp, but for some reason, to me, they just looked like the wrong two people to be hooked up. I mean he was snakeskinned down and sharp as a tack and she was kind of dumpy with glasses. In any case, we became friends.

They stayed in church, girl. I mean they were really tight with the reverend and his wife and were in church two and three times a week and on Sunday. She kept asking me to attend but you know I don't do church. I say all my prayers at home, in my partying spots and in my car. You know—God knows me extremely well and understands me and I don't have to present myself in church to have a relationship with him. Well, anyway, eventually Daphne began calling me and coming around my house when I was home and she was off from work. She was a stone Holy Roller and told me she and Wendell were pretty tight and happy. She said she was following God's and the reverend's instructions and even though she and Wendell were living together, there was absolutely no sex. I found that hard to believe, you know—how the hell are you going to lay up there with a man beside you every night and not get any? Humph. I couldn't do it. You know I would have rolled over and gotten me some even if I had to get on my knees afterward and tell God I was sorry.

Girl, Wendell seemed totally henpecked to me. He jumped every time she said anything. He really seemed like a nice guy, too. Even though I couldn't live the lifestyle they were living, I thought it was refreshing for a couple to be living in sin without sinning. That's hard to believe in this day and age, but maybe that is a good thing for people other than myself. You know?

Well, a couple of months into our friendship, Daphne explained that she and Wendell were officially engaged. She said they were attending classes within the church and after the classes were completed, they were having their wedding at the church. I was happy for her. I told her how proud I was of her that they were not sleeping together and all. Then she started praying for me—you know me and my wild self—and she explained how God would love me more and better things would happen for me if I were celibate and stopped fooling around until I had a real husband. I declined. We all know God loves me just the way I am.

Listen, girl, last month I had some car trouble and had to put my car in the shop. I was getting rides to work so it wasn't too much of a hassle. Well, the washing machine broke down one Saturday night and everything I owned was dirty and I didn't have my car. I didn't want to rent one just for that so I decided to grab a cab and get the wash done. I called the taxi company and they sent this fat White guy for me. He and I piled all the clothes in the car and headed for the all-night Laundromat. On the way there the driver started talking to me.

"Do you go to this Laundromat often?" he asked.

"No, I never go at all unless I have a comforter to get done or something big like that. I'm having some car trouble and my washer broke down so here I am. I'll be straight in a few days."

"Hey, I know a girl who works there—at the Laundromat. She's a friend of mine. Her name is Daphne."

"Oh, I know Daphne from the nailery. She is nice and also a friend of mine."

"Oh, you guys are really friends?" he asked.

"Yeah."

"Well, you know, I do a lot of favors for her. You know she has no car and works many nights there. She gives me a call and I pick her up and I give her a special rate. I can do that with you, too, if you ever have a problem getting anywhere."

"I shouldn't need that. My stuff will be in order shortly. I just ran out of underwear, sheets and towels, so I had to go this route today. Thanks anyway."

"Well, I'd just like to let you know that Daphne is something else. I have a real nice sexual thing going on with her. She is a straight-up freak, too. I mean highly sexed. I mean she fucks me like a maniac once I get her to my place. She's a nice fare," he boasted.

"That's interesting, I was under the impression she was engaged," I said.

"Yeah, he's a nice dude that she has completely under her control. He was working at the Laundromat, too. I know all about him and he knows nothing about us. Yeah, that Daphne is something else."

Lucy, I was floored. I don't know how I kept a straight face. After I got to the Laundromat I asked the owner who happened to be there if Wendell still worked there. He explained that Wendell was the nicest guy in the world and had been working the twelve to eight shift, but he had to quit because Daphne who also worked there on the seven to three shift didn't want him working nights because too many women came there and she felt threatened. The owner also said she treated him like crap. Humph. Girl, isn't that some shit? I cannot tell you how much praying she did at my house trying to convert me and rid me of my sins. I was mad as a bitch.

I called her the next day and very sweetly said, "Daphne, I was at the Laundromat yesterday. Girl, I had to take a cab because my car is down. I met a cabdriver who says he drives you home sometimes and he offered me a special rate because I said I knew you." She was silent. Couldn't say a word. Then she got all crazy and started asking questions like, "What's his name? What cabdriver? Did he say anything about me? Why would he mention me to you? I only ride home with him. I'm merely a customer. Exactly what did he say? He had a nerve mentioning I ride with him."

Lucy, I just let her go crazy and told her that he gave me no information other than he drove her home for a special rate and that if I needed him in the future, that rate would be available to me. I haven't heard from her since. I called her twice in two weeks after that and she never returned my calls.

Just a bit more news—as soon as I got back from the slumber party, I met a fantastic guy named Joel Millsman. Hold onto your seat—he has moved in with me. I'll give you more details on him later. I'll write to you next week.

See ya!!
Angie

Lucy was in shock when she read the e-mail; however, she absolutely loved it. Lucy was also ecstatic Angie had found someone and she was praying it would work out for her. Lucy would not dare breathe a word of it to Reba, Sonja or any of the gang in her hometown of Philadelphia, in case it fell through. A week later she received another letter from Angie.

Dear Lucy:

I'm back, and here is the scoop on Joel. We started dating about a year and a half ago. Well, it worked out fine and we really were happy. I saw him trying to do many of the things I had asked of him and I became not only quite comfortable with our relationship—shit, I was loving him a lot. He was attentive, a hard worker and we laughed a lot. I felt very secure and I was doing many things to make him happy. It was like a dream come true.

Joel had a complicated history. The woman he was living with for three months, Ebony, was the mother of their five-year-old son, but they weren't married. They shared an apartment about four blocks from where he worked, and he used to walk to work from home.

They had known each other over fifteen years, when he was stationed in DC in the military. Joel was married when he met Ebony. His marriage was rocky, because his wife, Stacia, was a piece of work and they separated. During this yearlong separation, Joel and Ebony had a weekend affair that produced a son, William. After this affair, Joel and Stacia decided to reconcile and Joel and Ebony didn't see each other again.

Three years later, Ebony contacted Joel to say that she had a son and he was the father. He asked why so long for the phone call and Ebony explained she felt since he and wifey-poo were back together, she had decided to go on with her life. After the call, she mailed Joel pictures of the child, who was a replica of his father. This flabbergasted Joel's wife, Stacia, even though Joel had been up-front when they decided to get back together. He had explained that during their separation he had only had one affair—the one with Ebony. Stacia could not stand the idea that Joel had another child and eventually Stacia filed for a divorce. They split and Stacia got everything including custody of their then six-year-old daughter, Danita. After the divorce, Stacia and Joel became great platonic friends and he remained a terrific long-distance father.

Joel was still living and working in Washington when Ebony contacted him again, two years after his divorce. She had recently been in another failed relationship and suggested that they try to get together and raise their son. After realizing he had some feelings for Ebony, Joel made a decision to move in with her and five-year-old William and give it a shot.

Things went fine during the "honeymoon" stage of the relationship, but Joel then began to see signs of trouble. Ebony was jealous and didn't want Joel to associate with his friends. She was a compulsive shopper, buying loads of toys and clothing for William—thus creating a lot of bills that Joel was paying. She was employed, but it was a very low-paying position at a supermarket and she couldn't afford to assist with the household bills. She was also a rotten housekeeper and knew nothing whatsoever about cooking a decent meal. Ebony's idea of dinner was fast food she obtained at the restaurant and brought home for William and Joel—who was working twelve-hour shifts in order to make ends meet. Things had gotten so bad in their relationship that he was sleeping in his son's bedroom, and she and William were sleeping together in the master bedroom.

During the third month of his stay, Joel received word that his father had suffered a stroke. Joel needed to take a trip to Denver. Upon hearing this news, Ebony was unhappy that he would be making that trip and started a fight with him. She felt it was an unnecessary journey and Joel should wait to see if his dad got better—or that his siblings should go. Joel loved his father deeply and decided to go anyway, infuriating Ebony. Five days prior to his departure to Denver, Ebony's behavior became worse and she argued with him, insisting he remain with her. During the weekend before he was to leave, Ebony became violent, throwing bottles, furniture, and breaking drinking glasses in the apartment. Joel was so upset with her that he left that Saturday. He attended my buddy Rochelle's wedding and that's where he met me.

He and I were tablemates and he was a basket case who found refuge in the good music, pleasant atmosphere, a delightful meal—and my company. Instead of returning home to Ebony, he opted to go home with me. I had listened to him all evening and trusted him—my gut told me he was pretty cool.

We arrived at my place a little before nine, had a wonderful time talking and I was becoming more impressed with him. One thing led to another and we ended up in the sack. This was something I'd never done—even as wild as I seem and all—I have never picked a guy up like that and slept with him. You know much of my personality is an act. I'm really pretty levelheaded. After this wonderful tryst was over— and I'm telling you he is something else between the sheets—I was embarrassed and convinced he'd never call me—this one-night stand again. I dug him but you know how that is and I felt he probably thought I did that sort of thing often.

"Listen, Joel. I feel funny about this and I want you to know that I don't do this sort of thing—you know, meet a guy for the first time and this happens," Angie said.

"It's cool. I don't think anything bad about you for doing this. It's what we felt like doing and you don't have to be ashamed or embarrassed about it. And I certainly don't want you to think your doing it has turned me off. I'm fine," Joel said, kissing her on the cheek as her head lay on her pillow.

"You're probably never going to call me again," Angie pouted.

"Oh, come on, woman. Believe me, I'm not looking down on you about this. I do plan to see you again after I get back from taking care of my dad. I'm not sure how long I'll be in Denver, though—he's pretty sick. If I'm gone too long, I can fly you in and out of Denver sometimes," Joel said in an effort to reassure her.

"No—I'm telling you I feel bad for real. I really want you to know I'm not a tramp. You know?" Angie said.

"I already know that. Come on. Relax," he said.

Angie continued to be distressed. Finally, she looked at him and said, "You just can't say it, so I will. I need to let you know that this is a one-night stand. I want you to get your underwear on, get your clothes together off the floor and get moving. Then I won't have to wait around to hear from someone who won't be coming back. I mean it. You've got to go."

Joel was in disbelief and his face showed it. "You've got to be kidding, Angie. Jesus. What's wrong with you? You need to chill. I'm here. I dig you—anyway. You got that?" Joel said.

"I said it's time to leave," Angie said as she got up and started picking up his things.

Joel lay on the bed staring at her. "Can I use the phone?" he asked.

"Whatever," she said, rolling her eyes at him.

Joel dialed a number and said, "Hey, how are you? What's happening?" He then listened to the person on the other end. "Where's my sister?" Joel asked. Then there was silence again. Angie was puzzled and was listening to the conversation.

"Tell her to call me tomorrow. I want to tell her all about my new girlfriend, Angie. I'm mad about her." When Joel hung up, Angie had a big smile on her face. He then made seven additional calls all over the United States, including one to his mother, giving the same information. On many of the calls, Angie was introduced to his relatives. After that, they made love again and she dropped him off at his apartment. He kissed her good-bye and entered the apartment.

Ebony was sitting in the living room when he arrived. "Where the hell have you been?" she asked.

Joel knew there was going to be a battle, but he nonchalantly said, "At a wedding with some friends. I needed a break."

Ebony rolled her eyes and blew up, shouting, "You've been gone for ten hours! You know better than that shit! Why didn't you call? You've never gone out in the three months we've been together—just work. You know this is out of the ordinary and you should have called."

Joel threw his arms up. "Ebony, do me a favor. Please don't start up. I'll be leaving in a couple of days and you won't have any more problems. In fact, I've thought everything over and I have no intentions of us being together anymore. I'll just stay here until it's time to catch my plane on Monday. I'm going to bed," he said wearily as he headed for his son's room.

"What! What do you mean telling me some shit like this? We're not breaking up," Ebony shouted.

Joel had about had it with Ebony and began pacing the floor. "Listen, Ebony. It's not working out and you know it. I'm tired of trying at it. This thing between you and me is worse than having another job. You know I'll continue to take care of William and support him. I plan to be in his life. I'm not running out on him. Just let me get out of here without a fight," Joel said.

Ebony shoved him against the living room wall and shouted, "You are just using your father as an excuse and I know it. The damn man is not that sick. That's what pissed me off—your family overreacting to it all. Hell, if it were that bad he would not have been released from the hospital. I'm sick of your family—a bunch of worrywarts. Every damn time I turn around one of your sisters or brothers is calling up here. Damn. Can you people make it a week without talking to each other? And, your mother—she needs to let you grow up. Damn. She calls up here asking you what you had for dinner, how the job is, how your day went—all that kind of stuff. Who needs that shit? I'm tired of it. That's why we have so many problems. It's that damn family of yours!" Ebony shouted.

Joel was livid and went to the closet to grab a suitcase. Ebony followed him and they tussled with it. He then took a deep breath and said,

"Ebony, you knew how tight me and my family were when we hooked up. I didn't just meet you. I've known you a long time, and you know my family and I keep up with each other. I'm telling you to get off this shit tonight. I'm going to bed." Joel slammed the door to William's room.

"It ain't over," Ebony screamed through the door.

He hadn't changed his mind when he woke up the next day. The first thing he did was make a call to Angie. "Good morning. How are you this wonderful Sunday morning? Just perfect for romance—rain crashing down on the windows. Miss me, baby?" Joel asked.

Angie was relieved to hear his voice and had a big smile on her face. "Hi, Mr. One-night Stand. I'm certainly glad to hear from you. Maybe I've indeed got a chance," Angie said.

"I'd say you've got a damn good shot at keeping me around. I just wanted to take a minute to call you. I can't talk long. I wanted to know if I could see you on Monday morning before I catch my flight. I'd like to take you to breakfast. I wanted to use today to take my son out since I'll be leaving. Do you have plans for tomorrow?" Joel asked.

"I have to work, but I can take off. What time would you like to get together?" Angie asked.

"I can be at your house by six in the morning. My flight leaves at three thirty," Joel said.

"Okay, you're on. I'll see you then."

They hung up and Joel felt better for a couple of reasons. He realized how much he dug her. He chuckled to himself remembering her trying to get him out of her house the day before. In no way did he think she was loose or a floozy. He really was interested in her. His thoughts were interrupted when Ebony stuck her head in the door.

"Well, I see you're up. There are some things that have to be done around here. I know it's pouring down raining, but William's car has to be put together. I paid four hundred dollars for it and he wants to ride the damn thing. Since you're not working today and will be leaving to-morrow, you need to put it together. This apartment is too small, so you have to do it outside in the rain. It just has to be done. So when you get yourself together, the box is in the closet. Also, what are you doing about our breakfast? Me and William have to eat," Ebony said.

Joel lay there in bed realizing how tired he was of Ebony ordering him around for the past three months. He thought, "Just one more day of this shit—I can take it." He said, "Okay, Ebony. I'm getting myself together. I'll get the car running for William. Just let me get showered, dressed and do breakfast, and I'll start on the car," Joel said.

"Okay," Ebony said.

After breakfast Joel said, "Listen, while I am putting that car together, could you run the dirty clothes over to the laundry room? I have to pack."

Ebony's eyes lit up in disbelief. She felt he had a nerve asking her to do his laundry after he was missing for ten hours the day before. She quickly replied, "No. I'm not washing any clothes—not after the way you've acted all weekend. Wash your own fucking clothes."

"No problem," Joel said as he got up from the table. He spent the next two and a half hours in the pouring rain putting the car together. When he finished he took William to a movie. When they returned home the phone rang. Ebony answered it and slammed the receiver down on the kitchen counter. It was Joel's sister Leigh.

"Hey, brother, I heard," she said with a chuckle. "Sorry I missed your call last night. You okay?"

"I'm cool. Getting ready to start packing. I'll call you when I get to Dad. Let me handle things there for a while and then you guys can come when you can. I've got it covered," Joel said.

"Okay—just call when your flight gets in. I'll fly home if you need me. You know we can start taking turns helping out with him at a moment's notice. All of us have informed our jobs. When you get tired, Joel—just holler," Leigh said.

"Okay—but I believe I'm good for about three months. We'll talk. Let me just get out there and see what's going on," Joel said.

"Have you talked to Mom today?" Leigh asked.

"No, but I know she was planning to call Dad today to check on him," Joel said.

"Okay—I'll give her a call. I'm also really glad Preston is being so good about Mom helping out with Dad," Leigh said.

"Preston is really cool. He doesn't care about that. He has to realize that Mom and Dad were together a lot of years and just because they couldn't make it together is no reason for Dad and Mom not to be friends. Preston is a pretty good man and a great stepfather. That's my man," Joel said as Ebony listened to every word and rolled her eyes while banging things on the counter. She was truly pissing Joel off.

"Okay, brother dear, I love you. Have a safe flight and I'll talk to you tomorrow night. Angie, huh? You're something else, boy. I can't wait," Leigh said.

Ebony immediately started on Joel when he hung up the phone. "Well, I see they are still at it—calling up here synchronizing watches and all waiting for you to leave me. I can't stand your family."

"Don't start," Joel said, looking in her eyes.

"Are you leaving me any extra money when you go? Just because you decided to take a trip, I shouldn't have to suffer for it. Macy's is having a sale and I want to get William some things. Let's talk about money," Ebony said.

Joel was pissed and felt Ebony was just one selfish and uncompassionate bitch that he was about through with—thank God. He said, "I just paid some bills, and the rest of the money I have I'm planning to use to get out of here. I want to stop at the Farmers' Market and pick up some herbs for my dad and a few other things he may need. You'll have to wait until your child support payment comes in the mail. The rent is paid and there is food here. I need the rest of the money I have and my next check won't be around for two weeks. You have to try to make it. Skip the sale at Macy's—the boy has a ton of clothes. There's stuff in his closet that still has tags on it."

"I *know* you are kidding! The stuff I want to get is on sale—good stuff that he can use later. Since you have a family emergency, why don't you have your job give you an advance on your next paycheck and you can split that money with me?"

He was through with this. "Ebony, I'm getting ready to wash my clothes and pack."

"That's it. You're not going. I've had it. I'm not suffering a loss because your father claims he's sick. You're not going anywhere!" Ebony said as she grabbed Joel by the arm.

"Let me go, Ebony," Joel calmly said. "It's over."

Ebony refused and began throwing Joel's things around in the bedroom. He walked out of the apartment and six blocks to the police station. Two officers accompanied him back to Ebony's and he got his belongings. He called Angie and a cab from the corner as the police waited to ensure that Ebony did not cause another altercation. He arrived in a half hour at Angie's.

Together they packed his things, had some serious talks over dinner and then he called his mom, who spoke to Angie and thanked her for helping her son out. After a night of passionate lovemaking, they fell asleep in each other's arms. When they woke up they headed for the Farmers' Market, had breakfast and shopped for things for his dad. He purchased some flowers for Angie and gave her a bunch of phone numbers to contact him in Denver, and she dropped him off at the airport. He promised to call her when he got to his dad's house.

Angie waited patiently for his call and it finally came. While Joel's plane was in the air his dad suffered a massive heart attack and died. Joel was at his mother's house, devastated and crying.

"Oh my God! I'm *soo* sorry. Oh, Jesus Christ, I feel so bad for you. Oh man, what can I do to help? Do you want me to come there? I can fly out there. Oh, Joel, this is terrible. I am *soo* sorry, baby," Angie cried into the phone.

"I think I'm okay. I don't know. I need to take a walk, I think. The neighbor found him. He had been at home all day. We had a person staying with him and he sent them away. He was trying to be so independent. I don't know what happened. All I know is they met me at the airport and told me what happened. I need to take a walk," Joel said.

"Listen, Joel, let me come there. Where is your mom? Let me talk to her," Angie sternly said. Joel passed the phone to his mother.

"Hi, Angie. We have a mess here. I got the call late in the afternoon after Joel's flight left. We have him here and will do the best we can. They were very close," Paulette said.

"Mrs. Millsman, I can come there if you like. I don't know what to do. I feel so bad for him—for all of you. You know I took him by a market before he left and he purchased all this stuff to bring back to make his father well. Oh boy—this is something else—so sad. Do you think I should come? I think Joel is in shock," Angie said.

"You know what—he has been through some stuff. I don't know how he keeps his head on straight. I heard all about Miss Ebony and I'm disgusted about that. Then the boy quits his jobs to come home and take care of his dad and *this* happens. I hope he doesn't lose his mind. I'm really grateful you were around to assist and comfort him. I've told my family all about you. We met Joel at the airport so he wouldn't go to the house and find his dad there like that. At this point I don't know what to tell you to do. Now he's outside walking around. Father's Day is next Sunday, too. Humph—that's going to be a trip. His brothers and sisters are getting themselves together to get here. This is a mess. I'm remarried but my ex-husband and I were on good terms. I'll do what I can to help," Paulette Millsman Marshall said.

"Okay—let me give you my phone number so you can let me know how he is. You can call me anytime. I have all the numbers there in case I need to reach him. Please give him a hug for me and let him know I'll come if I have to. Again, I'm sorry for your loss," Angie said.

"Thanks, Angie. I'll get back to you, sweetie," Paulette said.

Joel got through the funeral and remained in Denver helping to settle his dad's estate. Angie remained in Washington. After three weeks he and Angie missed each other terribly and Angie suggested that he come back to DC and move in with her. They had grown very close talking to each other numerous times during the days. A month after Joel's father's passing, Angie picked Joel up from the airport and they began living together.

They were an ideal couple and an enormous help to each other. They were both terrific cooks, shared recipes as well as preparing meals together and took turns cooking and waiting on each other. Unlike Angie, Joel was an expert at organizing and kept Angie's house in order. He was lousy at washing clothes and she was great at that. She sucked at computer knowledge and he was a whiz in that department and had begun teaching her the art of mastering that technology. They both had an incredible appetite for sex, an insatiable desire for each other and were equally imaginative in that area. Angie fussed over him like a mother hen, making fresh coffee for him and packing his lunches, something he had not been accustomed to in his relationships with his ex-wife and Ebony.

Joel had gone back to his old job and the two of them were falling in love. Joel's family adored Angie and she was crazy about them, too. Joel had let his ex-wife Stacia know how to reach him and that he was in a new relationship. He was continuing to be a great long-distance daddy to his daughter, Danita, who now resided in Syracuse, New York. He was forever calling the child, sending presents and educational toys. He continued to financially support his son, William—but he had not let Ebony know that he had returned to the DC area. He wasn't ready for a headache from her. He knew he would have to deal with it sooner or later, but he decided to get really settled in his relationship with Angie and then tackle Ebony. Ebony had placed a zillion phone calls to Denver when he had arrived there. She was apologizing for minimizing his dad's illness and for her behavior. He didn't want to hear it and his family was absolutely livid with her. Ebony continued calling Denver, leaving messages with Paulette for Joel to call her, which he never returned. His entire family kept his secrets that he was not only in DC, but back at his old job four blocks from Ebony's apartment. Lo and behold, Tisha Norton, Ebony's best friend, stopped in to purchase some items from Joel's company, and Joel was at the counter.

"Joel, I thought you were in Denver. When did you get back here?"

Joel was sorry as hell he was at work that day. He knew the shit was about to hit the fan. "I've been back a few weeks. Do me a favor, Tisha— don't tell Ebony I'm around. I need some time to think before I sit down to talk to her," Joel said.

"Mum's the word. When do you plan to call her?" Tisha asked.

"I'll do it soon—in a couple of weeks. Just keep your mouth shut and you'll be doing me a big favor," Joel said, praying she *would* keep her mouth shut.

"Well, where are you staying?" Tisha asked.

"With a friend," Joel replied.

Tisha raised her eyebrows suspiciously and asked, "What friend? Do we know him?"

Joel was beginning to sweat. He was tired of the interrogation and emphatically answered, "Nope. Listen, I've got some customers I have to get to. Let me ring you out," Joel said.

"I'm sorry about your dad," Tisha said.

"Thanks—look, I've got to do some work. Thanks for not saying anything to Ebony," Joel said.

"No problem," Tisha said, and walked out the door. He surmised Ebony would report to his job before the day was over.

"Good evening, Radnor Window Treatments. This is Ray. May I help you?"

"Good evening. This is Leigh Goodman. I'm Joel Millsman's sister and I'm calling from New Orleans. I know my brother is off work tonight. We have a family emergency and I have to reach him. Things are a bit crazy with my aunt unexpectedly dying in Denver this afternoon and I have to tell him. I'm so upset, I have lost his new number. Could you please give it to me? I cannot believe my family is going through this again. You know my dad just passed away. I need to get to Joel right away so he can help with these arrangements. I am so upset. I just got the news."

"My God! I am so sorry for you and your family. Joel is such a nice person. Let me go to the files and get his number for you. Just hold on," Ray said.

Ray returned, gave the number to Leigh and told her to tell Joel not to worry about work. He could have whatever time off he needed to attend to the funeral.

* * *

"Hello, may I speak to Joel?"

"Who's calling, please?"

"Ebony."

A surprised Angie said, "Hold on."

"Joel, Ebony is on the phone," Angie said as she passed the cordless phone to Joel, who was lying in bed next to her. He was shocked.

"Hello."

"What the hell do you think you are doing? Why haven't I heard from you? Who the hell is that who answered the phone? How long have you been back in town? Why haven't you called me or come back here? Are you crazy? You haven't even been to see William. I'm pissed. You'd better get your ass over here," Ebony screamed.

"Look, Ebony, I've been busy," Joel calmly said. "I was planning to come to talk to you and to make arrangements to see William. I just needed some time."

"Do you have time now? Come now. I asked, who the hell answered that phone!" Ebony shouted.

"How in the world did you get this number?" Joel asked.

"Don't you worry about it. I've got it and you'd better get your ass over here. We aren't done. Who the hell answered the fucking phone?" Ebony asked.

"I'll call you tomorrow," Joel said as he hung up on her.

The phone rang again and he picked it right up. "Ebony, stop this. Wait for me to talk to you tomorrow. Don't call back here again. Just call me at work if you have to talk to me. I don't want you causing any problems here," Joel said.

"I'll call there any fucking time I like. I have your son—remember him? You're probably fucking that bitch." Joel hung up on her again.

Ebony called back three more times, and the third time Angie answered. "Miss, you have to stop this. You have to deal with Joel at work. Do you understand? You cannot call my home again."

"*Miss,* do you realize I have his son and I am allowed to call there *be-*

cause of our son. Now, put him on the goddamn phone!" Ebony shouted. Livid, Angie passed the phone to Joel.

"What?" Joel asked into the receiver.

"Are you fucking that bitch?" Ebony asked.

"Not at the moment," he answered.

"Oh shit! You're asking for trouble now. I can't believe you brought your ass back here and moved in with a bitch! You'll be sorry, goddammit. I can't believe you're doing this. What do you have to say for yourself?" Ebony asked.

Angie was now sitting on the bed, looking disgusted. She was pissed at this intrusion. "I want to marry this woman I'm living with. That's what I have to say for myself. You got that?" he asked. He then hung up on her again.

The phone rang again and Angie answered. A child was on the phone asking for his daddy. Angie passed the phone to Joel, and he began talking to William. Ebony then snatched the phone from her son and said to Joel, "Put her on the phone." A tired and disgusted Joel handed the phone back to Angie.

"You shall not disrespect my child. You'd better understand that. When I call there, you get Joel and you stay out of our business. Now, I don't know what's going on there, but it won't be happening long. He has a family here and you're going to respect that. When me and my son call there—which won't be long because I'll have his ass back here soon—you get him to the phone," Ebony ordered.

Angie had had enough and said, "Let me tell you something. You have no idea who you are messing with. You'd better not call here again. You will find out exactly who I am in a couple of days and you'll be sorry. Don't you disrupt my home again. I'm serious. You'd better deal with Joel somewhere else."

"Good afternoon. I'd like to fill out paperwork regarding a Protection from Abuse Petition—you know—a restraining order," Angie said to the clerk at the courthouse.

"Sure, ma'am. Here is a set of papers you should fill out."

"Is there a charge?" Angie asked as she looked at the huge amount of paperwork that had to be completed.

"Yes, but you can check the box if you want the defendant to have to pay. You simply have to fill everything out and leave it here. Since you are here so late in the afternoon, your work won't go in until tomorrow. Then you are assigned a hearing for Thursday of this week. You can take the papers home with you, complete them and bring them back tomorrow if you like," the clerk said.

Angie flipped through the twelve-page application and said, "I'll bring it back tomorrow." She walked out.

"Help me fill these papers out. Give me all her information. Name, address, phone numbers, the works. I'll fix her ass for ordering me around," Angie said.

"What the hell is this stuff?" Joel asked.

"They are 'Leave me the fuck alone' papers. They are being filed with the court and she will not be able to call this house, bring her crazy ass here or come within three hundred fifty feet of either one of us. You'd better make some arrangements within the court for pickup and delivery of William for visitation, and he ain't coming here. That crazy bitch may let him come here and then try to say I molested him or something. You make your arrangements about him and keep him away from me. And sign the papers because you know the bitch is crazy," Angie yelled.

Joel knew Angie was not bullshitting and was surprised she was so smart and swift in her attempts to condense the situation. He immediately signed the papers and agreed to go back to the courthouse with Angie the next morning to have them filed. They did so and an initial hearing was set for the following Thursday. Angie and Joel pleaded their case and another hearing was scheduled in seven days. Service of the petition was filed upon Ebony and she appeared in court. The petition was granted and she was scared to death to bother them again. Joel's next move was to contact family court to apply for supervised visitation with William at the courthouse or unsupervised visitation at a location other than Ebony's home or his and Angie's residence. After the hearing and for the next two months, Angie and Joel never received another call from Ebony and she never came to his workplace or their home.

Joel and Angie continued having a great relationship with the exception of one thing—Angie was petrified of his use of alcohol and beer. Even though he insisted a couple of beers a night and a drink were no problem and merely a relaxation technique, she was worried. They had continued talks about it after she'd found he was doing this almost every evening after work. He wouldn't go out after work and come home loaded or anything like that, but he was drinking at home each night. She accused him of having a drinking problem and he was trying to convince her that a beer or two and/or a drink each night were far from a *drinking problem*. These talks escalated into arguments and often they went without speaking for a couple of days at a time. The more Joel would try to convince Angie he had no problem, her fears from a past relationship with an alcoholic, coupled with the fact that her own mother was an alcoholic, made her unable to relax and believe Joel was not in trouble.

One weekend Joel and Angie had a blowout about the drinking and were still angry at each other into the following Monday morning when Joel reported for work. His phone rang at work as soon as he arrived.

"Hi, Joel. How are you? I know I'm not supposed to call you but I needed to let you know that William had a medical emergency," Ebony said.

"What's going on? I still haven't managed to get the court papers for visitation. I do plan to resume seeing him. What kind of medical emergency did he have?" a concerned Joel asked.

"Well, they think he is developing asthma. He has to have some tests taken and we were at the emergency room all night."

"Oh, man. I'm sorry. What can I do? Is he in the hospital or at home?" Joel asked.

"He's here with me. We're home," Ebony said.

"Okay," he said, calculating. "I can come by to see him tonight. I'll do that. Let me know when and where his next appointment is and when the testing starts, and I'll be sure to be there for that, too," Joel said.

"Okay, I will. Listen, I'd like to run something else by you. I've been doing some thinking," Ebony said.

"Okay—hurry up and talk to me, I'm at work. What is it?" Joel asked.

"I don't know how things are going in your relationship or if you are still planning to marry your girlfriend," she said in a surprisingly calm voice. "I was wondering if you and I could give it another shot. I'd like us to get back together and for you to come back to live with me. I'd like to work things out—for us and for the sake of our son. What do you think?" Ebony asked.

Joel was struck dumb. He was silent, thinking of all the problems he was having with Angie. He also felt funny living at Angie's, because every time they had an argument and stopped speaking, he felt she wanted him out of there. He had questioned more than once whether his hooking up with Angie so quickly was the wrong move.

"Joel, are you still there?" Ebony asked.

"Oh yeah . . . yeah . . . I'm here. Listen, let me think about this and get back to you. I'm going to try to get by there tonight," Joel said.

"Hi, how was your day?" Angie said as Joel got into her car.

"It was okay. You still mad?" he asked.

"Nope, not really. I'm tired of it all right now."

"Listen—a couple of things happened today. I got a call from Ebony," Joel said. Angie's eyes lit up. Ebony had finally surfaced. It had been a long time and Angie couldn't wait to hear why.

"What now?" she asked. "What does she want, more money for child support?"

"No. William has a medical problem—asthma. He has to have some tests and I have to be in on that. I'm planning to go by to see him. The other thing is—she asked me to come back to her," Joel said.

Angie was driving the car. At this news she swerved violently.

"What! You've got to be kidding me. After all that shit she did, she asked you to come back to her? I can't believe it." She stared at the road ahead. "Humph. She is truly a piece of work. What did you say to her? You must have cursed her out," Angie said. Joel was silent.

"Come on, Joel, tell me the rest of this shit. What did you say to her?" Angie asked.

"Well, I told her I had to think about it and I'd get back to her." By this time Angie was parking in front of their house. She was steaming and marched into the house.

"Will you calm down? I had to tell you the truth. You know I am completely honest with you. I just told Ebony I had to think it over. Damn. Calm down," Joel said.

Angie leaned against the stove in the kitchen, and Joel sat on a stool. She looked into his eyes and said, "You mean to tell me after all we have been through together and after you attempted that shit with her and it turned out the way it did that you can consider going back to her. What about us? What about me? I'm pissed."

"Listen, Angie, you and I hooked up pretty fast. I've known Ebony over fifteen years," Joel calmly explained. "You and I are having *soo* many ups and downs and this is *your* house. When we go through our things here, I feel like you want me to leave. You have all these complaints about the way I do things. I feel I'm not good enough for you when shit gets crazy. I'm tired of arguing."

"Let me tell you something. No matter what we go through, if we can't make it, dammit—don't go backward. If you have to leave me and have no place to go, you ought to move into a fucking phone booth before you go back to that selfish wench. I'm surprised at you. It hurts me that you can even contemplate going there because you are supposed to love me. At least that's what you've been telling me these last five months. Do you love me? I need to know that."

"I believe I love you, but I'm not sure I am in love with you. You know there is a difference," Joel said.

"Do you love Ebony or think you're in love with her?" Angie asked, tapping her foot waiting for an answer.

"I don't know. I just don't know," Joel said.

Angie left the kitchen and went up to her bedroom. Joel stayed behind with a beer and then returned to Angie, who was staring out of her bedroom window. Everything that had happened between Joel and her was running through her mind. He had become part of her and she loved him no matter how many arguments they'd had about the drinking. He was not only her lover—he was her friend and confidante. Her ego was shattered and she wondered what the hell she should do or say about the bomb that had just exploded. Should she suggest that he return to Ebony? Should she fight for her man and their relationship? She had absolutely no idea how to handle this.

—

Chapter Fourteen

Paula

L"et's go, Paula, I'm back and it's lunch time," Jake said as he leaned against the wall of her cell. She got up and waited for him to unlock the door, and they walked away toward the kitchen.

"How was your vacation?" she asked as they proceeded down the hall.

"Fantastic. So much fun and relaxation. But all good things come to an end."

When they reached the kitchen, he sat on top of a large table and said to her, "You know the drill."

She retrieved the giant silver salad bowl from the shelf and then went around to the ice bin and filled it up. She set it on the floor and then got naked. She eased her ass into the ice, moving around until she could actually sit in it. It was *sooo* cold and this was *sooo* disgusting. She wanted to cry. She hated Jake. She knew it would take at least five minutes for her to be frozen the way he liked her. He sat and watched her every move.

"How did you make out with the warden?" he asked.

"Okay—it was okay. I did my job."

"Well, that's all over with now. I'm back. You won't have to fuck him anymore. It's *regular* duty now." He glanced at his watch, timing the freeze-up of her ass.

"Oh, so I'm done going to Warden Walt's office? You spoke to him and got the cancellation notice?"

"No, I haven't spoken to him, but he probably knows from the sched-ule I'm back. I'll clear it with him officially today or tomorrow."

Paula was disappointed. She liked being with Walt. "Okay," she said.

He looked at his watch again. "All right, Miss Paula—looks like you should be ready. Come on over now."

He stood up and pointed to his crotch and she fell to her knees. When that was over, she stood up and leaned against the wall, facing it, pushing her ass out, and he shoved himself into her from behind. It was so good he started singing "Old Happy Days." She loathed him. When that was over, he marched her back over to the bowl and grabbed a handful of ice and laid it on her vagina. She shivered and screamed from the cold. He massaged it in and then inserted his penis into her vagina while she lay on the kitchen floor.

Afterward he said, "Listen, I don't have the cake. My mom hasn't been feeling well so that will have to wait until next week. Let's get ready to bathe me."

She was pissed. She didn't move.

"Did you hear me, Paula? It's time for my bath."

"No bath—I haven't been feeling well," she said.

"Listen, bitch, don't you fuck with me. You wash my ass up *now*. Right fucking now—cake or no cake—you belong to me and you do what I tell you to do. I own your red ass and I'll keep it frozen whether I show up with a cake or not. Now get the soap and washcloths and towels and that warm water and wash your stench off me! You got that?"

"Fuck you!" she shouted.

"Have you lost your damn mind? What the fuck has gotten into you? You'd better hop to it before I make life extremely miserable for you around here!"

"Kiss my ass," she said as she began dressing.

Jake grabbed her around the throat and started smacking her. He shoved her onto the floor, dragged her over to the ice bowl and stuffed her face in the ice. She shoved him in the chest with her elbow and broke loose. She grabbed her sneakers off the floor and ran for the door. He caught her by her uniform and punched her in the face. He then grabbed his nightstick as he held her and hit her in the knees with it. Blood was oozing from her nose from the blow to her face. He stood over her as she was crippled and said, "Try some cute shit again like disobeying me and I'll really do you in. Now get your ass up and give me my bath." She crawled over to the bowl of ice, dumped it into the sink and ran the hot water into the bowl.

* * *

"I cannot stand his ass. I swear to God, Josie, I cannot stand him. I want to kill him," Paula said, lying on her bed.

"He is a real maniac. How in the hell are you going to get him off you?" Josie asked.

"I don't know. I'd better think of something before we kill each other in that kitchen. Look at my face. I look like a monster," she cried.

"What happened with the tape recorder?" Josie asked.

"Nothing yet. I don't know if Carlos is going to come up with it. I'm supposed to see him at six tonight."

"Maybe he'll come through. Do you want some ice for your face?"

"Hell no. I don't want to see another piece of ice as long as I live. I'm going to walk around looking just like this. I don't give a shit."

"Hey, Paula, are you ready to go to the library?" Carlos asked, standing at her cell door.

"Yeah, I'm coming," she said, getting up from a nap. She gargled with some Listerine, grabbed a mint and put it in her pocket and went to the cell door.

"What happened to you?"

"I fell. Isn't that what I'm supposed to say?"

"Maybe you should skip the library. You look terrible and you must feel bad. I can do without you. Can I get you anything?" Carlos asked.

Paula was surprised he was so concerned. "No, I don't need anything. Maybe I should go with you. The sound of your voice makes me feel better. At least I'll have that comfort. I feel like I'm going out of my mind. Sometimes this place is just too much to take."

Once they got in the library he sat and talked to her for a while. He explained he could not get the tape recorder, but he would think of something else to do for her upcoming birthday. She told him not to worry about it. She then went about her work with him, tears rolling down her face as he read to her. As he was walking her back to her cell, she said "Carlos, if you have an old Bible around your house, can I have it?"

"Paula, I'll bring it in tomorrow. Get some rest."

*   *   *

"Hi, I'm here to give the warden his mail," Josie said.

"Okay, I'll take it. Thanks," the clerk replied.

Josie continued to stand outside Walt's office with the mail in her hand.

"You can leave it with me," the clerk said.

"Well, I've never met him. I see him in there. I'd like to say hello. Can you ask him to come out?" Josie meekly asked. The clerk looked at her and sighed. She started to refuse but decided to be nice and went into Walt's office.

"Walt, there's an inmate out here who wants to meet you. She came from the mailroom to personally deliver your mail. Do you want to say hello to her or should I send her away? Are you busy?"

Walt looked up from the file he was going through. "Send her in," he said.

"What's your name? The warden is going to see you."

"I'm Josie—Josie Burgess."

The clerk took her in and said, "Warden, this is Josie Burgess. She has your mail." She then held out her hand for the mail and Josie gave it to her. She left the room.

Josie thought to herself as she sized him up, "He damn sure does look like E. G. Marshall on *The Defenders*." She imagined Paula and Walt getting it on. She wanted to laugh out loud, thinking about the stories Paula had told her.

"Hi, Josie Burgess—how are you?" Walt said, coming from around his desk and extending his hand. "It's quite nice of you to personally deliver my mail." He was checking her out, too, figuring this could be an extra piece of ass coming his way. He looked to make sure the door was closed. "Have a seat." Josie sat down.

"How are you doing here? Are they treating you okay?" he asked.

"I'm doing fine and I may be getting out in two years."

"Why are you here, Josie?"

"My husband beat the crap out of me too many times. So, a person like me, who never even had a traffic ticket, got fed up and did him in."

"That's sad. I guess you miss everyone in your life."

"You're exactly right. Well, I guess I'd better be going. I don't want to take up too much of your time. I just wanted to meet you because all the inmates say you are a good warden. It was my pleasure to meet you." She headed toward the door.

"Wait—can I ask you something?" he asked.

"Sure."

"Would you like to keep me company sometimes—in a personal way—up here in my office—privately?"

"I don't know. I kind of don't fool around. I'm not too adventurous. I'm low-key—not much experience, and you see I'm not pretty. You'd do better with someone else. Good luck."

"How about if we had some different kind of fun?" he asked.

He aroused Josie's curiosity. "What do you mean, Warden?"

"Call me Walt, and sit back down. Can I get you anything?"

"I want something, but it may be too much trouble for you."

"What is it?"

"You won't do it—forget it."

"Tell me, Josie. Maybe we can work it out."

"I am dying for a black and white milk shake. I would love one. It's lunchtime. Do you think you could get them to make me one?"

"That's not too hard a request. Let me call down there and have them bring it up here."

She smiled. "That would be terrific. I love everything black and white. I had so many clothes that were black and white before I came in here. My car was white with black interior. When I got married I had a black and white wedding. My favorite animal is a zebra. My best friend—on the outside, you know, at home—is Black. Isn't that something?" she asked. "My daughter even has a Black name—Sherikah."

"That's interesting," said Walt. "Let's see about that milk shake." He picked up the phone to make the order. When he hung up he said, "It's on the way."

"I hope it doesn't separate. You know—the ice cream from the milk? I hope they don't take too long getting it here."

"Let's get to know each other while we wait," he said, sitting on the couch and taking her hand.

"I'm really shy and embarrassed because I'm so inexperienced, sexwise. My husband didn't teach me a lot and had other women. That left me feeling inadequate. You know, Walt, I do have fantasies. Can I tell you one?"

"Please do, Josie," he said, gently rubbing her shoulder.

"You won't ever tell anyone, will you? I mean when you sit around with the boys, or you won't tell anyone here at the prison? Do you promise?"

"I promise, honey. You just tell Uncle Walt," he said, patting her hand.

"I want to have a kind of . . . orgy. You know, two women and a man—that kind. And I want it to be with a Black female and I want us to do all kinds of stuff to the man and make him scream. I want to be at one end of him and her at the other. That would probably be wild." She laughed. Walt was surprised, his eyebrows raised.

There was a knock at his door and the milk shake arrived. The food service worker brought it in and promptly left. Apparently Walt's clerk had gone to lunch.

Josie grabbed the shake and said, "It separated a little. Damn, I wish I could remix it a little. Do you have a glass or a cup, Walt?"

"Go out to Charmaine's desk. She has all kinds of stuff out there. Come right back, honey."

Josie hunted around and spotted an empty clean glass. She snatched it and returned to Walt. She started pouring the shake back and forth between the two glasses. "This worked out well—it's fine." She gulped half of it down, making sure some of it stayed on her lips. "Umm, kiss it off, Walt—let me see how you kiss."

Walt kissed her and said, "Everything tastes good. Did I do okay?"

"You did fine." She finished it and said lightly, "Well, I've got to be going. Lunch is over and the mailroom will need me back."

Walt's mind was racing with lust and he was intrigued at the thought of an orgy. He squeezed her hand and said, "Listen, Josie, I want to see you again. I can arrange your fantasy. Do you really want to do it? Are you sure?"

Josie imagined having a blast with him and said, "Yeah . . . I want to do it. I want to have some fun for once in my life. Just because I am stuck in here doesn't mean I have to be dead and unfulfilled—especially if someone like you is willing to help me."

"You're right about that, Josie." He moved away from her and went to review his schedule, flipping pages. "I want you to come here on Thursday at four thirty. I'll have something for you."

"Thanks, Walt—I'll see you then." She left, closing his door behind her.

Chapter Fifteen

Emily and Jared

Leo and Emily chatted as they made their way to I-95, headed for Rehoboth Beach. They were glad to spend some time together. Leo was crazy about Emily, but hated the fact that her schedule was so busy. Once they got onto I-95, there wasn't much traffic and Leo was soon zooming. He glanced over at her hair blowing. She was trying to control it.

"Reach in the backseat. There's a present for you," he said.

Emily smiled at him and retrieved a beautifully wrapped large box. "You are just too sweet. What is it?" she asked, placing it on her lap.

"Open it and see."

Emily carefully removed the ribbon and wrapping paper from the large box and then opened it. "Oh my God!" she exclaimed as she pulled a bright purple helmet from the box. It had a silver star on the front, and her name was done in silver on the back. It was gorgeous.

"I remember your telling me about your concussion a long time ago. I'm a good driver, but I'm making sure you don't get any head trouble on my watch. Also, I'm preserving your hairdo. I've got to protect my best girl. Put it on, let's check it out," he said.

Emily placed the helmet on and said, "How did you know purple is my favorite color? I love it!"

"I know because I *listen* when you talk to me, baby," he said as he took a quick look at her in the helmet. "Looks good," he said, grinning at her. He was wearing a fabulous pair of sunglasses he'd purchased especially for his car.

Emily looked in the mirror on the visor of the car and smiled approvingly. "You're damn right it does. This is something else! Thank you," she said, kissing him on the cheek.

They cruised for two and a half hours down long, skinny Delaware. They went for lunch and then began shopping. Leo bought her a mouthwatering lunch, a giant fish piggy bank by Mikasa from their outlet, a raincoat and an umbrella. Emily purchased an outfit for herself, a load of stockings and a pair of pajamas for Leo.

They had a nice day. On the ride home she said, "I know how much you care about me, and I'm glad you don't give me a hard time about Jared."

"Hey, listen, what's the sense in my being upset about a thing I can't change? No point. I enjoy you—that's that."

"There's someone else in your life, right?" she asked.

"Emily, to be perfectly honest," he said, taking his eyes off the road and looking directly at her, "yes."

"Okay," she said, "I don't need to know the details."

"And I'm not discussing them with you. You and me are you and me—when we're together—that's it," he said. She didn't open her mouth.

Back in Philly, he pulled up at the Warwick Hotel and had the valet park the car. He went up to the desk to register. Emily looked around and said to herself, "I live in hotels. Jesus, I need to get married or something so I can stay at home with a man." She thought about Jared as she gazed at Leo across the lobby. "He won't catch me in here, I bet." She then remembered Jared's words to her the first night he caught her with Leo, and she reminded herself she was following Jared's instructions to basically do her thing. Yeah, get some space, all that talking he did on Maritza's porch that night. Well, she looked at Leo and thought about the way he pampered her and the *little* things he did and she was happy Jared gave her his approval. She was keeping Leo, and she didn't give a damn who he had or what was going on with them. She'd played this role before and knew the drill. This was her thing.

"Come here," he said as soon as they entered their hotel room. "I'm gonna rape you."

"You promise, you really mean it?" she sweetly said.

Leo grabbed Emily and began snatching her clothes off. "Don't tear my shit up, man," she said, chuckling. His tongue was in her ear, and he had her ass cupped in his hands, squeezing it. He whispered, "I can afford to buy you some clothes. I'm a responsible person and I pay for my mistakes."

She turned his face around and shoved her tongue down his throat. He picked her up and leaned her against the wall, unzipped his pants, moved her panties to the side and entered her. They were both shaking with passion. When it was over, he laid her down on the floor, stared into her eyes and said, "Baby, you're gonna need the *poh*-leece before we leave here tomorrow."

Two days later, Emily appeared at the nurse's station. "Can you tell Sheila Toland that Emily is here to see her? I'm her cousin and it's important," she lied. The nurse paged a patient's room and advised Sheila.

Sheila walked up briskly, surprised to see Emily. "What are you doing up here, girl?"

"I had a doctor's appointment downstairs. I stopped by here to tell you I need you to make a run with me one day next week in the evening. When are you off?"

"I can do it Thursday night. Will that work?"

"I have to check on that and call you," Emily said.

"What's going on?" Sheila asked.

Emily had a worried look on her face. "I've got a little problem and I have a meeting to attend about it. I have to find out if it will be going on Thursday night. I'll call you when I know."

"Are you and Jared okay?' Sheila asked with a puzzled look on her face.

"We're cool. Look, I've got to go."

Sheila stood in suspense for a few minutes, wondering what Emily was doing. She then remembered she had another IV to insert and rushed to the patient's room.

Sheila answered the phone and Emily said, "Thursday night won't work. I can do Monday for the meeting. Can you?"

"Yeah, I can arrange it. I'll do a swap with another nurse. Where are we going?" asked Sheila.

"Let me tell you when we're on the way. It's a long story, but I need you. Just be patient, I'll give you the scoop. I'll be by your house at six o'clock Monday evening. We'll be out about three hours," Emily said.

"This sounds like something serious or wicked. I wish you'd tell me what's going on," Sheila said.

"Sheila, don't hassle me, okay? I love you but I'm not up for discussing this crap right now. See you on Monday."

"Okay," Sheila said. "Monday it is."

Jared's plane touched down. He was glad to be back in Philly. They'd been in London for ten days on tour. Jared called Emily as soon as he got to his house. "How's the love of my life?"

"She's hanging—where are you?"

"I'm home.

"What! So soon? You weren't due back for two and a half weeks."

"Ike Turner fired us."

"Fired you!" she shouted. "For what?"

"For being too good. He got pissed. We were supposed to be the warm-up group for them—you know? Well, we warmed the audience up too much and it got a little too hot for him. He became insecure, so we got booted out. He's not a very pleasant person either. So, we're home."

"What's Tina like?"

"She is a dream. She is so sweet, Emily, but they said she took a lot of shit from him. I saw it firsthand. He's rough, I hear."

"Oh man, that's a shame," said Emily.

"Yes, it is. And his band was really sorry to see us go. She has a great personality, too."

"So, when will I see you? I'll be home at least ten days before we get rebooked somewhere."

"How about we meet Friday at the Bellevue at one o'clock?" said Emily, all innocence.

"Today's Wednesday—that's a long time, baby," said Jared suspiciously. "What's up with the delay?"

"Well, I have to be at the boutique during the day tomorrow and that's four hours. I can't take off. I can't come tonight, you know that—

Horace has to go to work. You know you don't want to come over here and watch television because we won't have much privacy to do our thing. Friday is the best day."

"And you have to be back at Horace's by six o'clock Friday night for Renee—that makes it tight. I'm getting sick of this already. I feel like you're working me in."

"Oh, shut up—nobody even expected you back in town. You can wait a couple of days."

"Yeah, I guess I can. It's seven thirty—I'm getting some dinner and calling it a night."

"Okay, I'll call you in the morning," Emily said.

"Okay—not too early, though. I do have jet lag." They hung up.

Jared showered and headed promptly to Horace's house. When Emily answered the door, he said, "I came to watch television and have no privacy."

Emily walked into Sheila's house and said, "You ready?"

Sheila answered with a worried look on her face. "I'm scared to death. What the hell is going on?"

"Come on, I'll explain in the car," Emily said.

"Leonard, I'm leaving. See you around nine thirty," Sheila called.

When they got outside, Emily said, "We're taking your car."

"Okay, miss," Sheila said.

Once they got in and situated, Sheila said, "Okay, give it to me. I can't wait another minute."

Emily was flustered and had a forlorn look on her face. "Okay, I've got two problems. The first is, I'm six weeks pregnant."

"Whoa," said Sheila. "What are you going to do? What did Jared say?"

"He doesn't know. I'm thinking."

"What's the second thing?" asked Sheila.

Emily explained all about Rachael and how pissed she was that some gigolo was ripping that little old lady off. "So what meeting are we going to?" Sheila asked.

"We're going to Rachael's house. She lives in Abington. We're doing our detective thing like we did when we were trying to find Amber. We're going to sit our asses out there and wait for him to drive up. That stupid spineless Rachael is letting the bum come to see her tonight," said Emily.

"You mean to tell me that eighty-year-old woman won't stop seeing that piece of trash?"

"Affirmative," said a disgusted Emily.

"So what are we going to do if we find him there?" asked Sheila.

"I don't know. I haven't gotten that far yet," Emily said as she started the car and began driving.

"Are you keeping the baby or what?" asked Sheila.

"I'm mixed up on that right now. Let's not talk anymore about it."

They reached Rachael's house and parked across the street waiting for Mr. No-good Bum. Rachael had told Emily he was coming at seven o'clock. It was now six forty-five. They sat and waited. They waited until eight thirty and he didn't show.

"Okay, Sergeant Pepper Anderson," Sheila said to Emily. "What now?"

"Let's go. I've got to get home so Horace can go to work. Sheila, I'm writing down this address. I need you to come out here again for me, and I'll make some trips, too. I'm going to catch his ass sooner or later. Will you help me?"

"Emily, why don't you let this thing go? Jesus Christ. Rachael is so hardheaded. And another thing, she *wants* him. No matter how bad she says the situation is, she *wants* him. That's why she had a date with him tonight. Maybe you ought to back off."

"I can't let him take advantage of her like that. She's just old and weak."

"Yeah—old and weak with some prior injections of a Black peter— that's her weak spot," said Sheila. They both laughed as Sheila drove home.

"Hi, Rachael, what's up? It's Emily."

"Hi, Emily, how are you?"

"Just fine. How did your date go last night? Did he act any better?"

"He didn't come and he didn't call. What do you think about that?"

"What do *you* think about it?" Emily answered.

"I don't know. When he made the date he told me he was broke. I told him I wouldn't give him any money."

"Maybe that's why he didn't show up—you know he's using you."

"Yes, but I've said that to him before and he would come and I'd always give in and give him the money."

"Rachael, why don't you hire a woman companion to take you around and do things with you? You said you didn't mind not having sex."

"I lied. I like sex. I need it. I've been reading a sexy novel for the past two days and the characters are having wild and crazy sex. I'm all excited now. I want a male companion and I want him to spend the night, too."

An exasperated Emily replied, "Well, you need to look for another one because you said Mr. No-good Bum can't spend the night because he and his girlfriend live together."

"You're right. I'll replace him, but a bird in the hand is worth two in the bush."

"And that's exactly what you have, Rachael. A bird in your hand when you're with him and nothing in the bush. You told me that yourself."

"I know—I'll get things straightened out and get someone else. Meanwhile, I have something to ask you," said Rachael.

"What's that?"

"Well, in this novel I'm reading, this woman character tries all these things on this guy like gargling with really hot water and then giving him oral sex and using food with him and doing it in all positions. Have you ever had wild and crazy sex, Emily?"

Emily quickly reflected on her and Leo getting it on in Maritza's shower. "Yes."

"With whom?"

"I can't tell you that, Rachael."

"I've never had that kind of sex in my life. It sounds fabulous."

"What about you and your husband of fifty-two years—remember him?"

"Well, we just did regular stuff—boring to no end. Emily, tell me who you had the crazy sex with," said Rachael. "Do you still see him?"

"No," said Emily.

"Will you introduce him to me?"

Emily was floored and ended the conversation without even answering Rachael.

"Crazy nymphomaniac Rachael just called me," Emily shouted into the phone. "The bum is coming over Wednesday night—so he says. Can you go up there and wait for me? He's expected at eight and Horace has a date with his girlfriend, Jonita, that night and I have to be home with the kids."

"I swear I hate going up there. You make me sick. What do you want me to do if he shows up? Damn. The Abington police department is going to lock my ass up!" Sheila screamed at Emily.

"Oh, get ahold of yourself. I don't want you to say a word to him. Just write down his tag number. I'll run a check on the car and find out who he is and where he lives. Okay?"

"All right, I'll go. You're really getting on my nerves. What are you going to do about the baby?" asked Sheila.

"I don't know yet."

"Did you at least tell Jared?"

"Nope."

"Good-bye," Sheila said.

On Wednesday night Sheila arrived on time. Mr. No-good Bum's car was in the driveway and Sheila took down the tag number and left. She called Emily as soon as she got in. "Here's the tag number."

"What does this dude look like?" Emily asked.

"I don't know. He must have gotten there early because I was on time and the car was in the driveway when I got there."

Emily took down the tag number and hung up.

Jonita was at her desk going through medical reports, preparing for a deposition. She had been in her office since seven that morning. She sure was working hard these days. She would love to spend more time with wonderful Horace and her own family, but business was booming and time was tight. She was overjoyed to have such a nice boyfriend. It sure was a good thing he worked the twelve to eight shift because if not, she'd probably never get to see him. She looked forward to coming home some evenings and finding him there waiting for her—even if it was only for a few hours. She loved the quick dinners they shared some evenings and sometimes he'd even meet her at her office for a quickie on her couch. They had been dating over eight months and he'd taken her up to Boston for a weekend, to New Orleans and to the Poconos, and they had fantastic times on all of the trips. He was great with her nieces and her family thought a lot of him. There was no marriage or live-in talk—they were taking their time and enjoying each other. Jonita had a nice life, a secure job at a prestigious law firm and a responsible man who had a great sense of humor and an imagination.

The phone rang, distracting Jonita from her work.

"Hi, Jonita, this is Emily. I have to tell you something, and it has to be between you and me. Can you keep this in confidence?"

"What's going on, Emily?"

"Well, I don't want Horace to know that someone hit my car and cursed me out. He'll go ballistic. You know how he is. I just want to find out who the guy is and I can take care of it."

Jonita became very concerned and said, "Were you hurt, Emily?"

"No, I'm okay. There's not much damage to the car, but he was so cocky that I'm going to track him down and make him pay. I have his tag number. Can you help me?"

"Give me the tag number. I'll call a friend of mine who is a cop. Is it a Pennsylvania tag number?"

"Yes, it is."

"Okay, let's have it. I'll have the information for you shortly if he is working today."

"Are you going to tell Horace?"

"No, I've got you covered. What's Renee doing?"

"I dropped her off at preschool an hour ago. Here's the tag number."

"Oh, that's right—it is Thursday. I forgot she goes on Thursdays. Okay, I'll call you back. Sit tight."

Emily started a load of wash and the phone rang. "Hey, baby, what are you doing?" Jared asked.

"Nothing."

"We leave next week on Friday for Buffalo. You've got me seven more days. Do you want to run up to New York on Saturday and spend the night?"

"Yes, that sounds divine."

"If Sheila and Leonard are free, why don't you ask them to come, too. I'll pay their hotel expenses."

"Okay, I'll give her a call later and call you back. Are you and I still on for breakfast at the Omni tomorrow morning?" she asked.

"Yeah, that's cool. Come by here around ten o'clock. My mom is going with us."

"Great, I'll see you both at ten."

Emily stood by the phone staring into space. What the hell was she going to do about this pregnancy? Well, Jared wouldn't find out at brunch because she certainly wasn't telling him in front of Connie. Connie didn't have any grandchildren. Emily knew better than to mention this to her. She'd be delighted and even though she and Connie were the best of friends, Emily wouldn't be able to even discuss not keeping the baby. She had run through it all a million times, trying to make the right decision. This was definitely Jared's baby. She'd never let Leo touch her without a condom or her having her diaphragm in—even when they played the rape game. She wondered what Jared would say about the whole thing. She'd work it out next week, she decided. The phone rang, startling her from her thoughts. "Hello," she said.

"Emily, it's Jonita. I have the information for you. Grab a pen and paper."

Emily went to the kitchen drawer and snatched an old envelope and a pen. "I'm ready."

"Okay—it's registered to Leo Duffy at 5818 Woodcrest Avenue, Philly. You got that?"

Emily didn't answer. Her brain was suspended.

"Emily, are you there?" Jonita asked.

"Oh, I'm here, Jonita, I got distracted. You said Leo Duffy at 5818 Woodcrest Avenue. Right? Are you sure?"

"I guess I'm sure. That's the information he gave me. Was it a green LeBaron convertible that hit your car? That's what my friend said it was. We can run the tag for his insurance company. Do you want me to do that? I can do the form from here and send it to Pennsylvania Department of Motor Vehicles. I can handle it for you and won't charge you, and I *will* make him pay. You want me on this? We need to get your car estimated. I won't tell Horace a thing."

Emily could not believe this news. She was stunned. She was trying to get herself together as Jonita babbled on. "Listen, Jonita, thanks. And yes, that's the car. I can handle it from here. I really appreciate your help. I've got to run."

Chapter Sixteen

Purdy

*P*urdy stared at Ling-Ani, the girl with her and the baby with a bewildered look on his face. The baby began to cry and the mother pulled out her breast and began feeding the child. "This is my cousin Chung Soo and her daughter, Dr. Remington," said Ling-Ani. Purdy said hello to the woman.

"Chung Soo does not understand English," said Ling-Ani.

"Tell me how to say hello to her," said Purdy. She did so, and Purdy repeated the words the best he could in Chinese to Chung Soo and she smiled.

"Ling-Ani, will you fill me in on the reason for this unexpected visit tonight?" asked Purdy.

"I went home immediately after I brought you here. I had a long talk with my family and I explained everything you and I had discussed. Chung Soo wants you to adopt the baby." Ling-Ani repeated what she said to Purdy in Chinese so Chung Soo could keep up with the conversation.

Purdy kept staring at them and his mind was racing a mile a minute. This was going too fast for him, even though he had suggested it. "I have many questions, ladies," he said.

"How about we discuss it slowly?" said Ling-Ani.

"Yes, let's do that," he said.

He was dying to hold the baby, but didn't want to disturb the feeding, or go near the girl's breast. "Okay, Ling-Ani, let's get started. First of all, where is this child's father and what will he have to say about all of this? Was he at your family's home when this discussion took place?"

"Well, actually, we have no idea where he is. We have not seen him since she was about four months pregnant. He was afraid of getting into trouble because they were not married, and his family had him sent away. Neither he nor his relatives has ever contacted Chung Soo or my family again." As soon as Ling-Ani finished talking in English, she began in Chinese for Chung Soo's benefit. This was getting on his nerves already.

"Excuse my bad manners, would either of you like me to order something for you to eat or drink?"

"I'm okay, no, thank you," said Ling-Ani. She then asked Chung Soo, who said she was hungry. Ling-Ani grabbed a menu off the table and placed it in Chung Soo's hand. She began reading and then Ling-Ani picked up the phone and ordered a full meal for her cousin. Chung Soo smiled at Purdy to thank him.

The baby appeared content with the feeding, and Chung Soo put her breast away and began patting the baby's back so she would burp. She pulled a cloth diaper out of a small bag, wiped the baby's mouth with the corner of it and then walked over to the bed and laid the baby down to change her. Purdy stared in amazement. The child did not seem scrawny and was cute with large brown eyes and a thick head of brown hair. After the diaper change he looked at them both. "May I hold her?" he said to Chung Soo, reaching his arms out. She placed the baby in his arms. Her skin was as soft as cotton and her cheeks resembled two ripe peaches.

"What's her name?" Purdy asked.

"We call her Petal, like a flower—you know. I thought of it myself," Ling-Ani said proudly. Purdy smiled, being a lover of flowers himself.

"You never introduced me to your cousin," said Purdy.

"Oh, my apologies," said Ling-Ani. She then formally introduced the two in both languages. Chung Soo nodded and smiled. Purdy continued to play with the baby, intrigued with her. She was so tiny and beautiful, and he could not fathom anyone hurting this child.

"Tell me, Ling-Ani—and you take over this conversation in English between you and me and explain to your cousin after the discussion— what would she want, or your family want, in order for me to adopt Petal?"

Ling-Ani smiled and was pleased he was interested. "Well, we would want money and assurance that she would be well taken care of."

"Would she want to see or visit the baby?" he asked.

"No, she would let you take her and not interfere."

"She is willing to sign everything for a price?"

"Yes, Dr. Remington."

"And what would that price be?"

"What would you be willing to pay?"

"I've never done this before," said Purdy. "Do you have a figure in mind?"

The room was silent. Ling-Ani then spoke to Chung Soo. She sat thinking and then gave a number to Ling-Ani.

"Fifteen thousand dollars," said Ling-Ani.

Purdy looked down at the bundle of joy. He felt that was a small price to pay the mother and said, "Ask her if she is sure." Ling-Ani asked Chung Soo and she nodded yes.

Purdy began thinking about what the legal fees and expenditures might be and wished he were able to get in touch with Tony Garcia that moment, but felt it was a bad move to call him in front of them. "Her price is satisfactory but I have to work a lot of other things out. Also, I have to arrange for Petal to be examined. She has no birth certificate, correct?" Purdy asked.

"Correct, but there are other ways to go about it."

"Such as?" he asked, still holding Petal. He switched his gaze from the baby's big brown eyes as she sucked her thumb, to give Ling-Ani his full attention.

"Well, we were talking this over at my house, and since the father is not around and there is no record of the birth, Chung Soo could tell the airport personnel, or any authorities who questioned your taking the baby back to America, that you were the father. I could check around and ask someone I trust if we can do that. Also, I know a few lawyers here in the city who could help. What do you think?" Ling-Ani asked.

Purdy was speechless again. He wondered if it could be done that way. It seemed a lot less complicated than having lawyers in Philly trying to get it done.

"I need to do two things," he said. "I need to have this baby examined. Someone at concierge has the name of a doctor who can do that. I want to make sure she is completely healthy. Also, I'd like to speak with the lawyer you have in mind in three days. I can't see him any sooner because I have an important conference the day after tomorrow during the day. I can meet the lawyer in the evening here and he can explain everything to me and give me advice. You should try to arrange that," he said while tickling Petal's feet.

A knock at the door announced the arrival of Chung Soo's duck dinner along with a Coke, a strawberry milk shake, and chocolate cake with a scoop of vanilla ice cream. "She must have been famished," he thought to himself.

"Okay, listen, you do as much as you can do. Just in case we can't go the route of my taking Petal out of this country as my biological child, I'll have my attorneys in the States working on this. I was due to leave here on Monday. If anything happens and Petal does not pass her physical, I can't adopt her or take her with me. I am extremely busy with my practice and I do want to have a child, but I have to have a healthy one. You do understand that, don't you?" he asked.

"Yes, I understand, Dr. Remington," Ling-Ani answered.

"Then tell your cousin so she understands." Ling-Ani did as she was instructed, and Chung Soo, who seemed to be in heaven with her meal, agreed between gulps and bites.

"Okay, let me get some rest," he said as he handed Petal to Ling-Ani. "When she finishes her meal, you two get back home and we'll talk tomorrow. You and I still have a date, right?"

"Yes, I'll be here tomorrow."

Chung Soo looked up and noticed Ling-Ani with the baby and asked her a question. Purdy wondered what it was. Ling-Ani answered and turned in bewilderment to Purdy. "She wants to know if they can stay here until we are finished with all the business."

"That would be nice company, but not a good idea," he said. Ling-Ani relayed the answer to Chung Soo, and she frowned and said something back to her.

"She said 'Please,'" said Ling-Ani.

Purdy looked at the three of them with mixed feelings. Now he was questioning the entire thing. He had problems already. He looked at the baby and picked up the phone. "This is Dr. Pierce Remington in room 521. Do you have any vacancies?"

He arranged a room for them. The baby had only two diapers and the clothes on her back. Thank God it was eleven o'clock at night and the two diapers should last until morning, he thought. Purdy told Ling-Ani to return in the morning for him an hour later than she'd planned, and to come with two outfits for Petal, disposable diapers and whatever else she needed for two days. He also told her to tell her family to get some clean clothes together for her. He wrote a check for fifty dollars payable to Ling-Ani and told her to cash it at the front desk, and if she had any trouble, to call back to the room. He asked them to leave and made another call instructing the front desk to give them the key to the additional room and inform him of the room number.

Before he passed out he made a list in his mind:

(1) Birth certificate.
(2) Change the name to Pilar.
(3) Kid needs everything.
(4) Should I call Stefana for advice and help?
(5) What about a nanny?
(6) What if she is sick and I can't adopt her?
(7) Do I really need a lawyer in the states? Get in touch with Tony Garcia.
(8) Need an extra plane ticket.
(9) Need to wire money for the family.
(10) Need a car seat when I get to the airport for ride home.
(11) Breastfeeding—I can't do that—I need formula.
(12) How do you get the damn diaper on?
(13) Shots—she needs shots.

Then he questioned himself, asking, "How can I go sightseeing and ride the gondola with all this shit going on? Am I crazy?"

Purdy woke up the next morning and after having breakfast in the hotel dining room, he returned to his room and waited for Ling-Ani. She finally arrived at eleven o'clock with things for Petal. It was now two o'clock in the morning in Philly, and he couldn't call Tony.

"Okay," Ling-Ani said, rushing in, "I got this stuff and I didn't have enough money so I used some of my money to cover it—twenty-seven dollars forty-three cents in American dollars. Here are the receipts."

"I'll take care of it," Purdy said as he looked through the things. There were two outfits that seemed adequate, but nothing like Petal would be wearing if she were his.

"I have not talked to Chung Soo this morning. I didn't bother because she can't understand me anyway."

"I'll go to her room right now. I also brought a change of clothes for Chung Soo," said Ling-Ani.

"Okay, you go get that done and when you come back, we'll leave to do some sightseeing. I know we have a lot of business to attend to with the baby and all—however, I'm going to try to enjoy part of this as a vacation, too. We're still going out."

"That's the right thing to do, Dr. Remington. You should have some fun. I'll run and get them settled."

"Do me a favor before you go to their room. Stop at the concierge desk and pick up an envelope for me. I need that to make a call," he said.

"Okay, I'll be right back," said Ling-Ani.

While she was gone, he began contemplating the adoption all over again. Was he doing the right thing? Could he really get away with getting Petal out of the country as her biological father without going to a Chinese jail? He'd never been in any trouble before in his life. He couldn't wait to talk to an attorney in China about the project, and he also wanted to run it all by the attorneys that Tony might have located. He had made up his mind that whatever he needed taken care of in the States before he left China, he would not go through anyone at his office for anything. He didn't want them in his business and felt if he did delegate any responsibilities relevant to this matter, they would either be incapable of securing the correct information, or get it ass backwards. He also had no desire to hear their comments or opinions. As efficient an office manager as Jillian was, he didn't want even her on this. He didn't feel like listening to her mouth, either.

He could take care of the wire transfers himself, and he would call Mrs. Charleston to meet him at the airport with a car seat if indeed he got the baby out of the country. He'd also ask her to give him a hand with Petal until he got situated. He'd managed to get a lot figured out. He just had to talk to the right people and make a list of what else had to be done, such as obtaining an official birth certificate for use in the States, etc.

Ling-Ani returned to the room with the envelope and said, "Okay, I'm going to see about the baby and Chung Soo."

"Okay, come back with them when you're done. I have a couple of calls to make. Give me at least a half hour." She turned to leave and he said, "Make sure you bring them when you come back."

"Are you planning to take them with us?" she asked.

"No, I want to see Petal before we leave."

Purdy immediately called the doctor and made an appointment for him to check Petal out at four o'clock that afternoon.

As he waited for the women to return, he thought about how he would handle Jazz and Stefana. He surmised Stefana would be more of a help to him with advice on parenting because she was more mature and a lot less flighty than crazy Jazz. He smiled, thinking of Petal. He felt good about the decision he was making. There was no doubt about it. He hoped the baby was healthy. He was extremely excited about the idea of Petal in his life.

Chung Soo, Ling-Ani and Petal arrived at his room. Ling-Ani explained they had a restful night, and Chung Soo had ordered breakfast in her room. Purdy took Petal from her mother's arms, pleased that she looked so cute in her new clothes. He toyed with her tiny hand for a few minutes and then said he and Ling-Ani had to leave. Ling-Ani explained to Chung Soo that she should be ready to go to the doctor's office when they returned at three o'clock.

In the car, Ling-Ani asked, "Do you want to talk to a Chinese attorney? I have two numbers."

Purdy was glad she had reminded him and said, "Yes, I do, I should have done that before I left. When we stop for lunch, I'll make the call from the restaurant. Do these guys speak English?"

"Yes, Dr. Remington. Both speak English and I called both before I left the house, putting them on notice of your possible call, just in case one was not available when you called."

"Good work, Ling-Ani. We'll get to that later."

Purdy had a fantastic time riding the gondola and observing all the sights. He went to Tiananmen Square and also saw where all of the historic events of the twentieth century took place. He saw the portrait of Mao Tse-tung that hangs over the Gate of Heavenly Peace.

When they arrived at the restaurant, Ling-Ani was able to reach the first attorney. Purdy spoke to him, informing him that Chung Soo was single and had no contact with the child's father. He arranged a dinner meeting with the attorney at seven o'clock at a restaurant of his choosing. Purdy then passed the phone to Ling-Ani, and she took down the name and address of the restaurant.

The face-painting expedition was a gas, and Purdy was intrigued. He had tea with a local family and took a trishaw ride on the back streets of Beijing. They took a cable car to the highest point of the Great Wall and called it a day. They went back to the hotel late, 4:30, collected Chung Soo and Petal and dashed out to the doctor's office, Purdy carrying Petal. The baby was pleasant and he was feeling more comfortable holding her.

As they waited in the lobby of the doctor's office, Chung Soo nursed the baby, which reminded Purdy to get instructions on formula. There sure wouldn't be anyone in Philadelphia to do what her mother was doing. Finally they were called and all three went in for the visit. Petal was checked out thoroughly, and the physician asked Chung Soo a zillion questions. The doctor answered Purdy's questions regarding Petal going from breast- to bottle-feeding, explaining that Chung Soo could begin weaning Petal right away. He advised they should purchase Enfamil infant formula, which in his opinion was the closest to mother's milk, and alternate giving the baby breast milk at one feeding and bottled the next. He felt Petal should adjust with no problem within a few days. She was given two routine infant injections, which consisted of a vitamin K and the first of a series of three hepatitis B immunizations. They were advised that, at about age two months, she would require a

DTaP to protect her against diphtheria, tetanus and pertussis, and she'd need an OPV. Petal received a clean bill of health, and they all beamed with joy. Their first stop after the doctor's office was to the drugstore, where they pick up two six-packs of ready-to-feed bottled Enfamil.

It was six o'clock when they returned to the hotel. Chung Soo sat in Purdy's room examining the menu and then looked up at him for his approval to order. He nodded and she called room service. He thought she would never stop talking and was convinced that this kid was starving. The food was delivered, and he held Petal while her mother satisfied her apparent yen for American cuisine, gobbling up two cheeseburgers, a salad, French fries, apple pie and a strawberry milk shake. He shook his head looking at the thin girl. He guessed her weight at about a hundred pounds and he said to himself, "If I don't get out of China soon, I'll be bankrupt and she'll require a weight-loss program."

When she finished the meal, she and the baby left for their room, and he and Ling-Ani headed for the restaurant to meet the attorney. During the expensive seven-course dinner, the attorney promised that Purdy could get the child out as the biological father and a birth certificate could be obtained. His fee would be twenty-five hundred dollars to prepare the documents. It would look better if Chung Soo were present at the airport when Purdy left with the child. The attorney also advised Purdy that all information pertaining to the case would be kept confidential and done quickly to avoid problems with the government. He said he could have everything done within a week. Purdy declined and adjourned the meeting because he didn't feel right going that route. He didn't completely trust the attorney and the thought of something going wrong made him decide he'd better stick with Tony. He gave the attorney one hundred fifty dollars for his time, paid the check and left.

When they got back to the hotel, it was nine fifteen in the morning in Philadelphia, and he called Tony's office. "Tony Garcia or Alexa please. This is Dr. Pierce Remington calling from China."

"Hi, Dr. Remington, this is Alexa. I have some information for you, so grab a pen and paper so we don't waste time. I know this call is costing a fortune."

Purdy grabbed the hotel pad and a pen and said, "Let's go."

"Diandra Laveer does family law and seems to be the best. She is in Philly and has done many adoptions in China. Her number is 215-555-2200, and I've already spoken to her. She is high-powered and her fee alone will be twenty grand, but she can go through the Chinese government immediately because she has an excellent contact. If you pay an additional thirty-five grand to the Chinese government, you'll be supplied with all the necessary papers and a birth certificate to get the child out. She can have this done in three days. So the whole thing will cost you fifty-five. That includes everything and the mother does not receive any of the funds from the government if she is not married to the father. If she had a husband, they would receive five grand from the government. The Chinese government frowns upon unwed mothers and feels these women are out of control. Do you understand, Dr. Remington?"

"Yes, Alexa, I understand."

"Okay, one more thing," she said. "This adoption—if done through the Chinese government—will allow you under all circumstances to be the permanent legal single parent of the child. The mother loses all rights, cannot change her mind and is not informed of the child's whereabouts. She loses all rights whatsoever and is forever prohibited from bringing any legal actions against you or the Chinese government to gain access, visit, or communicate with you or the child in any way, shape or form. All documents to this effect shall be prepared for you by Laveer and signed by the Chinese government, and sets of documents will be filed in Beijing, Philadelphia Family Court and U.S. Immigration. Copies of everything also go to you and Laveer. So this is completely legit and airtight. No one can touch you with that child."

Purdy was thoroughly impressed with what Tony had accomplished. He could also see how efficient Alexa was and wished she worked for him.

"What about her plane ticket? Does she need one?" he asked.

"No. She's two weeks old. Daddy holds her."

"Good news," said Purdy. "Tell Tony I'll call Laveer. I'll be back to you guys. And tell Tony to get a bill ready for me for your excellent work on this project. Also, tell him that Pilar, the infant girl, is as cute as she can be."

"Glad to be of service to you, Dr. Remington. And there are a couple of other things," she said.

"Let's have 'em," he said.

"Tony said to let you know that he took the liberty of speaking to his sister Andrea. She is a twenty-three-year-old graduate student at the Wharton School at University of Pennsylvania. She is a very nice young lady and helps out Tony and his wife, Teighlor, with their three boys at home. She is on spring break now. Tony has asked her, and if you need Andrea, she can meet you at the airport in Philly, should you bring the child home. She can also stay at your house for two days to assist you until you get acclimated with the baby. If you need her, let us know and make sure we have your flight information. Tony also told me to tell you that you'll probably agree, excuse his language as I quote him: 'As usual, he is on the fucking ball 24/7.' He also said to tell you that if he sends Andrea that 'you'd better keep your hands in your fucking pockets so he doesn't have to make the kid an orphan for real.' "

Purdy, surprised, admired Tony's straightforwardness concerning his sister. He laughed and said, "Tell him I said thank you, I'm considering everything he said, and he is absolutely correct regarding the expert services he has rendered to me. He should also know I'm not a very obedient guy—however, I'll make an exception in Andrea's case. I'll speak with him soon. I appreciate all your efforts, too, Alexa."

"Garcia and Russell aim to please, Dr. Remington. Ball's in your court," she replied.

He then called Diandra Laveer to let her know he required her services. He collected her address and banking information and advised he would make arrangements to have her fee as well as the Chinese government's fee wired into her account immediately, since Petal had passed her physical. After that he placed a call to his office to advise he was having a superb time in China and that he might be two days late getting back to Philadelphia. Dr. Gelding should continue covering for him if he was delayed, he informed the staff.

Purdy called Alexa back to bring her up to speed on the retaining of Laveer and asked her to let Andrea know he would need her at the airport and he would get back to them with flight information.

The next call was to Continental Bank of Philadelphia to wire fifty-five thousand dollars to Philadelphia National Bank into the account of Diandra Laveer, Esquire. He then phoned her office and left word of the transaction. He and Ling-Ani then headed to Chung Soo's room to give her the news. Ling-Ani felt bad and was worried because she knew her family would not receive any money. Purdy sat down and explained the events of his conversations with Laveer to Ling-Ani and asked her to translate to Chung Soo. She also let Chung Soo know the laws and made sure she understood that the Chinese government would not give her any part of the money. She was extremely disappointed, but agreed that he could take the baby anyhow in fear that Petal would eventually be taken away.

Purdy then took his checkbook out, wrote a check for fifteen thousand dollars payable to Ling-Ani, showed it to both the women and told them that after all documents were executed by Chung Soo and/or her parents, the check would be turned over to Ling-Ani, as he knew Chung Soo was a minor. He also offered to make the check out to Chung Soo's parents, should they feel more comfortable with that. He told them to let him know later exactly how to write the check. Both women were lit up with huge smiles.

The deal was done. Purdy planned to have some fun in China for the next few days getting to know his new daughter. Her name would be Pilar Miriam Remington. Her middle name was chosen to honor his deceased mother, whom he still loved and missed dearly. Pilar would affectionately be nicknamed Petal, in honor of her biological family, and only her father would use her pet name. In public, at restaurants and at school, the affluent Dr. Remington's daughter would always be addressed as Pilar.

"Garcia and Russell, may I help you?" the receptionist answered as Purdy waited.

"Tony Garcia or Alexa please, this is Dr. Pierce Remington calling from China." Soon Tony came on the line.

"Hi, Pierce, how are you?"

"Hey, Tony, I'm fine. How are you, man?"

"I'm cool. I spoke to Ms. Laveer and I understand you've got a daughter."

"Yeah, man, and I love her to death. You did a bang-up job. I'll let you babysit some nights for me."

"You got it, anytime," said Tony.

"Listen, Tony, I'm calling to give my flight information. Grab a pen, man."

"I'm ready," said Tony.

"Okay. It's American flight number 1126 and I'll be in Philly on the twenty-fourth at 9:33 P.M. Can you get that information to Andrea? I guess you heard I'm going to be a good boy while she is at my house." He chuckled.

"Yeah, I heard. I appreciate that. I'll pass this info on to her. She's pretty good with kids, her nephews adore her."

"I'm sure I'll be pleased and I really appreciate your looking out for me. I need you to describe her for me so I can look for her. Make it short," Purdy said.

"She's five-eight and a beautiful slender redhead. You can't miss her in a crowd. That's it, man."

"Okay, Tony," said Purdy.

"I picked up a car seat, my gift to Pilar, and Andrea will have it. Is everything else cool? Do you need her to bring anything else?" Tony asked.

"No, we'll get the rest of her stuff when I come."

"See you soon," said Tony. They hung up.

Purdy looked down at Pilar who was lying on his hotel room bed. He had already fallen in love with her. Everybody had been paid and all the paperwork was in order. Tomorrow was the big day. Pilar had spent the last two nights in his room sleeping in his bed, and he had learned the art of changing diapers and burping, and had given her a bath. She was adjusting well to the formula. He hadn't told a soul other than Tony and Laveer that he had adopted Pilar. Ling-Ani had told Purdy that her family was house-hunting with the fifteen thousand dollar payment. Chung Soo was in good spirits, even though she was losing her daughter. He planned not to give her or Ling-Ani any information on where he resided. Neither of the women would accompany him and Pilar to the airport.

He'd done a little shopping, picking up a couple of outfits for Pilar, diapers and formula for the plane ride. The flight from Beijing to Chicago would be almost fourteen hours and then they were connecting in Chicago for a two-hour flight to Philly.

Pilar started to cry, and Purdy changed her diaper and grabbed a bottle from the six-pack. He went into the bathroom and, while cradling her, ran the bottle under the hot water in the sink until it was warm. He fed and burped her and she went to sleep. She really was a good baby.

"Hi, Dr. Remington, I'm Andrea Garcia. Welcome home." Purdy took a long look at Andrea and knew why Tony had to threaten him. "Wow," he thought.

"Hello, Andrea. I can't shake your hand—too much stuff I have here, thank God," he said, smiling down at Pilar.

"Let me see her. Can I take her?" she asked.

"Sure," he said, passing Pilar over to her.

"She is absolutely gorgeous, Dr. Remington. Congratulations, Daddy."

"Thanks, Andrea. Let's get the bags and get out of here. I'll get someone to help us."

The bags were loaded into Andrea's Ford Explorer and Pilar's car seat was in the backseat. Purdy had never put a child in a car seat in his life and was reluctant to place Pilar in it. Andrea noticed his apprehension and said, "I've had plenty of practice with Tony's kids and it's a snap. I'll put her in and you can watch. Tomorrow I'll transfer the seat to your car and make sure it is secure. Relax, Daddy," she said.

"Okay—I guess you know the ropes," he said hesitantly.

On the way home they chatted about his trip, the flight, Andrea's school and all the things he would have to do now that he had a child.

"Andrea, I know I'll need you to do some shopping with me. I have to get her room together, order furniture and all that stuff. Do you mind?"

"No, I love shopping. We'll make a list and get it all together. I can only stay over two days, however. I may be able to give you some time late afternoons and evenings after that. I know you have a lot to get together. You're going to have to apply for a nanny, right, or is your mother or a relative going to help out?"

"My mom and dad have both passed away. It's just me, but I can handle it all. I made a list of what I have to do, and you'll make a list of what you think I need."

"Okay, let's just take it step by step. By the way, what is she going to sleep in tonight?" Andrea asked.

"I'm going to fix a drawer up as a bed and put her on the floor by my bed. I have a couple of blankets in my suitcase. I plan to get her a bassinet tomorrow and then I'll see about the crib," he said.

"Okay," said Andrea. "Listen, you need to give me some directions now to your house or I need to pull over so you can drive."

"Pull over," he said.

When they pulled up at his house, Andrea was in awe. "This is lovely, Dr. Remington," she said, admiring the beautiful brownstone.

They went inside and got the makeshift bed together for Pilar. Andrea bathed her and fed her while Purdy showered and got into his pajamas. He had only a few pairs of those things because he loved walking around nude, but all that was about to change. He showed Andrea to her room and saw that she had everything she needed.

Purdy noticed the light blinking on his message tape indicating fourteen messages. He ignored it, glad no one from his office knew he was home. He hadn't even called Maritza or Stefana to say he was on his way home. He had been too busy with the adoption and the arrangements for Pilar. It was a little past midnight when they all retired—Pilar on the floor next to Daddy and Andrea tucked away in her room with her door open.

At twenty minutes after five, Purdy awakened to Pilar screaming her head off. Andrea ran in the room. "I've got her. Go back to sleep, Dr. Remington."

Andrea scooped Pilar up, grabbed her diaper bag and headed for the living room. She turned the radio on and found a station playing a little Kenny G. She quickly changed Pilar, heated her bottle and fed her, and they lay on the couch listening to the sounds. It was now a little past six o'clock. Purdy, still a bit nervous, grabbed his robe and headed downstairs. He observed them, smiled and said, "This is nice. Is she asleep yet?"

"Nope, she's jamming and enjoying the sights, too."

Purdy went over and picked his daughter up and gave her a tour of the first floor and basement of her new home. Those brown eyes were wide open and she was as quiet as a mouse. He then returned to the living room and told Andrea she could go back to her room for a nap and he would put Pilar down to see if she'd go to sleep. He needed a few more hours of rest and hoped Pilar would be agreeable to that. Pilar wasn't ready for the drawer and she and Daddy ended up falling asleep in his bed. Andrea came in to check on them and removed the child from the bed, placing her back in the drawer. She returned to her room.

Andrea lay in her bed for a while, restless, unable to fall asleep. She tossed and turned and listened to see if she heard the baby. Everything was quiet. She then got up and tiptoed back into their room, and all was well. She looked down at the sleeping angel and over at Purdy and walked back out of the room. She then took a look at the playroom and fell in love with it. She closed the door and played Pac-Man for a while and returned to her room. Before entering she stopped and looked back down the hall. She then returned to Purdy's room and he was knocked out. She gently eased into his bed.

Chapter Seventeen

Angie

*J*oel stood looking at Angie and said, "I'm all mixed up right now, Angie. I know I love you. I have a son who needs me. I'm worried you and I won't make it. I'm sorry I had to think this over. I need some time."

"Take some time to think. Do you want to think here or there?" Angie asked.

"I'll think here. Are you okay?" Joel asked.

"Yeah, I'm okay. I love you and while you're thinking this over—do it in the guest room," Angie said. That's as far as she could go. By no means was she going to be fucking him while he was thinking of going back to another woman.

Joel opted not to go to Ebony's to talk to her that evening or see William. He spent a night tossing and turning, missing Angie in his arms and trying to figure out the best decision to make for them all. The next morning they awoke and did their usual thing. Angie made coffee and his lunch and dropped him off at work. She reported for work and then picked him up. Things went on that way for three days and on Thursday, Angie and Joel began sleeping together again. He had gone to see William on Wednesday night and still had not given Ebony an answer. On Friday, Angie and Joel had a small spat that escalated into an argument because Joel had not reached a decision. Finally, since he could not make up his mind and kept advising her that he was indeed confused, Angie wrote him a letter suggesting that he go to Ebony's. She had had it.

Joel did not want to go, but Angie insisted. He had no car and she was not providing hers for the move. Joel arranged for Ray, a coworker, to move him to Ebony's apartment. When Ray and Joel drove off with Joel's suitcases that Saturday afternoon, Angie watched out of the window and cried. She was heartbroken.

Joel was having a tough time, too. Things were quite different at

Ebony's as opposed to Angie's home. William, though, was thrilled to have him around. Ebony was ecstatic and felt she was on her way to a husband.

Joel decided to use protection with Ebony—damn if he'd let her pop up pregnant. Ebony was trying to make him happy, but Angie remained on his mind. He thanked God Ebony worked two jobs and got in after ten in the evening.

Angie was a basket case and forgot how to work every gadget in her home. She noticed a few things he had left at her house and would cry every time she saw anything that belonged to him. Over that weekend she went shopping and that didn't help. She'd find herself in the men's department looking at items she knew he needed. She had not eaten a thing since he left. Every time she looked at the coffeemaker she started crying. She sent faxes to all of her close friends, including copies to Joel at his job, telling everyone they had broken up.

Things have changed. Joel and I have broken up and he has moved back in with the girl he used to live with before he hooked up with me. He explained to me they had some unfinished business and parted too quickly due to some misunderstandings, and because they have a five-year-old son, they needed to be together.

Joel and I had begun having some problems because I noticed and felt him drinking too much. After three consultations about this and him feeling a few beers a night and a couple of drinks a night are no problem, the third time I decided I could not hack that. We talked and I made the decision for him to move. Of course, I cared very much for him and I am feeling pretty low. He had given me a beautiful necklace for my birthday and on two occasions had asked discussed marriage with me over the time we had been together. This was a serious relationship for us both—I thought—but decided we needed more time to get to know and understand each other before a marriage could take place. So I nestled into the next best thing and was happy with that. It did not pan out—wasn't in the cards, as Leah, the tarot card reader, had advised me in July.

I am truly grateful for the time I spent with him and he indeed filled a void in my life. He was exceptionally nice to me and we had a tremendous amount of fun and companionship together. To be perfectly honest and up-front (you know how straight up I am) I am extremely disappointed and heartbroken at the way things turned out. You know I believe in "Whatever happens was meant to be" and "Nothing is a coincidence" and that God places people in your paths for many reasons and sometimes—just for a season. That is to teach us something.

Devin invited me to a party Sunday night at a bar and I am going there—need to keep busy. Just a couple of tears yesterday, and I believe they were shed because I know Joel is making a drastic mistake and you know what—that bothers me more than anything. But our heads are hard sometimes, and we just have to keep hitting them until we get it right.

Okay, guys—gotta run. Going to try to get a little housework and laundry done and make the party tonight.

Angie

By Monday morning, the beginning of Joel's third day away from Angie, he knew he could not be with Ebony. He was going out of his mind. He was happy to get to work where he found a telephone message from Angie that he immediately returned.

"You called me?" Joel asked, expecting Angie to start in on him.

"Yes, I did. I need you to get yourself together and come home." Angie sounded like she was worn out. "I'm tired of this thing now—you know, your being gone and all. We have to work it out. I'm miserable. Whatever you have to do to fix the situation there and get back to me— I need you to fix it," Angie emphatically ordered.

"Oh, just *fix* it? Do you realize you made me go over there? You wrote me a letter and told me to work things out with this woman and move back there. Now you want me to *fix it?*"

"Yes. I'm sorry. I did tell you that you needed to talk to her. However, I didn't actually *tell* you to move. I told you to go there and *talk* to her. Isn't that what the letter said?" Angie asked.

"You told me to *move* there. You know it. Now I'm there and you want me to move back." Joel was getting pissed because Angie was getting technical with him about what she said. He said, "Two months ago you got mad at me and I ended up at a hotel for a day. I'm not going through this stuff with you. When I went to the hotel, then you wanted me to check back out the same day and come back to you."

"Well, you've never done *everything* I tell you to do. Shit, I asked you to stop drinking and you didn't. You shouldn't have listened to me if I told you to move to Ebony's. You need to come home. We love each other, don't we?" She waited impatiently for his answer, not knowing what the hell he would say.

"Yes, I do love you, but does that mean that every time we have a disagreement I have to go? I'm not up for that—love or no love."

"Look, Joel, do you want to come back?"

Joel was silent.

"Look, you left some stuff here and I'm keeping it. The things remind me of you and I miss you. I'm not functioning here. I'm losing weight because I can't eat. I can't sleep. I sent you an e-mail. You need to check your in-box. I miss you and I'm tired of all this shit." An edge of sly humor entered her voice. "I want you to tell those people at your job you have a family emergency and have to leave right now. I'm coming there for you and we are going to have some marathon talks and iron all this stuff out. After that you can take my car and get your stuff and come home. It's as simple as that. Are you coming?" she asked.

Joel chuckled. Angie was hilarious. Her personality was the main thing that turned him on about her. He sighed and said, "Angie, let me get organized here. I just walked in the door. Give me an hour to call you back to let you know if I can leave."

"Okay, sweetie. I love you. I'll talk to you in an hour," Angie said.

"I love you back. Later," Joel said.

By then phone calls of support and condolences were coming in like crazy to Angie from her friends, who had arrived at their jobs and received her e-mail.

Joel was relieved Angie had called. He had realized over the weekend that he truly loved and missed her, too. He remembered the agony of being away from Angie while dealing with his dad's death in Denver and how he listened to his favorite song and was in agony missing her love. Joel knew he had to figure a way to get out of this mess with Ebony and get back to Angie.

Angie was happy after the call, feeling she had her man back. She sat thinking of all the things she could do to get through their problems. She knew she was in love with him. She wanted it to work out. She didn't want any man other than Joel.

As soon as they hung up, Joel checked his e-mail and found Angie's letters.

Okay. Let's break the silence. I'm getting ready to stop talking politely to you. The reality of this is kicking my ass and I bet you are miserable, too. I'm just being honest. But I'm giving you the room you asked for.

Every time I take the fucking trash out or make a pot of coffee, I'll probably be having a royal fit. Every time you put your fucking underwear on or take it off, you're gonna think about me and how I'd always snatch it off you. I know it and I know another thing—we both may have played key roles in fucking this thing up together, but you know what, buddy? We really love each other and I know it. So we'll both just have to suffer through this.

Every time you turn on the radio, you are gonna catch hell and so will I. It may be much easier on you because you have another person right now—but baby, one day you'll wake up and realize "that ain't it."

Don't think for a moment that I believe it was all lying down and getting up with us. Oh no, something was left there, baby.

But maybe this is the shit we have to go through in order to do this thing right another time in our lives. I say that because no matter how much I try to tell myself it's over, I'm singing the wrong tune.

We laughed too much together, we argued too much together and we talked too much together. We shared too much together—even though I'm not the mother of one of your children and don't have years of history with you. But we won't be able to discard those moments and events that happened between us—none of them—and they do count for something.

You'll find out we were meant for each other. No matter what time it is or where I am, you just come and you don't have to say a word. Nothing. Just take me in your arms and I'll know you've figured out where you are supposed to be and you'll work harder at being there. Then we'll deal with the rest. Out of respect (for this relationship you are in) and because I want to give you a chance to miss me and know what you had, as I am doing, too, I am leaving you alone to see these things.

We did not just happen to fall upon each other. I know better than that. You're scared, I'm scared, and that's just too fucking bad. But one thing I do know—there is a bond between you and me and it's just taking you a bit longer than me to realize it. And not for a moment do I believe that you do not love me as much as I love you. That's not my ego—it's my gut.

Angie

Reading the messages had a powerful impact on Joel. He noticed Angie's up and down feelings and mixed emotions and he was convinced she was literally going out of her mind missing him. He was flattered, impressed, surprised, grateful, relieved and certain of one thing—he was in love with her. He called a florist and had an arrangement of flowers sent to her.

She called well before they could have been delivered. "An hour and a half has passed and I haven't heard from you. Are you coming? Are you leaving work?" Angie asked.

"I can't leave. Two people called in sick. I've got to stay here. Pick me up here at four thirty this afternoon. What are you doing?" he asked.

"Nothing. I'm tired. I've been up for three days," Angie said.

"Angie, get some sleep and I'll see you at four thirty."

"Okay."

*　　*　　*

At four o'clock Angie telephoned Joel at work to say she was on her way. He told her that he had to work until eight that night. He advised her to call him when she was on her way. She did so and when she called was informed he had left for the night. She was flabbergasted! He had stood her up. All sorts of thoughts were running through her mind. She wondered if he was at Ebony's packing and would call her back to pick him up later. She didn't know if he had changed his mind and would not come back to her. She didn't know what was going on. She was worried. She was frantic, thinking that crazy Ebony may have really gone wild and killed Joel if he arrived back at that apartment and told her he was leaving. She reflected on all the stories she'd heard on the news of mates deciding that if they couldn't have a person, nobody else would, and maybe Ebony had done a murder-suicide. She wondered if he'd gotten disgusted with the entire situation and was on a plane headed for Denver or to one of his five siblings who were scattered across the country. She had no idea what the hell was going on. He did not call back that night.

Angie stayed up the entire night. She couldn't sleep and she couldn't eat. She went from "Fuck him, I don't care" to "Oh my God, he could be dead!" She contemplated calling the police and sending them to Ebony's apartment. Then she decided to mail the belongings he had left at her house to him at Ebony's. She considered showing up at his job when he reported at seven thirty in the morning and then decided to run away to Pittsburgh. She changed her mind about that and opted to wait until he got to work and she'd call him. By four o'clock in the morning she had showered, carefully applied her makeup, done her hair and gotten dressed. She got a bag and placed inside it the coats he'd left behind, the special alarm clock he treasured, and freshly done laundry. She went through the stuff in the bag and then decided he wasn't such a bad guy and felt sorry for him. She was worried about him. He was off his routine. They'd always gotten up together and she made the coffee and drove him to work. Now he was walking. The temperature had changed and she figured he was cold, with no coat. She went down to the kitchen and got his favorite coffee mug—the one with the top that kept his coffee hot—and placed it in the bag. Then she remembered how much he loved her fifteen-year-old niece, Shadiyah, and she grabbed the framed picture of Shadiyah off her mantel and added that to the collection. He used to pack his lunch every morning, so she went to the freezer and grabbed two frozen cheeseburgers and threw them in. Then she remembered how his feet got cold sometimes and she had purchased a really neat pair of sock slippers, so in they went. And his allergies—oh God, did he suffer with that. She raced upstairs to the medicine cabinet and snatched the Tylenol Sinus that used to be of some relief to his sneezing and congestion. Then there was the last videotape of the Tom Joyner *Fantastic Voyage*—the one she was on before she met him. He loved that tape and watching Angie shake her ass on there—so in it went.

Next she thought about his hands—those hands that used to caress her so many days and nights. She went to her closet and looked at an expensive pair of gloves she had purchased for his Christmas stocking. She took one of the gloves and put it in the bag. She purposely kept the other so he would always be reminded that he was missing something—her. Now the bag was complete and she had a full sack of his stuff. She was ready.

Angie looked terrific at five thirty in the morning. She sat in her kitchen and watched the clock on the stove. She and Joel usually left to take him to work at 6:50 every morning. She watched the clock until that time—an eternity of nearly an hour and a half. Then she left the house.

Angie drove up and down the road he should use to get to work. She talked to God every step of the way, praying he was not only safe, but that he'd come back to her. There was no sign of Joel. She was worried for sure then. She drove to his job and parked in the lot and watched for him. As she sat in her car, she observed Ray drive in and park. He had been to Dunkin Donuts. He saw her. This was the second time she had seen him in three days. He had come to her house to pick Joel up when he left her on Saturday. She thought Ray might call Joel and tell him that she was out there, and having that information, Joel might not come to work—so Angie drove off. She drove up and down the road and finally spotted Joel walking to work. She immediately blew the horn, stopped the car and turned it around. She pulled over and he walked toward the car.

"Get your ass in this car," Angie growled. He got in and just looked at her.

"Why did you stand me up?" she asked.

"I went to Ebony's, got disgusted and frankly tired of packing and moving. I went to sleep. I've had it," Joel said.

"What's up? You want to stay there? Is that what this is all about?" Angie asked.

"You know what? I'm worried about us. We've just got so much to figure out. I do love you. I want to be with you, but I can't have a lot of trouble."

"How much trouble am I?" Angie asked while kissing him. He moved her away, knowing she could get him aroused. She responded by trying to bribe him by saying that she'd buy him four cases of beer and a bottle of liquor—and understand he had no drinking problem.

"This is serious, Angie. Stop it. Also, you need to know that I haven't had a beer or any alcohol since I left you. We need to talk if I'm coming back there," he said.

"I've got it all figured out. You love me and I love you and we can't fight anymore and you'll just come back to me and I won't tell you to get out again and you won't tell me a bunch of crap about your being confused and you won't drink too much beer or alcohol and life will be wonderful. Now—how's that?" Angie asked.

He laughed and said, "You're a trip. I swear you are crazy. Did you have to e-mail everybody in the country? Damn. Everybody is in our business. I don't know what to do with you. This is a mess. What am I supposed to tell Ebony and William? You know I had to talk my way in there, even though she invited me to come back. I have to figure out exactly how to get out of this."

"Those people I e-mailed are my friends and I wanted them to know what was going on. I had to vent. I needed my friends to help take care of me. I was upset. If you want a way out of Ebony's place, just tell her you love me. Keep it simple and honest," Angie said.

He shook his head and kissed her. "I'll work something out," Joel said.

"Work it out soon—like by tonight. I've lost five pounds and I can't work the coffeemaker due to lack of concentration. Your mother is pissed off, and I had to take the trash out last night. I can't work a lot of stuff in the house and you fired the people who cut the grass. The grass is growing like crazy and the place looks a mess. I brought you some things," she said, as she noticed he had an empty coffee mug with no top on it. She pointed to his bag in the backseat.

Joel looked behind him at the large plastic bag and became immediately irritated. He said, "You brought my things to me?"

"Don't get mad. I really wasn't sure if you'd tell me to go to hell, so I brought the stuff with me just in case I would never see you again. Here, let's go through the stuff," Angie answered.

She went through every item, including his laundry that she had done the prior evening. The explanation of the one glove nearly brought him to tears. When she pulled out the cheeseburgers and announced she had brought his lunch, he said, "Have your ass at my job at three thirty. That is the only time I can get in and out of Ebony's apartment and take my stuff without her being there today. I mean, be on time. We'll get it out and I'll drive you back home with it. Then I have a meeting at work from five thirty to six thirty. I'll be home to you tonight. I love you. Now—let's get me to work and I'll see you later." Angie screamed with delight and hugged him, and then dropped him off at work.

"Joel, I need to talk to you. I'm worried. I saw Angie in the parking lot this morning. You'd better be careful. Is she a stalker?" a nervous Ray asked when Joel strolled in to work.

Joel chuckled and said, "No." He walked away without explaining anything to Ray. He just didn't feel like going into it because he was embarrassed that they were getting back together. As soon as Joel started to get organized for work the phone rang. It was his mother.

"What is going on out there?" Paulette demanded.

"I've had some problems over the weekend," Joel answered. He didn't need this shit this morning, and he knew there was going to be a fight with his mother. Paulette started in on him.

"Well, I've been on the phone all weekend with Angie. I couldn't even clean my house. Every time I turn around there's some mess brewing. You must be crazy going back over to that nut's house. You know she's loco. You couldn't have been that pissed off with Angie. Shit. Angie's the best thing that ever happened to you, and if you don't have sense enough to know it—I do! What's the matter? Do you have an attraction for bimbos or something? Maybe you need to be in therapy. And another thing—you can hook up with whomever you like, but you'd better keep them the hell away from me. Angie will always be my daughter-in-law. I'm surprised at you—having my baby, Angie, upset and crying all weekend. And this beer and booze—you'd better give it up, boy, before you lose everything you've got," Paulette shouted.

"Mom, I'm trying to work things out with Angie. I just got here. I just walked in the door," Joel said.

"*Work things out?* What's there to *work out?* Just get on your knees and beg her to take you back. Cry your eyes out to come back home—and that is *home*. She'll let you. Boy, don't you ever tell one woman you're thinking about moving in with another one. Are you *crazy?* Angie *should* have thrown your ass out of there. I know I would have. You'd better get yourself together and pray to God she takes you back. If she doesn't, at least you'll get to see her on Mother's Day and every other family holiday because she'll be right out here with me. That's *my* child and I already invited her—for the rest of her life. Poor Angie—running around there for five months cooking, cleaning, making coffee and packing lunches. I know she is pissed, too, since she was warming the bed up for you using that fancy electric blanket with no wires in it—and you've got the nerve to be thinking about going back to a lunatic who doesn't even give a damn whether you have a decent meal or not. I hope that nincompoop fed you fast-food tacos the entire weekend—and she probably did. Boy, you've gone from lobster to chicken nuggets and sugar to shit," Paulette shouted.

"I've got to get to work, Mom. Please hang up. I'll call you later."

"From where? Where are you going to call me from? It damn well better be Angie's house," Paulette shouted.

"Mom, can I go? I've got to work," Joel said.

"Good-bye," Paulette said as she slammed down her phone.

Paulette was absolutely livid—and scared. Angie was her dream daughter-in-law. Paulette had already been through hell with Stacia, Joel's ex-wife. In Paulette's eyes, Stacia was irresponsible and not a nurturing mother to Danita. Paulette had noticed during their marriage that Joel was the mother and the daddy. Stacia was always on the go taking classes, socializing with her friends and hitting the discos. Paulette was also convinced she'd be a lifetime student and Joel would not only be stuck with all the bills, but with the sole responsibility of Danita. During the marriage, this totally responsible son she had raised was working two jobs and caring for Danita. He changed the diapers, combed her hair, ran her to and from the babysitters—the works. Stacia was demanding and thoughtless. She couldn't help out much with the bills because she could only do part-time jobs and for one reason or another, never kept them.

No one in the family was impressed with her because she also had this aloof personality—she was the *shit*. Once they were having a family Thanksgiving dinner and everyone had met in New Orleans at Leigh's to get together and cook. Sixteen family members were at Leigh's the day before Thanksgiving preparing the food. Everyone was dressed casually in jeans and sweat suits, working together, washing meats and vegetables, and baking. Stacia arrived late dressed in a sexy red dress with spaghetti straps and heels. She perched herself on a stool and sipped wine as she watched everyone work their asses off. Paulette wanted to smack her off that stool. When it was time to look at family pictures, the family was shown pictures of Stacia from a long time ago when she was single and vacationing in the Bahamas—in a G-string. That night, Miss Queen of Sheba felt that she and Joel should sleep in Leigh and her husband's lovely bedroom instead of all over the place like the rest of the family. At about ten o'clock that night when everyone in the family was sitting around laughing and talking about old times and finishing up the tasks of the upcoming Thanksgiving dinner, Miss Stacia appeared in a negligee and high heels. She announced to the family that she was ready to retire and motioned seductively to Joel to leave the room. She then told everyone in the room she "needed her husband." Joel, who was having a great time with his family, was embarrassed, but went peacefully with Stacia to avoid a problem. Paulette wanted to raise the roof.

Joel was always covering up for Stacia and making excuses for her. Paulette knew when her son had gone to all the trouble to learn to braid hair, that there was a reason for that—Danita's lack of a mother's time and attention. As time grew on in their marriage, the entire family actually despised Stacia and merely tolerated her because she was Joel's wife. This wasn't a woman the family had been introduced to ahead of time and had the opportunity to bond with and get to know. Joel met Stacia while in the military and they quickly fell in love or lust and ran off and got married. Paulette and her family got a phone call that Stacia was the new addition to the family. Joel's sister Kendra had had enough of Stacia mistreating her brother long before any separation or divorce and impolitely cursed her out on one occasion and invited her to have a rumble at an Easter Sunday family gathering.

When Stacia and Joel finally separated, Stacia, being without Joel's income, moved in with her mother. Grandma then became a full-time babysitter, chauffeur, cook and hairdresser while Stacia happily dated and still attended college—at age twenty-eight. Stacia was living the life from September to June while Grandma had Danita, and Joel took care of his daughter full-time during the summer months. He never made a complaint but everyone knew he had married and had a child with the wrong woman.

The arrival of Angie into Joel's life brought relief and hope to Paulette. Angie was the light at the end of a long dark tunnel. Paulette trusted Angie and appreciated her thoughtfulness not only with Joel, but with Paulette and her entire family. Paulette loved chatting with her and felt comfortable with Angie—as if she'd known her all of her life. She adored Angie and her witty personality. The two of them became not only like mother and daughter, but they were girlfriends, too. Angie had also fallen in love with the gentleness of Paulette's demeanor, the way Paulette checked on her day to day and the motherly love she was bestowing upon her. Angie, who'd been estranged from her own mother off and on since she was a child, appreciated and welcomed having a mother in her life. Her relationship with Paulette had a closeness she had never experienced and she was grateful Paulette had come into her life. They had both agreed that they would have separate relationships—Angie and Joel, and Paulette and Angie. Paulette would just be damned if anyone was going to screw this up—not Ebony or William—and not even her son Joel, whom she loved dearly. And because she had grown to love Angie, she was going to do everything she could to make sure Joel was not only fair to Angie, but that he busted his ass to make her happy. Paulette Millsman Marshall loved and lived for her kids—the five she had conceived and given birth to—and Angie.

Joel was starting to have a bad day. He got some work orders ready and by eleven thirty his sister Leigh was on the phone.

"It's me. What the hell is going on?" she asked.

Joel sighed and said, "Hi, Leigh. I'm really busy. Can we talk later?"

"Well, just give me a minute. Mom called me and she is going out of her mind. She's been crying. What are you doing? Everybody is calling everybody—the whole family. Joel, you'd better get this shit straightened out or Mom says we are all coming there. She said this is a crisis situation and Angie is having a breakdown."

"Listen, I'm sick of this shit. I saw Angie this morning and I *will* get back to her. Jesus Christ. I can't take all this shit. Have any of you considered the fact that Angie made me leave? I didn't fuck this up all by myself. She had a part in it, too. However—let me ease all of your minds and tell you we are getting back together if you let me get off this damn phone long enough to get my work done and get out of here. I'll talk to you later," Joel said. He hung up.

Ten minutes after he hung up from that call, his stepfather, Preston, called. "Your mother is acting like a maniac. Listen, Joel, leave both those bitches alone—Ebony and Angie. That's my advice. I knew that thing with you and Angie wouldn't work out—you did it too fast. That other one is a serious nut case and should be hospitalized. Get the hell out of town, boy. Leave them both. All these broads are crazy—including your mother. You know your mother told me that if she were you she would have stayed there and taken Angie's shit just to have fresh coffee brewed every morning. Humph. Now you know she's out of her mind and not thinking straight. Split, man—run—go to Hawaii or Timbuktu, but leave there and don't ever call either of them again. If you need some money, hell, I'll send you some. Wherever you go, don't tell Paulette because she'll rat on you for sure, telling Angie. Those two are as tight as thieves. You better believe it, boy—your mother will sell you out. Next thing you know Angie will be knocking on your door ordering you around," Preston warned Joel.

Joel was cracking up laughing and said, "I gotta go, Preston. Thanks for the advice."

"Hi, baby. Listen—there's been a change of plans. Instead of three thirty, I want you to come here now. It's one o'clock and I have a break. Can you come now?" Joel asked.

"Shyrlee is here now—we're working on a project," Angie answered.

"I need you to stop the project. Bring both yours and Shyrlee's cars and meet me here right away. Once I get my stuff, you'll leave your car here with me and Shyrlee can take you home," Joel said.

"Okay—we're on our way." Angie said.

The two cars pulled into the rear entrance of the apartment complex. Joel got out of Angie's vehicle and went into Ebony's apartment. As soon as he was inside, fifty-five-year-old Shyrlee, a prison guard for twenty-nine years, whose hair was rolled up in those pink sponge rollers because she had a date that night, got out of her car and said, "Listen, Angie—you be the lookout guy. I'll help Joel load the stuff. Just watch. The bitch may be coming home early or something. Hell, we don't even know if she's in there. I hope she went to work today. Just watch everything coming around the corner."

Joel came out with a load of clothing—some stuffed in a suitcase and some in his arms. He passed them to Shyrlee. Shyrlee began packing everything in the back of Angie's car as Angie kept surveying the corner and the end of the driveway for Ebony. Joel returned twice with more things and finally he had gotten everything out. He went back in to lock the place up and Angie returned from the corner.

"Shyrlee, why isn't the stuff in your car?" Angie asked. Before Shyrlee could answer, Joel returned and was headed to Angie's car, ready to leave to go back to his job.

"Wait a minute, Joel. *You* have your stuff. Oh no. The stuff goes with *us*. Get that shit out of there. Oh no. I'm taking this shit with *me*," Angie said.

"Angie, I can bring the stuff when I come. Come on, let's get out of here," Joel said.

"Oh hell no. No fucking way. Take it out!"

They all then began unloading Angie's car and making space in Shyrlee's vehicle. Then they began reloading it in Shyrlee's car. As they were doing so, Shyrlee noticed a neighbor looking suspiciously at them all. The neighbor grabbed her cell phone off the table on her porch and began pushing in numbers.

"Oh shit!" screamed Shyrlee. "We'd better get out of here. That bitch could be calling the police thinking we're robbing the place or calling the wench who lives here. Angie, get that shit in the car and step on it. Can you fight? I mean, can you *bang* in case that bitch tries to stop us?" Shyrlee asked.

"Yeah, I can fight, but let's just get out of here. Bye, Joel. See you later, baby," she said, blowing him a kiss. They then jumped in the cars and sped off. When they got to the end of the driveway a car quickly entered and they barely missed hitting the vehicle. A woman jumped out and screamed, "What are you people doing with Ebony's belongings? We called the cops—Mildred called the cops on you! You're not going anywhere!" At that point Mildred, the neighbor, appeared with her cell phone and a butcher knife.

"Hold it, goddammit. Nobody goes anywhere," Mildred shouted.

Joel was parked in Angie's car, behind Shyrlee's vehicle. He got out and said, "Listen, we don't have anything that belongs to Ebony, and we did not rob the place. I was staying with her and I moved out. That's what's going on."

"Well, it's funny Ebony didn't know anything about this. I called her at the market. She is on her way here now. How do I know you don't have any of her stuff? Let's just wait for Ebony," Mildred said.

Shyrlee got out of her car and tackled Mildred, leaning on her and pinning her against the side of the building. Angie swiftly jumped into the car that was blocking them and moved it out of the way while Joel held the owner of the blocking vehicle. Once Angie had the car moved, Joel hopped into Angie's car alone and Angie and Shyrlee ran to Shyrlee's car. As they sped off, Angie threw the keys to the neighbor's vehicle out of the window of Shyrlee's car.

Joel returned to work. An hour after that, a petrified Ray approached him. "Joel—we have more trouble. Angie is back. I see her car out in the lot. This is getting serious. Is she all right? You know, I think something is wrong with her. I hope she doesn't do anything to you. Do you see the car out there?" he said, pointing. "It's right over there. See it? She may have her head down or be hiding somewhere on the property."

"Ray—relax. Everything is okay. *I* have that car. It's *me*. Okay?" Joel answered. A bewildered Ray stared blankly at Joel, and then walked away. He felt funny questioning him as to why he had the car.

Shyrlee and Angie laughed all the way to Angie's. They unloaded the car and put Joel's things in her guest room so he could unpack later. They then went out to lunch and laughed some more, wishing they could be flies on the wall when that wench Ebony came home and found Joel gone. Joel returned to Angie's that evening and they spent the entire night making plans to stay together and try harder at the relationship and work their problems out. Things were going great—no hitches and no bitches. All was quiet.

Angie answered her door on a wonderful summer afternoon to find a cute woman armed with gift baskets.

"Hi, I'm Janette Wilkins. How are you? I'm selling these baskets and the proceeds are going to the rescue mission—for the kids. Would you like to take a look at them?" she asked with a smile.

Angie looked down at the beautiful baskets and said, "They look wonderful. Yes, I'd like to check them out. Come on in."

The two women advanced to the living room with the four baskets. Angie delved in, examining and oohing and ahhing at the bath gels, sparkling ciders, exquisite soaps and candles. Janette began looking around the living room, complimenting Angie on having such a beautiful home. Janette moved over to the mantel and began looking at pictures there.

"You have a beautiful family. I guess this is your husband," Janette said, showing Angie a picture of Joel and Angie.

"No—that's my man. We're not married yet, but we live here together," Angie said.

"That's so nice. You two look incredibly happy. I'll be glad when I get hooked up. I've always wanted this. I've been pretty lonely," Janette said, placing the picture back in its place.

"Oh—take your time—don't hunt for anyone—he'll come. Look, I think I want these two. Let me grab my handbag to pay you. Excuse me for a second," Angie said, heading for the kitchen.

Janette immediately followed her. As Angie was rooting through her handbag she asked, "Janette, do you take checks, sweetie?"

"Yes, I do. In fact, I'm here on a *check*. I'm here *checking* on my man, bitch!"

Angie gasped and gazed in her eyes. She was stunned and asked, "What man?"

"The one you're living with, goddammit. That's my man. You broke Joel and me up, you bitch. You're a fucking home wrecker. I'm Ebony, goddammit! That's who I am. I'm William's mother, bitch—remember me?" Ebony then reached in her denim jacket pocket and came out with a revolver.

Angie was petrified and tried to remain calm, saying, "Listen, Ebony—you don't want to hurt me. Look, just leave and nothing will happen. I mean, I won't say anything about this. You want to stay calm. Let me let you out."

"I'm not going anywhere. Get your ass in that chair by the phone. Hurry up before I shoot you faster than I planned to."

Angie sat down in the kitchen chair and Ebony kept the gun pointed at her.

"All I wanted was a life with him. I couldn't have it because of you and his fucking family. All you guys do is make phone calls causing trouble. Then when he got himself together and realized he really loved me and wanted to be with me and William, you and his fucking family got in our business and fucked it up. I heard about you and your friend coming to my house and making him get his stuff. Well now I'm putting a stop to everything."

"Ebony—listen—you can have him back. He's just a bunch of problems anyway. We're not happy. I just packed his shit last week and told him he needed to be with his family—you and William. Listen—I'll talk to him and get him to come back. Just don't hurt me—or anyone," Angie cried.

"Don't give me that shit! You just told me you're marrying him," Ebony shouted.

"Well, I may have said that, but it's a lie. I was just showing off."

"Well, I'll tell you what—me and you are going to sit here for an hour until he gets home. Just me and you. I'm planning to kill you both," Ebony said.

In two hours and twenty minutes, Joel placed the key in the front door. He yelled for Angie and went into the kitchen. Without saying a word, Ebony immediately pointed the gun at him. "I'm going to kill both your asses."

Joel was stunned and stood frozen. He looked over at Angie crying as she looked at him. "Ebony, calm down, baby. You know you don't want to hurt anybody. Put the gun down. We can work this out."

"What the fuck can we work out when you're planning on marrying that bitch?" she said as she looked over at Angie.

As soon as Ebony shifted her eyes from Joel, he lunged for Ebony and they began struggling. He could not get the gun from her and when Angie realized it would eventually go off, she yanked Ebony by the hair. They all fell to the floor and the gun fell out of Ebony's grasp. Ebony reached for it but was not quick enough and it was Angie who retrieved the revolver. Joel and Ebony were still wrestling on the floor. Angie ran to the phone and called the police. When she returned Joel and Ebony were standing in the kitchen still tussling and Ebony had snatched a knife from the drain board. At that point and without hesitation Angie fired two shots, both striking Ebony and killing her.

When the police arrived Angie was trembling and screaming. After investigation and questioning, neither of them was charged in Ebony's murder. Joel's son, William subsequently came to live with Joel and Angie.

Chapter Eighteen

Reba

Reba had gotten in from work and was as tired as she could be. Doug was out of town on a business trip and the boys were busy doing homework and chores. She thought about Lucy. She certainly did miss her and was dying to see Dimitri. Reba thought Dimitri was the cutest kid in the world and was especially proud of him because he was her godson. He was now three months old.

Reba sat down in her home office and reminisced about how they had all gone down to Norfolk at the end of August and given Lucy a surprise shower. Lucy thought she was meeting Sonja that day to pick out a cradle that Sonja wanted to purchase to keep at her home for babysitting. Instead, Lucy found her mother, mother-in-law and the San Jose crew of Kevin's relatives and friends. His sisters and other members of his family were there from all over the country. The crowd also included the "Chateau Night On The Town Models" and coworkers from the radio station as well as the Philly neighborhood bunch hidden in Sonja's house. In order to keep it a total surprise, Sonja had even managed to have everyone get a ride from their hotels and homes or come by cab so Lucy wouldn't spot any cars on the property when she arrived. Sonja had also gone through Kevin and hired Bridgette, the astrologer. Lucy was blown away when she saw everyone. It was quite an event.

Reba started toward the phone to call Lucy, but then decided to write her a letter, thinking Lucy was probably busy with Kevin and Dimitri and she wouldn't have time to talk. Reba had a lot to tell her.

Hi Lucy:
   I hope all is well with you and Kevin and my little man. I miss him desperately. I thought I would drop you a line to let you know how fast my world is turning.

Lucy, when Dimitri goes to college, do not go to his dorm after he has moved in. You can move him in, you know, the first day he goes, but after that—stay away. Go to a hotel whenever you visit.

The first time I went there to visit, Nina met me downstairs at the door and I didn't even recognize her. She had only been there a month. Her hair was all over her head like she had never been to a beauty parlor. As soon as I saw her all I could say was, "What happened?" That's how bad she looked.

She had on clothes two sizes too big that I did not purchase. I asked her where they came from and she informed me, "Some boys gave me some clothes." It seems what we purchased and drove her down there with were not fit for the college freshman.

I just got back from my second trip to the University of Maryland visiting my darling daughter who begged me to come and pleaded with me to stay with her at her dorm. Worst mistake I ever made.

Once I got there and made a path so I could get into her place, I cleaned it up. How can a person who was raised up on clean linen, washcloths and towels always stacked up in the linen closet live like that? Unbelievable. But all her makeup was in order and placed in her cabinet—all those beauty products and bath gels were available.

Next, it's time to go shopping. She needs a rug to go on top of the rug that's on the floor, just so her feet don't get cold when she steps out of bed. Okay. We look at rugs. The Black American Princess picks out a beautiful crème-colored rug that resembles a polar bear—the thickness of it. Fabulous. It's the type of thing I'd put down in front of my fireplace with Doug and two good bottles of wine. This is what she has to have.

We get the rug and a bunch of other stuff to make life easier. Then we get back to the dorm and the mountain of dirty clothes is in the corner. Now it is time to go food shopping. Mommy has to buy the stuff, wash and season it up and put it in Ziploc bags. Thank God Peggy taught Mommy how to cook way back when. Then Mommy is supposed to fry some chicken for tonight's dinner. Okay. Mommy offers to take all the clothes to the Laundromat to get them all done at once. Daughter says, "Let's wait until tomorrow."

Now Mommy needs a nap and cannot have a nap because music from next door is blasting. Nina instructs Mommy to "just be cool." Mommy cannot be cool because the music is blasting all over the freaking college. You know what Mommy did, don't you? Mommy went the hell over there and threatened to call the cops. Music was off in a second.

Then Daughter, who has been sick all week (except last night at the disco), decides she is going to the football game. Leaves Mommy home. Mommy is told to watch a movie and stay in the house so she does not get lost in Maryland. Mommy obeys.

Knock on door. Nina gone. Mommy answers door. "It's John," he says. Mommy opens door and questions, "John?" John wants to know where Nina is. Mommy explains. John says, "Okay, but I came for the lotion." Mommy goes and gets one of three bottles of lotion and hands it to John. John says, "Oh no, I don't get the bottle, Nina just squirts some in my hand when I come by. I live next door." Mom squirts it in his hand and he leaves.

Nina returns home from the game. Mommy explains John came over. Nina instructs Mommy never to give John the bottle. He is on the basketball team and goes to school for free and messes up all his money that the college gives him buying jewelry and crap and he can always only have a squirt of lotion. Unbelievable.

Okay. Now Mommy and Nina are sleeping in a twin bed. Nina offers to sleep on the floor but she has been sick all week and Mommy brought down an electric blanket because she had the chills and was freezing to death when she called from college four times on Wednesday night and twice on Thursday before she left for the disco (the disco that Mommy never knew she went to) after she called home. Mommy finally takes the floor and sleeps on the polar bear. His name is Gilbert.

Mommy explains to Nina that she will get up at five a.m. and go to the Laundromat to do the clothes. Nina says, "No way" and she does not want Mommy to wash clothes because her friends' stuff is mixed in and Mommy might mess someone's clothes up. "Okay. We'll wash the clothes when you get up—together," says Mommy. "Okay," says Daughter. Mommy wakes up anyway at five and tries to sneak away with the dirty clothes. Nina sees Mommy and puts a stop to it. Tells Mommy to *"lie down and wait around, she'll get up."* At noon, she, the Black American Princess, awakened. Now Mommy needs a shower and asks where she keeps the clean towels. Mommy is informed, "No clean towels." Mommy is pissed. Mommy has had it and threatens to run away to Aunt Nicole's in DC and steal a shower and some peace of mind. Nina won't hear of this. She goes down the hall to her girlfriend's and asks for a clean towel. She has none. Then Nina explains to Mommy that she did not know Mommy would need a towel, and if she had not been sick all week she would have done the wash. Mommy packs up. Nina starts scurrying around and finds a gigantic beach towel—it's clean—and gives it to Mommy. Problem solved.

Okay. Now it is time for brunch and Mommy goes through the dirty clothing before going out the door. Mommy gathers washcloths and towels and puts them in a trash bag to take to Aunt Nicole's to wash. We get there and we go to Clyde's (the Black American Princess's favorite elite spot for brunch.) It's Mommy, Aunt Nicole, cousin Shyraun and new Auntie Gayle (Mommy's new best buddy) who just loves the Black American Princess to death. And of course Auntie Gayle has been so worried about Nina being sick and she wants to make sure she gets some TheraFlu for her illness and we must shop for it though it's pouring down raining while we are out. So, Mommy puts in a load of wash and we all head out the door.

After a marvelous brunch, the Black American Princess needs clothes. So we all go shopping and have a great time. Mommy already dropped $293 at B.J.'s before leaving Annapolis to visit Daughter Dear, $404 after she arrived and now we are shopping for jeans and tops. Okay. Done shopping after Auntie Gayle helps poor Mommy out with the bill after her credit cards are maxed out. Now Mommy goes back to Aunt Nicole's to fry chicken and dry clothes for the Black American Princess. By now the BAP is really sick again and has to lie down while Mommy cooks and folds clothes. Oh, she did help Mommy fold the clothes, but she was feeling really badly and needed to get back to the dorm to do her schoolwork.

Okay. Mommy loads the car up and takes the BAP back to the dorm. Now it is telephone time for the BAP. It seems she recovered some after the wash was done. Mommy has a chat with Nina. "Listen, Nina, I believe I should take the rug home. This is not the right place for Gilbert. You will destroy him. He is too nice a rug. You won't take care of him. He will be ruined." The BAP has a heart attack and a fit about keeping Gilbert. She starts pulling money out, trying to pay for him (and she comes up with the cash). Is this not my child? Mommy got so mad she told her to keep the freaking rug and her money and shut up. Mommy makes her bed up on the floor, goes to bed and gets up at four a.m. Mommy drives back to Annapolis, goes straight to her office when she hits town, works, then goes to her shrink (whom she needs desperately that day), then home. When Mommy arrives home, she turns her answering machine on. Nina is screaming into it, "Mommy, Mommy! They made a mistake here, they are putting me out of my room, and they said someone else is moving in here!" Mommy tells her to work her own problems out. She calls back in two hours and everything is fine and she is not being moved.

Mommy has peanut butter crackers for dinner because she is too tired to cook. Doug and the kids eat KFC. Mommy goes to another part of the house to sleep where she cannot hear phones ringing, takes a Xanax and conks out.

Mommy wakes at five a.m. Now buddy Marietta from Chicago is on the machine screaming. She has some deal working that will do something to make her a millionaire and she's looking for me to tell me all about it. "Where are you?" she is screaming into the answering machine. I call Marietta and indeed she has found a celebrity and that person is working a great deal for her second novel and this one is not Oprah—she found some new stuff, an additional deal, and the person luvs her novel and she is too excited for words. I listlessly reply, "Okay, I'm so happy and proud."

"Just okay?" Marietta thinks I have gone crazy. "Aren't you happier than that?"

I explain life over the past six days—in detail. Marietta is Mommy to two beautiful adult angels—private school, college and the works. She's been through it all and understands exactly what I am going through. She excuses me for not being enthused and screaming with joy.

She also explains to me that she has "been that route" and I was never, under any circumstances, to go to the dorm again. "That's bad for parents," she says.

Mommy will never stay at Nina's dorm again. By the way, she is living large there, the place is actually very nice and she has private quarters. That's the scoop of my weekend.

Love ya!!
Reba

Three weeks later Doug and Reba were sound asleep when the phone rang at six thirty a.m. Doug answered it and the voice at the other end said, "Douglas or Rebecca Ransome please, this is Washington Adventist Hospital in Tacoma Park, Maryland, calling."

"This is Douglas Ransome."

"Mr. Ransome, my name is Claudia Wayman and I'm a nurse. We have your daughter, Nina Penster, in our emergency room. I'd like to discuss her condition with you prior to your speaking with her. She asked me to call you." Reba was sitting up looking at Doug trying to figure out who was on the phone.

"Hold on," Doug said as he looked at Reba. He put the phone down and said to Reba, "It's the hospital near the college calling. They have Nina there."

Reba grabbed the phone frantically and said, "This is Nina's mother, what's going on?"

"Your daughter has been seriously injured. She arrived about twelve thirty this morning and we have treated her."

"What happened?" shouted Reba. "Has she been in a car accident or what? What's going on? How is she?"

"She's been attacked."

Chapter Nineteen

Paula

"ey, Warden, how are you?" Jake said as he entered his office.

"I'm pretty good. How was your vacation?"

"I spent too much money and had too good a time. Then the old lady started getting on my nerves. You know how it goes. Glad to be back to work. How did you make out with Gray?"

Walt's face tensed up; he nodded and said, "She did okay. She's a nice enough girl."

"I wanted to check to make sure she did her job. I'm back now and I can take her off your hands. I just wanted her kept busy while I was away to keep her out of trouble," Jake said.

Walt stared at him. "Since you're so friendly with her, can you tell me what kind of an 'accident' she had? I heard she is pretty banged up and said she had an 'accident.' "

Jake's face tensed up and he shook his head. "She never mentioned a thing to me," he lied.

Walt looked Jake hard in the face. "Okay, I guess everything comes out in the wash. By the way, she can continue on here. I'm personally okaying it. I'll have a chat with her and find out what happened. I don't need any lawsuits in the house—in case something fell on her or anything like that occurred," Walt said.

Jake was relieved Paula had kept her mouth shut. "I'll try to find out something, too, and if I do, I'll let you know. I can get you someone else—personal—for yourself. You can do better than her," Jake said.

"No—don't go to that trouble," he said with a wave of his hand. "I can manage with her."

"I think it's a bad idea. She's really trash. You're a high-up man—forget that. I'm bringing a real gem I already checked out. I insist."

"Look, Jake—don't try to boss me around. Gray stays. I want her here tomorrow and Thursday at four thirty, and I also want her here three days a week. If I come in on weekends, I want her available to me. I don't give a damn about work detail or anything. You got that? And if I find out a ton of bricks didn't fall on her and some crazy corrections officer beat the crap out of her, they will answer to me. Between the two of us, we'll find out who fucked her up. I don't like that kind of stuff."

"Let me see what I can do and get back to you," Jake meekly said as he was leaving.

"I thought I would die! It was so funny!" Josie screeched while talking to Paula.

"Oh my God," Paula said. "I would have loved to have been a fly on the wall when you were in his office. This is too funny. Why didn't you tell me you were going to do that shit?"

"I don't know. I just got so mad when I saw what Jake the Snake did to your face. When I went up there with the mail, I had intentions on telling Walt about it. Then one thing led to another and I kind of started playing this game with him. Then I got on the black and white shit, and next thing I knew he had a plan for him and me to accommodate each other. It was a trip—milk shake and all. And guess what?"

"What?" asked Paula.

"I lifted *this* from Charmaine's desk when I went out there for the glass," Josie said as she reached in her uniform pocket and pulled out a handheld Dictaphone with a tape in it. She handed it to Paula.

"Oh shit! You *are* good! Thanks, Josie. I'll get some respect with this." They laughed.

"Listen—I believe he's going to have the orgy on Thursday. He's probably going to ask you to be in it. I never told him I was your roommate. Even if he finds out we are roommates, we can have him believing you never told me about you and him. I never mentioned your name to him."

"Okay, let's just be cool. I can't believe that zebra shit. You are crazy," said Paula.

*   *   *

"Paula, let's go," said Jake as he stood at the cell door. She rolled her eyes at him and got up to leave. When they got down to the kitchen, she went for the bowl to fill it up.

"Hey, Paula—forget the ice today. Let's have a talk."

She was shocked. "I'd rather not talk to you. Let me get my work done so I can get back to my cell."

"Listen, lighten up. This is going to be a good day. How is your face? I'm sorry I beat you up."

"Apology accepted. May we get on with it or can I leave? Take your pick."

"You're going back to the warden on a permanent basis. I arranged that for you as a peace offering and because I was a jerk to do what I did. You'll be with him a few days a week starting tomorrow. I really talked up for you because I felt you really liked him. I got a vibe like that from you, so I did you a favor. He really didn't want you and I talked him into it. So you owe me. Now if he asks you what happened to your face, you tell him you lost your balance. You didn't trip over anything and your face went into the concrete outside. Nobody was around to help you and no one saw you fall."

"Do you think Walt is stupid? There are twelve hundred women in this fucking prison. Don't you know he'll know somebody was out in that damn yard? Do you think he thinks I can just walk around outside with no supervision and all the other eleven hundred ninety-nine in-mates are somewhere else? Is it my *backyard*? You must think Walt is a fool."

"Walt is a fat fool and he'll believe anything you tell him if you tell him right. Now, you owe me. I also called my mom and she's baking you a cake tonight and I'm not making you ice up or blow me and I won't even fuck you today. So, do we have a deal or not?"

Paula looked him right in the eye, poked him in the chest with her index finger and said, "I don't want to be with you anymore and your mother can take the cake and stick it up her ass."

Jake balled his fist up in a rage. He then got a flashback of his con-versation with Walt and got control of himself. He coolly said, "You have to do me. I'm just letting you off today. If you don't do me after that, and if you give me a hard time—something could *happen* to you around here. You know what I mean?"

"I need to go, Jake."

"First tell me what the deal is. Are you going to tell Curly you fell?"

"Who is Curly?"

"Curly is that fat fuck upstairs who thinks he runs this place. He's sadly mistaken though, because I run this shit. I call him Curly because he looks like the guy in the Three Stooges, and he's stupid."

"I happen to think he's a nice guy."

"Who gives a fuck what you think? You ain't so smart either—that's why you're in here. You just get this thing cooled out if he asks you anything or I'll arrange a *real* accident for you. You're dismissed. Let's you and me take a walk back to your cell."

Paula sat in her cell thinking and wondered what the hell she was going to do. She really didn't trust Jake because he was crazy. She always had a lot of fun with Walt when she was with him, and she loved the fact that she could control him. She was sick of being in prison, and the thought of doing another three years made her nauseous. The only thing that made her laugh was the fact that she might be chosen by Walt to do the orgy thing with Josie and that would sure enough be a gas—the two of them making him do all kinds of idiotic things. She wished she could blackmail Berman and get him to bust her out of the joint, but he talked too much for her to try to get him to do anything like that. She had pictures of herself and Walt that she didn't know what the hell to do with because she needed him for an ally and thought she'd better not fuck up with him. Carlos was nice to her, but he was too smart for her to get over on him. Jesus Christ, she thought, what was she going to do? It was now time for her to have a visit with her mom.

The interview room was gigantic and loaded with adults and children visiting the inmates. Many of the female inmates had absolutely no respect for themselves. It was nothing to catch an inmate sitting on her man's lap having sex or groping each other. There were wooden chairs placed in corners and a few couples even had coats covering them up— as they were trying to be discreet. The place was a horror and children were running around everywhere. "Hi, Paula. I brought you a care package. Just a few things and a couple of books," Fannie said.

"How are things going, Mom?"

"Well, bad. Oscar is acting a complete fool. He won't give me much money and he doesn't come straight home from work. He's being a real bastard. Me and McNight are still doing our thing. Oscar keeps threatening to leave. I haven't seen the kids. That mean old Horace, who has a new woman I hear, a lawyer, won't bring them over. How are you making out?"

"I wish a giant riot would erupt and everybody could escape. I hate this place."

"You can't find a boyfriend?"

Paula raised her eyebrows and said, "I have four boyfriends. They are part of my problem here."

"Did any of the lesbians try to get you?"

"No, not yet. I guess my boyfriends have them scared to death."

"Who beat you up—what happened to your face? I was waiting for you to say something. It looks pretty bad."

"One of my 'boyfriends' got upset with me."

Fannie was outraged and said, "Tell on him. Then it will stop."

"If I tell on him, I'll have bigger troubles. Look, Mom, can you go and talk to a lawyer and see if you can get me some money from when the supermarket accused me of stealing?"

"Two years passed. Did you forget that? You can't sue those people. You waited too long. Forget that. What do you need money for, anyway?"

"For when I get out of here, and in case I want some things for while I'm in here."

"Well, I have no money—I get no checks anymore. I have no job and Oscar is acting a fool. Take your care package. Has Amber or Sydni written you any letters?"

"No, thank God. I'm done with kids—at least with those."

"That statement sounds funny to me, girl. What are you up to?"

"I'm getting pregnant."

Fannie's mouth dropped open.

"Are you out of your mind?"

"Nope, I'm getting pregnant. That will be my ticket out of here."

"It's time for me to go, Paula. I don't even want to hear the rest of this shit." Fannie shook her head and left.

"I've missed you, Walt—how are things going?"

"Hi, Paula, I've missed you too. Are you doing okay?"

"I'm fine."

"What happened to your face?" he said as he put his hand on her chin, surveying the bruises.

"I got hurt."

"How?"

"I fell in the yard. I tripped and stumbled and went into the cement."

"Those are some nasty bruises. Let me get some ice."

Paula shuddered at the thought of more ice. "No, Walt, please—no ice. I'm okay. Really, I'm fine. Don't get any ice," she cried.

"Paula, have you been to the infirmary about this?"

"No." She sat on the couch and started crying. "Listen, Walt, I'm just here to please you. Let's get started."

"I want to talk about a couple of things. The first thing is I need to know how this happened. You have to tell me."

"Why are you acting so concerned? You didn't even want me to come back to spend time with you. Jake had to beg you. I thought you liked being with me."

"What are you talking about? I told Jake I was going to continue seeing you. He tried to talk me out of it, but I put my foot down."

Paula was shocked, then mad. "Are you serious?"

"Yes, I am. I ordered him to bring you here to me."

Paula was pissed off. She wanted to curse Jake out. She reached in her uniform pocket and took the tape recorder out. "Listen to this. Just sit there and listen to this, Walt."

Paula had taped her entire conversation with Jake from the last time they were in the kitchen. Walt listened to all the names Jake called him and heard Jake admit to beating Paula. Now he was pissed.

"Okay, I'm glad you brought that to me. I'll deal with Jake. Listen, I need a favor from you. I want to know if you have any problems with me doing a threesome. I have another inmate. Can she be with us? Do you mind?"

Paula's face showed surprise. "I'm not a lesbian. Do I have to—you know—let her—do things to me?"

"No. I'm the star of the show and I'll start off in my diaper—the way you like me," he said, smiling.

"Oh, so you like that diaper shit?"

"I love it. I put one on at home for my wife the other night."

Paula was floored and started laughing. "You've gotta be joking, Walt. What did she do?"

"She called my doctor and she begged me to go into therapy. She thinks I'm going nuts."

"So, you've listened to it all and you know I know what happened and you know I know you lied. We understand each other, don't we?" asked Walt.

"Warden, I'm sorry. I have a problem. I should not have hurt her and I apologize for all the things I said about you. I was just mouthing off and trying to be a big shot. Please accept my apology."

"You're fired. If anything happens to Paula after you leave—if there are any 'accidents'—your ass is going to jail and I'll make sure there is an 'accident' as soon as you get there. Get your ass out of here and tell your mother 'Curly' said those fucking cakes better keep coming. You make sure you personally deliver them to Charmaine once a week. Since you won't be working for a while, you'll have time. That's it—you can leave," Walt said.

Walt had his office decorated with balloons and had a cake. He had two six-packs of wine coolers. It was Paula's birthday and Josie was there, too.

He had his diaper on and his pacifier in his mouth. He told Charmaine to go home early.

Kool and the Gang sang "Celebrate" and Stevie Wonder sang "Happy Birthday" from the stereo. It was party time. Josie and Paula laid his fat ass down on the floor and took turns going down on him. One poured the Smirnoff's down his throat, and the other licked it off his body. Paula would sit on his face a while and then Josie would take over. The ladies then took turns letting him screw them.

With a wink at Paula, Josie took out a pair of eyeglasses and put her hair up in a bun. She was now the schoolmarm. "Let me teach you how to count, Walt," she said. She shoved one of her breasts in his mouth and then the other. She sang, "One titty—two titties," and then Paula came over singing, "Three titties—four titties," pushing hers damn near down his throat. The two of them stood up and rolled their asses around and sang, "One ass—two asses," and then they got him off the floor and stood him up in the middle of them and sang, "Three asses."

"Sing it, Walt—three asses," Paula said as they all shook their butts, and Walt sang along. They all then put candles on the birthday cake, and Walt and Josie sang "Happy Birthday." They all ate cake as naked as jaybirds, singing and dancing. Walt was having the time of his life. When that was over, Walt pulled a gift-wrapped box from under his desk. Paula opened it up and it contained two sets of clothing, including shoes. They were jeans, T-shirts and sandals. Walt said, "Put your shit on, ladies, goddammit, it's dark outside and party time! I'm taking both of you out. *Outside*. Outside to a *restaurant*, and to a *club*. We're going dancing tonight. Don't worry, we're out of here tonight. Get dressed! I've got everything arranged and you're walking out of here with me."

Chapter Twenty

Purdy

Purdy never felt Andrea's arrival into his bed. He was knocked out. She snuggled up next to him and lay there. Her face rested under his neck with her long red mane falling on his chest. She began massaging him and he didn't respond. She gently moved her hand down and found the slit in the front of his silk pajamas. She massaged his penis until it became erect. Still sleeping, he mumbled, "Stefana, Stefana baby. Umm." Andrea continued, and when he was fully erect she carefully got on top of him and placed him inside her. She began kissing him and his body moved with hers. Purdy moaned, calling out Stefana's name. Both his hands were running through her hair. He moved his hands from her hair to grab her ass, pulling her closer inside him. She came and began whispering, "Oh my God, Dr. Remington, oh my God."

When he heard "Dr. Remington," he opened his eyes and looked at Andrea. "What the hell, what the fuck! Oh shit—you're not Stefana! Oh shit! Andrea! What the hell are you doing?" He pushed her off of him. Pilar started crying as he jumped off the bed, gaping at Andrea. She couldn't move. She stared at him. He was so angry he banged his fist on the expensive walnut chest behind him. Noticing that Pilar was crying, he ran over to pick the baby up.

"I'm sorry, Dr. Remington," Andrea said sweetly.

Purdy paced the bedroom floor with Pilar, cursing. "Andrea, Andrea, Andrea," he moaned. That's all he could say.

He walked out of the bedroom to the living room looking for Pilar's diaper bag, and put the crying child on the couch to change her diaper. Andrea walked down the stairs and headed for the kitchen to get a bottle. He was sitting on the couch, trying to quiet Pilar, when Andrea came with the bottle.

"Want me to take her?" she asked.

"Yeah, why don't you? You just took her daddy," he said sarcastically.

Purdy went back to the bedroom and lay on his bed, staring out of the window. He was pissed and ashamed. After his promise to Tony, god-dammit, this shit happened anyway. Damn, he was dreaming about Ste-fana. This shit was not to be believed. He didn't know what he was going to do about Andrea. Maybe he should just throw her out. He knew if Tony ever found out he would hate him. He looked down at Pilar's makeshift bed, and then he ran back to the living room.

"What do you use for birth control?" he said as softly as he could not to scare Pilar. "Do you have a diaphragm or are you on the pill or some-thing? Shit, I can't handle two kids. I'll go out of my mind for sure."

"I use condoms," she answered.

He reached into the slit of his pajamas and pulled his penis out. "Well, where the fuck did you put the one that was supposed to go on *this* be-fore you raped me?"

"Well, I hadn't planned this. You know, it was kind of spur of the mo-ment, like an experiment," she said.

"A fucking experiment?" he screamed. "Does this look like a god-damm test tube to you?" he said, holding his penis out to her.

"No. It's much more attractive," she said.

He wanted to smack her. "I swear to God if you're pregnant I'm going to kill you!" He stormed out of the room headed back to his bedroom, thinking, "As bad as my luck is, she'll be pregnant and I'll have two ba-bies screaming their heads off." He then returned to the living room and said, "And another thing: I better not have anything like a disease re-sulting from our little tryst."

His phone rang and he almost picked it up, but then remembered it was not time to talk to people in Philly. He had things to do. There would be two more days of no answering the phone. It was now 8:35 in the morning. It was time to start moving on what he had to collect for Pilar.

He showered and dressed and returned to the living room. Andrea and Pilar were gone. He searched around and found them in the base-ment watching Mr. Rogers.

"Andrea, we have to talk," he said softly.

"Okay," she answered.

"That thing that happened cannot happen again. Not ever. Your brother is a great friend to me and specifically asked me to be a gentleman with you. I tried to do that. Tony must never find out about this. Now, tell me, what am I going to do about your helping me with Pilar? Maybe, under the circumstances, I should not have you here."

Andrea sighed and ran her fingers through her hair. She rested her forehead in the palm of her hand. "I apologized for what happened. I don't know what got into me. I've never done that before, honest to God. You just looked so sexy and peaceful lying there, and I've been impressed with you because you're so sophisticated. I had something—I guess an attraction or something. I don't know how to explain it. I'm mixed up about it, but I promise I'm sorry and it won't happen again. I'd like to stay and I'll behave."

Purdy didn't know what to say to this gorgeous creature. He never thought he'd see the day when he would chastise someone for making love to him. This shit was bizarre. "Look, let's forget this ever happened and start over. Give Pilar to me. I'll bathe and dress her while you get ready. We have to go shopping."

Andrea went over to him and with a small smile meekly said, "Okay, so I'm forgiven?"

"Yes, Andrea, you're forgiven—but you better not be pregnant and I better not be burned."

"By the way, who's Stefana?" she asked as she stood up.

"None of your business. Let's get going. We'll go out for breakfast."

They got started and purchased everything from baby monitors to thermometers. They also bought a brass cradle that hung. It was exquisite, and they got linen and blankets, decorating it in pink and white eyelet fabric. He also picked up doubles of things for the basement, and in case Pilar spent an evening being babysat at Tony's, with Peggy Kinard or Mrs. Charleston. Purdy spent over two hundred dollars in CVS on eyedroppers, suppositories, baby aspirin and anything else he would need for routine care or in an emergency.

At noon, they broke for lunch at Fridays. The staff and patrons made quite a fuss over his bundle of joy. They came home to dump their truckload of stuff and then went to a specialty store to pick out Pilar's bedroom furniture. It would arrive in six weeks. When they got home, it was a little after four o'clock. Purdy fed and changed Pilar and she went out like a light. He then called Tony and let him know all was well, thanked him, and let Andrea talk to her brother. He didn't place one call to any of his friends or to his office. When Andrea got off the phone he said, "What do you want for dinner?"

"Anything will do. I can cook us something if you like."

"Are you a good cook or shall I order something? I'm too tired to start a meal," he said.

She thought for a moment, looking at all she had to do. "Order out, because I really should get busy setting things up and putting stuff away. You don't have much fresh food here anyway. I already checked things out. I don't feel like going to the market. Let's order a pizza and some salads from Pete's. They're near here. Will that do you?"

"That will be fine. Can you get them on the phone?"

"Yeah, I've got it covered," she said, going for the phone book.

Purdy went upstairs and ran the shower. He put on a pair of jeans and a shirt and lay across the part of the bed that was not covered with items they had purchased. He looked down at Pilar as she slept. He was mad about that kid. She was going to have a great life. He wondered if he was going to be able to use Andrea after the two days. She was good, but he was truly pissed with her and prayed to God Tony would never find out what happened. He imagined Andrea having a little too much wine at Thanksgiving dinner with her family or some other family gathering and telling Tony. Tony would want to kill him for sure. Damn. He wished he could be up-front and tell him about it, but felt that might be a bigger mistake.

He planned to call Stefana in a few days to tell her about Pilar. Maritza was all over his answering machine, but she would just have to wait. He had a list of things planned for the next day and they were:

(1) Get a life insurance policy on Pilar and have her placed on his medical insurance.

(2) Have his will changed and designate a trustee and a care provider

in case something happened to him.

(3) Call an agency to arrange for a nanny.

(4) Get a pediatrician.

(5) Buy a golden retriever puppy and find a trainer.

(6) Install video cameras in the house and motion detectors all over the property, including all windows.

(7) Find a playgroup and make sure he got her there twice a week so she could be around other kids.

(8) Install a fish tank in Pilar's room.

It would certainly be a busy day tomorrow and he'd be on the phone all day.

After dinner, he went to the basement to relax, and Andrea acted like an employee and stayed out of his way. She really did a great job setting up the nursery. It was cute, but he had a ways to go with it. He couldn't wait until her furniture arrived. He had a restful and uneventful night, and the next day he took care of everything on the list and was waiting for callbacks. He was still screening all calls.

On Wednesday morning, Purdy awoke at five thirty in the morning. He bathed and fed his daughter himself and then he dressed for the office. When he and Andrea met at the front door, she had prepared a diaper bag complete with everything Pilar would need. Purdy grabbed the infant seat that his daughter was sitting in all dressed up, put the diaper bag around his shoulder and grabbed his briefcase. "Okay, Andrea, follow me out to the car."

Andrea assisted him by holding the diaper bag and briefcase as she watched him carefully place Pilar in her car seat. She then put the diaper bag in the passenger's seat and handed him his briefcase. He placed that in the backseat, got in the car and headed for his office.

"Good morning, everyone, I'm back," he said as he entered the main office.

"Hi, Dr. Remington," they all said in unison, staring in surprise at the baby with him. Desiree, a clerk, peered in at her in the infant seat.

"Whose is this little angel? Where did you get her from? Is her mom on the way in?"

"She's my daughter, and I'll explain later. Dina—here, take my keys and go out to my car. I left a diaper bag out there that I'll need." She looked at him like he was crazy.

"Dr. Remington, what's going on? This isn't your baby—stop playing. Whose baby is this?" asked Karla, a secretary.

"I told you she's mine," he said, and walked away to his office. Desiree returned with the diaper bag, placing it on the floor of his office, and stood there frozen. Purdy was taking the blankets off Pilar, along with her sweater and hat. Desiree couldn't move. She was stunned. "Dina went down to therapy for a chart. She told me to bring you the bag."

"Desiree, what is wrong with you?" Purdy asked.

"Where did you get that baby? Let me see her."

He proudly held her up and said, "Desiree, meet my daughter, Pilar Miriam Remington. You'll get more details later this morning. I need my schedule so I can set up an office meeting."

By this time Karla had buzzed Jillian, the office manager, and she came running into Purdy's office. She halted when she observed him sitting behind his desk holding Pilar. "Jesus Christ, she is beautiful," she said. "Karla said she was yours. Is that really true?"

"Yep, and I'll explain later. Tell one of the male therapists to come here and give him my car keys. There's a playpen in a carton in the hutch of my Jeep out there and I want it brought in here and set up in this office."

"When did you buy a Jeep?" Jillian asked.

"I rented one yesterday. I *need* the playpen," he sternly said.

Jillian picked up the keys and left, shaking her head. Purdy opened the diaper bag and counted the bottles of formula and water and checked to make sure it contained baby wipes and everything else Pilar would need. It was complete. He took one bottle of the ready-made formula out of the bag, along with her bottle warmer, and placed them behind his desk on his credenza, so they would be easily accessible when it was time for her feeding.

Desiree came back with his schedule and read it to him while he checked to see if Pilar's diaper was wet. This was a trip for Dezi because she had worked for him for four years and never saw a sign of him wanting a baby. This just wasn't him. Purdy got up and changed Pilar on the couch and Desiree stood speechless. "Dezi—please tell me if I have a break for about thirty minutes anywhere so we can have a short staff meeting this morning." She looked at the schedule.

"No breaks." She finally recovered herself enough to tell him the office schedule.

"Okay—everybody is eating lunch one thirty until two thirty and the meeting will be during lunch. That means therapy, billing, trauma, main office staff, transcribing, and therapy exercise staff. The meeting will take place in the conference room adjacent to the exercise equipment. I want everyone there on time and at one twenty I want someone called from therapy—a male—and I want Pilar's playpen brought down there from this office for that meeting. You got that?" Purdy asked.

"Yes," she said.

She was surprised at the way he was ordering her around. That wasn't like him. She obeyed and left the office, going around and telling everyone to be at the meeting.

After Purdy finished changing Pilar, he placed her back in her infant seat. She was bright-eyed and wide awake, looking around. He checked his schedule and saw he had a patient in about fifteen minutes. He lifted Pilar up from the infant seat and carried her out to the wall-to-wall fish tank in the lobby. He explained all the colorful tropical fish to her. By then he could hear that the playpen was being erected in his office. The staff was watching him, dying to take Pilar out of his arms and play with her.

On the way back to his office he stopped at the desk and said, "No calls from Maritza or Jazz Fleming. If she calls, I'm still out of the country. I'm not answering my private line either, and if any people call from companies regarding orders I placed for baby items, put them through. If anyone calls here about a puppy or training a puppy, put them through, too. If an agency calls about a nanny or babysitting, get me right away. Otherwise, take messages for me all day."

"Dr. Remington?" said Jillian

"Yes."

"Can I hold the baby?"

"Nope. This is our quality time. Maybe later." He walked away, headed to his office.

As soon as he left, the office staff started gossiping amongst themselves, asking each other questions like, "What the heck is going on? Where do you think he got her from? I wonder if he really adopted her? I can't believe he did this! How in the world is he going to raise a baby? Maybe he got somebody pregnant a long time ago and kept his mouth shut. He probably bought her on the black market. I'd like to see what he does with her when he gets ready to go on one of those trips when he gets pissed off with all of us. Did you see him changing a diaper—I couldn't believe it. I wonder how much he paid if he bought her? I wonder if the mother is here in the States? He'd better be looking for a full-time nanny. I just can't believe he brought her and all that baby stuff here to the office. He must be in a midlife crisis. This shit is a trip. He had to be planning this for months. She is absolutely gorgeous. I wonder what the big meeting is about? Dr. Remington with a baby? I guess she'll be drinking formula at that fancy French restaurant downtown—Le Bec-Fin. Can you see him up nights with a baby and not one of those wild women he has? A dog? Do you believe he's getting a damn dog? All the thing has to do is shit on the floor or on one of those to die for Oriental rugs he paid a fortune for and that mutt will be out of there, as clean as Purdy Remington is. Dr. Remington has gone crazy. He probably got drunk off all that good wine he drinks and bought her while he was intoxicated in China and got stuck with her and had to bring her back here."

Purdy used the last five minutes of his free time explaining to Pilar about the beautiful floral arrangements in his office. He softly told her the name of each flower, its color and origination, and took a petal off a tulip so she could smell it. He then spoke to the flower and said, "Petal, let me introduce you to my Petal." She began crying and he knew she was hungry. Just then the phone buzzed. It was Dezi saying she was bringing his patient in. He asked her to let the patient wait and to come into his office. When she arrived, he looked at his schedule and said, "Go out there and ask Mr. Jackson if he has a cold or any flu-like symptoms and come right back here with the answer."

She checked with the patient and came back. "He said no, not at all. He's just here for a follow-up because his left hand is continuing to bother him."

"Okay, just do me one more favor and plug that bottle warmer in the corner over there."

"Bottle warmers need water in them," she said.

"I know, I already did that. See that bottle of Evian there?"

She smiled and shook her head. "You're really on this thing, Dr. R," she said.

"Thanks. Now bring Mr. Jackson in, but first take his temperature. If he has a temp, don't bring him in here because that is a sign of infection."

When his patient came in, he found Purdy feeding Pilar while sitting behind his desk. After listening to his patient's complaints, Purdy buzzed Dina and told her to set Mr. Jackson up with a specialist for an examination of his hand. He also told her to escort him to a treatment room. When the patient left, Purdy burped Pilar, checked her diaper and put her down in her playpen for a nap. He then turned on the baby monitor, grabbed the other part of it, closed his office door and locked it and headed for the treatment room. He grabbed Karla and said, "Take these keys and stay in my office until I come back."

He set the speaker on the table of the examination room and hit the switch. He then examined his patient while listening closely for any signs of Pilar crying. Everything was cool. He wrote Mr. Jackson a prescription for Motrin 800 and returned to his office, leaving the monitor there. When he entered his office, he wrote a note to buy a few more sets of monitors for every exam room. He then picked up his voice recorder, which had been on while Mr. Jackson was in his office, and buzzed Jillian, telling her to come to retrieve the tape and have the office notes typed up. Normally, he handwrote the events of office visits, but he couldn't do that and feed his baby.

He saw five more patients, and Pilar slept through all of them. His little princess was such a good baby for Daddy. He screened all patients for colds, paranoid that Pilar would catch something. Two patients admitted they had the sniffles, and he apologized to the hilt and scheduled them as quickly as he could with Dr. Gelding.

A male therapist arrived at Purdy's office precisely at 1:20 for the playpen. Purdy lifted Pilar out and placed her in her infant seat on top of his desk and told her to look around while Daddy got ready for lunch. Purdy buzzed Karla and asked her to go down to the kitchen and put a Stouffer's stuffed peppers frozen dinner in the microwave for him and bring it, silverware and napkin to the meeting for him with a bottle of water. He then grabbed his baby, changed her diaper and headed for the meeting.

The conference room was filled with his forty employees. "Good afternoon, everyone, it's nice to see you. Thanks for altering your lunch time for this meeting. First, I'd like to introduce all of you to my daughter, Pilar Miriam Remington." He gently picked her up from the infant seat and showed her off. Oohs and ahhs came from everywhere, and people lined up and crowded around to see her better. He let that go on for five minutes and then calmed them down.

"The reason for this meeting is to inform you about my daughter and advise you of some new procedures. Get settled and listen carefully. I am toughening up around here and there will be a lot of new rules. I'd like to keep you all on. However, if I have problems, you will have to find other employment. I have decided that Pilar will be brought to this office every day. I want you all to know that I know you mess around a lot of time here. I'm sick of finding information in charts that does not belong there. There are too many personal phone calls coming and going. Documents lie in the fax machines for hours without being taken out and given to me. You people arrive late to work often, and that has to change. The billing department can get more bills out, and my money can get here a lot quicker if you're not fooling around. The physical therapy department needs to stop having so many personal chats with my patients so that other patients can be seen without waiting so long. I don't need you therapy assistants conversing with the patients about books, movies and their night life while they are on the machines. Unless they are having a problem with the equipment, let them exercise. Don't get my program mixed up with Happy Hour. The office staff needs to expedite setting up the appointments for MRIs and specialists as quickly as they can and give the information to the patient. Also, follow up with the patient and the doctor to make sure they arrived there and get their reports to me. And another thing, all of you need to stop leaving your dirty dishes in the kitchen. If you can't comply, don't use the kitchen. Okay, let's move on."

The staff was astonished, listening to him come down on them. They were silent and paying very close attention to the new Dr. Remington.

"Since my daughter will be here and you people have so much free time, all of you will have additional job responsibilities. This won't exactly be a day care, but you'll have responsibilities to help out with her. I am having video cameras installed throughout this place, too. The large lounge will become a room for Pilar. I will have it completely done over by a decorator. When it is set up, every one of you will be responsible for watching her for fifteen minutes a day whether she is asleep or awake. Diapering and feeding will be handled by whom I designate *only*, and I will advise who will be doing that. In between my patients, I will have her. At no time will Pilar be unattended. A schedule will be posted in her room and in each department. I want it adhered to. So, all of you people will be taking care of *three* infants."

Everybody froze, stopped eating their lunches, stunned expressions on their faces. He really had their attention then. They wondered whether he had adopted some more kids and they were coming later. Jillian's head sank, convinced he had lost his mind for sure.

"I am not kidding. I will have two additional infants coming in. I will find the kids myself and they will come here for free and their parents will drop them off and pick them up. It is important to me that she has friends and is not alone during the day. If she or one of the other kids gets fretful during your shift or is crying uncontrollably, or you think anything is wrong, I am to be interrupted *immediately* by phone, or send a worker down to my office and I'll come down here. If anybody doesn't like it, let me know now and I'll give you unemployment or whatever else you need. Two days a week for half a day her nanny will be here to assist."

Now people were muttering and sulking and sighing. Some were giving eye contact to others. People were shaking their heads and some were laughing. Remarks were being made like, "This is unreal."

Dr. Remington ignored them and continued, saying, "We're getting a dog. It will probably be a golden retriever. I'm having him trained by experienced trainers that teach dogs that go to hospitals and doctor's offices to visit the sick. They are extremely well behaved. I'm trying now to get that all set up, and the trainer will be here with the dog whenever he is here. He and the dog will be living at my home until he is fully trained and housebroken. Okay—there's more.

"You will all have your temperatures taken here each day that you report to work. I realize I specialize in rehabilitative medicine and people do not come here for treatment of colds and things of that nature. However, you are my employees and my lifestyle has changed and we're now working around children. I plan to take every precaution so that my staff and I don't infect them. If anybody doesn't like kids or has any problems with what is expected of them, I'm telling you to let me know now. Does anybody have anything to say?"

They were all stunned. Dr. Pierce Remington was definitely a new man. Nobody asked to be fired or laid off and, to his surprise, nobody quit. One worker said, "Since you're having babies here, can I bring my daughter?"

"I'm sorry, but I am selecting the kids myself through Children's Hospital of Philadelphia. I know someone there and they will help with that. I'm not looking for a sick child, but I want to assist parents who have sick children. Many parents with a sick child have other children who are well, and they need help because they have to spend much of their time at the hospital and at doctor's offices with the child who is ill. I would be helping by providing care for the well child free of cost. I know the parents would be relieved and more at ease knowing their healthy infant is being babysat in a safe environment, such as a doctor's office. I don't even want to start bringing staff's kids in here because I can't accommodate all of you and what I'd do for one, I'd like to do for all. Any more questions?" Purdy asked.

Another worker commented, "I'm confused with the dog part of it. The dog is going to be pissing and crapping all over the place, and you are going to have a fit with us."

"The dog will be trained by a trainer, and he will have full responsibility for it. You see that room over there?" Purdy said, pointing across the room. "It will be used for training the dog. Until he is adequately trained, he won't be roaming around. It is important to me that Pilar has a pet, so he has to be here.

"Another thing," Purdy said. "I will have books in Pilar's room and you guys can read to her and her buddies while you're with them, and there will be all kinds of toys. If they are all asleep when you come for your shift, you can clean up or read the paper or talk on the phone. I don't care. Just be in there if you are supposed to be. Does anybody mind doing this?"

A worker stood up and smiled. "I think it's a great idea and I'm glad to help, Dr. Remington. She is as cute as a button and I'll love doing this. I'm happy."

"Thanks, Tina," said Purdy. "Okay—we'd better finish up lunch and get out of here. Thanks a lot, everyone—and if anyone has any problems, let me know. One last thing—if you come on your shift and Pilar is not here, she is in my office, maybe getting a diaper change, or the nanny or I took her for a stroll around the grounds. She should be no other place. None of you are to take her anywhere. She is *never* to be taken off these premises by any of you. Do not remove her from this room. If you come for her and she is not here, come to my office and check or buzz me to make sure I have her, or the nanny does. You all have to sign in for your shifts with her and sign out. Always write in your name and the time. If you screw it up, I'll fire you no matter how much I like you, how bad you need a job or how long you've worked for me. You'll do this correctly or you'll go. No bullshit."

Purdy returned to his office, fed and changed Pilar and put her down for a nap. He picked up the phone and called Andrea at her home.

"Hi, Andrea, it's Dr. Remington."

"Hi, how is it going?" she asked.

"It's going just fine. I'm mailing you out a check for six hundred dollars, and I have another job for you."

"Shoot," she said.

"I have forty employees. I want background checks done on all of them for child care. I have an agency that I'll give all their information to and they'll take care of that. I'm getting memos out to my staff to fill out the forms."

"So what do you want me to do?"

"This is confidential. Okay?"

"No problem."

"All right. This is the scoop. I'm going to give you the names, addresses and birth dates of all my people. I want you to call all pharmacies in their neighborhoods and give the pharmacists their names. Be slick. I know you know how to do that. We want to find out if they are on any medications, so you'll have to give their info and find out the prescriptions that they are on. Now you know some pharmacists will probably have no record of the person or any meds. That's okay—I just want info if there *is* info. Also the big pharmacies like Drug Emporium, Eckerd, CVS and Rite Aid have to be checked. You should also call the hospital pharmacies in their neighborhoods and the big hospitals like Hospital of the University of Pennsylvania, Jefferson and Pennsylvania because lots of times people go to those places if they are sick simply because they trust them. Don't forget about the VA Hospital, too—the one on Woodland Avenue. We also have a prescription plan here and I'll give you that info so you can check through them. I am not taking any chances. This project is important. My staff will be helping out with Pilar and I don't want anyone handling her who is taking antidepressants, nerve meds or meds for being psychotic. You know, you never know what kinds of problems people have. Damn if I want something happening to Pilar and then the person says they've been upset or they were abused when they were younger and have problems. If anybody here is crazy or upset or anything close to that, I'm getting them out of here. You got that? You should know how to worm this info out of these pharmacists without letting them know what you're doing. Okay—there will be one more project for you to do for me and I have to set that up. I'll get back to you on that one. Can you handle this stuff?"

"Yep, I've got it covered. Just get the info to me and I'll start working on it."

"Thanks a lot, Andrea," he said.

"Dr. Remington, I talked to Tony today, and he said he and Teighlor and the kids wanted to come by there one night next week to see Pilar. He told me to tell you to call him."

"Okay, I'll call him tomorrow."

"Hello," the voice on the other end of the phone answered.

"How is the most beautiful girl on the planet?"

"Oh God, you must want something," she answered.

"How are you, baby?"

Her voice sounded delicious. "I'm fine, Purdy. It's nice hearing from you. How have you been?"

"Pretty cool. How are you and that man making out? You know, the one I'm insanely jealous of?"

"Okay, really okay," Jade answered.

"You sure? You know if he gives you any trouble I can make one phone call and have all *three* of his legs cut off." She laughed.

"You're still crazy, I see. Now don't go cutting up my husband-to-be, Purdy. I got engaged two weeks ago," Jade answered.

"Congratulations, baby—when's the wedding?"

"Gotta wait about a year—need save-up time."

"I can dig it. Listen, I've got the flowers covered for the entire affair. Just pick out whatever you want for whoever, whatever or wherever and tell the florist to send the bill to me. No carnations either—go for the good stuff."

"I love you—honest to God I do. Thanks. Now, tell me what the hell you want today. I know it's something."

"As a matter of fact I do need you. Listen to this. I've got about forty employees and I need thorough background checks done on all of them. Since you work for City of Philadelphia, Criminal Listings, you are my woman."

"Damn, did something happen over at your office or at home or something? This sounds serious."

"Well, I have a new young baby in my life and I am a bit nervous about people. I'll give you all the details later on the baby. Let's just get this straight now."

"Okay, let's have it."

"I'll have someone call you and give you all the names, addresses and birth dates of my people. I'm giving her your home number because this will take a lot of time. Her code name will be 'Isabella.' If she ever calls you either at home or on your job, she'll be Isabella. I want you to run full checks to see if they have had any hearings, been in jail, on probation, waiting for a hearing—anything and everything. I especially want to know if they have any history of child abuse in any form or fashion. Even if they smacked a kid around, I want to know about it. If any of them are manic-depressive, crazy as hell, been in jail and/or committed a crime, I want to know if it is in your system. Cross reference with the probation department separately, too. Then get somebody in Civil Listings to do you a favor and check for complaints that they either filed against someone or that were filed against them. If there are complaints, get copies of them and go through them—you know—the text. Find out what happened. Give your reports to Isabella and she'll go through the stuff again and then alert me if she has to. You got that? Am I putting too much on you?"

"I've got it, baby. How much time do I have?"

"Start when you can and finish as quickly as you can. You can send stuff piecemeal to Isabella. When you send her the envelopes or drop them off or however you guys run this thing, anyone you want me alerted to—buy some red stickers and put one on their envelope. Make separate manila envelopes for each person's stuff. Even if a worker is clean, put the notes in an envelope. If a person is completely clean, put a green sticker on it. People who are up in the air—like a minor problem or something we need to discuss—code their envelope with a yellow sticker. Are we clear, baby?"

"We're clear."

"Okay, I can't get downtown, but I'll leave an envelope at the front desk of my office with your name on it. One of the secretaries will find it for you when you stop by. It's expense money."

"You don't have to pay me."

"Yes, I do," he answered firmly. "You may have to grease somebody's palm in Civil to get this job done. Just remember to be as discreet as you can. I don't want you to end up working for me."

"Okay, but tell me what happened," she said.

"I'll tell you the rest when we meet for dinner soon—I'm bringing the baby to dinner at your house, and you're cooking. You can have your man there—I promise to be nice, and we can discuss this stuff in front of him."

"I'm getting off this phone now because you have given me too much information today. I cannot imagine you playing daddy. You're something else. I can't wait to meet her. What's her name?"

"Pilar Miriam."

"Miriam—you named her after your mom! That is *soo* sweet. I'm *soo* proud of you. Tell the baby her Auntie Jade cannot wait to spoil her to death."

"Okay, baby, I've got to split. Expect a call from Isabella and I'll call you about dinner."

Purdy then called Andrea back, gave her Jade's information and instructed her to make the call within a couple of days.

When Purdy got home that evening he found a small gift-wrapped package in his door. The card read "To Daddy from Pilar." He opened it and it was a tape of the song "Thanks for Saving My Life" by Philadelphia's own Billy Paul. He surmised Andrea had left it. After getting settled he stuck the tape in his stereo system in the living room while holding his child. He listened to the words and a couple of tears rolled from his eyes. He replayed it and sang the words to his daughter as she smiled. This was their song.

Thanks for savin' my life
For pickin' me up
Dusting me off
Making me feel like I'm living again

Purdy knew the two of them were meant for each other.

Chapter Twenty-one

Reba

"Nina was injured at a dance at her college," the nurse said.

"A dance? Was there a fire and she got trampled by him, or a fight or what? What happened to her?"

"She was assaulted by a man at the dance. She has a concussion and has suffered injuries to her ribs and left wrist."

"Oh my God!" shouted Reba. "We are on our way. Please give me your address and some directions." Reba scanned the bedroom for a pen and paper. She found one and wrote the information down.

Doug and Reba jumped up, and as they dressed Reba told Doug what the nurse had said. They were out of the house in fifteen minutes and on their way to the hospital.

"Nina, baby," Reba called as she and Doug rushed to her bedside.

"What happened to you, sweetie?" asked Doug, kissing her forehead.

Nina lay there with an intravenous needle in her arm and a bandage on her forehead. "A guy beat me up at a school dance."

"What!" screamed Reba. "Beat you up—who the hell is he? Is he your boyfriend or something?"

"No, Mom, he was just at the dance. He doesn't go there."

"Why did he do this to you—what happened?" asked Doug.

"I don't know him. He was in the ballroom with the rest of us. He asked my friend Natasha to dance on a slow record and she wouldn't dance with him. Then he yanked her and started shoving her around and she got away from him. After that, he came up behind me and grabbed me by the waist and was humping on me. I got away from him and started walking away looking for Natasha and spotted her. Then he snatched me from behind and turned me around and punched me really hard in the neck. He belted me a few more times and threw me across the ballroom floor. I went flying." Nina started to cry.

"Who is this asshole?" asked Doug. "Do you know him?"

"I've never seen him before. I told you I don't know him."

"What did the people in the dance do?" asked Reba.

"They got an ambulance for me and then they locked the doors to get names and stuff. I've been here all night."

"I've got to get to a phone and talk to the police," said Doug. "Reba—you just stay here."

Doug went to the desk of the emergency room and started asking questions. Then he got a number for the police department.

"Hello, my name is Douglas Ransome and I'm the father of Nina Penster. I'm at Washington Adventist Hospital and my daughter is here because she was attacked at a dance. This happened last night at the University of Maryland. She is a student there, and I would like to talk to the officers who took the report or have any information relevant to this matter."

"Hold on please, sir."

In a few seconds a man answered, "Sergeant Harry Brantley."

"Good morning, Sergeant Brantley, I'm Doug Ransome and I'd like to get all the details regarding an occurrence at University of Maryland last evening. My daughter, Nina Penster, was assaulted at that dance."

"Hold on, Mr. Ransome, and I'll get that file." Doug impatiently waited until Brantley returned to the phone.

"Who hurt my daughter?" asked Doug.

"I can't give you details like that, sir, as it's still under investigation. We have to collect statements from all the witnesses, including your daughter and her friend."

"Was this guy a student at the college? Is he in custody? Has he been arrested and charged?"

"Well, sir, he is not in custody and no arrest warrant has been obtained as yet. We were waiting to get the statements, and because your daughter has been hospitalized, we haven't gotten hers yet. We plan to talk to her today and interview her friend who was also assaulted by the young man."

"I asked you if he is a student at the college," Doug repeated.

"Sir, he is not a student at the University of Maryland."

"How old is he?"

"He is nineteen and resides in Maryland. We know where to find him."

"I'm going to have a talk with my wife, the doctor and my daughter. If you need a statement I'll try to arrange for you to come here today. I want him in custody. I will call you back."

Doug returned to Nina's room and informed them of his conversation. Reba got up and talked with the hospital staff. They agreed that Nina could give the statement if she felt up to it, but not to pressure her.

The two detectives entered the room and exchanged greetings with Nina, Doug and Reba. Reba was silent and looking at her child. This hurt her deeply, to simply imagine Nina being beaten and hurled across a ballroom floor after she had been molested by some low-life punk who came to a university function, not even a student, assaulting and abusing her daughter. After the meeting was over and Nina had signed the statements and complaint, the officers left.

Reba spent the night with her daughter in the hospital. Nina was discharged the next day. Reba delivered Nina to her dormitory to change clothes, and then they headed to the police station to file a restraining order against the young man. Nina was petrified of him and cried throughout that ordeal. Reba then arranged counseling for Nina, spent another night with her at the dorm and the next day returned home. Two weeks later the Ransome family and Nina received notification that a hearing would take place in six weeks.

The feisty Reba seemed worried, was not sleeping and was constantly checking on Nina. She was severely depressed herself; she seemed to be in a cloud. Nina was experiencing many of the same feelings and was terrified of attending any school functions. She was seeing her therapist twice weekly and was encountering breathing problems, which were labeled panic disorder. She was having concentration problems and was losing and misplacing things. She was on medication for panic disorder and migraine headaches. Her grades were falling, she was afraid to go on campus at night and she dreaded the upcoming trial. Reba kept assuring her that things would work out and the young man would be incarcerated for what he had done to her. She and Reba were almost constantly on the phone comforting and consoling each other. Reba stayed worried and upset. One evening Nina called home and said "Hi, Mom, it's me. I have something to tell you."

"Jesus, what happened now?" a frantic Reba asked.

"Well, Mom, it's not all that bad—there's a bad part to it and a funny part. Since we are always protesting and pissing and moaning about all the stuff that happened, I need to share this story with you."

"All right, let's have it."

"I went into DC today after classes to do a little window-shopping and go to an early dinner."

"What happened, Nina?" Reba said sternly.

"Well, after dinner I stopped at a bakery and bought some cookies and then I caught the train back to school."

"Did the freaking train crash or something, Nina?"

"No, Mom—no accidents. But I sat down next to a man and got situated. Then I took out one of my schoolbooks to study."

"What did the man do—feel you up?"

"Listen, Mom, can you just wait and let me tell you what happened? Jesus Christ, you keep interrupting me. I'll tell you what happened. Can you let me finish a sentence? You are crazier than me."

"I'm sorry. I'll shut up. Don't take all day."

"Okay. So, I began reading my book and eating cookies from my bag. The man reached over to the cookie bag and just took a cookie and started eating it. I couldn't believe it! He didn't even ask. I assumed he was crazy and you know I don't want to meet any more maniacs."

Reba was really getting worried now and said, "Nina, look, what the hell happened, are you okay?"

"Listen to this. He ate the cookie. Then when I had finished mine, I took another one from the bag. It was sitting next to me. Then he took another. Then I thought, 'Oh my God, this *is* a nut'—but I wasn't going to say a word to him because I was scared he really *was* crazy. To make a long story short, we kept going and got down to one cookie left. He had shared almost the entire bag of nine cookies with me and never said a word! Then he picked up the last cookie and I thought, 'I know this man is not going to eat my last cookie.' Well, Mom, he broke it in half and gave me half and never said a word. I was fuming! My stop was coming up and I started gathering my things. I reached over to my left for my purse. Beside it was a bag of cookies—the bag of cookies *I* had purchased. Mom, I had sat down on that train and started eating that man's cookies thinking they were mine and he never said a word. I hadn't realized mine were on the other side of me. I picked up the bag and was *soo* embarrassed and handed the bag to him and apologized. He told me I could keep them."

Reba burst out laughing and then Nina joined in.

"Hey, Nina—you'd better keep going to therapy for that concussion. You've got problems, baby."

It was almost quitting time for him at the station when this fine chick pulled up for gas. Damn, she was a masterpiece. She instructed him to fill the car up with unleaded plus, got out of the car, switched into the store area, and purchased a pack of cigarettes and a soda. She then returned and stood watching him pump the gas. She sure did look good in that black leather miniskirt and short matching jacket. She also had a nice set of headlights of her own, he thought.

"What's your name?" she said, looking him up and down as he pumped the gas.

"Eddie Parker."

"Well, Eddie, you're the cutest pumper I've laid eyes on in a long time. Are you a free man?"

"Free as a bird, baby."

"What time?" she asked as she took another swig of the soda.

"I'm off in about ten minutes. What's your name?"

"Carmen Rogers. You like what you see?"

"Affirmative, baby. What are you doing tonight—how about a date with the pumper?"

"Where do you like to take your dates? What are your hobbies?" she responded alluringly.

"I do clubs, picnics, restaurants, libraries—take your pick, Miss Carmen."

"I like Giraldo's on the strip for a club and the food is okay there. Do you know that spot?" she asked.

"Yeah. Around what time could we hook up? You want to meet me there around nine o'clock tonight?" he asked.

"See you then," she said as she switched slowly back into the store area to pay for the fill-up. She then returned to her car, winked at him and drove off.

Eddie got his belongings and headed for his apartment. He took his time—he had nearly three hours to kill before his date. He went through the stack of mail and complained about the bills and then went to his closet to select an outfit that would make this Puerto Rican piece of ass know she had finally hit the jackpot. She was fine enough to make him go straight and stop running the streets and roughing up everybody. Yeah, she just might be his chill-out pill.

He arrived at Giraldo's twenty minutes early, ordered a wine cooler, decided to drink slowly and watched the door for Carmen. She arrived promptly at nine in a black skintight minidress and high heels. Her long brown hair was pulled back off her face in a ponytail. She was built like a brick shithouse and he was falling in love with her just watching her walk toward the bar searching for him. He held his hand up to let her know he was there. She walked over to him, squeezed his hand and sat down.

"You look great," she said, running her index finger up the sleeve of his mahogany-colored leather jacket.

"Well, I believe God himself sent you to me and you look incredible for the second time today," he responded, kissing her hand. "Why don't you order whatever tastes good to you?"

"Cabernet Sauvignon please," Carmen instructed the bartender. Eddie had no idea what that was. The bartender returned with the glass of red wine. Carmen lifted her glass, as did Eddie, and she said, "To a hopefully warm friendship."

"So, Carmen baby, what is up with you—what are you about, where have you been all my life, and are you a free woman or just out making your man mad tonight?"

"Well, I'm a dancer at night—off tonight, thank God. I attend computer school during the day, I've been in DC all my life looking for you, and there is no other man at the moment. What's your story?"

He flashed a gleaming smile and thought, she's cooler than a Popsicle.

"I'm single, living in Hyattsville and making up my mind what I want to do about everything in my life, which happens to be nothing right now. I'm pumping gas to pass the time and keep from being homeless," he said.

"What happened to the lady?" she asked.

"I got fired for noncommitment," he said, taking a long swig of the Smirnoff Ice.

"You have problems with that, huh?" she asked.

"Wanna dance? They're playing our song," he asked.

"Wanna answer my question before you tire me out?" she asked.

"Let me think about it while I watch you move," he said.

"Okay—deal," she said.

They headed for the dance floor and her body seductively responded to the crooning of Barry White. They returned and she picked up her wine glass and summoned the bartender for a menu. They ordered dinner, he ordered another round of drinks and they continued to chat.

"I don't have any real commitment problems, I simply hadn't found the correct wonder in my world. You know what I mean?" he said.

"I don't know if I believe you because you're so fine and I'm sure many have crossed your path determined to make you happy. You sure you didn't just fuck up?"

"You're brutal," he laughed, shaking his head from side to side.

"Just honest, Mr. Parker. Just an honest Sagittarian doing an honest day's interrogation."

They finished their meal and drinks and headed back to the dance floor to enjoy slow dancing to the Miracles' "Ooh Baby Baby." Eddie was totally intrigued with Carmen.

"Well, it's getting late," she said after the dance. "I'd better get ready to head home, I've got school tomorrow—remember I'm the computer whiz."

"Okay, I'll follow you home to make sure you get there safely."

"That's not necessary—I know my way and I can take care of myself," she said, switching while walking ahead of him.

He ran to catch up and followed her to her car and said, "I insist. Let's go together, sweetie—you've got the perfect date."

They left the club and headed to Carmen's apartment. When they arrived, she parked and so did he, and they got out of their cars. Standing on the street, he didn't want to leave her and said, "I need to use the bathroom and the phone."

"Who do you have to call, your mother?"

"Yeah, my mother is waiting for me to check in. She hasn't heard from me all day. Can I use your phone?"

"No."

"Come on, Carmen, don't be so cold."

"For all I know you could be a not-so-nice guy."

"Oh, I'm the person you've been looking for all of your life—remember? Let me call my mother and she'll tell you herself."

Carmen walked toward her door and he followed. When they got in she pointed to the phone and the bathroom. She sat on the couch and waited for him to pick the phone up. He headed for the bathroom and then returned and sat on the couch.

"There's the phone—hurry up," she said.

He grabbed her into his arms and kissed her. She pushed him away. "Not so fast, buddy. First date. Rule of first date is nothing happens—*nothing.*"

He was irritated and said, "Why did you come on to me damn near all day?"

"I did no such thing."

He grabbed her and kissed her again, shoving his tongue in her mouth and attempting to get on top of her. He positioned himself on her and began to grind on her. He was panting.

"Eddie—you need to get off of me!" she shouted. "I'm not having sex with you. No—stop!" He went into a rage.

"Listen, bitch—stop playing and give it up!" he shouted. "You've been trying to give it to me all day! Don't turn into Ms. Goody Two-Shoes now!"

He lifted her dress up and snatched her underwear off, tearing it. She gave him a good shove and got away from him, running and screaming around the apartment. He chased her, knocking over a table, a lamp and the phone in the process. He finally caught her by the back of the dress and threw her on the floor, pinning her down. She yelled and could not move him. She bit him, and he was so angry he punched her in the face. When she grabbed her face, he inserted his penis in her and raped her. He was so engrossed in it that she was able to pull the telephone cord and press 911, while continuing to scream, never talking to the officers on the other end. In ten minutes Eddie was scurrying around for his things and calling her names as the police were banging on the door. Eddie Parker was arrested and Carmen was taken to the hospital and treated for rape and the bruises to her face.

Edward Parker always walked around dressed to kill and bullying every girlfriend he had. He met most of them in the local clubs in Maryland or at the colleges. He had absolutely no respect for women. He had two sisters and a mother in Hyattsville, Maryland. This high school dropout worked at a gas station pumping gas and had always been in trouble for one thing or another most of his life. He blamed everything that he was ever in trouble for on his mother and father—who happened to be quite respectable people who had just taken a lot of crap off their spoiled son. His parents were now divorced and had been for the past four years. His father couldn't hack it anymore arguing with his wife and going through changes with Eddie. It took its toll on the marriage, literally breaking it up.

Now Eddie was sitting in jail not only being charged with rape, but also saddled with that case of beating up some bitch named Nina Penster. That was a bad break, but she probably thought she was cute and she deserved the ass-whipping she got at that dance. Who the hell was she to reject him? He'd had a feeling he'd get off on that case with that big-time lawyer his mother had hired. His mother's best bet was to help him, or he'd act like a maniac and wreck her house or threaten to set it on fire. That would truly make her terrified and miserable, which would inevitably ensure her assistance with the Penster case. He really hadn't planned to do any of that stuff, but his back was against the wall with what happened at the dance and he was going to need some help.

Now he had this new mess. He was sick of these damn chicks looking down on him. All they had to do was go along with him—but no, they always had to make trouble. Now this Carmen girl was going to be a pain in the ass and cause him more aggravation. He sat in jail and thought about how he'd awakened the morning before and started to call in sick and changed his mind. He wished he had never laid eyes on Carmen.

Eddie was an Aries and those people have an entire set of problems. They have to be top dog—incredibly huge egos. They just have to be *it*. They are usually very smart and independent people. They also have a reputation of being as financially tight as Dick's hatband. They are the type of people that if you crack the door for them, they kick it in and try to take over. They can be as cold as ice. They thrive on attention and are unlike the Leos who love attention—the Aries *have* to have it.

In their profession, or if they own or operate a business or have a job—they are great at it. These people are far from lazy. Because they are insecure, they are jealous people. The men have a very low opinion of women and are capable of treating them horribly—unless they are truly smitten. They will demand control and are notorious for using women. If they are head over heels in love with a woman, these customary traits don't really surface and they are vulnerable and loving to the mate. They are actually also very naïve people and you can feed them all kinds of bullshit if they are in love with you. But if you've got the regular Aries man, you'll catch hell with him.

When they walk into a room, meeting, party—whatever—they expect to be treated as if they are the only one there—by *everyone*. If that doesn't happen, they feel rejected and will react in any way from pouting and sulking to actually getting a big-time attitude. The men usually love their mothers a great deal and will do anything for them. They are typically clean, the men wear funny colored socks many times, and they hate dirty dishes in the kitchen sink. The men have extremely freakish sexual habits and love toe-sucking, watching people have sex, transsexuals, orgies, pornography, threesomes—anything goes.

Carmen was discharged from the hospital around three o'clock in the morning and was escorted by police to the station to file formal charges against Edward Parker, including a restraining order. After all the paperwork was completed, she was driven back to her apartment. As soon as she arrived she undressed, showered and put her pajamas on. It was after five in the morning when she picked up the phone and dialed a number.

"Hello," the voice answered.

"Hi—is this Reba?" Carmen asked.

"Yes, Carmen, it's me. How are you?"

"It's done. I'm home and I'm okay. He's in jail and I'll give you the details tomorrow. We'll meet at our special place."

"Navy Yard," the voice on the other end answered.

"Horace Alston please, this is Reba Ransome calling."

"Hold on, ma'am."

"Hello," Horace answered.

"Hi, Horace, how are you?"

"I'm fine, Reba—what's up?"

"I just wanted to thank you for the business contact you hooked me up with. I'd also like to let you know that they scored tonight."

Chapter Twenty-two

Emily and Jared

I'm getting bored, Emily," Connie said as Emily, Jared and she had brunch.

"Well, why don't you get a little job or volunteer at a hospital or something?"

"I just may," Connie said. "I'm tired of sitting in the house all day."

"Wanna travel with us, Mom? You could be our wardrobe assistant or something," Jared offered.

Connie had a frown on her face and said, "I'm not hanging around with you guys; I'm not that desperate." She turned to Emily. "So, Emily, how are things going with you, baby? I don't see much of you anymore. You've got the boutique and the kids. You're a busy lady."

"I really am, Connie," Emily said.

Looking over at Connie, Emily felt guilty knowing she was carrying her grandchild. Connie would love having a baby around to keep her company. But Emily could not discuss the pregnancy.

"Know what, Connie? I'll check at the store to see if they need anyone to do the books or something. You may even be able to do that from home. Retail is sometimes a dangerous business and I don't want you in the store. If Dominick has anything, I'll ask him to pass it on to you. Jared can also check at his office for you. We'll see.

"Look, you guys, I can't stay a long time with you. I have to be at the boutique today. Connie, I'm going to call you. Jared, I'll get ready for New York. Give me some kisses, guys, I've got to run."

After Emily left, Connie said to Jared, "I love her—you know that? There is something so special about Emily. You ought to marry her, Jared. She really does love you, too. You'd better grab her up, boy, before someone else does. Are you ever going to divorce Stephanie?"

"Yeah, probably. I don't know. I've never said a thing to her about

Neal not being mine. I simply send the money. I don't bring it up because I don't want to hear the story. I would have never figured Stephanie for that."

"Well, you know what they say, son—those quiet ones will get you. I knew it when I looked at him. I knew he wasn't a Wells. Then she left him with me one day and Emily came over and looked at him and didn't say a word. She knew it, too. I got sick of Stephanie bringing that imposter over for me to babysit, so I told her that my arthritis was kicking up and my nerves were bad about you guys doing so much flying around, and I asked not to babysit anymore. I felt like an idiot watching him, knowing she deceived you, and while I was watching him—who knows—she was probably with another man. I wasn't letting her make a fool out of both of us."

"Well, Mom, I have to take some of the blame. You know I had Emily much of the time when Steff and I were together."

"Did that stop her from putting a rubber on while she was getting back at you? Coulda gave you the heebie-jeebies and made your little ding-dong fall off. Then you would have really been in trouble."

Jared, still being terrified of sexually transmitted diseases and embarrassed with the conversation, said, "Okay, Mom, don't start talking about that stuff. Finish eating. This discussion is over."

Connie cracked up laughing and said, "Pay the bill and let's go to the movies."

"Okay, Mom—the movies it is."

Leo answered his telephone, delighted to hear from Emily. "Hey, sweetie, you just made my day. What's going on with you?" he asked.

"I want to see you. Can you arrange that? Can it be tonight at your place? I'm sick of hotels."

"I would love to have the honor of your company. What time is good for you?" he asked.

"I can't get there until midnight. I don't want Horace to have a fit and he has to go to work. I'll get my brother to come over after he leaves. I have to be out of your place by four and back home by five. Don't try to keep me there all night, Mr. Sexpot."

"I'll be good—and quick. I can't wait 'til the midnight hour," he said.

Emily rang Leo's doorbell and impatiently stood waiting for him to answer. "Hey, you fine thing," he said when he opened the door.

She kissed him on the cheek and headed up the stairs to his second-floor apartment. She threw her jacket on the chair and sat on the couch. He sat next to her and took her hand.

"Do you want a glass of wine or anything?" he asked.

"Yeah, I'll have some wine."

As he went to retrieve it, she kept her eyes on him. She loathed him. She imagined Leo with Rachael and saw images of him being paid for his "services" at the end of his "shift." She reminisced about her being in his car—the one Rachael had purchased—and she knew he was not a student at Temple. She wondered how he could have done such outrageous acts. He was definitely Dr. Jekyll and Mr. Hyde, and she couldn't wait to surprise him with the news she had uncovered.

He returned with the wine and sat down beside her, kissing her on the cheek. He put his hand on her thigh, but she pushed it away. She got up instead and walked toward the kitchen.

He was bewildered. "What's the matter with you? I thought you missed me. Instead, you seem to be in deep freeze," he said.

"I'm upset with you," she said as she took a sip of the wine.

"What did I do?" he answered.

"You did Rachael." He was struck dumb and surprised. She had indeed dropped a bombshell on him. He tried to be cool.

"Look, Emily, I shouldn't have to explain anyone I see to you. We've been over that. Did you forget a person named Jared? You know, the guy who sings to you?"

She gazed at him from across the room. She took a swallow of wine and blurted out, "I'm not ripping Jared off. I'm not charging him to fuck me. He's not paying my tuition to Temple. Shall I go on?"

He had never seen her angry, and her behavior alarmed him. He knew he had better come up with something to calm her down. "Oh boy," he said wearily. "Listen, Emily. Come here, baby, let me talk to you." He got up and tried to take her hand. She snatched it back.

"Get off of me! I'm ashamed of you!" she growled. "I cannot believe you could be a con artist and take advantage of a little old woman who was lonely because she lost her husband. You are cruel. I don't ever want to see you again!"

"Emily, please, let me explain. There's a lot I need to tell you."

"Goddammit, I don't even want to listen to it! You make me sick! What kind of a person are you? That woman is going to lose her life's savings fucking around with you."

Leo was getting pissed now. How did Emily have all this information? He didn't dare ask her how she found it all out. Whatever the case, it made no difference now. He was in hot water up to his eyeballs with Emily.

"Do you want to leave now, Emily, or will you let me talk to you?" he asked as he threw his hands up in the air and headed for the couch. "Just do one or the other."

She looked at him, shaking her head and tapping her foot. She had mixed emotions. She wanted to hit him upside his head with a frying pan. She wanted to choke him, cursing him out at the top of her voice. That would ease some of her pain, and walking out on him might make her feel even better. She didn't know what to do about listening to him.

She thought about the night she met him and the flowers he sent and the helmet he'd given her. She was mixed up. She picked up the wine glass, drank it straight down and said, "Talk to me and it better be good, motherfucker."

"I had a part-time job thirty-two hours a week, taking care of a cancer patient in the suburbs. I worked through an agency. I did my job well and her husband died anyway. Rachael seemed heartbroken, lonely, and was living alone. She approached me three days after he died—on the third day that they sat shivah. You know that's what they do when Jewish people pass away. People come over for seven days to the home and pay their respects. I was there helping her out."

Emily didn't interrupt, so he went on. "After shivah was over, she asked me to stay on, assisting her around her house. She is seventy-five years old, and her kids and relatives all live out of town. I needed the money and stayed on. She wanted me to take her places—like shopping at first. Then it was to dinner. Next, she decided she required me to go to the movies and plays—stuff like that. I said okay. She was paying me for my time, putting gas in my car and footing the bill whenever we went out. Then she explained that she desired to sleep with me, and she started playing around touching me. I declined. I flat-out said '*No.*' "

Emily was studying him as though she wasn't sure whether to believe him.

"She kept pressuring me and explaining that I could be her 'companion.' She was throwing all kinds of money at me. She started encouraging me to go back to school and she'd pay for it, and then she suggested I should have a better car. I started obliging her with sex. However"—he held up his head—"That wrinkled-up white old body made me sick to my stomach. I started staying away."

He cursed to himself. He didn't like what he had to say next.

"She coaxed me back by calling, saying she needed my help at the house and she had no car. She claimed she was helpless. She said she hated driving and would not purchase a car for herself. Then she went to a dealership and purchased my new car in a further effort to rope me in. She presented it to me—she had paid for it in cash and it was in my name. I tried to tell her I couldn't accept it. She insisted, and finally I took it. In return she wanted me to perform oral sex on her and screw her almost all the time—every time we saw each other."

Leo then took a break, refilled his wine glass, sat back down on the couch and lit a cigarette, blowing smoke in the air. He put his feet up on the coffee table, took another drag of the cigarette and took a big swig of wine. Emily sat speechless on top of his kitchen counter. He continued.

"She started calling me day and night, sending notes to my house. One day she called me thirteen times! She had pornographic books and she was looking stuff up in novels, trying to do what characters in erotic books were doing. She would have a list of 'duties' prepared for me sexwise to do when I arrived. I just couldn't hack it. When I'd refuse, she'd go down on me, crippling me into changing my mind. Sometimes I'd get there and that old woman would be butt-naked when she opened the door. Emily, that little old lady is a trip. Trust me."

Emily's face was drawn into a frown, but she looked like she was going along.

"She tried to monopolize *all* of my time. She was literally worrying me to death, driving me stone crazy. Emily, she became a nightmare and a pain in my ass. Finally, I told her I'd had a girlfriend a while back, and we had gotten back together and I couldn't spend any nights at her house. She said that was okay. Just come after work and stay a few hours each night." He ran a hand through his hair.

"She kept on with the money. She was such a pain in the ass that I not only accepted all she gave, I asked for more because I couldn't stand her. So that's how it all happened. For the last month I've been standing her up. When she calls to make a date, I say I'm coming just to get her off the phone and I don't show."

He sat up again to tell the last ugly part. "Early this week she called to tell me that if I didn't come over, she was going to the police and tell them I had conned her out of a lot of money. She lives in Montgomery County. Those White cops would have hung me, so I went there one last time and I told her that was *it*. She freaked out and started threatening me again and pulled out some more cash. I told her I was going to the police myself and getting an attorney to get her to stop harassing me. I also informed her I was going to try to find out if I could file a sexual harassment suit against her, since I was her employee and she was attempting to fuck me to death. She was paying me by check sometimes and I knew I could prove something because of that. I told her I'd get a restraining order keeping her from contacting me and if I ended up getting into trouble—so be it. That's my story and believe me—she is a real piece of work."

"That's still no excuse for you—" Emily said, but he cut her off.

"I know what you're going to say and maybe you feel that way. Hell, maybe you are entirely right—maybe I was dead wrong. Okay, I *was* dead wrong, but shit, I believe I earned that damn money—every cent of it. Have you taken a look at that old damn White woman or did you just speak to her on the phone?" he asked. Emily didn't answer. She was too busy chuckling, imagining Rachael, naked, holding those "instructions" at the door when Leo would arrive.

"I've met her," Emily finally answered.

"So, do you think I earned it?" he asked. She didn't answer.

He started again, saying, "These damn White people get on my nerves with what they want. She wanted companionship at a price, and we've been paying out all our lives to White people—double the regular price for everything merely because we are Black—and you know it. And we've been sweating for their asses since they got us out of Africa. So, since she wanted Black companionship, my time and my sweat, I made the old lady pay. And don't forget, she *wanted* to pay. She offered, suggested, was willing to and actually *begged* to pay. Call me whatever you want, because yes, I charged the old bag whether she was truly grieving for her dead husband or not. Think about it, Emily. As soon as the old man died, she approached me. How long was Rachael actually in distress? I don't think it was too long, baby. She probably had it in her mind to jump my boots the first day I started working there and just didn't have the nerve to do it—the horny bitch." He took another gulp of wine and refilled the glass.

Emily kept staring at him, trying to understand the entire scenario. Leo's actions weren't excusable to her, but she wasn't as upset as when she'd heard the news from Rachael. And Rachael—Emily was beginning to feel differently about her after hearing Leo's story.

"Leo, are you seeing anyone other than Rachael and me?" she asked.

"No, I don't have time for anyone else. Hell, I'm working a full- and a part-time job and I've got you. I went back on with the agency after I got rid of Rachael," he said, putting his face in his hands.

"So, you lied to Rachael about going to Temple and all the other classes?" asked Emily.

"Yep, I took the school money and spent it and I didn't take any classes. That old bat couldn't have believed I was in school anyway. She didn't care—she just wanted to be humped. How the hell could I work, see her and go to school? If she was really concerned about whether or not I was attending Temple, all she had to do was call there and check. I bet she never did that. I'm so sorry I got mixed up with her, I don't know what to do. Brothers are always crying about Black women and how controlling they are. Shit, that old Jewish woman has been more of a pain in the ass than any Black woman I *ever* had. Like I said before, I earned every dime of that bread and I'm not sorry, giving it back, going back to her, or going through any more shit with *you* about it. She wore me out so bad I don't even want any more cash from her, and I *need* money. If you wanna walk because you can't handle what happened, I'll be devastated about losing you and I'm sorry to have disappointed you, but I'll keep moving. And I'll be quite honest with you—someone else could come into this picture with us even if you stay because I won't wait around alone all the time while you and Jared do your thing. I know I'm second in your life, but I'll be damned if I'll be second in mine. I've got to look out for number one, you know?"

Emily put the wine down, grabbed her jacket and said, "I've got a lot on my mind. I've got to run."

"Hello," an awakened Sheila answered her telephone.

"It's me," said Emily.

"What time is it? Jesus Christ, what's wrong?" asked Sheila.

"I need to know if you have to work today."

"Yeah, I'm working seven to three. Why?"

"Well, we have to hook up tonight. I have a plan. I'll call you around noon at the hospital."

Emily undressed and went to bed. It was three fifteen in the morning. She tossed and turned until she got to sleep, and awoke about ten o'clock. Renee was gone to school and she sat figuring what the hell she was going to do about the pregnancy and Leo. She made breakfast and did a couple of loads of wash and called Sheila back.

"Listen, Sheila, either I need to come over to your house this evening or you need to come here. You have to do something with me tonight."

"What?"

"I can't tell you now, and I'd rather you came here. Can you do it?"

"What time tonight?" Sheila asked.

"It has to be after Horace goes to work so that means I need you to come around eleven thirty."

"Aw, come on, Emily, please God, what the hell are you up to? If I come there then I'll be up half the night. I have to be at work at seven in the morning. Jesus Christ, what the hell is going on now?"

"Can you switch days and get someone to work for you? It's important. Can you take a vacation day or something?"

"You are a pain, Emily, with all your missions. You make me sick. Can't you get somebody else to do it—whatever the hell it is?"

"I can't trust anyone else with this. I need you. Please. Go see if you can get off. If you do it, I'll take you to the Hyatt for dinner whenever you say and I'll pay for everything, and—I'll keep the kids a whole weekend for you whenever you want. I swear."

Now it was sounding interesting to Sheila. A much needed break from motherhood. "For real—the Hyatt *and* a weekend?"

"Yep."

"I'll call you back. Let me see if I can do a switch and get off."

"Okay."

Emily waited impatiently, and in an hour Sheila called back saying she was coming.

Emily headed to South Street and did some shopping and then rushed to get Renee from school. They hit the park and McDonald's and then returned home. Horace had cooked dinner and wasn't there. He was probably with Jonita, she thought, and hoped he would be going to work from her house. They quickly jumped back into the car and rode out to Grandpa Oscar's job at the gas station.

"Hey, Oscar," Emily yelled out as she parked the car.

"Hey, Emily, baby. It's so good to see you. I see you've got my little chicken with you." Oscar opened the door so Renee could get out. He scooped her up and hugged her. He then proudly shouted to his fellow employees, "Come on over here and see my family. I've got my granddaughter." The guys came over and exchanged pleasantries with Emily.

Emily got out of the car and hugged Oscar. "How are you doing, Oscar? I've been meaning to get out here sooner, but I've been so busy. I have an extra job."

"Well, you've gotta make money, baby, I know that. How is my Amber doing, and have you heard from Sydni?"

"They're both fine."

"What's my man Horace doing other than working?"

"Well, he's got a girlfriend, you know, Jonita, and she's a lawyer. We like her a lot and she's nice to the kids."

"That's nice, baby. I'm glad. I wish I could find me a girlfriend. I'm leaving Fannie. I made up my mind to do that. She's still hoarding every dime she can and treating me like a piece of crap. I'm getting out, baby."

"You really mean that, Oscar?" a surprised Emily asked.

"I'm dead serious. I looked at a room to rent last week."

Emily fell silent. She was thinking. "Oscar, I may be out of line, but I want to run something by you if you really are planning to leave Fannie. Can we talk?" she asked.

"Please talk to me," he answered.

"Listen, I met a woman I'd like to introduce you to, but I've got to explain a few things first. First of all, she's a White woman. Does that bother you?"

He smiled. "I have no problems with that. Who is she and how do you know her?"

"I met her in the park and she lives close to us. Her husband died a few months ago. She's nice and pretty lonely. She has a giant house in Abington—down the road from us."

"You're really going to introduce me to her?" he asked as his eyes lit up.

"I will if you want me to. I don't want to break up your marriage, though."

"Do me a favor, chile, please break it up," he answered.

Emily laughed and said, "Why don't you come by the house on Sunday? Call me when you get up and I'll take you to her house. Her name is Rachael. I think the two of you will like each other. Another thing— whatever happens, don't you tell Fannie on me."

"Hell, you don't have that to worry about. You're doing me a favor. I hope the lady and me hit it off. How long was she married?" Oscar asked.

"I can't remember, but I think about thirty-something years," she answered.

"Okay, baby. See you soon," Oscar said as he kissed Renee and Emily. They drove off.

"Open the door, it's me," Sheila shouted as she rang the bell at eleven thirty that night. Emily opened the door.

"Hey, pal, come on in."

"Okay, what's going on?" Sheila asked as she took her coat off. She flung it on the couch and gazed at Emily, standing there with a scarf around her head and wearing a pair of giant hoops. "Why are you wearing that stuff?"

"Look, Sheila, come over here to the table. I have to talk to you."

They sat down at the dining room table. Sheila noticed a deck of tarot cards and an instruction booklet on the table. "What are you doing, Emily?" a bewildered Sheila asked.

"Listen, I've got problems and I'm going to try to work them out. You know everybody says I'm psychic, so I want to read these cards and see if I can get some things figured out."

Sheila burst out laughing. "You might be a little psychic, but you are *definitely* crazy. Goddammit, are you losing your mind? Now you're turning into a gypsy. Humph. I can't believe you had me take off work to listen to this shit. Why didn't you simply let me make you an appointment at the lady's house that read my cards way back when?"

"I may have to end up doing that, but I'm going to try to do this myself. I'm going to learn to read these cards."

Sheila shook her head in disbelief. "So what do you need me for and what the hell is your problem?"

"Well, I figured I'd practice on you. I've been reading the book this evening so I'd know some of the stuff."

"Shit! You ain't practicing on me! Do I look like a guinea pig to you?

Damn if you're gonna start flipping those damn cards around not knowing what you're doing and fuck my life up. Oh no, goddammit. I'm going home!"

"Oh come on, Sheila. Shit. I can get it down. I just need to practice. Nothing's going to happen. Stop being such a punk."

"You know I'm no punk, but this shit is *dangerous* if you don't know what you're doing. You could fuck around and put a spell on me or make something bad happen. I don't want to do it."

"Look, I'm following the instructions. All I have to do is light the candles and—" Before Emily could finish her sentence, Sheila cut her off.

"Light some candles! Oh no, goddammit. I *know* I'm getting out of here now!"

"Will you stop screaming before you wake Renee up? Jesus Christ. Relax. We merely dim the lights and light the candles and you'll shuffle the cards. Then I'll flip them and read each card. If I don't know what a card means, I'll look it up in the book."

"Emily, what are you trying to find out?"

"Well, I am making a decision on having the baby, and I'm making a decision on what I want to do about Leo."

"What happened with you and Leo?"

"Well, I never got a chance to tell you, but he is the one who was seeing old sex maniac Rachael."

"What! You mean he is the gigolo? Oh my God! How did you find out? Did you go up to her house and catch him or something?"

"No, girl—*you* caught him. That tag number you gave me—I traced it and the car was his."

"You've got to be shitting me. Damn! Does he know you know?"

"Yep. I went to his place and confronted him. It's a long story—it's deep, and Rachael is mostly the problem. However, I have a lot going on and I need some help making decisions."

"Did you ever tell Jared about the baby?"

"Nope."

"Are you afraid it may be Leo's or something, or are you not sure which one it belongs to?"

"No way, this is all Jared's. I never let Leo touch me without protection. This is definitely Jared's baby."

"So why the cards? What's the problem?"

"I'm not sure what will happen if I have the baby. It's not only a big responsibility, but a lot of changes will have to be made if I have it. Another thing is me and Jared are so on-again, off-again with getting settled together. Suppose he is messing around or something on the road or goes off again to one of those camps or something? I'm just not sure. And Mr. Leo—oh boy. He loves me to death, so he says. I could excuse him for Rachael, but I don't think I should do it. I have another plan for Rachael, too, and I'm all screwed up and I want to learn to use these cards to guide me."

"Well, I believe you and Jared are going to be stuck together whether you have the baby or not, or learn to read those damn cards or not. I'll make an appointment for the lady to read your cards. She may be able to get all of your questions answered," Sheila said.

"She can't read them every day or night. I want to be able to check on myself."

"Emily, please—don't make me do this. I'm scared. I don't like this."

"Look, let's just try it for a while, and if you get too scared, I'll stop. Let me practice on you. Okay? Remember, the Hyatt *and* a weekend."

Sheila looked at Emily and all that stuff on the table, and then thought about the Hyatt Founders Room and a weekend away from the kids with her husband. She sighed and reluctantly said, "Okay."

Emily lit a white and a purple candle. Then she turned all the lights off. She gathered the cards together and shuffled them, then handed them to Sheila for reshuffle. "Cut them," she ordered.

Sheila cut the cards and looked petrified as Emily read the instructions, grabbed a composition book and a pen to take notes and began placing cards on the table in accordance with what the book said. Once she got the cards placed correctly, Emily began looking up the meanings of each card.

"Okay, your first card is the four of Pentacles which means—let me look it up—okay, it means 'you're turning in a circle and you have reached a deadlock.' " She wrote the information down. "Now, I wonder what that really means—you know what you're supposed to do?" Emily said, reading and trying to figure it out.

Sheila sat there looking at her like she was crazy. "Do you think you can get me out of the fucking 'circle' before I have to go to work at six in the morning?" she asked sarcastically.

"Shut up! You're breaking my concentration," Emily snapped. She continued searching the book for more details on the first card and couldn't figure it out. "Let's skip that one," she said, moving to the next card on the table.

"Okay, now we have the Empress in the number two spot, which means 'don't do anything.' "

"We *aren't* doing anything," Sheila said.

"Look, what I'm trying to tell you, dummy, is that the second position on this card right here says, well, it means 'to fill the matter at hand with life, to bring something new into the world and let it grow.' "

"Sounds like you ought to be having the baby to me. Doesn't your baby have to grow?" Sheila asked.

"Not so fast—we've got other cards to check," said Emily.

"Okay, the next card is the four of Cups in position three," Emily said. "Let's check that out."

Sheila was scared with those candles going, and Emily was getting on her nerves. "What does that card mean, Emily?" she asked, tapping her foot.

"Well, let's see. It tells you something is important. It is an "Instead" card. Hold up, I'm trying to get this. Let's see, the third position means 'instead' and it says in the book here, 'show that you are insulted and cross or pay attention to valuable opportunities despite all other distractions and take time to cure your hangover." Emily wrote that down and said, "Umm, I've got to concentrate more on this one, I don't understand."

"The damn cards are telling the truth because I *am* angry and cross, and it is an 'instead' card and I'd rather be home *instead* of here. I'm about to leave your unable-to-read-tarot-cards ass. And by the way, I don't have a hangover—in case that stuff is pertaining to me," Sheila yelled.

"Look, Sheila, I'm doing the best I can. Hell, I'm no expert on this stuff. Do you want to read the book while I try to figure out the cards and write the stuff down? Do you want to work together?" she snapped at Sheila.

At that point Horace opened the door and walked in. He was shocked to see them both at the table at one fifteen in the morning, and they were stunned to see him home early.

"What are you doing home?" Emily asked.

"I don't feel good and I left work. What the hell are you two doing? Hi, Sheila," Horace said. He started turning on lights.

"Why the hell are you guys sitting in the dark and why the candles? Emily, what the hell is on your head?" he said as he walked over to the table.

A nervous Emily replied, "Umm . . . Horace, we're playing a game."

"What kind of game, with candles?" Then he looked down at the cards on the table.

"You two are in here playing gypsy? Jesus Christ, two damn witches. You'd better stop this shit." He then grabbed all the cards and the book and ran out the back door to the trash can and threw them out. When he came back in, Sheila was laughing hysterically.

"Emily, get that damn scarf off your head and don't you ever bring any of that crazy shit in this house again. Blow those damn candles out!" Horace yelled.

"I was just having a little fun," Emily said, immediately blowing out the candles.

"You can't have that kind of fun in *here*. That shit is creepy and people shouldn't be doing it. I don't like it. I mean it, Emily, don't you let me catch you with that stuff in here again. I'm surprised at you, too, Sheila. What have you done—gone from beating people up to putting spells on them? Don't tell me you're over here trying to put a spell on your dead husband. Damn, that poor man is never going to be able to rest in peace. Or has Leonard pissed you off now? Have both of you gone crazy? I'm going to bed. Don't take those cards out of that trash. I mean it. Don't play with me."

When Horace went upstairs Emily said to Sheila, "Make me an appointment with the lady."

"Okay," said Sheila, still laughing, "and you're still watching the kids an entire weekend *and* taking me to dinner. I showed up and it's not my fault you got busted. I'm going home."

Chapter Twenty-three

Amber

Horace, Amber, Jonita, Renee and Sydni went on their first Caribbean cruise. It was actually Amber's eighteenth birthday present and Horace decided to make it a family affair. They sailed out of Miami, Florida, on Majestic Caribbean Cruise Lines. It was a magnificent ship bound for Puerto Rico, St. Martin and a private island called Labadee, located off the coast of Haiti. The ship had a spa, hair salon, a rock-climbing wall, an all-night pizza joint, a casino and an ice skating rink. They had Broadway shows, bingo and all sorts of activities on board.

Horace had also brought along Amber's best friend from school, Savaun, and paid her way, too. He and Jonita had their own cabin, and the girls stayed alone in a separate cabin.

When the ship docked in St. Martin, they took a tour of the island, and then Jonita found a beautiful bed and breakfast that was on the beach. This delightful place had a giant porch restaurant built onto the property overlooking the turquoise ocean. The food was mouthwatering. They had the manager show them the rooms, and they were absolutely gorgeous, with old-fashioned four-poster beds and wardrobe closets. The beds had sheer white curtains draped around them from top to bottom. They got brochures of the place and planned to return there in the future to stay for a week.

One night back on the ship, Savaun and Amber were in the disco and two guys, Philippe from Trinidad and Victor from Jamaica, who worked on board the ship, began talking and dancing with them. The girls had seen them around the ship, since they were employed as bartenders in one of the lounges. Most of the people on the boat were White, and the only Black people they met, the only people who paid any attention to them, were the Black crew members. They learned all about how these workers came from impoverished countries and were paid a mere fifty dollars a month for working, but received free room and board for their services to the cruise lines. They lived off tips from the passengers and their small salaries. They worked long hours, often double shifts, and worked eight months on board the ship and then got off for six weeks to return to their homelands. It was interesting to the girls to learn all about these working conditions, and many times they felt sorry for the crew members.

One night Victor and Philippe invited them to go to see the observation deck, and they accepted. It was incredibly dark, and there were a lot of other people out there. They got a whiff of marijuana when they entered the deck and noticed another group of people. Amber and her friends got into a private corner and began talking. In about ten minutes a security guard arrived onto the deck. He began shining lights on everyone. They knew he'd probably smell the marijuana and haul those White people off to the ship jail or someplace like that. Even though they weren't doing anything, Victor and Philippe became frightened. Victor took his uniform shirt off and placed it over his head.

"What are you doing that for?" Amber asked.

"Amber, we'll get in trouble if we are caught with you and Savaun. We're not allowed to have anything to do with the guests," he answered.

"Well, we're not doing anything except standing here like everyone else, relax," Savaun said.

Still the two appeared scared to death. A light was then shone on the four of them and a security guard came over. "Get against the wall!" he shouted. Victor and Philippe moved over and leaned against the nearby wall. Savaun and Amber stayed put.

"All of you get against the wall!" he screamed. Savaun and Amber became terrified and obeyed.

"Get out your work passes. Get your crew passes out—all of you!" shouted the guard. Victor and Philippe got their passes out and handed them to one of the officers. The officers looked at Savaun and Amber and said, "I *said* give me your passes."

"What passes?" asked Savaun.

"Your work passes—your ID—get them out right now. You are in big trouble for being out here!"

"We weren't doing anything. How can we be in trouble?" Amber answered.

"Don't play games with me. You know you are not allowed here and you are in big trouble. Get the damn passes out so I can identify you properly when I write you up!" shouted the guard.

"We don't have a pass," said Savaun.

"Oh, so you're traveling around the ship at four o'clock in the morning with no passes? You know you're in deep shit now."

"Why don't you go over there and interrogate those people who are smoking marijuana and leave us alone?" Amber shouted back at him.

He looked across the deck and said, "You four better stay your asses right where you are until I get back."

He walked over to the crowd and they heard him say to all the White people there, "Now I know you have grass and I'm letting you go. You can't smoke grass out here. Okay?"

He then walked back over to them. "Okay, give me the crew passes, girls."

"Look, mister, we don't know what the hell a crew pass is," Savaun said. "And another thing: Why are you yelling and screaming at us and treating us differently than you did those White people who were actually *breaking the law* by using narcotics on your boat? You should be arresting them and not fucking with us innocent Black people. I'm going to report your ass."

"In about an hour, you're not going to have a job, and I'll personally see that you are taken off this boat and sent back to whatever godforsaken country you came from. You got that? Now give me the fucking pass!"

"We have no passes, you asshole," Amber screamed.

"Okay, that's it. I'm running you all in," he said as he snatched Amber by the collar of her blouse and pushed the others off the gate.

They were all taken to an interrogation room on the eighth floor of the ship. He marched them into the office and sat them down. Victor and Philippe were crying and trying to explain that they had done nothing wrong and were begging not to be written up. He then asked Savaun and Amber for their passes again. When they told him again they had none, he grabbed their pocketbooks from them and dumped them out onto a table. He immediately spotted two blue cards. He grabbed them up and stared at them in astonishment. "You two are passengers?"

"Damn right," Amber said. "African American citizens of the United States of America. We are *passengers* who don't *happen* to work for Majestic Caribbean Cruise Lines. You got that, buddy? And as an extra bonus we are traveling with another United States citizen who happens to be an attorney."

Then it was he who was petrified. "Listen, ladies, I apologize. I just figured because you were, well, not Caucasian, well, that you, well, were crew members. You are free to go. Please accept my apology."

"Oh, we are *all* free to go?" Savaun asked sarcastically.

"No, these two are still in trouble because they had no business with you. I have to write them up."

"So they are losing their jobs for walking us onto the deck?" Amber asked.

"I cannot discuss that with you. However, you two can leave."

"Why don't you forget writing them up?" Savaun asked.

"They broke a company rule. You two must leave."

Savaun and Amber left the office and went storming to Horace and Jonita's cabin. It was now close to five in the morning. Horace answered the door and listened to the story. He was horrified. He picked up the phone and called the main desk. He said he wanted the captain of the ship and he wanted the head of security as well as the security guard who detained the kids. They said they had to call him back.

Horace and Jonita got dressed and they all went down to the lobby desk.

"I'm Horace Alston and this is my family."

Jonita cut in. "I'm Jonita Holden, Esquire, an attorney."

"Good morning, everyone, I'm Lorenz Batiste. What can I do for you?" the clerk asked.

"I called about twenty minutes ago. I explained to someone down here that I wanted to speak with higher-ups of Majestic Caribbean because my girls were detained by security personnel about an hour and a half ago," Horace said.

"Just a moment, Mr. Alston. Let me check in the back. You must have spoken with Pedro, who is also on duty."

In a moment Pedro arrived. "Good morning, Mr. Alston. I took your message and I have phoned the people you wish to talk to. I was told they are trying to arrange a meeting in the afternoon."

"You're going to arrange a meeting now, that's what you're going to do. Get them on the phone for me now. And by the way, where are the two young men who escorted my girls onto the observation deck?"

"They are presently unavailable."

"*Make* them available, and give me their names and where I can find them on this ship. I mean I want the location of where they actually *live* on this ship."

"I apologize, sir. I cannot give you that information."

"Let me tell you something, Pedro. You'd better get someone down here to talk to me who *is* allowed to give out information. You people held, searched and scared the hell out of these kids, and someone is going to answer for it. Now, Pedro, it's telephone time—use it," Horace demanded, pointing at the phone.

Pedro called all personnel Horace requested, and then they sat down and waited. In an hour a gentleman appeared who introduced himself as the assistant to the captain, and another man identified as head of security was with him. They explained to Horace and the rest that Victor and Philippe would not be charged or "written up," and that they could not divulge any other information or their last names. They also explained that they couldn't reveal the name of the security officer who detained the girls and that he was "unavailable." The assistant captain explained that Amber and Savaun were assumed to be crew members because they were with crew members in uniforms. He further explained that it was Majestic Caribbean's policy that employees not associate with passengers in any way, shape or form, other than providing a service. Horace listened. He was pissed.

"Is it your 'policy' to merely smack the hands of passengers who smoke marijuana on board your vessels?" asked Jonita.

"No, ma'am."

"Then why weren't those White people hauled off and placed in detention?"

"I honestly cannot say. I have to look into that, ma'am."

"I suggest you do so, sir. And why is it that we cannot have the name of your security officer who held these passengers for being on the observation deck?" Jonita asked.

"Because we need to investigate more, and it's not our policy to give out crew members' names."

"Well, they all have badges, don't they? And I was introduced to you and Pedro and others here, all of whom were not involved. Seems to me we need all parties involved at this meeting," Jonita said.

"Ma'am, we have apologized and promise that the two crew members who escorted your children onto the deck will not get into any trouble and will keep their jobs. Can we just leave it at that?" There was silence as Jonita and Horace studied the strangers sitting in the seats around them.

"We'll leave and file a formal complaint later. This discussion is over. Good morning," Horace said as he motioned for them to leave.

Throughout that day they could not find the guys at their regular workstations. Amber had gotten their cabin telephone numbers and called them. They told her that they had been taken off duty for the remainder of the cruise and were not allowed to talk to any passengers. When they returned home, Jonita filed a formal complaint against the cruise line and they were compensated for being detained by being given another cruise whenever they wanted to take it. Horace and Jonita were still pissed and vowed to take their asses to court.

Things were going really fast for Amber when she returned home. Her prom was in a week and it was being held at the Ritz Carlton Hotel in Center City. Her date was Maxwell Sutherland, another senior at her school, and they were platonic friends. She hadn't been out on a real date with a real guy since Horace got rid of Dante.

She had a beautiful white stretch limo and an absolutely scandalous gown that Peggy Kinard had designed. It was red glitter spandex with a V-neck and formed a small circle at the bottom. She was voted the best dressed at the prom. They had a wonderful time and left there to go bowling and rode around after that in the limo. They ended the night having breakfast at Sheila's favorite spot, the elite Founders Room at the Bellevue Hyatt. Amber made it home a little before noon.

All of her college applications were in and she had been accepted to every college she applied to, which included Dartmouth, Boston University, NYU and Hampton. Amber chose NYU and would be leaving on June first to get a head start by taking summer classes. Her high school graduation was scheduled for June tenth but she would have to return from college in order to attend it. She couldn't celebrate the graduation that afternoon because she had to rush back for classes. It was an exciting time for her.

Horace, Jonita and Amber had been doing so much shopping for her dorm prior to her leaving, and she had a lot of fun doing it with Horace and Jonita. Sydni was very excited for her, too, and had promised she would spend some time with her when she could get leave. She was stationed at Lackland Air Force Base in Texas.

Amber was looking forward to living without any supervision, but was glad that she was a mere hour and a half away from home. She also knew that her friends and family would come to see her because New York was such an exciting place—full of entertainment. She couldn't wait.

"Amber, I don't know how in the world you are going to fit all of these things in that tiny dorm room, and you know we're probably going to have to move you out of here after summer session because they will switch your room," Horace said as he was hauling boxes and suitcases up to the third floor.

"We'll fit the stuff in as best we can. Whatever won't go just won't go. Let's pray they don't switch my room," Amber said.

Everybody was huffing and puffing by the time they got her moved in and Renee was determined she was spending the night. Her roommate had not arrived yet, and thank God the place was air conditioned because it was eighty-two degrees. After they got everything situated and had dinner at Fridays, they returned her to her dorm and left for Philadelphia. Amber thought Horace was going to cry when he drove off.

She felt she was a grown-up now. She had her own checking account and her name on one of Horace's charge cards. She was to be on a budget and have a meal plan. She'd get an allowance of four hundred dollars a month. Horace advised she was not working anywhere until after the first year. She had to concentrate on her schoolwork. He had provided her with every necessity and a few things she just *wanted*. She also had two round-trip train tickets to get home in case she got homesick. She was so lucky.

Her major was cellular molecular biology—doctor stuff, but she was up for the challenge. Amber got so homesick she went home in two weeks for a weekend. She enjoyed seeing her friends who were still at home. She went home two more weekends, calmed down, and became more adjusted to being away from her family and friends. She liked New York and there was plenty to do. She saw a couple of plays on discount days, hit the movies and had a pretty decent roommate, Nyla, who was from Michigan and was majoring in broadcast journalism.

It seemed like the summer flew by. Soon all the kids were at school for fall semester, and she met a lot of people. They went to a few discos on the weekends and hit some interesting restaurants. She was doing really well in her classes. Then it was time to return home for winter break. Amber was looking forward to the holidays and Sydni was coming home, too. They had a great Christmas and New Year's and Amber returned to school in mid-January. Before she could look up, it was time for spring break.

"Hey, Daddy, it's me," Amber said.

"How are you, baby?" he asked.

"I'm doing fine. I love New York."

"Great, what's up?"

"Well, how is everybody? Let me talk to Renee," Amber said. Horace put her on the phone.

"Hey, Renee, what are you doing?" Amber asked.

"I'm working on a puzzle and I went to the painting place and made a butter dish for Emily. I like that place. Wanna take me there when you come home?"

"Okay, I'll do that. How is school?" Amber asked.

"It's okay. I have to go almost every day and the bus comes for me. I like the bus."

"That's good, Renee. Let me talk to Daddy."

"Bye, Amber, I love you."

"I love you, too, and I'll be home in about sixty-five days. You cross them off the calendar. Okay?"

"Okay, Amber. Bye." Horace took the phone from Renee.

"Listen, Daddy, can you send me some money? A few of us girls are going away for spring break in a couple of weeks," Amber asked.

"Where are you going and who are you going with?"

"Well, I told a few of my friends, Millicent, Nyla and Stacia, about that nice place where we had lunch in St. Martin and we decided to go. Can I go?"

"Are anyone's parents going?"

"Nope—just all of us eighteen-year-old adults who can take care of ourselves."

"You're not going."

"Why?"

"Because I said so and I'd like an adult to be there—you know, one over thirty—an old decrepit one with some sense."

"The people who run the hotel are adults."

"Don't be smart, Amber—I'll come through this phone."

"You are so lame. Everybody else's parents are letting them go."

"You're not going out of the country at eighteen without any supervision. That's *that*."

"Well, what am I supposed to do for spring break?"

"Come home or go to Disney World or something. I'll let you go down there, but you're not going out of the country by yourself just yet."

"Will you give me money to go to Disney World?"

"Maybe."

"I have to check it out and see if I can find some friends who want to go there. I'll call you back later, or tomorrow. You make me sick, Daddy. You are too overprotective."

"Too bad. I love you, and call me when you get something else figured out."

"Good-bye," Amber said.

Two days later Amber called Horace back. She explained she had found two friends who wanted to go to Disney World and she needed six hundred dollars.

"Who's going with you?" Horace asked.

"A girl named Janice Tyson who's in my theater class and Lesley Crowe from my biology class."

"Where are you guys staying down there?"

"The Peabody. You know that nice hotel that the ducks go strutting through the lobby twice a day."

"Oh, I remember that place. I like it there and it's safe and it'll be fun for you guys. Those ducks are really cool," Horace said.

Amber could see Horace grinning in approval. "Yeah, it is a beautiful hotel, Daddy, and did you know they have a hotel in Memphis, too?"

"Oh, so you did your homework on the place?" he asked.

"Yep—you know me. I'll need about six hundred dollars for my share of the room and tickets to the parks. I've got about two hundred fifty dollars saved up so I can buy food and junk with that."

"What about the airline tickets?" Horace asked.

"Janice's mom is going to charge all of them on her credit card and let us pay the bill every month."

"That's a good idea and will teach you some responsibility, too. Yeah, I like this trip, baby. I'm not worried at all. Tell Janice's mom I said thanks and I'll send you the money right away. Now what are the dates you are traveling?" he asked.

"I'll be leaving New York on April first and returning to New York on April seventh."

"Okay, baby, I'm going to get out of here and get this money to you. I'm sending an extra hundred dollars. Bring back T-shirts or something for Renee, Sydni, Emily and Jonita."

"Okay, thanks, Daddy, I'm out of here. I have a class in about a half hour."

"Ladies and gentlemen, please fasten your seat belts, and crew, please prepare for landing. The temperature is a fabulous seventy-eight degrees. We'll be touching down in fifteen minutes. The local time is five fifteen."

They went to baggage check and got their luggage. They were in awe of the beauty of St. Martin. They grabbed a cab and headed for the Governor's Palace. Amber was playing tour guide while in the cab. The taxi pulled up at the hotel and they entered the wonderful bed and breakfast that she had first visited with her family. They walked up to the lobby to check in. The bellman came to escort them to their room. As they turned to follow him they walked down the wooden stairs of the old-fashioned porch restaurant. It was breathtaking.

They heard someone call Amber's name and turned around.

"This sure doesn't look like the Peabody in Orlando and I haven't found any ducks since I got here. Dante, you don't look much like Janice or Lesley," Horace coolly said.

Chapter Twenty-four

Purdy

"Hi, Jazz, I'm home," Purdy said into the phone.

"Hey, sweetie pie. Welcome home. I've missed you. You just got back?"

"Yeah, it's been a long trip and I'm glad to be home. What's been going on with you?"

"I've been working like a slave. I have two new clients. One has a fabulous home in Dresher, and the other bought a house at Twentieth and Green that is being totally renovated. I've been swamped. How was the French fry city and Chinatown?"

"Amazing. I had a great time. The only things that bothered me were the long flights, but I'm cool."

"When will I see you? You've gotta be missing me—sleeping alone all those nights," she said.

"Yeah, I've missed you, too. Would you like to meet for dinner tonight?" he asked.

"Sounds terrific—where?"

"The William Penn Inn. Will that do?" he asked.

"It sure will. See you around six thirty?" she said.

"Let's make it seven, and can you make the reservation?" Purdy asked.

"I got it. See ya."

Purdy *was* missing Jazz now, but he knew Pilar was about to blow her mind. He was curious as to how she would react. He'd never seen her with any kids.

He was tired from getting up nights and just wanted to go home, take care of Pilar and get his ass in the bed, but he had to deal with Jazz. It was time.

He looked over at Pilar, sleeping in his office. He sure would be glad when the workers were finished hooking the room up at his office. They had started and were working nights and weekends. A Pergo floor was being put down because he didn't want a carpet that would harbor germs. The painters were starting the next night, and he had a carpenter coming in to put up shelves, racks and built-ins. He wondered if he'd ever get a seventeen-thousand-dollar watch again. He'd already taken fifty grand out of his American Fund account to cover his expenses since the baby's arrival in Philadelphia. The decorator was coming to do her thing in five more days. "Damn," he thought, "kids really do cost a fortune."

He retrieved his appointment calendar and started flipping through the pages. He wanted to have some dates selected because he had to talk to Stefana and he had plans to visit her in about six weeks. He would love to surprise her and take Pilar down to Barbados, but they agreed a long time ago to not making any unexpected visits to each other.

"Hello, miss," he said into the phone.

"Hello, sir. Welcome back to the City of Brotherly Love. How are you? Tell me all about it," Stefana said.

"Hey, baby. I had a dream about you the other night."

"And I take it you're still dreaming?" she asked.

"You got it. What's happening?"

"The usual. Business is a bit slow for some reason."

"So, you're starving and bankrupt?" he asked.

"Almost. You know anybody who needs some diamonds and rubies, or perhaps a few emerald bracelets?"

"Let me check and get back to you on that. I do need a pair of ruby earrings—very tiny, with posts. They're for an infant. And I can use a set of cuff links for my attorney. I want a black stone for the cuff links. Pick some things out and discuss them with me."

Stefana said with a bubbly voice, "You are *soo* generous when you give gifts. I'll check my stock and if I don't have them, I'll get them for you. What's the tab going to be?"

"You can go twelve if you have to."

"They won't be that much. Who are the earrings for?"

"Pilar."

"Whose kid is Pilar?"

"Mine."

"Okay, I'll sit here patiently and wait for you to tell me the next lie or fantasy," she said.

"I'm serious, Stefana. She's my kid."

Stefana stayed silent, knowing he really must have had something deep going on in Philly and she wasn't prepared for that. She was uncomfortable because he hadn't shared the relationship with her, or the pregnancy.

"Wanna talk about this?" he asked.

"Only if you're comfortable doing so. You know me—I don't make waves, pry or ask too many questions," she nonchalantly replied.

"Come on, Stefana, relax."

"Okay, let's have it," she said coolly.

"While I was away I adopted an infant. She's Chinese, almost five weeks old. I brought her back with me. She is beautiful, healthy, adorable, keeps me up all night and is spending every dime I have. Her name is Pilar Miriam Remington and I am in love with her. I'm also the best damn daddy you'll ever meet. In fact, I change diapers, give baths and bring her to work with me every day. How do you like that?"

Stefana was thrilled and screeched, "I love that! I'm shocked! I'm impressed, and I can't wait to meet her. When can I come back?"

"You just left here—remember? I'm coming *there* with Pilar. Go get your schedule to check your buying trips."

Stefana ran for her book and sat down to get comfortable. "Okay—what do you have?" she asked.

"Well, I'm looking and you know I just got back here. I have to stay a while because I'm having a playroom done here at the office and I'm working on a staff project. I can't get there for at least a month. Okay—so now we're going into November."

She said, "I'm in California for the week of Thanksgiving, got a buying trip in Italy the first week in November. Can you do November tenth?"

Purdy flipped his pages. "No, Dr. Gelding is away that week. I can do the seventeenth through the twenty-second."

"Deal," said Stefana.

"Now we have to talk because I can't haul all my crap down there. I'll need a playpen, and find a stroller so I don't have to bring mine. I'll have everything else. We'll talk about it all another time."

"Okay, Mr. Mom. I'll see you on the seventeenth and I'll talk to you soon. You have a nanny, I presume?"

"She starts in two days—thank God. I've had someone helping me out. I'm handling things."

"Okay. Know what else, Purdy?"

"What?"

"The rubies are on me."

"That's sweet and extremely generous. I'll give you all the details later. I've got patients to see."

"Adios, man."

"See ya," he said.

"Hi, Mrs. Charleston, this is Dr. Remington. I'm calling back to let you know that I'll definitely need you tonight to watch my daughter. Can you be there at five thirty?"

"That's fine. I'll see you then," she answered.

"Okay, I should be back by ten o'clock and you've got the option of sleeping over or driving home." They hung up.

Purdy opened the large manila envelope that he'd received from the agency that was doing the background checks on his employees and retrieved the blank forms. He looked them over and buzzed Jillian, telling her to come to his office for them and distribute them to all employees and to keep one for herself. He told her they were to be completed within two days and returned to him.

Jillian picked them up and immediately passed them out to personnel, leaving notes in each department for staff members who had not arrived or were off to report to her office for their forms.

Purdy went through his messages and had one from the organization that trained the dogs. They had a trainer and wanted Purdy to call. He did so and arranged to meet with the trainer over the upcoming weekend at his home. Everything was rolling. He got through the day and left the office at four thirty headed for home.

*   *   *

"Good evening, Mrs. Charleston, I'm glad to see you," Purdy said as she walked in the door. He took her coat, hung it up and led her into the kitchen where Pilar was in her infant seat on top of the huge island counter. "I'd like you to meet Pilar Miriam Remington," he said, beaming with pride. Mrs. Charleston smiled with delight as she gazed at Pilar and lifted her out of her seat.

"My, my, my, she is a pretty thing, and this outfit is adorable. You must be in heaven with her."

"Indeed I am. Let me show you around quickly. I wrote down a lot of instructions to help you along. I also indicated on the notes where I'll be having dinner and the phone number in case there is a problem. She had a bottle at four o'clock and will probably want another one between seven thirty and eight."

"Okay," she said.

"Now let's take a tour of the house quickly. Of course, I'll show you her room and where all her things are. She gets a bath at night before bedtime and all her bottles are ready-to-feed Enfamil. She drinks her milk warm. Be sure she burps."

Mrs. Charleston smiled and said, "Dr. Remington, I raised four kids and each of them is as healthy as a horse. Relax."

Purdy had a worried look on his face. "I'm sorry, Mrs. Charleston, but this whole thing is new to me and I'm still a bit nervous about it all. Don't mind me—just try to put up with an inexperienced doting father."

"You'll be fine and *we'll* be fine," she replied.

They quickly got through the house tour. He stopped to make a call to Tony's office to tell him that the following Thursday at seven would be great for a visit with his family to meet Pilar. He then dashed out to make his way to the restaurant. That would be a forty-minute drive at least, but an awesome place with great food.

Jazz was seated in the lobby when he arrived. She looked stunning in a crème-colored suit and coral accessories. Her gorgeous hair was in an old-lady bun with gold barrettes around it. As soon as he saw her hair, it reminded him that he had to get some barrettes for Pilar.

"Good evening, Miss Fleming."

"Good evening, Dr. Remington." He squeezed her tightly and kissed her.

"Missed me, huh?" she whispered in his ear before the embrace ended.

"Yep, baby, I missed you. Come on, let's have dinner," he said as they approached the hostess to request their table.

"So, who's going to go first?" Purdy asked after they ordered a bottle of wine.

"You go first. I told you my news on the phone—two new clients, remember?"

"Yes, congratulations, baby. How are they to work with?"

"Well, the one in Dresher is a neurotic pain in the ass, but the Green Street one is pretty cool and will let me do my thing. I also negotiated a great fee and am excited about Green Street because I can really strut my stuff there and get wild. The guy is intrigued with me. Okay—tell me all about your trip."

Purdy explained the face-painting expedition and Jazz lapped that all up, wishing she were there. She loved the fact that he'd done the gondola thing and laughed out loud when he told her how much chocolate he bought and ate in Paris. The wine finally arrived and they had looked over the menu and ordered.

"Jazz, I have to talk to you about something that is very important," he said. She looked up at him, the gay expression draining from her face as she expected trouble. She felt the trouble had a lot to do with what she found on the chocolate-colored sheets before he left for New York.

"What's up? Am I about to be fired?" she asked.

Purdy was taken aback that she thought that and said, "No. I need to let you know that I have done the totally unexpected. I adopted a child while I was away."

She gasped. "What! A baby! You've gotta be kidding. When did you decide this? Where is it? Is it a girl or a boy? How old is it? How did you get all that done? Did you go away just to do that and didn't tell me?"

"Calm down, Jazz," he said as she gulped her wine down and then looked at him like he was crazy.

"Talk to me, Dr. Spock," she demanded.

"Listen, Jazz, I'm fifty-two years old and my life is basically pretty empty. For the past couple of months I'd been thinking about adopting a child. I hadn't made up my mind; however, when the situation presented itself to me in China—I know this sounds crazy—but I went for it. I'm extremely happy with my daughter. She is a month old and I'm absolutely crazy about her. I brought her back here with me, and she is at home in her room. Her name is Pilar Miriam Remington."

Jazz remained silent, overwhelmed with the news. "She's at home with *whom*?"

"A friend of mine is babysitting."

"Who? What friend?" a suspicious Jazz asked.

"An older woman whom I've known for years."

"Older than *me* or *you*? Is it someone you used to date or someone you run around with now—when you're not with me?"

"No." Purdy knew the shit was on. It was coming. "Jazz, Mrs. Charleston is slightly older than me. She and I have never dated."

Jazz didn't believe him. The entire conversation was disturbing to her as well. It was all going entirely too fast for her. This was *soo* out of the ordinary for Purdy Remington, and she couldn't believe what she was hearing. She was mixed up, overwhelmed, confused and frightened everything would end with them. She was immediately jealous and insecure and she pondered how this thing would play out in their relationship. The waiter brought their entrees, but she couldn't touch her food.

"How do you plan to take care of this child and run your practice and your trips? You can't do it all alone. I'm going to have to move in there before it is all over with," she suggested, to get a feel of what his plans were and if she'd be included in the raising of the baby.

When she made that statement, he knew he had to talk fast because she would definitely not be moving in with him. He explained all the plans he'd made at the office and with an agency for a live-in nanny. She listened carefully and each word he said made her more insecure about their relationship. She hadn't had much time with him prior to all this, and she knew what little she had would be cut down. She was worried.

"Tell me something, Purdy. Just where do I fit into this?"

"I plan for us to keep seeing each other, and I hope you understand that this is a very serious commitment for me."

"The commitment to me or to Pilar?" she asked.

He paused, knowing a fight was about to begin. "The commitment to the baby is what I was speaking about. I plan, if you're up for my new lifestyle and will have me, to continue to date you. You know I'm crazy about you, and nothing has changed with that. I'll just have to allocate my time between you, Pilar, my practice and my traveling. I've been honest with you about what kind of man I am. I think I've been fair and I've treated you well. You knew all along I had no plans of marriage for us. I enjoy things the way they are with you, but you and I know we have our differences and how we go at it most of the time. However, I do enjoy you, I have a lot of fun the majority of time and I want us to continue seeing each other. What do you want to do about this situation? Do you want to hang or walk?"

She was thinking, and stirring her wine with her finger. He waited for her to respond.

"I need to think about all of this. This shit is too much for me tonight. Were you planning to have me back at the house tonight? When had you planned to introduce me to your daughter?"

"Mrs. Charleston is there and I don't know if she is sleeping over or going home. Tonight may not be a good night for you to be there if she's sleeping there."

"Get up and go to the phone and call your house to see what her plans are," she ordered.

He did so and came back to the table. "She's leaving when I come home."

"So, what do you want me to do? Do you want me there or not?"

He looked at her and he knew he wanted her. He imagined how all of this had to be making her crazy—hell, it was making him crazy. He'd actually shocked *himself* adopting Pilar. He picked up her hand, kissed it and said, "Miss Fleming, would you do me the honor of accompanying me home, meeting my new daughter and spending the night with me?"

She smiled and said, "Yes, Dr. Remington."

"Hi, Mrs. Charleston, I'm back," Purdy said as he and Jazz entered the house.

"Hi, Dr. Remington."

"Mrs. Charleston, let me introduce you to a friend of mine, Maritza Fleming."

"I'm pleased to meet you, Miss Fleming," Lola Charleston said as she extended her hand to Maritza.

"It's my pleasure," Maritza smiled and said, relieved that she was a real "older" woman.

"How did things work out with you and my little princess?" Purdy asked.

"Just fine. She is something else and so beautiful. She's also actually a very good little girl. She does like music—just like you said in your note to me. She's asleep in her room. She went out like a light a little before nine so she'll probably be up for a feeding between twelve thirty and one."

As they were talking, Jazz was surveying the place and was surprised to see all the baby gear around and so neatly arranged. Purdy sure appeared to be organized with this thing, she thought. She was dying to see Pilar and headed up the stairs.

"Wait, Jazz, let me take you up. Just have a seat, sweetie, while I finish up with Mrs. Charleston."

Maritza was pissed. She didn't like the fact that already she had no say-so. She walked back to the living room frostily and sat on the couch.

"So, Mrs. Charleston, do you have anything else to tell me about tonight, and can I depend on you to help in a pinch again?"

"You certainly can. I'd like to talk to you about that tomorrow if you get a chance. I have a suggestion."

"Okay, before you leave, I just want to make sure she drank at least the four ounces of her bottle. And you did remember to place the soiled diapers in the trash bin on the deck off the kitchen, didn't you?"

"Pilar drank four full ounces, burped like a pig, and the diapers are outside."

"Did she have a bowel movement?" he asked.

"No. I did give her a bath and lotioned and powdered her down. She's also got Vaseline on her little heinie."

Purdy's face showed relief and satisfaction. "Thanks for a job well done, and here's something for your trouble. I'll give you a call from my office tomorrow."

"Good night, Dr. Remington, and good night, Miss Fleming," she said as she walked out the door.

Purdy followed her to her car where she turned and said, "I want to be her nanny and that's why I wanted you to call me. I love her."

Purdy smiled and hugged her. "Let's talk about it tomorrow. Drive safely," he said.

"Okay, Miss Fleming, are you ready to meet the little lady who runs the house?" he said as he entered the living room.

"I can't wait," she said as she headed toward him. He led her up the stairs and into Pilar's bedroom. He turned on the night-light, which was exquisite—all white, with a beautiful shade with tiny pink pinpoint roses on it, and small ballerinas circling the round base. He took Jazz's hand and whispered for her to be quiet and led her to the cradle. Jazz was speechless, looking down at the sleeping beauty with the gorgeous brown hair. "Purdy, she is something else. I want to hold her. She looks so soft. Congratulations, Daddy."

"Thanks, and I tell you, she is the love of my life—but don't wake her up, baby. I'm trying to keep her on a schedule, and she doesn't always go right to sleep when she wakes up in the middle of the night."

"Her room is gorgeous already. You put this all together in a day?"

Purdy glanced around and admired the good work of Andrea. "No, not exactly. We've been home four days. I didn't have time to talk to people. I had too much to do. I've really been totally overwhelmed."

"You mean you've been home *four* days and I'm just getting here?"

Purdy evaded that question and said, "Let's get out of here, Jazz, before Pilar wakes up." He gently kissed the baby and they headed for his bedroom.

"Jazz, please don't start up about anything. I've been running around like a chicken with its head cut off for almost three weeks. Give me a break. I can't handle it tonight. Get your stuff off and get in this bed before she wakes up."

He then made sure his monitor was turned on so he'd hear Pilar and set the alarms in the house, which included motion detectors. Jazz eyeballed his every move and began to feel she was not going to be able to handle fitting into this thing. She made love distractedly and fell asleep in his arms.

At twenty minutes to one in the morning Pilar started yelling her head off. Purdy jumped up and went to her room. He scooped her up, grabbed her diaper bag and headed for the kitchen. He placed her bottle in the bottle warmer and proceeded to the living room. He put the Kenny G tape in the stereo and changed Pilar's diaper. By this time Maritza was standing in the living room watching.

"Do me a favor, Jazz, and grab her bottle out of the warmer in the kitchen?" he said.

She went for it, and when she sat it down on the coffee table she said, "You should give her the formula room temperature. Also, that music may make her stay up longer. Maybe you shouldn't have the music on."

Purdy shot a disapproving look and said, "Thanks for the advice, but I think warm milk is better and Pilar loves Kenny G."

Maritza began looking through the tapes and abruptly stopped. "Can I feed her?"

"Sure you can, come on over."

She took the baby from him, cradling her in her arms, and then placed the bottle in her mouth. Maritza was in awe of her beauty and her tiny soft body.

"Exactly how and from whom did you get her?" she asked.

He told her the story, and she couldn't believe it or the fact that he was able to effectuate the whole thing in such a short amount of time. He never discussed the financial end of it with her, as he felt that was confidential.

"So she is really yours, signed, sealed, delivered and untouchable?" she asked.

"Yes, Jazz, she's all mine."

Purdy was watching them like a hawk from the love seat on the other side of the room. Maritza was enjoying feeding Pilar and wished she were closer to them both.

"Jazz, when she gets through two ounces, try to burp her. Is she there yet?"

Maritza checked the bottle and then placed Pilar on her chest and gently patted her back. Pilar let out a burp and Maritza continued the feeding.

Purdy continued to watch. He missed feeding his daughter. "Let me take her. I haven't spent any time with her all night," he said.

"You have her all the time—let me feed her."

"I miss her, give her to me."

"You are so selfish. Come on over and get her. You make me sick," she said.

Purdy took Pilar, and Maritza got up and started checking the place out. She went to the basement, inspected the kitchen deck and then went back upstairs to Pilar's room, investigating and looking around in her closet to check her wardrobe out. "He must have spent a fortune already and there's no furniture yet," she thought. She went into his bedroom and peeked in his drawers for additional things and then advanced to the Pac-Man playroom, which was filled with additional baby stuff. She shook her head. By the time she returned to the living room, Purdy was dozing off and Pilar was on his chest as quiet as a mouse. She patted him gently and removed the baby from his arms. "Let's go upstairs," she whispered.

She placed Pilar in her cradle as Purdy supervised and then they returned to bed, had sex again and passed out. At six thirty Pilar was crying and Maritza rushed to get home to get ready for work. As she left, she glanced at Daddy, who was doing his thing again with his daughter, and said, waving good-bye, "I'll talk to you later."

As soon as Purdy put Pilar down in his office, it was temperature-taking time. It was a riot, with all the people and all those thermometers, and employees were laughing, joking and complaining. By two in the afternoon three people had come to Purdy's office and asked to be laid off before filling out their background check applications. He surmised they all had a checkered past and was relieved they made the decision to leave. He assured them he'd sign for them to get unemployment.

At four o'clock he got a call from the agency regarding the dog trainer and was informed the dog was coming in two days. He called Mrs. Charleston and after speaking with her at length, he hired her to take care of Pilar. She'd be moving in in two days and also agreed to come to the office two days a week for half a day. He called the agency and cancelled the nanny, but told them not to be surprised if he called for help in case Mrs. Charleston was ill or needed time off.

As he was about to leave the office Jazz called, saying she wanted to spend the night. He declined and she argued. He stood firm on his decision and she informed him he was selfish, thoughtless and mean and she wasn't speaking to him until he found a way to make her happy.

He got his gear and his baby together and they headed for the car dealership. He had to purchase a Jeep, a minivan, or something. He was definitely buying a vehicle that night. He'd make arrangements to have the car delivered to his house the next day. His Ferrari was too small for everyday use, but he did have a car seat in it for when he and Pilar went cruising.

Three weeks had flown by and things were working out great. Pilar's room at the office was completed and splendid, staff was complying with everything, Pilar was gaining weight and her buddies from Children's Hospital had been coming for a week. He'd found a three-month-old girl, Margot, and a four-and-a-half-month-old boy, Ian. He and Pilar would be leaving in four weeks for Barbados. Andrea had nabbed four employees who were on heavy antidepressants and nerve medications.

Jade came up with two red alerts who were gently dismissed and she was still working on her project. Pilar was intrigued with the new gorgeous blonde Daddy had, Bailey, a nine-week golden retriever. Now that he had the trainer living with him, every room in Purdy's house was occupied. Purdy would be happy when the dog trainer had Bailey completely trained and could leave the house, freeing up a room. The arrangement would then be that the trainer would come at five thirty in the morning, feed and walk the dog, and then Bailey could come to the office with Pilar and Purdy and stay the day. Then he'd have staff walk Bailey a couple of times during the day. Purdy could feed him at night when they returned home and he and Mrs. Charleston could take turns walking Bailey each night. He had it all figured out, but estimated it would take at least four to six months to get Bailey trained. He was positive he would lose employees who would probably quit when they inherited dog duties. He also noticed many people on his staff actually seemed happy with their new duties and having the kids and the dog around.

Stefana was checking with him a couple of times a week for updates on how things were going, and Maritza's moods fluctuated. Many times during the days she would come up to the office unexpectedly and play with Pilar in her room, pleasantly asking questions of the staff, and sometimes she would bring a toy or two. She had requested several times if she could take Pilar out for a day and he always declined. Because Maritza was so flighty and had so many wacko friends, he didn't trust her out in the world with his daughter. She had spent a few more nights with them at his house and seemed to enjoy Pilar.

Four weeks finally passed and Purdy was packing for Barbados. They were leaving the next morning and he was elated. Stefana was also very happy they were coming. They arrived in Barbados and she met them at the airport and actually jumped up and down when she saw them. She immediately took Pilar from his arms when they got to her. They sped to her house. She had supplies all over the place, and a gorgeous pair of ruby earrings.

"When are you getting her ears pierced?" she asked.

"Pretty soon, probably after Christmas. I don't want her enduring any pain throughout the holidays."

Stefana was thoroughly impressed by his devotion and love for the child and the fact that he was so organized and on top of things. She admired him for taking fatherhood on. The second night of their visit, Stefana took them both out for an early dinner and they returned to her beachfront house, which was adjacent to her shop, at seven thirty p.m. When she opened her door, her house was filled with business associates, neighbors and friends, and they all shouted, "Surprise!" There were fifty-four people inside bearing gifts, as they had all been invited to Purdy's surprise baby shower. Stefana's favorite restaurant took care of the food and sent a staff to wait on them. It was a superb occasion and, because Stefana was so well liked and gave a lot of business to the locals, they presented her dear friend with an array of gifts, many of which Stefana and Purdy decided to leave in Barbados so he wouldn't have to haul so many things down for upcoming trips. He received everything from washcloths to furniture.

They had a fantastic visit and she enjoyed showing them off to her friends and the locals in Barbados. She was truly proud of her man. The next seven days flew by and she actually hated to see them leave.

"You call me soon and take care of my girl," she said as she kissed them both good-bye. "I'll be sending the things you want to take back from the shower in a couple of days. I'll have them delivered to the house."

"Thanks for everything, baby, and we'll try to get together in February. I'm sure Tony will call you loving the cuff links, too."

Two days after he arrived back, he and Maritza had dinner together and she confessed to him she was in love with him and wanted him to think about them hooking up permanently. This turned into a long conversation of her offering to help raise Pilar and calming down with her riffraff friends. She was sincere and he was appreciative, but explained again that because of their age differences and personalities he didn't think it would work out. He was also honest to the point of telling her that he actually just wanted it to be him and Pilar. He wasn't looking for a mom for her and he let Maritza know that.

She was not only disappointed—she was heartbroken and her ego was crushed. She was so upset she threatened to end the relationship for good. She told him she was going to think about it—but she did accompany him home and spend the night with him.

When they got to his house, Purdy quickly took Bailey out for a walk and Maritza began looking around. In Pilar's dresser drawer she found an envelope, which contained pictures of the baby. They were great shots and she began going though them. She then came to many pictures of Purdy and Pilar with an attractive blonde. There were photos of Pilar and the woman alone, Purdy and the blonde alone, the three of them on the beach, in a boat and in restaurants. There were pictures of the woman feeding Pilar in a kitchen and shots of her bathing the baby. She also came across the pictures of the baby shower showing all the gifts and people who attended. As she flipped through the photos she noticed one of the three of them in front of a shop. The bright red awning on the business had in bold white letters, STEFANA'S OF BARBADOS. Maritza was outdone! Purdy had himself a Chinese baby and a White woman! Damn!

Chapter Twenty-five

Emily and Jared

*I*t was a beautiful boat and the Knightcaps were jamming, singing all their hit tunes to the passengers on board for the celebration of the wealthy Celeste and Charlie Adlam's fifth wedding anniversary. Just as they broke, a fierce jolt sent everything and everyone flying. A second crash into the boat occurred, capsizing it.

Jared was in the waters of the Atlantic Ocean, off Myrtle Beach, South Carolina, swimming, screaming and terrified. He looked for the Knightcaps and spotted Lee and Damon but could not find Rodney or Kelly. The seawater was going down his throat and he was trying to get to the boat to hold on for his life. He tried to yell to Lee and Damon, but the waves kept overpowering him. Passengers and crew were everywhere in the water. Jared felt himself being pulled down into the water and he wondered if his brother had already drowned. A small shark approached and a school of fish surrounded him. They all had him cornered. He tried to swim away, but he couldn't. He looked around and fish were everywhere. The shark zoomed in to bite him. Jared closed his eyes and screamed. He kept yelling for help.

"Jared!" Connie screamed. "What's the matter? You're having a nightmare. Wake up, boy." Jared was shaking like a leaf.

"Oh man, oh Mom, this was a real nightmare," he said, holding his head in his hands.

"What the heck were you dreaming about?" Connie asked.

"All these fish were around me. All these fish had me and a shark was getting ready to bite me."

Connie stared at Jared. "Fish, huh?"

"Yeah, we were performing on a boat and it overturned, Mom."

"Jared, do you have to work on a boat? Is anything like that really booked?"

"Yeah, in about three months." She stared at him.

"Well, I know I don't have to tell you what to do about that gig, you can figure that one out pretty easy. Somebody is pregnant. When you dream about fish, a baby is on the way somewhere. Better give Emily a call or look at her real good next time you see her. If you've been in- volved in any other extracurricular activities—and you know what I mean—you might want to check with those young ladies, too. I'm also going to say something to your brother and Lee when they get their butts back here from God knows where they are, because *somebody* is pregnant. Fish don't swim around in dreams for nothing, especially in Black peoples' houses." Connie then walked out of the room and went back to bed.

Emily picked up a grinning Oscar on Sunday and drove straight to Rachael's. Oscar observed the property as they rolled into the driveway and could not believe his eyes. "Emily, you're introducing me to a rich woman!" he exclaimed.

"Well, she's not exactly rich, but she can hold her own," Emily an- swered.

They rang the doorbell, and a smiling and dressed-up Rachael an- swered. "Come right in." She hugged Emily and shook Oscar's hand as she sized him up for a moment. The three went into the living room and sat down and Rachael offered iced tea. They accepted. While she was preparing it, Oscar looked around and gave Emily a thumbs-up. Emily smiled as Rachael returned.

"Rachael, as I told you, Oscar is a dear friend of mine and is in the process of moving. He's currently living in North Philadelphia. He is Renee's grandfather," Emily said.

"Oscar, tell me some things about yourself," Rachael said.

"Well, I work in Upper Darby at a gas station and have been there over thirty years. I work six days a week, and I like the job and the peo- ple I work with. I'm there during the day and am home around six thirty in the evenings. I'm off every Sunday. I have a wife and I'm leaving her because she's not too honest, not too much fun, and to be truthful, I've been miserable with her for a long time. I'm looking for a place now and spoke to someone last week about renting a room not far from where I work. Tell me some things about you," he said.

"I was married fifty-two years and my husband died five months ago of cancer. I live here alone. I have three children and they are scattered in New York, New Jersey and upstate Pennsylvania. I like going out to dinner, running around with Emily when she can find the time for me, and I love the theater and reading. I joined a bereavement support group to help me with my depression. To be honest, I really want to get into a relationship with a gentleman who likes to have fun and wants to have a close association with a woman."

Oscar was impressed. "I've never been to the theater, I might like that. I don't drive because I can't get a driver's license. I can't read or write. Does that bother you?"

"It bothers me if you don't want to learn. I can teach you," she said.

"Well, you see me sitting here and I want to know what you think. Do you think you'd want to spend some time with me? I'd like to learn to read and write, too."

"Would you like to go out for coffee sometime?" she asked.

Oscar smiled. "I'd like that just fine, Rachael."

"Okay, how do we communicate? You seem to be still living at home with your wife," she said.

"Well, I have a card from my service station. You can call me there. Maybe one night after work we can get together, or I can see you next Sunday," he offered, handing her the business card.

"For our first date, we'll meet somewhere like downtown. I can take the train there. I have your card and I'll call you soon and we'll pick a place not hard for either of us to find. Does that sound okay?"

He took another swig of his tea and said, "That sounds fine."

They all then talked a little about her grandchildren, and she showed him pictures of them. He bragged about Renee, Sidney and Amber. They seemed to be hitting it off well, Emily thought.

Emily stood up to leave and told Oscar it was time to go because she had to meet Jared. Rachael said, "You know, Emily, if Oscar doesn't have plans today, why don't you leave him here? We can go up to Jenkintown on the bus and look around and also pick up some books from Barnes and Noble that I can use to start teaching him to read. I can show him how to get the bus back to Philadelphia." Oscar looked at Emily for approval.

"Have a great time, guys, I'm out of here," Emily said, not knowing if Rachael would immediately throw Oscar into her bed.

"All right, Mom, Emily will be here soon. Are you okay? Do you need anything? We're going down to Atlantic City to play the slots. Are you sure you don't want to come?" Jared yelled down to Connie, who was watching TV in the living room.

"I'm staying home—you guys go on and have fun." In ten minutes Emily arrived. When she walked in, Connie got up and hugged her, trying to notice during the hug if Emily felt "fat." Connie was definitely suspicious.

"Emily, baby, how are you doing? Have you been feeling okay? Getting along all right?"

"Yes, I've been fine, Connie. What about you?"

"I'm doing the best I can. I still want a job. I'm bored. Didn't I tell you that the last time I saw you?"

Emily laughed. "Yes, you did and I haven't found you anything yet. I'll get to it. Where is everybody?"

"Your boyfriend is upstairs getting ready, Rodney is in Boston with somebody he met and Lee left out of here telling me he was going to New York and would be back tomorrow night. Are you hungry?"

"What do you have, Connie?"

Connie thought to herself, "Hungry—that's a sure sign of pregnancy."

"Come on in the kitchen so you can raid the refrigerator," Connie said, grabbing Emily by the hand. Emily made herself a roast beef and cheese sandwich and put a couple of spoonfuls of potato salad in a bowl.

"Don't you want more food than that? Put some more potato salad in that bowl."

"Come on, Connie, I'm not starving to death. This is enough. Jared and I will get something down the shore."

"Okay, just don't get on the road hungry," Connie said, staring at Emily's stomach.

Jared entered the kitchen and kissed Emily. "Are you ready to win the jackpot, baby?"

Emily shot him a smile and said, "Certainly, Mr. Wells."

"Then let's get out of here. Bring your food and eat in the car."

"No, give me a few minutes with this—then we'll leave," Emily said, sitting down at the kitchen table.

Jared and Connie went back to the living room. When Jared sat down, Connie whispered and pointed. "She's in there eating—that's what they do." She then pointed to her own stomach.

Jared smiled and flagged her off, whispering, "You are *sooo* crazy, Mom."

On the ride down, Emily and Jared discussed the group's schedule and chitchatted about minor things. They finally arrived, and Emily lost all her money and some of Jared's. They went to an early show at Caesar's. They got a room and made passionate love. Jared noticed that Emily was either absolutely on top of her sex game or missed him, but in any case the sex was incredibly good.

On the following Wednesday evening at four o'clock Emily was sitting in front of Leah, the psychic and tarot card reader, at her home in New Jersey having her cards read. "Okay, Emily, here we go," Leah said as she placed the cards on the table after Emily shuffled and cut them.

"Let's go," a curious and nervous Emily said.

"The five of Wands here is reversed in the twelfth house, which means 'secrets' and 'self-undoing.' I see a lot of upheaval in your life. Your life has never been stable, and that has caused much unrest for you. I also see here with the Knight of Pentacles that you have a lot of skills and can be dependable and skillful at work even though things are chaotic around you. You'll *always* be able to land on your feet. Knights signify change, movement and opportunity. In your first House is the six of Cups, which signifies your *goals* in life. What that tells me with the two cards is that you really are still clinging to the past on things and relationships. I see six months from now you could find yourself wanting to retreat alone—

being away from people. I also see you seeking answers about who you are and what you want in life, and maybe you keep looking back in the past and maybe that's *not* where you want to go. I see there is definitely a conflict financially. I don't know how you are doing—looks like your financial situation will change in a couple of months. I see a job coming for you with more work than you had before. The eight of Wands is the card here, which signifies 'good news soon' related to work, and it falls in the sixth house, which rules health and work. I see too in the fifth house of children, there is indecision here. I have your moon in the fifth house, which means you have to make a decision with regards to children, and it looks like your plans for this are on hold. As far as your own house—it looks like a lot of decisions regarding your home and family have to be made. Don't procrastinate. The Page of Cups card has appeared, which indicates a proposal for marriage or a pregnancy. There is a procrastination surrounding how this can affect your life. I see in the seventh house, which rules partnership, the Knight of Wands. You have a lot of Knights cards. There are four up here, which signify major changes in your life. You are particularly upset about a man. He is a very spontaneous, ardent and passionate man and he is an adventurer. He does a lot of traveling. He is an air and creative sign. I see there is a lot of stress, upsets and sleepless nights about him. I see another person here—you see, two people are coming up. One is more secure and stable. He is a lot more practical and reliable and he comes up as the King of Pentacles. I see right now, though, that there is discord between you and him, and you feel very insecure about him. The four of Pentacles reversed here crosses over his card, demonstrating your insecurity about him. I feel like what's happening is you haven't focused on goals and the things *you* wanted, and that's causing problems for you. I see, too, in the near future, that you may cling to the past again—but then I also see that you're going to have an epiphany, which really is a realization that you can't go on like this anymore. I also see that you have to learn to take care of your own burdens and not let other people dump on you. You must be very assertive and aggressive about this. These two cards relating to this are my Native American cards, which are your spiritual lesson. One of the challenges I see for you is to be aware of the new messages coming in that speak of having new projects and goals you want to pursue and not let indecision and negative influence stop you. This shows me in the cards combined of Page of Wands and the five of Swords (reversed) as well as the two of Swords (reversed). When a card is reversed it means a delay or a block in that particular card's meaning. I see a celebration around you and maybe an upcoming wedding or a large party or gathering. I also see in this Star card, which has come up, that you should not let go of your dreams. Continue to pursue them. You are a very psychic and intuitive person, which is signified by the High Priestess card. Even though things are dark right now, you are moving into a much happier time. Things aren't as bad as you think. Stand your ground and push for what you want because the seven of Wands card is here for you. I see a birth of a child that will make you very happy. I also see fraternal twins—yes, a boy and a girl are coming. Do you have any questions, Emily?" asked Leah.

Emily sat motionless, as her brain was exhausted from trying to keep up with Leah and she was intrigued with all the news. She was stunned that this woman knew so very much about her—or that the cards turned it all up right in front of her face. Twins? Jesus Christ. Discord—that was damn sure Leo's ass on that table. Also, Jared's problems or her protection of him often felt like "dump" stuff. And people dumping on her? She believed that was Rachael Feiner, too, because she called Emily every other day moaning and crying about being lonely and pissed because she couldn't get her "companion" to come around.

Emily paid Leah forty dollars and said, "I don't have any questions and I have to go home and get my life together. You are an excellent reader and I'll thank Sheila for sending me to you and will pass some of your cards around."

Over the next seventeen days, Emily listened to the reading and contemplated what to do. Leo had called her four times and she wouldn't see him. She never told Jared or Connie about her pregnancy.

"Hey, baby, I have a meeting in New York tomorrow afternoon. Can you go up with me to keep me company? We have to leave here at nine in the morning and I plan to come back home after that. You game?" Jared asked Emily.

"Yeah, I can swing it. We've just got to be back here in time for Horace to go to work. Yeah, I'd better go because I have to babysit all weekend next weekend for Sheila and Leonard. Okay, I'll go. Are we taking the train?"

"Yep. We have to be on the 9:40 train. My meeting is at one o'clock. We'll have lunch at Tennessee Mountain before my meeting. Okay—I'll see you at the train station. Bye," Jared said.

They played Uno on the train up there and then while they were having lunch at her favorite restaurant, Jared looked at Emily, whose fingers were full of barbecue sauce, and said, "You're a mess, you'll really have to clean up before we get to the meeting. You are one rib-eating child."

"You know I love these things, Jared. I'm so glad you brought me here," she said, licking her fingers.

Jared looked at his watch and said, "Hurry up, Emily."

"Okay, I'm done," she said, putting the last bone down. "Let me run into the ladies' room and clean up and then we'll leave." Jared also dashed into the men's room to wash his hands. When they met back at the table the waiter brought the check. Jared looked at Emily and said, "Now, you don't smell like barbecue sauce, do you?"

"No, I don't, they've got this great lemon soap in the ladies' room. Smell it." She put her hand under his nose.

"Umm, does smell good." He kissed her hand. With his other hand, he immediately placed a glittering diamond ring on her finger and abruptly said, "Marry me."

Emily was floored. The ring was glistening and Jared was smiling. She started thinking about what the card reader said and was amazed. She stood up and bent over and kissed him. "Yes, Jared, I will marry you. Now, let's pay the check so you're not late for your meeting."

"You are my meeting," he said, smiling.

"You tricked me! You are *soo* clever. You're something else." By then she was in his lap with her tongue down his throat. After the kiss ended, he said, "So, when do you want to tie the knot?"

"Well, you know we have to wait a while because you have to get the divorce."

Jared then asked her to sit in her seat. He reached in his briefcase and handed her a document. "Is that what you are concerned about?"

Emily read the document—the divorce decree—and screeched, "When? How? You never said a word! How did you pull this all off?"

"Your man is the smartest sign in the zodiac, you know—an Aquarian. Aquarians know that in the state of Nevada you can get a divorce in two weeks if there is no property to settle and no custody issues. You don't even have to be a resident of the state, either. Aquarians are also extremely psychic individuals and know when their fiancée is pregnant."

Emily was very surprised to hear this from him. She wondered how he knew. Her facial expression asked the question.

"Let's just say a little fishy told me. And this Aquarian happens to love his fiancée very much and is delighted he's going to be a father. And another thing—because I'm in love with you with or without my baby, I would have married you anyway. I'm not a fool, Emily."

Jared had paid a pretty penny for the spectacular affair. The Ritz Carlton Hotel in Center City Philadelphia was packed to the gills. He threw his weight around, being a Knightcap and all, and the wedding was held in two weeks on a Wednesday at four o'clock in the afternoon.

Peggy had worked like a slave to have the four gowns completed in two weeks. Emily's gown was a masterpiece of white silk satin with a deep V neckline. It held every curve of her body and had tiny bows with hand-beading in a straight line from her butt to the end of the train. Her stomach was as flat as a pancake. The headband in her hair was also accented with beads, and it fitted snugly across her forehead and around her head. A small veil was attached to it. She was a magnificent bride, mind-blowing, and dazzled the guests.

The Knightcaps, minus Jared, were the most handsome groomsmen the ladies had ever seen, as Damon and Lee guided Sheila and Rodney and Kelly escorted Regina down the aisle. As fine as those ladies were, they needed two men—extra protection. Sheila was stunning as Emily's matron of honor, wearing a tangerine chiffon gown ribbed at the bodice with spaghetti straps. It fit tight from the top of her waist to the thighs, and the sheer chiffon flowed down the middle of the front to the mid-calf of her legs. It draped in the back down to the floor. Sheila was drop-dead gorgeous.

Emily's sister Regina wowed the crowd in the same shade in silk satin, an off-the-shoulder gown which fit like a glove down to the knee. It completely exposed her lovely legs, and from the back of the gown hung a short train of the exquisite fabric.

Little Renee stole the show when she traipsed down the aisle, walking too fast, pitching flowers all over the place, in a floral print gown with warm colors of mint, yellow and of course, tangerine. Horace had her hair done in exquisite braids at Baka International, Philadelphia's leading braiding salon. She was gorgeous and just too adorable.

The ceremony was short and sweet for the crowd of over two hundred, which included many of the Knightcaps' fellow entertainers such as Bobby Womack, Pieces of a Dream, Patti Labelle, Blue Magic, The Stylistics, The Manhattans and Billy Paul. Emily's brother Earl was as proud as a peacock watching his dad give Emily away. His mother started crying even before the ceremony started. Everyone from the neighborhood was also there, including Oscar and Rachael, Horace, Jonita, Amber and Sydni. And of course Lucy, Angie and Reba were basking in pride. During the reception it was announced that there were surprise guests in the house, and everyone stopped partying to find out who it was. The announcer then introduced Ashford and Simpson and they went onto the stage. The crowd roared. They congratulated the bride and the groom and then Nick Ashford made a speech.

"It is Valerie's and my pleasure to be at this affair. We've had the opportunity on two occasions to work with the Knightcaps and have formed a warm friendship with not only the groom, but with the entire group as well. One thing we've never seen the Knightcaps do is perform with a female. You know, I think the Knightcaps have really been male chauvinists, not ever letting a lady sing with the group." The crowd started booing the Knightcaps and demanding a duet. Nick continued.

"So, tonight we are changing all of that. Jared will sing a song with a lovely lady." The crowd began cheering and chanting, "Valerie—Valerie," with Patti Labelle standing up front applauding the guests, additionally energizing the already ignited group of people.

Valerie moved up and took a microphone, satisfying the crowd. She then looked into the crowd at Jared and motioned with her index finger for him to come to the stage. The crowd began roaring and applauding all over again. She then looked at Emily and said, "You too, *Mrs. Wells.*" Emily strolled slowly to the stage, giving everyone another opportunity to check that gorgeous gown out.

The band began warming up. Valerie passed her microphone to Emily and Nick released his to Jared. In a few minutes, the musicians began the theme song, which belonged to Mr. and Mrs. Jared Wells. Nick and Valerie moved to the rear of Emily and Jared and positioned themselves in front of additional microphones to sing backup. Staring at her husband, Emily belted out the first words to their song and Jared eventually joined in.

> *And for love's sake*
> *each mistake you forgave.*
> *And soon both of us learn to trust.*
> *Not run away*
> *it was no time to play*
> *We build it up and build it up and build it up.*
> *And now it's solid*
> *solid as a rock.*

Chapter Twenty-six

Amber

Dante looked up at Horace and thought he would get diarrhea right there in the restaurant. Horace's eyes were glued on him. Amber was scared to death, too.

"Daddy, oh boy," Amber said. "Oh boy . . . how did you . . . why . . . Dante, well . . ." She kept stammering and could not get a complete sentence out. Amber was stunned and in shock.

"Let's have dinner," Horace said. "Let's go right over to this table that I have been sitting at since ten o'clock this morning and have some food. Come on, both of you, let's go." Dante and Amber slowly moved over to the table, remembering the last time they were in a restaurant with Horace. The bellman was standing there and Dante went over to him and told him to hold it with the luggage and take it back to the lobby.

When they sat down, Horace motioned for the waitress, and when she came over to the table, he asked her to bring some menus. She returned with them and took orders for drinks.

"Okay, who's going to go first to clean up the lies?" Horace asked, looking at both of them.

"Mr. Alston, I apologize for your having been deceived again and I am involved. Our last meeting was a catastrophe and I'd like this one to run a lot smoother," Dante said.

"Keep going, Mr. *Date*," Horace said sarcastically, looking into his eyes.

"Well, I need to let you know that I didn't continuously see Amber after you ordered me to leave her alone nearly three years ago. We had not seen nor talked to each other for a long time. I ran into Amber at Barnes and Noble in Jenkintown over the Christmas holidays."

"Which Christmas holidays? What year?" asked Horace.

"These past holidays, after Amber started college. I was on winter break from school, too."

"Keep going," Horace said.

"He means *after* I turned *eighteen,* Daddy," Amber cut in. Horace looked at Amber and rolled his eyes. He then shifted his gaze back to Dante.

"Well, Mr. Alston, Amber and I were glad to see each other and we began talking and she let me know that she was extremely disappointed when she was informed that I was married with two children." Horace's expression changed because *he* was now caught in a lie.

"Dante, I did tell my daughter that, and it was a lie when I said you were married. However, I would have done anything to keep my sixteen-year-old child out of the claws of a twenty-four-year-old man. I won't apologize for that."

"I understand, sir," Dante said. "I'd also like to let you know that it was then that we started dating and we spent the remainder of the Christmas holidays doing some fun things and it was me who took her out for New Year's Eve. I've also gone up to New York to her college twice on weekends since then to visit her and I care a lot about her. I liked Amber a lot from the very day I met her."

"What do you like about her?" Horace asked.

"Well, she's not wild and crazy. She's more mature than many girls I have met and dated who are older than she. She has scruples, common sense, class, and she wants to get ahead. I love her sense of humor, the fact that she is not only book-smart, but street-smart, too. She has many talents and a great deal of compassion. You have done a fine job in raising her. She is a survivor with whom I am thoroughly impressed."

"So, have you been sleeping with my daughter?"

"Daddy, please, will you stop it!" Amber growled.

"Shut up, Amber, let the man answer. Seems like I can only get true answers out of him—you lying little rascal." Horace reminded him, "Dante—I asked you a question."

"I've never slept with Amber."

"Okay, so you came all the way down here to beautiful and romantic St. Martin to start?"

"You know what, Mr. Alston—I don't know. I don't know if it would have happened here. I certainly wasn't coming here demanding that or especially for that reason. If it's just sex I need, believe me, I can easily find it with others and would have saved a lot of money, too. I clean up pretty well, sir, and have no trouble securing young ladies to accompany me places. Also, in this day and age, sex is a commodity cheaper than chicken. I'm neither hard up to find it, nor impressed with a woman simply because she can supply me with it. She's got to come with more than that. Amber and I have to feel our way through things, and sex is a decision that will be weighed by both of us. I have no desire to pressure her into anything. She's not only my girlfriend and love interest— she is my friend. That's why I have *this*," he said as he held up his hotel room key.

"And, I have *this*," Amber said, as she held up hers. "Separate rooms, Mr. Detective. So what do you have to say about that, Columbo?" Amber asked.

Horace smiled and then started laughing. "Amber, you are something else." Then they all started laughing. The waitress returned to the table for the dinner order which they gave and continued talking.

"Dante," Horace asked, "what have you been doing since I called the police on you three years ago?"

"I've been working at another BMW dealership since you got me fired from the other one, and I moved into a house in Center City. I don't own the house, but merely rent a large house with a group of other college students. I am presently attending the University of Pennsylvania School of Law and I'll graduate in two years. I'm on the dean's list."

Amber was proud of Dante and noticed an expression on her father's face showing surprise and approval.

"Go, Dante. Go, Dante. Go, Dante," Amber chirped.

Horace started laughing and shaking his head. "Amber, I can spend a ton of money on education and efforts of refining you, but I'm convinced in the end you'll still remain a little hoodlum." Dante and Amber laughed.

"Well, listen, this is the way I feel about this situation, Daddy. You know what, you just hover over me like I'm a little baby. I'm sick of all the rules all the time. I am eighteen years old. I'm no dummy. Now, Dante is a respectable gentleman and a nice guy. I like him. He's not one of those jerks with his pants hanging off his butt without a job or any ambition. He is older than me—so what. Hell, I'm older than me. I'm refined, smart and mature and I'm going to attract sane and responsible guys older than me. I'm not a bimbo. I could have done a lot worse than Dante—you know that. Why don't you relax and trust me and let me grow up? Let go a little, Daddy. Trust me and give me some credit for having some sense.

"I wouldn't have lied to you if I hadn't felt I *had* to. I wanted to tell you all about us—I wanted to share it with you because I was excited and happy—but I *know* you, and *you* know you, so I kept my mouth shut so I could be happy and enjoy my first boyfriend. So the truth is—it's your fault you've been in the dark, not mine."

Horace knew she was right and he was pissed that she was. Amber was tough and he knew she was maturing and developing into someone who could stand up to him—making sense. For the first time he realized that he was not going to control her forever.

"Okay, so now what?" Horace asked.

"Well, I'd like to stay here on my vacation in peace and without your ordering any of Dante's body parts cut off. You know what I mean?" Amber said.

"Listen, Mr. Alston, I don't want this to be a big mess, either. We planned a nice trip and I've paid for two round-trip tickets and these rooms. Do what you like and I can take the loss on everything. I just don't want trouble. But I assure you, I will respect your daughter and I will be her friend. I can't say what will or won't happen down here, but I promise you I really care for your daughter. She is the only person I am seeing and I'm serious about her. I'm going to leave after dinner and get a shower and change my clothes. I'll see you later if you're still here. For now, why don't we stop talking so much about life and where everyone ought not to be and with whom and move to a more pleasant subject? Take a look at that beautiful ocean, all that sand and the palm trees. Let's relax."

Horace stared at him and realized that he really did like the guy, but was convinced he would end up having to kill him. Dante was just too damn smooth for Horace. "Okay, Dante, let's have a nice dinner," Horace said.

Dante breathed a sigh of relief and said, "Excuse me, I may be twenty-six years old, but I still have to check in with my parents. I'll be right back."

As he got up to leave Amber said, "Tell your mom and dad I said hi and I'll call them when I get back to school."

Horace was floored. As Dante walked away Horace looked over at Amber, shook his head and gazed into her eyes.

"You think you're so slick, don't you?"

"What do you mean?"

"The Peabody Hotel and all that duck shit. We found out your butt was lying." Amber laughed.

"How did you find out, Daddy?"

"Emily. That's how I found out. You know how she is. She started walking around the house saying, 'Something just doesn't seem right. I swear I believe Amber is up to something.'

"Then I started thinking about everything. You didn't really put up much of a fight switching from St. Martin to Disney World. And I kept remembering the look in your eyes when you first saw this place and how you kept saying you wanted to come back here. So I called the Peabody and indeed they had a reservation for you. Then I wasn't sure what you were doing so I called here and they had a reservation for you, too. I couldn't figure it out and I didn't want to accuse you of lying because there was a possibility that you had forgotten to cancel this place, or the other girls you told me about in the beginning could have been coming anyway on that reservation."

"So what else did you do, Columbo?" Amber asked.

"Well, the bottom line is Emily, Jonita and Renee are in Disney World at the Peabody—flew down last night to wait for your ass to show up and I took the Governor's Palace in St. Martin."

Amber was shocked he went to all that trouble to check up on her. "You are a freaking trip, Daddy. Unbelievable—and it must be quite costly for you playing detective."

"You've got that right, and you're going to pay me my damn money back when you get your degree and start working. Jonita and them will be in Orlando for a week. I'm having Jonita draw up papers on your ass and you'll sign a promissory note to pay me back every dime of my money or I'll take your butt to court when you become Miss Doctor. We've all got the same taste level, baby. So right about now Emily and Jonita are probably down in Florida eating dinners in all those fancy restaurants and ordering bottles of wine, too. And Renee is no doubt begging for everything in that park. You just better hope they don't purchase Mickey Mouse himself, because you're picking up the entire tab for seven nights in sunny Florida. You'll also be paying for whatever I spent to come here, and whatever I do while I'm in romantic St. Martin. Since you're the one who wanted to deal with some ducks, quack on what I just said and don't think because I don't have a college degree that I can't count and don't know how to keep up with receipts. I'm getting my money back from you—I promise you that. Keep all this in mind the next time you even think about lying to me about where you're going and who you're going with, because 'Columbo' will be on your trail. Better tell your lawyer boyfriend you'll need representation, because *I've* got Jonita."

Amber's head sank. She wanted to strangle Horace and said, "By the way, what do you think about my lawyer boyfriend who's on the dean's list and not only stood up to you, but also outtalked you?"

"To be perfectly honest, I have to admit I do like the guy. I liked him three years ago but I couldn't let him have my baby."

"He's cute, too, ain't he?" she said.

"Yeah, Amber, he is a nice-looking guy."

"Go on, say it, Daddy—I did good, didn't I? Come on, shove me my props."

Horace laughed and said, "Amber, this is okay with me. It has to be. I can't do anything about it. God knows I can't police the two of you. I can honestly say, though, I'm not worried about Dante with you. I think he's okay. You did do fine for a first boyfriend. You've got my blessing." He bent over the table and kissed her.

"Thanks, Daddy. I love you. I'm sorry I couldn't trust you enough to tell you the truth. He really has treated me very well and he respects me."

"So—you've met his parents?" Horace asked.

"Yes. Over the holidays he took me to meet them. We all went out together to a family party on New Year's Eve. We had a great time. His mother came up to New York alone to see me, too. She likes me a lot. We went shopping in New York and to see *Bring In Da Noise Bring In Da Funk*. It was great. She doesn't have a daughter—Dante is an only child. It felt good spending that time with her—like my having a nice mom—you know.

"She is an English professor at Villanova. She's funny. She told me this story about Dante bringing this girl home that she and her husband hated. She reminds me of you. She couldn't get rid of her and ended up telling her that Dante had another girl pregnant and the girl's mother had come to her house pissed off. It was all a lie. She had me dying laughing. She didn't like the girl because she worked at the lottery place taking numbers and didn't want to go to college. The girl kept telling Dante and his mom that she was going to enroll in college and never did. His mom said she didn't want her son dating someone with no drive or ambition because she had worked too hard on him. Dante got mad at his mom for interfering and lying and told her off and she made him move. So he is living in Center City. She is really proud of him. They made up. He loves his parents," Amber said.

"Where do they live?" Horace asked.

"They live in Philly off Lincoln Drive in one of those gigantic houses. It is awesome. They have to live in the City because his Dad is a city employee and there is a rule that you have to stay in Philly if you work for the City. His dad runs the medical department or something for the City and part of their family is the Dwight Evans Barbecue business. You know, they have a couple of restaurants. His uncle owns that company."

Horace looked at this girl, whom he had rescued from everything, and he was indeed proud of who she had become. She had come a long way since she had first come to live with him when she was seven years old and he had to put that dreadful Paula out of his home because of her evil ways. He was glad he got Amber back at fourteen and that he'd been instrumental in turning her life around. As he sat and looked at her he envisioned her in the white lab coat with the letters monogrammed on it: "AMBER ALSTON, MD"

Dante returned to the table and said, "Well, everything is cool at my parents' home and I saw the waitress on her way with what looks like our food. Let's eat—dinner's on me."

Chapter Twenty-seven

Purdy

Three days after he returned from Barbados Purdy received a call from Andrea.

"Hi, Dr. Remington, I received another red alert today. This is our fifth and it's serious. Do you want the details now or shall I call you tonight at home? Are you busy now?"

"I'm with a patient. Is it really serious?"

"Yes, this one will require immediate attention," Andrea answered.

"Okay—can you meet me for dinner at six o'clock at Scoogi's on Bethlehem Pike?" he asked.

"I'll be there," she answered. They hung up.

Andrea was sitting at the bar when Purdy arrived, carrying Pilar in her infant seat and her giant diaper bag hanging from his shoulder. Andrea jumped up to assist him, taking Pilar and requesting the hostess to get them a booth. They got seated and organized and Andrea removed Pilar from her seat and held her.

"Open this," she ordered, dropping a large manila envelope on the table with her free hand. Purdy studied the report and complaint and read Jade's handwritten notes. Also inside were Andrea's notations from two pharmacies. Purdy was surprised at what he was reading and shook his head as he continued studying the material.

"You're right, this is a hot one. I'll take care of it first thing tomorrow. Gerald Willis. I'm shocked. Nice fellow, I thought."

"Well, he must have gone off the deep end. He was probably very much in love with the girlfriend or jealous of her son or something. In any case he did kick her behind really good and stole the baby. The boy was missing for four days. That's not good for us," Andrea said.

"I see he's been on a few medications and at one point was on Stellizine. That's a rough one. He's been off that for a while and is on Valium now. I see the latest prescription was filled last week," Purdy said as he continued reading. "I'm so glad I have three people working on this stuff because all of my employees filled out applications when I hired them. Now we both see that the information on the apps was not checked out thoroughly. This guy has a record and has been in jail. Either he never disclosed it on his application or no one followed up."

"He probably never put it down. I know if I were an ex-con, I wouldn't tell a potential employer," Andrea said.

"Well, whatever," Purdy sighed, "we know it now and I haven't gotten anything back from the agency running the checks. You and Jade are doing a great job. How is it going with you and the pharmacies? Are they giving you a hard time when you call for the medications?"

"Not really. I usually try to get a male or anybody who speaks a foreign language. Most of the time they have a hard time understanding me and they're busy and just want to get rid of me. If the person I'm checking on is a female, I act like I lost my latest prescription and don't know the name of it. If I call about a male, I act like he's my husband and we can't find his medication or I say I lost it or something. If I have problems, I call back on another shift like I'm calling from the doctor's office with a new prescription and want them to look up the old one for some reason. Look, people don't want to be bothered and they give information to merely make me go away so they can work. I'm doing fine. Okay—that's the most I have now. I'll call you if I get anything else. How was Barbados?" she asked.

"It was the best trip I have taken in a long time and Pilar had a ball getting spoiled to death." Purdy didn't want to get into discussing Barbados or Stefana so he motioned the waitress to take their order. After dinner they parted and he went directly home.

At 9:25 in the morning Gerald Willis was standing in Purdy's office, having been summoned from his desk in the billing department.

"Sit down, Gerry," Purdy said.

"Good morning, Dr. Remington, is there a problem?"

"As a matter of fact there is," Purdy said. "I have to cut right to the chase."

"Okay, sir," Gerry replied.

"You know I've been having background checks done and it's come up that you have a criminal record and have been incarcerated." Gerry put his head down.

"Dr. Remington, I wanted to come to talk to you about that, but I was afraid of losing my job. A lot of things happened a while back and I have been straight for the past year. I'm sorry I didn't tell you or Jillian when I was hired."

"I accept your apology and I, too, am sorry that you had problems in the past. However, under the circumstances, I'm not comfortable with your working here, especially with the children here on the premises." Before Purdy could finish Gerry stood up, looking directly into Purdy's eyes.

"I swear I would never harm Pilar, Margot or Ian. I need my job—I really do. I know I look bad having taken my girlfriend's son and run away with him, but I was so angry with her at that time that I just wanted to get back at her. I had been helping her out with her son for about nine months while we were seeing each other. She hurt me by having an affair and the kid's father was never around. He never did anything for him. She started carrying on with another guy and taking the boy over to his house. I got pissed and went postal. I'm fine now and we don't see each other anymore. I swear to you I would never do anything like that again," he pleaded.

Purdy studied Gerry and he truly did feel sorry for him, but he wasn't taking any chances with Pilar or the other kids. "I'm sorry, Gerry, I really am, but I cannot keep you on. I'll lay you off so you can collect unemployment but that is the best I can do," said Purdy.

"What about when I apply for another job? I have to give this place as a reference. What will you say?"

"Gerry, with the information I have received, I wouldn't be comfortable okaying you to work around any kids. I think your best bet is not to give my office as a reference. I'll sign your papers for unemployment and give you four weeks severance pay in case your checks don't start right away. I need you to leave here immediately."

"This is not fair! This is just not fair. It's not my fault you brought those kids here and that dog and changed all the rules around! I've been a good worker."

"Don't get crazy in here, Gerry—especially while I'm in the middle of writing this check," Purdy said, looking into Gerry's eyes. Gerry calmed down, knowing he needed that money. Purdy then completed writing the check, ripped it from his checkbook and handed it to him. He summoned Jillian and asked her to walk him to his locker to get his things. While they were gone, he called Brady Emerson, a six-foot-four, two-hundred-twenty-pound physical therapist, and told him to go to Gerry's locker and escort him out of the building and watch him drive off or get on a bus. He then dictated a memo to Dezi to type immediately and give to all staff members that Gerald Willis was no longer in his employ and was not allowed on the premises.

Maritza finished up her meeting and called Purdy's office. "Hey, it's me. What's happening?" she said.

"Same shit, different day. How are you?" he asked.

"I'm good. Wanna hook up tonight?"

"I can't. I have to go to my attorney's house tonight for dinner. I can see you tomorrow night. Will that work?"

"Can we have dinner at your house instead of going to a restaurant?"

"Okay, I'll ask Mrs. Charleston to cook," he said.

"I can bring something over," she said.

"No, don't do that. Mrs. Charleston is a fantastic cook. Any suggestions?"

"I'm craving fried chicken again. That's easy, too. Ask her to do that, some scalloped potatoes and a salad. How's my little girl?"

"She's fine. She's in her playroom bossing the staff around. You'll see her tomorrow night. Let's do six o'clock," Purdy said.

"Okay, see you then. If you get a chance, call me before you go to bed," Maritza said.

"We'll see. I probably won't get home until about nine from Tony's and I have to get Pilar to bed and tonight I have to walk Bailey."

"I thought the trainer walked him at night?"

"He normally does but his mom is in the hospital and he wants to stay there most of the night and come back to my house by five in the morning. I gave him the time off."

"Okay, I gotta run. I'll see you tomorrow and maybe talk to you tonight," Maritza said. They hung up.

Maritza stared at the phone and thought about those pictures. She wanted to confront him, but figured if she did that it would only cause a giant feud between her and Purdy. That could ultimately result in their being estranged—at least put them on nonspeaking terms for a while. That would surely give that White bitch more leverage. Maritza decided not to start a fight and to keep her mouth shut if it killed her.

Teighlor Garcia prepared an absolutely scrumptious dinner for Purdy, and the entire Garcia family was dazzled by Pilar. Purdy arrived with gifts for everyone and Tony screeched with delight when he was presented with the onyx cuff links that Stefana had found. Purdy had fun playing with Tony's kids, Nicco, Luca and Carlo. They were all as cute as they could be and loved having Pilar around. After dessert, an exhausted Purdy patiently played a board game with six-year-old Nicco and four-year-old Carlo, and baby Luca, who was five months old, looked on. Teighlor and Tony were busy drooling over Pilar and threatening to steal her.

When Purdy and Pilar were leaving, Tony walked Purdy to his Range Rover, thanked him again for everything and assured him that Pilar was welcome anytime to play the role of baby daughter Garcia. Just before Purdy drove off Tony said, "Listen—I know about what happened with you and Andrea. She told me the whole story. You know I wanted to kill her. I apologize. I'm ashamed of her." Purdy was speechless.

"Drive home, man—no comments necessary. Don't make this any harder on me than it is," Tony said. A stunned and relieved Purdy headed for home without saying a word. He got settled at home and passed out—without calling Maritza.

*   *   *

"Hi, everybody," Maritza yelled as Mrs. Charleston led her in. Maritza was carrying a beautifully wrapped box. Purdy came from the kitchen to greet her.

"Hey, baby, how was your day?" he said as he kissed her.

"It was fine. I have a gift for Pilar," she answered, smiling and holding up a gift-wrapped box.

"Well, come on and let's give it to her. She's in the kitchen supervising," Purdy said. Maritza followed him into the kitchen and went right to Pilar, who was on the counter. She threw her coat off, flung it on a chair and put her purse down. She handed Purdy the box and scooped Pilar out of the chair. "Hey, sweetie, what have they been doing to you since I last saw you?" she cooed. Purdy smiled.

"I've got a little something for you. Daddy should open it. It sure smells good in here, Mrs. Charleston. Rumor must be correct that you can really burn," Maritza said. Purdy immediately opened the box as the women looked on. He pulled out an adorable swimsuit in colors of watermelon, black and green. It was exquisite.

"Thanks, baby. Pilar, tell Maritza thank you," he said. Maritza gently planted a kiss on Pilar's cheek.

"I was wondering if you had talked to the Y about swimming lessons?" Maritza asked.

"Too soon. She has to be six months—I checked it out. I've got it on the back burner," he replied. "She'll really be a hit in this," Purdy went on, holding the swimsuit up. Maritza felt inadequate again, as she just couldn't come up with anything suggestion-wise that Purdy had not covered.

She, Purdy and the baby then went into the living room and she played with Pilar while Purdy went through her diaper bag and began adding items needed for the following day. In twenty minutes they were all sitting down at the dining room table having dinner, and Bailey was lying down on the floor next to Pilar. It was a pleasant meal that included dog trainer Bruce Hedgins, and afterward Mrs. Charleston cleaned up everything while Purdy fed and bathed Pilar.

Purdy and Maritza watched a movie and went to bed, and when Pilar woke up for her two o'clock feeding, Maritza told Purdy to stay put and she would handle it. Purdy declined and got up anyway to take care of her, letting Maritza help. She was pissed and felt useless again. She then thought about that damn White woman and wanted to curse Purdy out for choosing Stefana over her to take care of Pilar.

Staff was still buzzing about the dismissal of Gerald Willis and everybody was on their toes. Employees were starting to come to Purdy's office telling him all their domestic business and life histories, and he was hearing all kinds of crazy stories. They ranged anywhere from slight arguments they had with their spouses and significant others to problems and arguments on past jobs. One girl came in and explained that her father had killed her mother thirteen years ago and was questioning Purdy as to whether the murder would have any effect on her job. It was a trip. It seemed like they were all being careful and shaking in their boots.

Two weeks later, Purdy came home to find that all the things that he wanted from the shower had arrived. He had a great time going through them with Mrs. Charleston. She was really impressed and already she thought of Pilar as her granddaughter. She was absolutely mad about her and took excellent care of her. She had already started Christmas shopping for Pilar even though the baby wouldn't know what the holiday was. She was almost four months old.

Purdy walked into his office, dropped Pilar off in her playroom and checked his schedule. This was Wednesday; he was open until seven that night and his appointment list was packed. Jesus. He'd be tired this evening. Thank God Mrs. Charleston was coming in the afternoon and he'd send Pilar home with her. He poured a cup of coffee and told Dezi to start sending the troops in. They were nonstop.

At 11:20 Yvette Bryant, who worked with trauma patients, came to his office.

"Dr. Remington, where is Pilar? She's not in the playroom."

Purdy was shocked. "Are you sure?"

"Yes, I'm sure. I reported for my shift. Ian and Margot are there. Pilar wasn't, so I came here thinking you had her."

"Wait a minute," said Purdy. "Who's in the playroom with the other two now?"

"I grabbed Holly and told her to stay there."

Purdy's patient was listening to the conversation, and he also looked concerned.

"Mr. Powers, excuse me, you see I have a situation here. Can you go out to the lobby desk and tell Dina to put you with Dr. Gelding? Here's your chart—give it to Dina." Purdy then grabbed the phone to buzz Jillian, who had feeding and diaper duties.

"Jillian, do you have Pilar?"

"No, she's in her playroom."

"No, she's not!" He slammed the phone down. He went to the lobby office looking for Karla, the other designated diaper changer and feeder. She wasn't there. "Is Karla changing or feeding Pilar somewhere?" he asked Dezi.

"Karla went to the bank," Dezi answered.

"Did she take Pilar with her?"

"No. What's going on?"

By now everyone was alarmed. Purdy and Yvette ran out of the lobby and stopped in all the departments and checked the kitchen. No Pilar. They went to Bailey's area and she was not there. Then they went to her playroom, finding only Ian, Margot and Holly. Purdy was frantic— absolutely scared out of his mind. He got on the phone and called his home. Mrs. Charleston answered.

"Mrs. Charleston, did you come by the office to take Pilar home? We can't find her."

"What? No! I don't have the baby. I'm not due there until one o'clock! What do you mean, you can't find her?"

"Just what I said. I have to go." He hung up and Mrs. Charleston ran for her coat and headed for his office.

Purdy snatched the log off the wall in the playroom and examined it. He then muttered, "The last person signed in to watch the kids before Yvette was Nathan Fuller. Where the fuck is he?" Purdy then went looking all over for him. He couldn't find him anywhere. He buzzed Jillian for his home number and called his house. While he was doing that, Yvette stood on a chair in the playroom trying to get the tape out of the video camera so they could run it back to see what happened there.

There was no answer at Nathan's house.

Purdy ran in to assist Yvette, and as they were on their way back to his office, Nathan came down the hall carrying a large bag of dog food. Purdy screamed, "Where is my daughter, and what the hell are you doing with that bag of dog food?"

"What's wrong with you, Dr. Remington? I'm only doing what you told me to do," Nathan said.

"What are you talking about? I didn't tell you to do anything. I haven't seen you all morning. I can't find my daughter and you were the last one with her," Purdy yelled.

"Listen, I don't know what's going on. I was told that you wanted me to go to the market for this damn dog food," Nathan said, holding the large bag up. "I did it. What the hell are you yelling at me for?"

"Nathan, who told you Dr. Remington needed dog food?" Yvette calmly asked.

"His girlfriend. The one who comes here sometimes. She came to the playroom and said Dr. Remington said for me to go to the store for this dog food because we were out. She gave me money and said she would watch the kids until I got back."

For a few seconds Purdy stood in the hallway looking at Nathan in amazement. He then went through the office lobby, passing his staff, all of whom looked bewildered and were conversing among themselves trying to figure out what had happened to Pilar. He went into his office and closed the door. He immediately placed the videotape into the VCR and ran it back, searching for Jazz. He watched and listened as she advised Nathan, "Dr. Remington wants you to go get dog food." Purdy watched Jazz hand Nathan money. He was stunned. The tape then showed Jazz lifting Pilar out of her swing and placing her in her infant seat. She then grabbed her diaper bag and left the playroom with the baby.

Purdy immediately grabbed the receiver of the telephone and called

Jazz's house. He let the phone ring twelve times but got no answer. He then called her office and she was not in. He was going ballistic, but he sat down and tried to figure out what she might be doing or thinking. He contemplated calling the police. However, he didn't want her arrested.

He reviewed his entire association with her, realizing she was a mere twenty-three years old. She was immature, impulsive and flighty, but he did not believe for a moment that she would actually hurt Pilar. He had no other numbers to try to locate her and had none of her friends' telephone numbers. He wondered if she and Pilar were off to the zoo or in the park. Perhaps she was showing Pilar off to her friends or a client, he thought. Maybe she was just stealing some time with her because he wouldn't permit her to take her out alone. He had no idea and gave up, knowing he really didn't know what she was doing or why. He was still extremely uneasy with the situation.

When Mrs. Charleston arrived in his office ten minutes later, she stopped in front of him, speechless. She finally asked, "You still don't know where she is, do you?"

"No, I don't, but Maritza does have her," he answered.

"Maritza? Thank heaven! Oh my God, I'm relieved. I was scared out of my wits. I guess they'll be back soon—or is she bringing her back to the house?"

Purdy was silent. "Well, why are you looking so forlorn? At least Maritza has her," Mrs. Charleston said.

"I'm worried because I'm not so sure they are just out for a while."

"Oh, Dr. Remington, stop worrying. Maritza is a sweetheart. They're probably just out having a good time."

Dezi and Yvette then came into his office. "What the heck is going on?" Yvette demanded. "Where is Maritza? I know you've called her by now."

"I can't find her. I'm thinking," Purdy said as he stared at the three women. He then continued and said, "Do me a favor and leave right now. I've got a lot on my mind." They all left his office. He then buzzed the lobby office and asked Karla to cancel his appointments for the day, left the office and went straight to Jazz's house. He waited there over two hours, but they never arrived. He called back to his office. No calls had come in from her. He hated to phone the police, knowing that if he did, she'd be arrested on kidnapping charges.

"Is that good, my little boopy?" Maritza asked as she put a little barbecue sauce from her spareribs on Pilar's tongue. "I know you get sick of drinking that warm milk all the time. You need some variety and a little spice in your life, don't you?" she asked Pilar while sitting in the booth of her favorite rib spot, the Rib Crib on famous Germantown Avenue. Pilar seemed to be in heaven when she tasted the sauce.

"All right, hurry up, Maritza, I don't have all day. We'd better get out of here before we're late," Dredge said.

"Okay, just let me change her diaper and we're leaving. Do you have everything?"

"Yeah, hurry up."

"Hey, Tony, this is Pierce Remington. I have a gigantic problem," Purdy said into the telephone from his living room.

"What's up? Is Pilar sick or something?"

"Pilar's been taken from my office this afternoon."

"What! I know the police must be on this. Have they found out anything at all?"

"I haven't called the police because a young lady that I have been seeing has taken her. I have it on tape and I can't find her," Purdy said. He then explained to Tony why he hadn't yet called the police.

"Umm . . . ," Tony said, "I don't know how to call this one. I'd say give her another couple of hours and then call it in to the police—unless you think she may hurt the baby. You've got to do that if she doesn't hurry and bring her back. Keep calling her. Call me back as soon as you have her—or if she doesn't show up. You're certain Pilar's not in danger with this girl, aren't you?"

"Honestly, I don't think Maritza is dangerous. Maybe a little insecure and jealous—but she wouldn't hurt the baby."

"Okay—I'll wait to hear from you." They hung up.

Purdy continued to telephone Maritza's house and still got no answer. At four thirty Purdy's phone rang and he lunged for it.

"Hello."

"Hi—it's me and Pilar."

"Maritza!" he shouted, and then remembered how upset she got when he called her that and calmed down and said, "Jazz, what the hell is going on?"

"I'm pissed. I have Pilar because you're selfish."

"Jazz, bring Pilar home or tell me where you are so I can come there."

"I'm not ready to do that. You're going too fast for me."

"Is my daughter all right?"

"Don't yell at me," she said.

"Jazz, you know you have to bring me the baby. Now stop playing games. I've been worried all day. Why did you do this?"

"Didn't I just tell you why? You've made me feel helpless, inadequate and out of place since you adopted her. You refuse to let me in, you know? And why didn't you tell me you had someone else?"

Purdy had no patience to walk Maritza through his decisions. "Listen, Jazz, this is all a long story that we can't discuss now. Right now, all I want is my baby. I'll answer any questions you have after I have her back. Don't make me get you into any trouble regarding this. Don't make me do it, Jazz. We can work this out, baby, just bring Pilar to me or tell me where you are."

"You know, Purdy, all you care about is yourself. That's probably why you adopted Pilar. She's just another play toy for you—just like me."

Purdy, knowing how much he loved Pilar, became irate. "Listen, god-dammit, you better get my fucking baby to me or I'm having your ass arrested!"

Maritza hung up.

"I'll need your baby's birth certificate and your boarding passes," the attendant said to Maritza.

She handed them over and waited impatiently. The documents were checked and Maritza was assigned a seat. Dredge handed the small suitcase carry-on to Maritza and said good-bye as she boarded the plane. Maritza and Pilar got seated and waited for takeoff. It was a smooth flight and when they landed it was ten thirty at night. Maritza gathered their things and grabbed a cab. "Palm Beach Hilton," she told the driver.

Maritza was exhausted from the events of the prior day and night. She was bathing Pilar. She knew she'd be in hot water with Purdy, but what the hell. She was sick of his selfish two-timing ass. Let him worry himself to death. She got Pilar dressed and ordered breakfast from room service. After that they headed for the beach. After a few hours of that, she gave Pilar a bottle and put her down for a nap. She snoozed with her and they got up at three o'clock. They went through the lobby and outside and got into a cab.

When the cab pulled up at their destination, Maritza gathered the baby and all their belongings. She looked in the window of the shop and then walked in. The clerk walked up to them, and they exchanged pleasantries.

"What's your name?" a smiling Maritza asked the clerk.

"I'm Stefana, the owner. Can I help you with something?"

"Can you hold my daughter while I look around?" asked Maritza.

"I'd love to," Stefana said, reaching for Pilar and cradling her in her arms.

Stefana looked down at Pilar and was alarmed. "Is this your baby?" a suspicious Stefana asked.

"Yes, my husband and I adopted her. Isn't she beautiful?"

"She certainly is," Stefana said as she glanced down at Maritza's hand and noticed a diamond ring and a wedding band on the third finger of her left hand. Stefana was shocked.

Maritza stared into Stefana's eyes and growled, "Listen, bitch, I know all about you and my husband, and if I ever find out that you've had them down here again, I'll set this fucking jewelry joint and you on fire—you got that? Don't you let Purdy—Dr. Pierce Remington—get your ass killed. You'd better leave us alone. This is the last time you better ever have my baby in your arms."

Maritza then snatched Pilar and her diaper bag and strutted out of the store. She hailed a cab and went back to the hotel.

Purdy lay on his bed replaying everything in his mind. Jazz surely had some problems, but he had no idea she was so infatuated with him. She was so alive, independent and feisty that he didn't figure her feelings to be so strong. Then he thought about all the precautions he had taken to secure Pilar's safety against strangers and people he worked with, and when she was actually taken, it was by someone very close to him. He was outdone!

He was hoping his instincts were right and Maritza was not dangerous. He prayed Maritza wouldn't do anything crazy, like hide for the rest of her life or kill herself and Pilar. An array of fears was dashing through his mind.

He couldn't even get out of bed to go to his office. His entire existence was at a standstill. He was frozen and could not make himself call the police. Tony had called him twice demanding he report Jazz, but he just couldn't do it. Mrs. Charleston had gotten herself all worked up again and went to her own house to be miserable until she got word on where Jazz and Pilar were. Bailey, who was used to lying down near Pilar, had been walking around aimlessly for over twenty-four hours. Everyone from the office had been calling him at home since he'd left the prior day. Everything was fucked up. He could not imagine where they could be. He'd even driven around to some of the neighborhoods where Maritza's loony friends lived, looking for them. He also went to that Jamaican bar to see if she had the baby in there. No luck.

He had a horrible sleepless night. He had gotten used to taking care of Pilar during the night, and he was now off his routine. That damn off-the-hinge Maritza—he wanted to kill her.

When the telephone rang, Purdy grabbed it on the first ring. "Hello."

"Hi, Purdy, we need to talk about your wife," Stefana said.

"I have a crisis here and no *wife* in my life, Stefana. I'm not in the mood for games, baby," he abruptly said, letting her know he meant what he said.

"I'm calling to tell you that your *wife* is down here with Pilar. She just read me the riot act."

"What? You've got Pilar down there?" he screamed.

"I don't have Pilar, but she was here with a woman who told me she was your wife."

"Where are they?" he shouted into the phone.

"I have no idea. They showed up here about fifteen minutes ago. The woman walked into my shop with the baby." Stefana then told Purdy what Maritza had said.

"Stefana, I'm leaving here right now for the airport. I'll see you when I get there. In the meantime, please call every hotel down there and see where *Maritza Fleming* is registered. I'm on my way. I'll explain all the details to you when I get there." He hung up.

Purdy couldn't believe this. He wondered how in the hell Maritza had pulled this entire thing off, including finding Stefana. He was flabbergasted as he threw a change of clothes in an overnight bag and grabbed his wallet and keys. As he was about to leave, the phone rang. He ran to answer it.

"Don't bother getting a flight to Barbados. We won't be here. I know your blond bitch probably called you by now," Maritza said coolly.

"Jazz, baby, please—listen, stop this, *now*. I haven't called the police yet. You are not in trouble. Just bring Pilar home or meet me somewhere and everything will be okay. Come on, Jazz, you know you don't want to be in trouble."

Jazz started crying. It was the first time he had ever heard her cry. "I hate you. I just hate you. I'm sick of everything—all this mess. I would have had you a baby. I really would have had one. We could have shared her. We could have worked our stupid problems out and we would have been okay. But no—you had to have somebody else *and* Pilar all to yourself. You are *soo* selfish and mean."

Purdy was angry, scared and worried. "Jazz, baby—listen—we'll work this thing out. You know I'm crazy about you both."

"Who? Me and the blonde?" she snapped.

"No, sweetie, you and Pilar. Pull yourself together, baby. Do you want me to come and get you guys?" he asked slowly.

"I don't know," she whined. He knew she was softening up. He felt he could persuade her to give in.

"How is Pilar? Is she having fun, sweetie?" he asked to lighten things up and let her know that he was more relaxed with her having the baby.

"She's okay. She's been eating well and I've really taken good care of her. I let her get in the edge of the water on the beach and we rode around down here sightseeing. I'm doing good with her and she likes me. She hasn't been crying. I even took her to listen to a calypso band on the beach. You said she likes music."

"That's great, Jazz. If you aren't coming back now, when are you two planning to come home?"

"I'm not sure."

"Then why don't you let me come down there and the three of us can stay for a couple of days?"

"You'd do that and not start a bunch of shit?"

"Yes, I'll do that. Where are you two staying?"

"I don't know if I want to tell you that right now. I need to think. I may leave here. I just don't know."

"Do you want to call me back, sweetie—when you feel better?"

"Maybe."

"You know Pilar has her checkup tomorrow afternoon. She's due for her first shots here in the States. You know she hasn't had an immunization since I brought her from China. That's important, sweetie. Also, you know you're in a foreign country and people could have anything over there. Should I call the doctor and reschedule her appointment? What do you think I should do?"

"You really didn't call the police on me?"

"No, do you think I want you in jail?" he said, trying to get her into a joking mood. "If you go to jail, who am I going to argue with? Mrs. Charleston doesn't like to fight."

"If I let you come to get us, will you go by that Stefana's place and end it with her—do it in front of us? Will you cut it off?"

"Jazz, I'll do whatever you want, baby. Do you have everything you need down there for Pilar?"

"Yes, I went shopping a little before I left and I got milk and diapers and two outfits for her. I bought her another bathing suit, too. I also got her some vitamins."

"What kind of vitamins?"

"Flintstones drops are all I could find." Purdy's head sank. She needed a better vitamin. He didn't know a damn thing about the Flintstones vitamins. Instead of criticizing Jazz, he said, "Good job, girl, you are on the ball. Now, can I come to get my two babies?"

"Maybe."

"Listen, Jazz, go to the hotel desk and reserve the room for three more days. I'm going to get packed and grab some extra things for Pilar. I'll get a flight right away and I'll see you later. Just tell me where you are. Do you have enough money? I can wire you some until I get there in case you and Pilar want to do some fun things. I also have to check the flights to see what time I'll get in. Do you guys want to meet Daddy at the airport?" Maritza was quiet, thinking, and her silence was making Purdy more nervous.

"Jazz, are you there, baby?" he asked.

"Yeah, I'm here. I have money. Okay, I'll do what you said. I'm at the Hilton on Palm Beach. You call me back in room 313 and let me know what time your flight gets in. Me and Pilar can come to the airport. You're not mad, right?"

"No, baby, I'm not mad. You guys have fun. Jazz, be careful of the sun, you know? You guys don't want to get sunburned. I'll call you later with my information. If you aren't in your room, I'll leave you a message. Be careful if you meet me at the airport—mosquitoes. Did you get any sunblock for Pilar since you were on the beach today?"

"I dabbed some on her. I bought some at the hotel gift shop." Pilar then started to cry and Purdy heard her.

"Purdy, I have to go. I have to feed her and change her diaper. I'll talk to you later. You're really okay—right? You're not angry and you're not going to start a fight or call the police? Right?"

"Right, Jazz, I'll see both of you tonight."

Purdy sped to the airport and checked in for a flight that would be non-stop from Philly to Puerto Rico with a change of planes that would take him on to Barbados. He made a few phone calls while waiting, including calling Jazz's hotel and leaving his flight information for her. Purdy was a nervous wreck throughout both flights and extremely impatient. Finally, the second flight landed. He gathered his belongings and got off the plane. He rushed through the airport searching for Jazz and Pilar and spotted them in the baggage area. He rushed over to them, careful to hug Jazz first, and then scooped Pilar up from her infant seat. Jazz's facial expression showed worry as she looked around for police. She saw none and was relieved.

"Hi, Purdy," she said, and then put her head down.

"Hi, baby, it's so good to see you. I'm glad you met me. Come on, let's get out of here," he said, carrying Pilar in his arms, his bag across his shoulder and Jazz's hand in his free hand. They hailed a cab and got in.

"So, how did the day go after we talked?" he asked while kissing Pilar, who was fast asleep.

"It went okay. I took her to the aquarium—it's just a little one, but I took her to see the fish."

"That's nice. She likes looking at the tank in my office," he said.

"I want to go straight to Stefana's and get everything straight," Maritza said.

"Jazz, it's after eleven o'clock at night. Let's do it in the morning. And you know we need to get Pilar in bed. We shouldn't be dragging her around too much in the night air with the mosquitoes and everything. Let's get settled at the hotel and deal with Stefana in the morning. I don't even know if Stefana is home tonight," he said.

Jazz was silent, a little pissed because she wanted Stefana dealt with immediately. She rolled her eyes and said, "All right—tomorrow morning, as soon as we can get ourselves out of the hotel."

"You've got it. How was dinner tonight? Where did you eat?" he asked.

"I found a local place not far from the hotel and we went there. They had jerk chicken and it was pretty good. I fed Pilar there, too."

Purdy was worried again and wondered if Pilar had chicken, too. "How did you heat her bottle there?"

"I ran it under the faucet in the restroom."

"Where was she when you were doing that?"

Maritza had no idea Purdy was testing her. "I had her sitting on the toilet in her chair. I know what to do," she said proudly.

"Okay, looks like we're here," Purdy said as the driver pulled up.

They got out. Maritza led him to their room. Purdy undressed Pilar, changed her diaper and grabbed a nightgown from his bag and put it on her. He then placed her in the middle of the king-size bed and placed the covers over her. He took the pillows and placed one on each side of her. Maritza silently watched.

"Give me her diaper bag so I can go through it," he said.

"It's all in order, I have all the things she needs in it," Maritza answered.

"I know you probably do, but I have a few things, too, and I'm just used to going through her bag. It's a routine thing for me. How many bottles of formula do you have?"

Maritza surrendered the bag and said, "I've got seven bottles left."

He thoroughly checked the bag and when he was through he turned to her. "Okay—what's the deal? When are we leaving here? Did you extend the reservation?"

"What do you want to do?" Maritza asked.

"Well, honestly, I'd like to get back by Saturday—that's two days away. And I rescheduled Pilar's appointment at the doctor for Saturday. You know, she has to get her shots. Would us leaving here on Friday be okay with you?"

"Well, okay, but—well—I wanted us to stay longer—but I guess we'd better get her back. Okay, we can leave Friday."

Purdy said to himself, "Thank God."

After going through the bag, he took a shower and got into bed. Maritza got in next to him and snuggled up to him.

"Jazz, let's not get started with anything with Pilar in this bed. In fact, don't you think it would be better if you slept next to her, too, on the other side of the bed? That way, we'll be sure she doesn't roll over onto the floor."

"I feel like having sex. Can't we just get a quickie here and be careful? I've missed you."

"We get too wild and you know it. We can get to that another time. You can wait—you maniac."

She laughed and said, "We could do it in the bathroom or on the floor."

"Jazz, I am so tired from all the crap that's gone on and those flights— I'm not up for another adventure. Get your butt on the other side of that bed and go to sleep next to your daughter."

Maritza was so glad to hear him refer to Pilar as her daughter, and also felt more secure that he was not angry with her. She kissed him and cheerfully hopped over to the other side of the bed. At twenty minutes after two in the morning Pilar awoke for her bottle and Purdy fed and changed her. She went right back to sleep.

It was a little past eight thirty when Pilar woke up again. They all got up for the day, dressed and had breakfast in the Hilton restaurant. When they returned to the room, Maritza said, "It's time to go to see Stefana."

It was 12:20 when the cab pulled up at Stefana's shop. Before they exited the cab, Jazz said, "I told her we were married," and held her hand up to him with the set of rings on it.

He pretended to be surprised. "Nice set of gems. Where'd you get them?" he asked.

"QVC—Diamonique," she answered. He shook his head and laughed.

Stefana had an expression of total shock when they entered the shop. "Hi, Stefana," Purdy said.

"Hi, Purdy, how are you?"

"I'm okay. I need a few minutes—can you talk to me?" Maritza was silent.

"Come with me to the back so we can have some privacy," she said, moving toward the door of her shop to lock it. Once that was done, she headed for the back and he started to follow her. Maritza was right behind them, carrying Pilar.

"Stefana, I need to introduce you to my wife, Maritza, and this is *our* daughter, Pilar."

"I met your wife yesterday," Stefana answered, looking at Jazz. Jazz rolled her eyes at Stefana.

"Listen, Stefana, I'm sorry I neglected to tell you I was married. It was wrong to deceive you. I should have handled that better. I shouldn't have cheated on my wife either, and I was wrong. I'm in a marriage, and therefore I have to cut all ties with you. We can't even be friends. Please accept my apology and understand that I'll never get in touch with you again. Are we clear?"

"We're not clear just yet. I have a few things to say before you *clear* out of here. First of all, you've got a lot of fucking nerve being a pathological liar as well as a pain in the ass having your wife show up here. You had plenty of opportunities to let me know you had a family—that you were attached. This pisses me off to no end. You make me sick. As far as I'm concerned, you're a fucking insecure coward. Add those things to the list I just gave you. Now, I want you to get your daughter and Mrs. Pierce Remington out of my shop and my world as quickly as you can. Don't you ever even entertain the thought of my calling your Black ass again for anything. Now, goddammit—we're *clear,* so get out."

Purdy was astonished at her language and her behavior. Jazz looked like she was terrified and kept her mouth shut. Stefana then marched to the door, unlocked it and held it open while Purdy exited with Maritza and the baby.

They got back in the cab and headed to the hotel. In the cab Jazz said, "Damn, she is a real bitch. You must be glad as hell you found out what she was about. Humph, she had a lot of nerve going off like that. It's a good thing I came down here so you found her out. Well, at least you've still got me," she said, looking directly at him. "And you call my Jamaican, Puerto Rican and Black friends loco? You went and got yourself a crazy White woman. Humph." Purdy didn't say a word.

He took them to the pool, out to lunch and on a tour of the island. When they got back, he put Pilar down for a nap and gave Jazz two hundred dollars and told her to go shopping for herself and then gave her another forty dollars and told her to bring back some more formula and diapers. He then called the airlines and made reservations for them to leave on a Friday early morning flight back to Philadelphia.

* * *

"Hey, Mrs. Charleston, we're back. We've got your little girl," Purdy yelled as he entered his house with Jazz and Pilar.

Mrs. Charleston ran from her room and grabbed Pilar out of her chair. "How's my dumpling doing? Where've you been, baby? I missed you so much," she cooed to Pilar.

"She's been having a ball with Maritza in the islands. How are you, Mrs. Charleston?" Purdy asked.

Mrs. Charleston smiled at Maritza. "I'm fine now that I've got my girl back. Hey, Maritza, how are you, sweetie?"

"I'm good, Mrs. Charleston. Glad to be back," Maritza said. Maritza was relieved Mrs. Charleston was not angry with her.

"Look, you guys, I'm going to get all the stuff out of the car. I'm starving. Can you guys get some food together?" Purdy asked.

"Sure," said Mrs. Charleston. "Come on, Maritza, help me out in the kitchen. Bring the baby's chair." Maritza followed Mrs. Charleston into the kitchen.

Purdy got everything in and went upstairs to shower and empty the luggage. He came down in an hour. They had dinner together and Bailey was happy to see Pilar. After dinner Maritza helped Mrs. Charleston with the dishes. Purdy was settled in the living room, playing with Pilar, when the doorbell rang. He got up to answer it.

"I'm Sheriff Herman McGhee. I'm here to see Ms. Maritza Fleming," the uniformed gentleman said.

"Come right in," Purdy said.

McGhee held up an envelope and said, "I have these papers to serve on Ms. Fleming. Is she here?"

"Yes, she is. I'll get her," Purdy answered, leaving McGhee in the foyer.

Purdy entered the kitchen and said, "Jazz, there is someone here for you."

Surprised, Jazz said, "Who the hell could be coming by here for me?" She swore it was Dredge and she was going to kill him. She walked toward the front door and saw McGhee in uniform.

"Goddammit, you liar! You are such a liar! You tricked me. I cannot believe you tricked me, you bastard," she screamed at Purdy. He never said a word.

"Ms. Fleming, I'm serving you at this time with a restraining order. You must appear in Philadelphia Family Court. The date and time of the hearing are in these papers. You should obtain an attorney. This order also prevents you from coming within two miles of minor Pilar Miriam Remington, and it includes members of her household, these premises, and the office of Dr. Pierce Remington. Do you understand?"

Maritza rolled her eyes at Purdy and said, "I understand, sir."

"At this time I must escort you from this house," the sheriff said.

Maritza went to the living room and grabbed her suitcase and her coat. She then said, "I have no way to get home. My car isn't here."

"Unfortunately, Ms. Fleming, I'm not a taxi service. If I put you in my vehicle, I have to take you to the police facility at the Roundhouse."

Maritza stood tapping her foot, and her eyes pierced Purdy's.

"I need to call a cab. Can I do that?"

She and the sheriff both looked at Purdy for approval. Purdy stared back at her and said, "I'll call her a cab. She should wait outside for it."

"I'll stay until the cab comes for her. I'll be outside with Ms. Fleming," the sheriff said. Maritza strutted out of the door.

"Hello," she said into the phone.

"Hi, sweetie, I'm home."

"You made it back safely—thank God. How is Pilar?"

"She's fine. That was a remarkable performance you put on. You're something else."

"Was I too hard on you, you know, calling you Black and all?"

"Well, I am Black, and you did what you had to do and it all worked out. Thanks."

"What's going on there now?" Stefana asked.

"The sheriff is outside waiting for a cab to take Maritza to her house."

"She wasn't arrested?"

"No, I didn't want it that way. She's not a kidnapper and she isn't dangerous. I don't want her locked up. I wanted a restraining order keeping her away from us—that's enough. We'll have to go to court. That's sufficient punishment and I, too, have learned a lot. Maritza's too young—

twenty-three—and not very mature or experienced. She reacted the way she did because of her lack of those things. She's not a bad person. She just made a horrible decision. If she were older, she would not have done that. I *had* to do something about what she did because had I not, and she had completely gotten away with it all, it would probably have happened again. Also, by my employees knowing about it, any of them could have tried something like this and felt I wouldn't come down on them. An example definitely needed to be set to keep everybody in check. And who knows who the hell people discuss things with. Any Joe Blow they told, or any female I'd date in the future could have gotten wind of it and tried that same shit. I'm not going for it. My daughter is too precious to me. It's almost over now, thank God. I know I can't see Maritza anymore because she's not stable, and it's not even worth it because I never planned to marry or live with Maritza. It wasn't that kind of thing for me. It wasn't serious. I really am sorry this all happened."

"How do you feel about losing her?" Stefana asked.

"I will miss Maritza, for sure. She is fresh, fun and spontaneous. She has a crazy sense of humor and she's not bad in bed either. However, she is not the girl of my dreams and quite frankly I believe I'm too old for her. I've explained this to her many times. I was honest and up-front. I just neglected to tell her about you. If I thought she could have handled you, I would have been up-front about that, too. I must have made the right decision in hiding that because look what she did—appeared on your doorstep."

Stefana was listening carefully to every word he said, not knowing what the outcome of his conversation would be.

"Are you there?" Purdy asked.

"I'm here," Stefana answered.

"Listen, Stefana, I need time to absorb this shit. You can't imagine what I have gone through in the past four days. I've been totally overwhelmed with events. I've been worried about mosquitoes, health concerns regarding Pilar, I missed her terribly and I've been dealing with a wacky woman, concentrating on stroking her—gently—in an effort to keep her cool so I could get my baby back. I'm okay though. Listen—

give me a few weeks to calm down and to get through this court thing and I'll talk to you then. Does that sound okay?"

"Sounds reasonable to me. I understand," she said.

Purdy walked outside and noticed that Maritza and the sheriff were still waiting. He gave Tony a call. "Hey, man, it all worked out. I don't know how to thank you. You've turned into my guardian angel."

"You'll think I'm the devil when you get my bill. Everything went smoothly at the house, too?" Tony asked.

"Yes, not a hitch." He then explained how everything went down once they got to his home.

"Great. I have your set of court papers at my office. Now, one other thing," Tony said.

"Shoot."

"Remember I told you to be careful you did not sleep with her? I hope you were able to avoid that because if you slept with her after she committed this type of crime, the court could throw it out if we ever decided to file kidnapping charges, and the court could also deny the permanent stay of the restraining order. That works just like divorce cases. If you file an action against your spouse, then you voluntarily have sex with them, everything stops on the complaint. You know, everything becomes null and void."

"I didn't touch her, Tony," Purdy said.

"And let's just hope she doesn't understand all this shit or get an attorney who explains it to her. If she lies, we could have a problem with this thing you're trying to do with the restraining order. Then we have to go for kidnapping. We could also have a problem with the kidnapping thing because you know I never called the police department regarding kidnapping charges. I knew if they got into it, she was going right to jail—no ifs ands or buts about it. The feds would have met her at the airport and carted her away."

"Okay, Tony. I understand everything and I'll see you in court. Send the papers here to my house and I'll mark the date on my calendar. How are Teighlor and the kids?"

"Everybody is fine. They went over to my dad's to visit. I haven't said a word to them about this. It's up to you if you want to tell Teighlor. If you decide to do that, just be prepared for her to yell, lecture you on the company you keep and hit you with something—like an object from our kitchen. She's gonna blame it all on you, trust me. If I were you, I'd keep my mouth shut and be glad it's not going in the newspapers. She's crazy about Pilar. Just a warning, buddy. I'm out of here."

Epilogue

Dear Lucy:

Well, this is the scoop: My life is crazy as usual. Doug left here last night taking the boys to Disney World for a week and they all tore the house up washing and packing before they left. I got up at six a.m. today. That's late for me. I noticed three brown marks on my legs and thighs. It looked like dried blood. I wasn't really shocked because I had fallen down a few stairs the other day and thought I'd get some bruises. I really didn't have time to research the thing because my assistant Elvira was coming over to the house to help me with some paperwork. She was due at my house at one o'clock. Since the house was a complete wreck, I was running around trying to get it clean for her. I was cleaning toilets and sweeping, etc. I was out of control on a roll trying to pull the place together. She had never been to my house and you know how that is (friends coming for the first time and you don't want them to think you are a slob). I should have been walking around picking up after them as they were messing the place up, but I simply did not have the energy. I have been working like a slave the past few weeks at my job. So, to look good for Elvira, I was forced to run around like a bat out of hell.

I ended up sleeping in Nina's bed last night—missing my man so much I didn't even want to sleep in our bed. I fell asleep reading in her bed. This morning I pulled back the covers and saw all these brown spots that looked like blood on the sheets. I got scared. I looked down at the three marks on my legs and thighs. I thought, "Oh my God, what's this? I must have a terrible disease." Oh shit! Then I looked around at my house and said, "Well, dying will have to wait—I have to get this place cleaned up."

I snatched the covers up off Nina's bed and stopped for a moment to examine the blood spots. They were kind of caked up. I started to smell the spots and they smelled minty. Then I remembered that I had been eating a box of Junior Mints in the bed before I fell asleep. Am I going out of my mind, or what?

I heard about all the things going down in Philly. It's a trip. Sheila and Emily called me about that shit with Maritza stealing that doctor's baby. I was shocked. You know, she's always been so cool and indifferent about everything (so I hear) and it was a mindblower to know she fell so hard for Purdy Remington. She should thank her lucky stars they didn't get her for kidnapping. They had a hearing girl, (so I heard from Sheila) and the Judge told her she was going to jail if she ever went near that baby again. Humph. I heard that Dr. Remington is totally in love with that kid. Rumor has it he may marry that White chick who comes to visit sometimes.

Isn't it a trip and a blessing that Oscar Porter finally got up enough nerve to leave Fannie? I heard he is living the life in the "burbs" with that rich white woman who loves his last year's dirty drawers. Remember he brought her to Emily's wedding? Girl, Emily told me that they were vacationing in Palm Springs, California, last month and Oscar can read his ass off now. Peggy said every time she sees Fannie, she looks like she wants to kill somebody. And that Amber—I can't believe Horace did not commit mass murder when he caught her and Dante in St. Martin. That damn Amber—always slick as hell. I talked to Horace. He called me. Girl, he said he stayed down in St. Martin as long as they did and he was rooming with Dante while he was down there—sleeping with one eye open making sure Dante didn't exit the place in the middle of the night to visit his sweetie, Amber. Horace said he signed up for every snorkeling, Jet Ski activity and sightseeing tour they did. He said he was so sick of that damn disco he wanted to kill the DJ. He had me dying laughing telling me how he was hanging tough with them down there. He said that trip kicked his ass so badly Jonita had to rub him down with Ben-Gay when he got home. He said Amber and Dante probably sneaked some pieces somewhere on the island after he passed out a few times from sheer exhaustion, but he did the best he could to prevent it. He said no matter how nice that guy *was, how many schools he graduated from, how polite and well-spoken he was, what a great family he came from—he wasn't leaving his baby down there with his twenty-six-year-old ass. Girl, they all rode the plane together back to Philly when the vacation was over. That damn Horace is something! And Amber and the guy are still hooked up. Maybe it's real love. She just better keep her ass in college and be a doc-tor or Horace will kill her for sure, as much money as he is spending. I wonder if he is going to marry Jonita. I like her a lot.*

I was so sorry to hear about Angie ending up in a mental facility for four weeks as a result of watching that crazy girl, Ebony, try to gun down Joel. I'm glad she's out now and I'm praying for her.

I'll be glad when Emily has the baby. She and Jared bought a house not far from Horace so she could still take care of Renee without a has-sle. They invited Jared's mom to move in with them, but she stayed down in the neighborhood.

Listen to this shit. Did you hear that the warden at State Women's got busted for having two of the inmates out on the town? Girl, it was on the news. They were all as drunk as hell in a bar! Girl, one of the women he was out with was Amber's mom. Yep, Paula Gray. I don't know who the other chick was that was with him. Unbelievable. And guess what. After a full investigation, the warden didn't lose his job! They made a martyr out of his ass on TV. It seems Paula Gray had got-ten her ass whipped by a guard in the prison and the warden was pissed and fired the guy. To smooth things over and make her feel better, he took her and one of her buddies out on the town for her birthday. Yep, he did the "goodwill" thing and the public loved it. You know all the stories that come out about inmates being mistreated and all—well, looks like that Warden fell into a pile of shit and came up smelling like a rose. I guess whoever dimed them out and sent the Feds to the bar really felt like a fool when they saw them all on TV being treated like royalty. And to boot the Warden had an exemplary record at the prison for the last thirteen years and they were drooling all over him about that, too. Speaking of jail—Sheila said Lenora will be getting out soon. I wonder if she is coming back to live with them.

Sheila said Emily is on a mission to find her brother Earl a nice girl-

friend. I did see Earl checking Terri out at Emily's wedding. Maybe that might work. Terri is pretty cool and Earl likes kids. We'll see.

By the way, we made out just fine at court with the guy who beat up Nina. His ass went to jail because he had raped some other girl after he kicked Nina's butt and he was arrested on the spot. When we got to court there were two cases against him. I'm glad his ass is in the tank and not scaring the shit out of my baby.

I gotta go, girl—kiss my baby, Dimitri, for me. Say hi to Kevin and I'll talk to you later.

Luv ya!
Reba

Connecting

~

Adrienne Bellamy

A CONVERSATION WITH ADRIENNE BELLAMY

✤

Q: What inspired you to write Connecting *and what questions did you ask yourself when you were working on it?*

A: My first novel, *Departures,* was such a hit and inspirational to so many people that quite frankly, I had to write its sequel. Since *Departures* was such a tough act to follow, I was worried I wouldn't be able to intrigue my readers and fans a second time. Because of my outstanding reviews of *Departures* and the fact that so many of my fans were waiting so impatiently for *Connecting,* my questions to myself were "Can you do this again?" and "How in the world are going to do it?"

Q: Purdy is an exceptional character. How was he developed?

A: In the year 2001, my youngest daughter and I were involved in a near fatal car crash. Both Alia and I had serious head injuries and cognitive problems as well as multiple physical injuries. There was very little we could do for ourselves. We came under the care of an excellent doctor who specialized in physical rehabilitation. From the onset of our visits with Dr. Jerry Murphy, I found that he was not merely interested in bringing my daughter and me to a full recovery, but he always managed during our consultations to teach us something that had nothing to do with medicine. We learned about flowers, the opera, fine wines and foods, and great spots in the Caribbean. He corrected us if we mispronounced or misspelled a word. He was interested in my daughter's plans for college. My being an astrology nut, and knowing my stuff, I felt safe and secure learning from this Aquarian. After all, I *was* in the best of hands being led by a person born under the smartest sign in the zodiac. I am not one who is easily impressed and in fact, I have stupid people rage. The more I met with doctor Murphy, the more I appreciated his wisdom and I was inspired to create Purdy, his character. He undoubtedly had affection for children, so I loved creating the character Pilar.

Q: *There are many characters in this novel. Who is your favorite character and why?*

A: This is a hard one but I am forced to go with four people. Sorry. I love Emily because of her aggressiveness in her relationship with Jared. I am intrigued with her protection of her man. I am thrilled how Reba emerged from being such a timid woman to becoming more self-assured and in control. She desperately needed her self esteem. Horace is my hero and my favorite parent in the entire world. He hangs tough over and over again disabling people from interrupting the well built stability he has achieved for Amber and his other two daughters. Last but not least, I love the way Paula is operating the employees of the prison system. She is truly a gas.

Q: *What was your vision when you began writing* Connecting? *What got you started when you actually began the first paragraph?*

A: The vision was a "gotta be awesome' *Connecting*. I knew I had to come in with a bang. I had to snatch my audience at the front door of *Connecting* and I knew I could rely on Paula to get the job done. So, I placed the beginning of the novel in her capable sexy hands, among other parts of her body. As usual, she came through with flying underwear.

Q: What was the hardest scene you had to write in Connecting?

A: The Purdy chapters were the hardest. I had to show many sides of him. It was also necessary that I pay strict attention to the marvelous plot at the end and the sequences of events that led up to it. It required my utmost concentration.

Q: What were your favorite chapters and scenes in Connecting?

A: Hands down—they are the tarot card chapters involving Emily, Sheila and Leah. They are totally hilarious and I love the fact that they are an instrument to reach and teach my readers about one of my very favorite hobbies.

Q: Were any of your characters actually derived from real people?

A: Yes. The characters are: Purdy, attorney Anthony J. Garcia, Rachael, (our near-eighty-year-old nymphomaniac), and Joel.

Q: Are there certain times during the day that you write? Do you ever get writer's block?

A: I believe six weeks was the longest period I ever experienced. I am a writer who will not write if I don't feel I have good material. Many times material would come to me while I was driving. I'd try to retain it by jotting a few words down at a stoplight or often just turning around and going back home to my computer if I was on a personal errand.

Q: How much of Connecting *is based on your own experiences?*

A: About six situations in the book. A few scenes were written almost exactly as they happened to me. Others I prepared from a little that occurred and then I'd simply blow it out of proportion adding fictional events.

Q: Are you working on other projects?

A: I have completed my third novel, *Arrivals,* a sequel to *Departures* and *Connecting.* Some of the characters from *Departures* and *Connecting* are featured in *Arrivals* and I have introduced new ones who will not only knock your socks off, but cause you to laugh hysterically. I have begun a fourth novel titled *Illusions* that takes us totally out of the *Departures* neighborhood. Keep watching for a spin-off of Lenora's character in a book titled *The Donation,* and, have just completed the research for a book entitled *Epiphany* which goes totally out of the *Departures* family. I also have a project on hold which is a long awaited Astrology book that many fans have been begging for. I was inspired to write about astrology as many of my readers simply luv the stuff and are pleased with the little "taste" they received in *Departures.* I plan to get back to the *Departures* neighborhood characters by writing an additional sequel to *Departures* in 2005.

Q: At any point in your writing of Connecting *did you know how the book would end?*

A: In *Connecting* I honestly had no clue other than the fate of Pilar.

Q: Can you tell me some of the ways you get material?

A: Much of my material I receive in my dreams—while sleeping and I get a lot while I am driving my car. Also, often a small event will happen to me or a friend or family member and will trigger me.

Q: Can you share with me some of the compliments you have received from your readers?

A: People love my work because it is easy reading—no giant words that a not so articulate person would have to have a dictionary next to them while reading. This makes my work appeal to all types of people. I purposely watch the words I use so all will understand. I've also been praised for my descriptions of people, places and things. Many readers have said, "I've never been there but I felt I was there after you described it." My readers also like my characters because they can relate to them. Many say, "I'm Reba or "I know these people!" I have a cousin who acts just like that!"

Q: What chapter or scene in Connecting *caused the most controversy, discussion or sparked the readers?"*

A: There are two. The tarot card chapter, Rachael the nymphomaniac, the Scorpio chapter and Reba's daughter Nina's cookie chapter.

Q: Who are your favorite writers?

A: Wally Lamb, John Grisham, Vincent Bugliosi, Terry McMillan and Danielle Steel.

Q: Did you learn something about yourself when writing this book?

A: I learned that I like my characters and I am like them in so many ways. I like Sheila because she is no-nonsense and will fight. She will do battle every time and come up the winner. I love Horace because he never gives up. I love Amber because she emerged from a ghastly life prior to coming to live with Horace and she is a normal teenager—with tricks for her parents—just like they all have. I love Amber because she is book and street smart.

Q: You write a lot about astrology. How do you know so much about it? Have you studied it?

A: I have read up on astrology for years. I am not an expert. I find it intriguing and I totally believe in it. In all my relationships, (co-workers, bosses, lovers, friends and relatives) I have used the assistance of astrology to guide me in the way I handled those relationships. I have raised and handled my children using astrology. My daughters are Leo and Aquarius—exact opposites. The Leo I have to handle with kid gloves. I have to request, ask and be gentle with if I want something done. She requires praise. Whenever I would make commands—nothing got done. I had to realize and understand that lions are king of the jungle and we are their loyal subjects. We are beneath them. Knowing my astrology and their personalities, I knew how to approach her. Praise and flattery will always put you ahead with them. The Aquarian with the bad temper always did me in. However, I also knew I had the smartest person in the zodiac in my house. I had to learn to deal with her belligerence, which is part of her characteristic. You'll always walk on eggshells with an Aquarian female, even though they are true humanitarians. They will always belong to a group of something. Maybe it will be a church, cult, sorority, or singing ensemble.

QUESTIONS FOR DISCUSSION

❖

1: Parenting is one of the most important topics in *Departures*. What characteristics make a good parent?

2: Purdy seemed to have it all prior to Pilar. Why do you think he teamed up with her? What do you think he really wants? Do you think there is any real depth in his relationship with Stefana? Do you think it is fair how he treated Maritza?

3: Relationships are a major part of *Connecting* and all are very different. Compare the relationships of Joel and Angie, Purdy, Stefana and Maritza and Emily and Jared. Which is your favorite and why?

4: How do you feel about Emily's relationship with Leo?

5: Discuss the different ways in which the lives of these characters might progress.

6: Shock us with a statistic relevant to book.